Garden OF Dreams

# Garden of Dreams

# Leslie Gould

WaterBrook
Press

GARDEN OF DREAMS
PUBLISHED BY WATERBROOK PRESS
2375 Telstar Drive, Suite 160
Colorado Springs, Colorado 80920
*A division of Random House, Inc.*

ISBN 1-57856-636-3

Library of Congress Cataloging-in-Publication Data
Gould, Leslie, 1962-
  Garden of dreams / Leslie Gould.
    p. cm.
  ISBN 1-57856-636-3
  1. Gardening—Fiction. 2. Friendship—Fiction. I. Title.
  PS3607.O89G37 2003
  813'.6—dc21

                                    2003000612

Printed in the United States of America
2003—First Edition

10 9 8 7 6 5 4 3 2 1

*This book is dedicated to my husband, Peter.*

*You've given me so much.*

# Acknowledgments

Thanks to Sally Quimby, R.N., and the nurses on the oncology floor at Legacy Good Samaritan Hospital, Portland, Oregon; Karol Waits, R.N., oncology floor at Rogue Valley Medical Center, Medford, Oregon; and Peggy Peterson, hospice nurse, for their medical expertise. My deep appreciation to Emily King and Donna Gabrielson for sharing their cancer-related stories.

My gratitude to Libby and Chris Salter, Holly and Alfred Frakes, Kate Commerford, Cindy Monte, Laurie Snyder, Kathy Fink, Becky Berg, Val Bennett, Linda Hohonshelt, and Nancy Brannen for their friendships and insights. Special thanks to my book group and fellowship group members who have challenged me to grow in faith and love all these years. Much appreciation to my writing group members for adding clarity to these pages and to Stanley Baldwin and Nancy Ellen Row for much-valued editorial suggestions. Thanks to my editor, Erin Healy, for her excellent work and overall encouragement.

My heart of thanks belongs to my husband, Peter, and our four children. God has blessed me beyond my dreams through you.

Each friend represents a world in us,
a world possibly not born until they arrive,
and it is only by this meeting
that a new world is born.

ANAÏS NIN

*Part One*

Wait for the LORD;
be strong and take heart
and wait for the LORD.

PSALM 27:14

## 1

"Rob," Jill said. She stretched an arm across the bed and patted her husband's bare chest with the back of her hand. "Simon's awake."

Rob rolled toward the wall.

"Get the baby," she said, turning to look at the clock: 6:15 A.M.

She slapped at the monitor, dragging her finger along the switch, silencing the frantic wails and scratchy bursts of static.

"If you get him now, Hudson and Liam might sleep longer. Let the dog out too, okay?"

She heard Rob's feet slap against the wood floor, one at a time. She heard him pull on his sport pants and make his way around the bed and out into the hall. She imagined him trudging up the open staircase to the boys' room. He'd been out of town for the past two weeks—he'd forgotten how early Simon awoke.

How many times had she been sick during the night? Four? Five? She remembered Rob getting up with her the last time at 4:30. "This is some nasty flu bug you have," he'd said.

She hoped it was just a flu bug.

Jill pulled the violet floral duvet up to her chin, rubbed the soft cotton against her face, and rolled over on her side. The morning light illuminated the wall. The bureau was covered with black-and-white photos. Rob and Jill on the beach in Argentina, the Atlantic behind them, Rob's surfboard between them. Hudson as a newborn. The three boys in Lithia Park. A best-friend picture of Jill and Caye hamming it up while on a cross-country ski trip at Lake of the Woods. Caye's husband, Nathan, shot the photo while Rob broke trail across the frozen lake.

On the wall, to the right of the bureau, hung Jill's favorite painting. The figures were small and abstract. Two women on a porch. Children in the yard. A garden. It was her painting. Her house. Her life.

She felt the urge to call Caye, but she wouldn't. Not now. Not yet.

Her lower back hurt. Her stomach roiled, turning the nausea up her throat churn by churn. She hated for Rob to miss work, but she couldn't get to the doctor on her own. Not today.

She knew Caye would take the boys. That, at least, was a given.

Caye leaned over the yellow Formica counter, both hands wrapped around her coffee mug, and gazed out the kitchen window. The morning sun filled the backyard. The grass looked like a sheet of emerald. The just-open blooms of the white dogwood fluttered outside the window like a lace curtain in the breeze.

She was dressed in a pair of old Levi's with the knees ripped out and a blue sweatshirt splattered with white paint. Two gold clippies held her short reddish hair back from her face. Her yellow gardening clogs waited at the back door.

Caye had just dropped seven-year-old Andrew off at school. Audrey sat at the breakfast-nook table and kicked the heels of her black rubber boots, inherited from her big brother, against the bench seat. Her plaid skirt stuck in bunches to her ivory tights. She pulled the Chutes and Ladders game board out of the box.

Nathan had tilled the plot against the fence the evening before. Caye would plant zucchini, peppers, lettuce, spinach, carrots, and tomatoes. In the back, along the cedar fence, she would plant the sunflowers. The image of the flowers' faces bowing gently in the summer heat made her smile.

"Come play, Mama," Audrey said, unfolding the board onto the table. She jerked her head from side to side; her chestnut pigtails brushed against her face.

Caye stared at her daughter. Chutes and Ladders wasn't what she had in mind.

Audrey's fourth birthday was tomorrow. Caye added *bake a cake; decorate like a daisy* to her mental to-do list.

"Mama!"

"Just a minute, sweetie. I'm thinking about the garden," Caye said, turning her head back to the window.

"Pumpkins!" Audrey shouted, her brown eyes wide.

Caye had forgotten the promise she'd made to Andrew and Audrey. By the end of August the far corner of her perfectly square yard would be a jungle of vines.

"Right. Pumpkins."

Every year her best friend, Jill, teased her about the garden.

"All those vegetables," Jill would laugh. "You'd think we were at war."

Jill's large Victorian home above the Boulevard had a yard twice the size of Caye's. Jill grew only flowers and herbs. She bought her organic produce at the grocery store. Caye liked the idea of a victory garden. She imagined the Railroad District, where her bungalow was located, full of vegetable plots fifty-five years ago.

Caye shifted her focus to the window box in front of her and the drooping red, orange, and yellow tulips. Jill had given her the bulbs last fall. Now the petals were fading and falling into a weak pile at the base of each stem. The black stamens were exposed and nearly naked.

Caye planned to cut the waning flowers and tuck the leaves behind the red geraniums and white and blue lobelia that she would plant by noon.

She took a sip of coffee and smiled. It was a perfect day.

"Mama," Audrey whined. She flicked the blue arrow of the game spinner and sent the piece of cardboard across the table.

It was a perfect day, except that Audrey was driving her crazy.

"I never imagined a four-year-old could talk so much," Caye had complained to Nathan the night before. Andrew had never been a chatty child—he was a doer, building with LEGOs, drawing cowboys, turning his bedroom into a fort.

"She was made to talk," Nathan had answered. "That's how her brain is wired. Besides," he said with a chuckle, "she takes after you."

Caye hoped Audrey would busy herself playing in the sandbox

while she planted the vegetables, took care of the window box, and cleaned out the leaves that had blown under the raspberry bushes during the winter. She would garden and then bake the cake, and continue, she knew, to obsess about the job, the paying job, that she had interviewed for yesterday.

On any other warm spring day, she would have been on the phone with Jill planning a picnic in Lithia Park. They hadn't waded in Ashland Creek yet this year; maybe today would have been the day. She imagined the kids jumping and yelling and scrambling up the cement steps from the dappled creek to the sunshine in the park.

She would not call Jill until afternoon, late afternoon.

Yesterday, after the interview, Caye had phoned Jill. Caye measured her enthusiasm as she talked about the position selling ads for a travel magazine. "That's so not you," Jill had blurted out. "If you feel like you need to go back to work, why don't you go for what you really want to do?"

They didn't finish the conversation. Jill's baby woke from his nap; Caye needed to pick up Andrew.

As she pushed Audrey in the umbrella stroller to the school, Caye realized that she hadn't asked Jill how she was feeling. Jill had been run-down since Simon was born ten months before. Her milk had recently stopped.

"Awhile ago," Jill had answered as they were sitting in her garden earlier in the week and Caye had asked when she'd stopped nursing Simon.

"Are you pregnant?"

"Not according to the test."

The sweet lullaby scent of the pink cherry blossoms dusted the air around them. Audrey, Hudson, and Liam stripped rusty-colored flowers off the camellia bush and flung them at each other, littering the brick walkway with the fading, curling petals. Jill's black Lab puppy, Scout, jumped from falling flower to falling flower.

The day had been overcast; Jill had worn sunglasses.

"Allergies," she'd said when Caye asked about that, too. "They're really bad this year."

*It's the in-between year—this year 2000.* Caye took another sip of coffee. The last year of one millennium or the first of another, depending on who was counting. It felt like a year hanging in time, a year of uncertainty for Caye—the year between staying home and going back to work. If not this job, then another by year's end. They couldn't keep scraping by on Nathan's teaching salary.

When Audrey was born, Caye had only intended to stay home a year. She never expected her leave would stretch into four years. Jill, quite honestly, was the reason she hadn't gone back to work sooner.

Audrey whined, "Mama, you never play with me!" She flicked two orange pawn holders off the table. Caye wanted to sweep the entire game into the garbage. She took a sip of cold coffee and gave Audrey "the look."

The phone rang.

Audrey hurled three cardboard children to the floor.

"Pick up the pieces," Caye commanded as she headed to the phone.

She checked the caller ID: Rob and Jill Rhone.

Caye instantly forgot her thoughts of a moment ago. Maybe they would go to the park today. She *would* have a chance to explain to Jill why the job possibility really was a good thing.

"Hi," Caye said in her sunny-day voice.

There was no greeting, just Rob's hoarse voice asking, "Can you come get the boys? Jill's sick."

"What's wrong?"

"She's been throwing up all night. I have a call in to the doctor."

Caye hesitated, adjusted her plans again. No park. No gardening. A day—at least a morning—alone with four little children.

"I'll be right over."

Caye dumped the last swallow of coffee into the empty sink, rinsed the cup, and put it in the half-full dishwasher. "We're going to get the boys," she said to Audrey. Maybe Jill would get in to see the doctor right away.

Audrey picked the pieces of the game off the floor and table, crammed them in the box, and slammed out the back screen door, boots flying down the steps, chasing Abra, Caye's ancient calico cat.

Caye drove up A Street to Oak in her old Toyota wagon, and then darted along the little overpass above the Plaza. Below stood the statue of the pioneer, the "tree of heaven," and the entrance to the park. Just up the hill were the Shakespeare Festival theaters and the towering Mark Antony Hotel.

The Plaza was the heart of Ashland; she saw it anew every time she drove through it or by it, even on this quiet Thursday morning, even though she had lived in Ashland for seventeen years. As she waited at the light to turn onto the Boulevard, she craned her neck, looking beyond the Plaza, and noted the clouds rolling in from the southwest, slipping over the foothills of the Siskiyou Mountains, threatening the blue sky. The light turned green; she pushed on the gas and then turned left by Briscoe School, or "Not Andrew's School" as the younger kids called it, and hurried up the hill.

Jill sat on the edge of her bed with a cup of peppermint tea cradled in her hands. The duvet was wadded behind her, leaving the tired-looking lavender sheets exposed. Rob had poured the tea into one of her Royal Copenhagen blue china cups and brought it to her with no saucer. He'd also buttered the toast. The smell of the butter, even though the plate was on the dresser, made her throat thick.

Jill's dark wavy hair hung loosely around her face. The odor of vomit hung in her nose.

"Caye's on her way," Rob said, poking his head into the room. "Do you think she'd keep the boys this afternoon? After we're back from the doctor? So I can go into work?"

Jill didn't answer.

Simon was at the door, wiggling his way through. "Ma-ma-ma-ma," he chanted as he quickly crawled across the floor; he grabbed the leg of Jill's flannel pajamas with fierce determination and pulled himself to his feet.

"Hey, you," she whispered, looking down.

"Here, I'll take the tea," Rob said, reaching toward her.

"No. The baby."

Rob slung Simon over his shoulder and headed out the door.

Jill noted Rob's irritation. She knew how much he hated it when she was sick. It wasn't just the inconvenience. He didn't know what to do. He didn't know to hold her hair back, to give her a glass of water to rinse her mouth. He didn't understand how hard it was for her to take care of Simon, how hard it was to keep trying to explain what needed to be done for all of them.

After being coddled beyond reason by her mother when she was ill—and then practically ignored the rest of the time—Jill found Rob's aversion to sympathy refreshing. Except when she really was sick.

She stood and put the tea on the dresser, looked again at the toast, and headed down the hall to the bathroom.

❧

Caye let herself into Jill's Victorian house, peering through the leaded glass window as she opened the door. Audrey slipped around Caye and planted herself in the middle of the living room and began kicking up her feet, showing off her boots to the three boys. The brothers wore matching blue-footed pajamas and looked like oversize stuffed toys. All three had blond hair and blue eyes—Hudson's straight hair was beginning to darken, Liam was a towhead with loose curls, and Simon's fuzz was nearly white. Hudson and Liam bounced on the living room sofa. Simon sat in the doorway to the hall—on the fringes of the burgundy Oriental runner—crying. Tears slid down his face, and drool cascaded around his two bottom teeth, over his lower lip.

The dog came bounding into the living room from the hall, brushing past Simon, barking at Audrey. Caye hoped that Scout, at eight months, was done growing.

Simon held up his arms; Caye picked him up and felt the wetness of his diaper against her arm as he leaned his compact body against her. He stopped crying. He smelled of sour spit-up and all-night urine. Caye ran her hand over his smooth head.

"Hi, little guy," she said. "Hi, to you big guys, too," she added, signaling with a quick jerk of her thumb for Liam and Hudson to get off the couch.

The periwinkle brocade drapes were drawn; the living room, painted a bluish-gray with a white alcove ceiling, was cold and dark. She pulled the drapes, switched on the Tiffany lamp in the corner, and turned up the heat.

"Where are your mama and daddy?" she asked.

"Back there." Hudson pointed through the doorway.

Caye heard heaving as she headed down the hall. She tapped quietly on the bathroom door and said calmly, "I'm here."

"We'll be out in a minute," Rob answered.

Hudson, Liam, and Audrey tumbled off the couch when Caye walked back into the living room.

"Go get dressed."

"We're hungry," Hudson whined.

"You can eat at our house." Caye shooed the boys and Audrey up the cherry-wood staircase and followed with Simon. All three of the boys slept in the turret room, or castle room as they called it, Liam and Hudson on bunk beds and Simon in the crib. The other upstairs rooms were used for a playroom, a guest room, and Rob's office.

Jill thought it was good for the boys to share a room.

Caye yanked the rings on the three eggshell-blue shades and zipped them up the windows. Simon startled each time. The neighbor's cedar tree across the street filled most of the view, but around the edges she could see the east side of the Rogue Valley.

Jill had painted white clouds on the faint blue ceiling. A mural of a stone wall with turtles, butterflies, frogs, and dragonflies on a sage-green background surrounded the room.

Caye rummaged through the boys' drawers. No clean socks for Hudson or Liam. The dirty-clothes hamper was full. Caye put Simon in his crib; he started to cry again as he pulled himself up against the rail and thrust his foot through the slats.

"Come down," Caye said to Hudson and Audrey, who had perched on the top bunk. Hudson jumped from the top rung of the ladder.

"Don't you do it," Caye told Audrey, her eyes leaping the distance to her daughter. "Come down the ladder."

Audrey rolled her eyes. Caye ignored her.

Caye gave Hudson his clothes. "Put them on."

"I can't. Mommy does it for me."

Caye knew this wasn't true.

"Give it a try; Audrey will help you," she said, thinking that offering Audrey's help might inspire him to be independent. It didn't. He wiggled out of his sleeper pajamas and then lifted his arms for Audrey. She yanked the shirt down over his head and knocked him over. They both fell on the floor giggling.

Caye peeled off Liam's mushy Pull-Ups, turning her head from the acrid smell. She put a new Pull-Ups on him, not wanting to hassle with big-boy underwear, and then his orange shorts and yellow T-shirt. He needed a bath, but it would have to wait. He walked to the closet and pulled out his yellow rubber boots. "Like Audrey," he said with a smile and sat on the floor in front of Caye.

Audrey wrinkled her nose. "No, Liam. Mine are black."

Caye pulled the yellow boots on Liam's bare feet.

Simon continued to cry as she changed his diaper and then lifted him out of his crib. He banged his head against her chest and pulled on her shirt. "Poor baby," Caye cooed, kissing his head, the fine strands of hair caressing her lips. She wiped the tears away from below his big blue eyes with two swipes of her index finger.

༄ༀ

Rob threw a tea bag in the garbage as Caye and the kids paraded into the kitchen. Last night's dishes sat in the sink with half-eaten corn dogs, mustard, and ketchup dried on the plates. Rob had obviously fixed the meal. He must have stopped at the store on his way home from work. It wasn't the kind of food Jill kept in the house.

"How is she?" Caye asked.

"Not any better."

"Maybe you should just take her to the doctor's office. Don't wait for the call back. Especially if she's getting dehydrated."

Rob's blond, bushy hair was uncombed. His gray eyes were dull. He hadn't shaved. His white T-shirt was wrinkled. He didn't answer.

"What about the dog?" Caye asked. "Should I take him?"

"He'll be okay," Rob answered. "We won't be gone long." Rob started toward the door.

"I need the car seats," Caye said.

"The Suburban's unlocked," Rob answered, looking over his shoulder.

Caye put Simon on the slate floor and handed him a rubber spatula from the drying rack to chew on.

"Where are Simon's sippy cups?" Caye called out, opening the cupboard beside the sink.

"Sippy cups?" Rob stopped in the doorway and turned around.

"And formula?"

"Does he use a cup?" Rob asked. "Isn't Jill still nursing?"

"No," Caye said.

"Is she pregnant?"

"She doesn't think so," Caye said, feeling befuddled. *Why hadn't Jill told Rob she thought she might be pregnant?*

"The test was negative," Caye blurted out. She immediately regretted her hasty tongue. Heat began to rise under the collar of her sweatshirt and up her neck.

Rob pressed his forefinger against the bridge of his nose. "I don't know where she keeps the cups and formula," he said, looking hurt. "Try over the microwave."

## 2

Jill climbed into the Suburban. Rob put the vehicle into reverse and backed out of the parking place at the clinic. They headed toward Medford, over to Rogue Valley Medical Center, a fifteen-minute drive.

"Tests," the doctor said. "It's time for more tests." Two days ago their doctor, a new family-practice doc, said he thought it was a virus. He'd ordered more blood work—the results hadn't come back yet.

Three weeks ago he thought Jill was anemic. And he was right; she had been. Today he said that it might be her gall bladder, maybe hepatitis C. Had she been exposed in Argentina? But probably just a virus, a liver virus. He'd seen it before—a mild case of jaundice from a virus.

Rob stayed in the waiting room and worked on his laptop during the appointment. He looked surprised when the doctor came into the waiting room with Jill and said they needed to head over to Rogue Valley Medical Center for more tests.

Their doctor had already called an internist in Medford to take her case.

Jill closed her eyes as they sped by the foothills to the west. Mountains covered with trees and topped with spring snow rose above them. To the east, dry, prehistoric hills with spines like dinosaurs stretched themselves out of sight.

She'd felt cradled by the contrasting geological giants these last four years. Nurtured, cloistered, protected. She finally felt as though she belonged, as though Ashland was a place to be from, to say, honestly and proudly, *I'm from Ashland.* Ashland was where she wanted to raise her family, paint, create a garden. But, as in the original

Garden, a serpent lurked here, waiting, scheming, hiding among the blossoms.

All along she'd meant to tell Rob—but hadn't. She hated to think of it as a secret, exactly. In her mind it was simply a fact she hadn't yet revealed. She'd come closest to telling Rob when they were in Argentina, when Hudson was three months old. She was exhausted, frightened. They sat on the beach, an umbrella shading their first-born. "I want to go home," she had said.

Rob asked why. She said it was the baby. What if something happened? What if they couldn't get the right medical help? She started to cry.

Rob asked if it was postpartum depression. She'd never been a worrier. What was going on?

She didn't tell him she was suddenly terrified of dying—of leaving her child motherless.

Two months later, they were living in one of her mother's rentals when she realized, or more accurately Rob realized, that she was pining for Ashland. She and Rob had stopped in the little town after their wedding on their way from Portland to L.A. Rob wanted to show her the college, Mount Ashland where he'd worked on ski patrol, the Shakespeare Festival, his favorite deli with the outside seating along the creek, the Plaza, and Lithia Park. The town enthralled her.

Even with her eyes closed, she knew—by the timing of when they turned onto the Boulevard—that they were passing under the train trestle. She thought of the purple pansies planted in the median.

A few minutes later Rob accelerated as he pulled the Suburban onto the freeway on-ramp. Jill opened her eyes and fumbled in the pocket of her fleece for her sunglasses.

She thought about the boys with Caye. Safe. Well cared for. Caye was more than an auntie to them. She was a second mom.

The image of her garden rushed into Jill's mind. She had made the garden wall the focal point—seven feet of weathered bricks supporting purple wisteria. Earlier in the week, when she and Caye sat in the garden admiring the tulips and early tree peonies, she'd wanted to talk about her old fears. But she had held back again. For months, really for years, she'd wanted to mention it to her friend, in passing, as if it were no big deal, which it wasn't, not really.

In L.A., right after she and Nathan had returned from Argentina, she went for a checkup and broached the subject with her doctor. "Take care of yourself," he said. "Eat right. Exercise. Go ahead and have another baby. Chances are you'll be just fine."

"Is it genetic?" Jill had asked.

"There's no evidence that it is," the doctor answered. "And you're young. Put it out of your mind."

She also told their first family-practice doc in Ashland, who had just retired. He also told her it wasn't genetic. Most recently she'd told their new doctor, after she kept feeling under the weather.

So if it wasn't a big deal, why hadn't she told Rob? Or Caye?

Caye would have dug and hunted, gone on the Internet, ordered books from the library, asked more questions, made it into a tornado of an issue. Caye would have hounded her, asked how she was feeling every day, pressured her to go to the doctor, then to a different doctor.

And she had gone to the doctor. She'd taken the iron tablets—but they hadn't helped. She'd only gotten worse.

Rob reached over and patted her leg.

"I'm sorry you're sick," he said.

Jill squeezed his hand. "Sorry you're missing work."

She couldn't get any more rest than she was getting now—and still take care of the boys. They could hire a nanny. Maybe Stephanie, who baby-sat two mornings a week, could come every morning. Marion, Jill's mother, would probably pay for the added expense.

Jill had decided to wait a year to landscape the north side garden. And she wouldn't start trying to get pregnant again soon—as she had planned.

They passed the pear orchards, zipping by the symmetrical rows of trees covered with tender green leaves. The terrain was drier on both sides of the freeway now. A green dusting of spring grass covered the hills. It would soon give way to brown. Although Jill could not see it at the moment, she was aware of Mount McLoughlin, snowcapped and majestic, to the northeast, standing guard over the valley.

Caye sat down in her rocking chair with Simon and the cup of formula. The baby wiggled against Caye's chest and closed his eyes.

As she rocked the baby, Caye thought back to when she'd first met Rob. She never would have imagined as she sat behind him in econ that his future wife would be her best friend. Nathan and Caye had gone to college with Rob at Southern Oregon State. Rob was spontaneous, smart, and fun. He majored in business with a minor in computer science. After graduation, he moved back to Portland and worked for Intel. Several years later they heard he was living in Buenos Aires.

Nathan and Caye married and stayed in Ashland. Nathan took a job teaching middle school social studies in Medford; Caye took a job in the sales department of a software company. She kept working after Andrew was born, but when she was six months pregnant with Audrey she cut back to part time. They'd gone to a church in Ashland after they were first married, but they attended less and less after the pastor Caye liked left. Soon they weren't going at all.

They'd just started going to a church in Medford when Caye met Jill. It had been Nathan's idea to attend—he was determined to find a home church for his growing family.

Caye decided to try the Wednesday-morning mothers' group at the new church. She put Andrew in the children's program and then joined the other moms in the social hall. One woman said hello to her. That was it. No one else even smiled.

The next Sunday she sat reluctantly in the same social hall with Nathan during Sunday school. Fifteen minutes into the lesson, Rob entered the room. Beside him walked Jill. She wore a long black skirt, a bright blue silk blouse with three-quarter length sleeves, and strappy black sandals. She carried a blond-haired baby on one hip and a large black leather bag over her other shoulder.

Caye and Nathan raised their eyebrows at each other in one of those unchoreographed moments of acknowledgment. There was Rob. Rob Rhone. Right in front of them. Who would have ever thought?

Rob didn't notice them—or at least didn't acknowledge them.

Caye watched Jill. Her wavy dark hair flowed down her back; her blue, blue eyes shimmered as she smiled in a carefree way and stepped around Rob and into the row of metal chairs. Jill was slim and tall, at least five feet nine inches. Caye, at five feet three inches, admired height and envied women who carried it with poise and confidence. Rob was also tall—well over six feet. He wore his blond hair short and bushy.

Jill carried the baby in an effortless manner. The little boy looked to be around a year old. He was perfectly balanced on his mother's hip, supported by one arm. It looked as if she could carry him that way forever without growing weary.

They sat just ahead of Caye and Nathan. Caye watched as Jill pulled brightly colored Discovery Toys out of the bag for the baby and then retrieved them from the floor after he threw them. Unable to keep him occupied, she lifted her blouse, and the baby began to nurse.

Too interested in the people around him to keep his head under his mother's blouse, the little boy kept pulling off to shriek. Finally Jill gathered him and the large bag, smiled at Rob in defeat—or perhaps victory—and walked out of the hall.

"I have to go to the rest room," Caye whispered to Nathan.

Caye caught up with Jill in the foyer and introduced herself. "I'm Catherine," she said with a dimpled smile, and then added, "but my friends call me Caye."

Suddenly she realized, as Jill offered her hand, that she was famished for a friend.

"Pleased to meet you. My name is Jill. And this is Hudson."

"Jill and Hudson Rhone—I presume," Caye responded as she shook Jill's slender hand. Instantly she felt embarrassed. Was she being too forward? Too overbearing? She could feel patches of red crawling up her neck.

Jill laughed. "How did you know?"

"My husband and I went to college with Rob. In Ashland."

Caye's embarrassment somersaulted into self-consciousness. Jill's chic leather sandals and bag looked foreign—Italian—and expensive.

Her clothes had a designer look. Caye was wearing a red, long-sleeve maternity top that Nathan had given her for Valentine's Day, blue leggings, and a frumpy pair of scuffed black flats. Her brownish-red hair hung limply around her chin, accenting how fat her face was with the added pregnancy weight.

Jill smiled a full-bodied, embracing smile. "I'm so, so happy to meet you," Jill said. "I've been praying for a friend."

Caye wanted to sit down on the gray industrial carpet and cry.

Before the church service started, Rob and Nathan joined them in the foyer. Rob and Jill had moved to Ashland because he'd taken a job with a computer-consulting firm that had its headquarters in town. A computer friend of Rob's from college worked there and gave him an "in." Rob was the kind of person who always had an "in."

He and Jill had met in Buenos Aires. "It was love at first sight," Jill said. Caye wondered if Jill knew how many different girls Rob had dated during college.

Rob asked Caye and Nathan if they liked the church they were visiting. Caye wrinkled her nose; Nathan nodded. Rob and Jill laughed.

"We're trying a home church next Sunday. It's called the Fellowship," Rob said. "The couple who lead it were friends of ours in Argentina. Thomas and Joya are their names. Want to come with us?"

※

Simon finished the formula and then threw the cup before Caye could stop him. It bounced off the river-rock fireplace in Caye's living room and landed on the flagstone hearth. Caye kept rocking, willing the baby to sleep.

He turned his face, with his eyes closed, toward Caye. She thought of how tired Jill had been. Her weight came off quickly after Simon was born—in fact it looked as if she'd lost more than she'd gained.

"Mama," Audrey said. Hudson and Liam stood at attention behind her in the doorway to the hall.

"Mama," Audrey whined again. "We're bored. Will you play with us?"

"Maybe later," Caye said, knowing she wouldn't. "Go play in

Andrew's bedroom. Play with his LEGOs. I'm going to put Simon down for his nap in your room."

Caye fed the kids peanut butter and grape jelly sandwiches on white bread for lunch. Audrey pulled her sandwich apart and ran her index finger through the goo.

"Don't eat your sandwich that way," Caye said.

Audrey licked her finger. Caye imagined the peanut butter under her daughter's fingernail and the yeasty way her hand would smell. "Stop it," Caye said.

Audrey put the sandwich back together and smashed it on the table with her palm. The dark-purple and brown mess oozed out of the sides of the bread and onto Audrey's hand. Caye resisted the urge to yank her daughter off her chair and give her a swat.

"Eat," Caye said.

She was beginning to worry. Why hadn't Jill called?

Caye picked up the phone and tried Jill's cell.

No one answered.

Audrey sat in the eating nook and pouted. "I'm really not hungry," she said. "I really want to play."

"Leave your sandwich on the table," Caye said. "You won't have a snack until you finish it."

Hudson looked at Audrey with sympathy. Jill never made her boys finish a meal. The two children raced down the hall to Andrew's room while Liam finished the last bite of his sandwich.

Caye checked on Simon and then ran down the basement stairs and brought up a laundry basket of towels to fold at the dining room table. Her house was a square box. Two bedrooms downstairs, one bathroom, a living room, dining room, and kitchen, and one bedroom upstairs and a large landing. The floors of the house were covered with old-growth pine.

The house was a worker's bungalow built below the Boulevard for a railroad family. Caye and Nathan had bought the house three months before Andrew was born. They were ecstatic. They had saved and saved.

Nathan painted the interior walls a faint, pale-lemon color and the outside light gray with daffodil-yellow and forest-green trim. He'd sanded the floors. He found a metal light fixture with colored rhine-stones for the dining room at a flea market, and hung Caye's black-and-white photographs taken in Lithia Park in the living room. They purchased 1940s furniture at estate sales. They dubbed the style "funky bungalow."

They landscaped the backyard, creating flower beds and garden spaces, and mapped out a play structure for their kids. Caye imagined gardening while the children played with each other in their match-ing outfits. In her fantasy, which was influenced by Nathan's desire for a "good-size family," there were four: two boys and two girls, making the fact that they had two bedrooms for the kids a perfect fit.

Caye loved the Railroad District. She imagined how it had bustled years ago, trains coming and going, vendors selling pears and apples, carriages taking passengers up to the Plaza. After the train route was moved to the east side of the Cascade Mountains back in the late '20s, the District had dwindled, but in the last several years the neighborhood had begun to pick up again. A park was built just two blocks away, right along the tracks. Bakeries, cafés, and shops brought the old storefronts to life again.

When Jill and Rob moved to Ashland, they first rented a house south of town—a fairly new split-level home with an attached double-car garage. "I can't stand all that perfection," Jill would say. "All those beige walls. It's so boring. I want a different color in every room and nooks and crannies and a garden that's worth working in."

Jill hated the house.

"I want an older home," she'd say when she was over at Caye's, and naturally Caye thought that Jill wanted a place like hers. Caye imagined the Rhones moving into a house on her block, or at least close by, and every time one went on the market she picked up a flier.

Caye carried the towels into the bathroom. It was time to go get Andrew. She'd have to wake Simon. Why hadn't Jill called?

She left Hudson's car seat at the house. She'd have to double buckle the big boys up front. Nathan would not approve. She would not tell him.

"Auntie Caye," Liam said as she fastened his booster seat, "where's Mommy?"

"I'm Dr. Miles," the man said to Jill, reaching for the clipboard on the end of the bed. He quickly scanned Jill's chart and then asked about medical and family history. Jill answered his questions matter-of-factly, keeping an eye on the door, expecting Rob to barrel through it any minute, back from lunch in the cafeteria.

Dr. Miles jotted some notes and then said he'd order more blood work immediately and a CAT scan for the morning.

"I just had blood work done," Jill said. "Call over to Ash—"

"We'll do blood work here," the doctor answered, "and a CAT scan in the morning."

"What are you looking for?" Jill asked.

"Any abnormalities."

"Like?"

"Like anything." He snapped the chart shut and left the room.

Rob walked into the room a moment later; Jill told him the doctor had ordered tests.

"What tests exactly?" Rob asked.

"More blood work." Rob nodded. "And a CAT scan," Jill added nonchalantly.

"A CAT scan? Jill, that doesn't sound good. What is he looking for?"

She shrugged. "He wouldn't say. Call Caye to see if she can keep the boys for the rest of the afternoon, okay?"

"I'll call from the lobby," Rob said. "I need to walk around some more."

Jill thought of her boys. By now they'd be playing with Andrew, following him around. Except Simon. Simon would be tenaciously clinging to Caye. Poor baby. Poor Caye. Simon seemed to know before any of them that life had taken a sudden downward turn.

By the time they returned home with Andrew, Simon and Liam were both crying. Audrey held her hands over her ears as she ran into the house shouting the words to "Jingle Bells."

Immediately alliances shifted. Hudson betrayed Audrey by slamming her out of Andrew's room. Audrey stomped down the hall, dragging Liam with her. Andrew came out of his room to comfort Audrey. His round glasses slipped halfway down his nose as he invited his sister and Liam back to play with the LEGOs. Hudson stood in the hall, hands on his hips. Hudson, at nearly five, was almost three years younger than Andrew was and nearly as tall.

Bouncing Simon on her hip, Caye checked the caller ID. One call from Rogue Valley Medical Center.

Alarmed, she pushed the memory-two button for voice mail.

"It's Rob. I need to talk to you." His message sounded tense.

Bewildered, Caye walked into the living room, the phone still in her hand, and sat down to rock Simon. She tried Rob's cell phone. No one answered. She wondered if she should call the hospital and have Rob paged. She wanted to call Nathan—school had just ended—but didn't want to be on the phone if Rob tried to call again.

Rob. Caye tended to say his name as two syllables. In her opinion, Rob never helped Jill enough with the kids and the house. He happily let Jill manage their domestic life; he had no idea how hard she worked. It was obvious when Caye first met Jill that Rob adored his wife. Caye could tell by the way he looked at her, the way he kissed her, the way he held her when they hugged. It had been months since Caye had noticed Rob eyeing Jill as she crossed a room, or since he'd brought her flowers, or a gift from one of his many business trips.

"I feel like I don't have any time for Rob," Jill had said last winter when Simon was seven months old. "And I've become such a lazy lover."

"It will get better," Caye said. "Simon's still little. You're up nearly every night." None of Jill's boys were good sleepers.

"Rob's been acting weird," Jill continued. "Restless. He's unhappy with his job. He'd like to move back to Argentina. He doesn't call me twice a day when he's out of town like he used to. Last night, when I was trying to talk, he said I should talk to you, tell you my story, he couldn't keep track of every little detail."

Caye had felt uncomfortable.

But now she wondered if it had felt more smug than uncomfortable. Jill had a better house, more talent, more kids, more money. But Caye, she was sure, had a better husband.

Nathan and Rob, although amiable, had never clicked the way Caye and Jill had. The two men spent time together, were content to double-date, even play tennis together, but had never become fast friends. Nathan was responsible and serious, predictable and cautious; Rob made him nervous.

Rob could hardly sit down for more than a few minutes at a time. He always had some idea or project brewing, something in the works. "It's that computer mentality," Nathan had said once. "Even when he's sitting at a desk he's off somewhere. Inside a computer. Jumping from site to site, program to program."

The phone began to ring, startling Caye. She jarred Simon as she clicked the blue On button. It was Rob.

"They're going to do more blood work," he said. "And a CAT scan. I'm sure they think it's something bad, really bad."

And then he began to cry.

## 3

Caye checked on the kids. Andrew had put on *Muppet Treasure Island*—at Hudson's request, Caye was sure. All four were on the living room floor transfixed by the TV.

She gave Simon a graham cracker and took him and the phone out into the backyard. He gnawed the cracker and then wiped the crumbs, mixed with his spit, on Caye's shoulder. The day had grown somber and chilly; the wind was picking up, forcing the top branches of the big-leaf maple to scrape and screech against the roofline.

She decided to call Nathan first. Then she'd call Marion, Jill's mom, as Rob had asked her to. She quickly dialed the number to her husband's school. The school secretary transferred the call to Nathan's room.

"The doctor ordered a CAT scan," Caye blurted out. She felt alarmed. Confused. Afraid.

"Hold on," Nathan said. "What are you talking about?" Caye knew it drove Nathan insane when she started in the middle of a story.

"Jill's at Rogue Valley—at the hospital. Rob says the doctors think it's bad."

"I thought she had allergies."

"It's more than that. They're doing a CAT scan tomorrow—more blood work today."

"But they don't know what's going on?"

"No." Caye knew Nathan wanted facts. "Their doctor thought it might be hepatitis or a liver virus. Or something else." *There are no facts. Not yet.*

"Well it doesn't sound like we should be alarmed."

Caye felt the heat rise in her neck.

*Not alarmed?* At times she greatly appreciated Nathan's calm, logical approach. This was not one of them. They were talking about Jill. Next to Nathan, the kids, and her parents, Caye loved Jill more than anyone else in the world. And something was wrong; Caye knew it.

"They have her on the oncology unit."

"Why?"

"Rob said they use it for overflow."

"Then it doesn't mean anything," Nathan countered.

"Would you call Joya?" she asked. She could hear the defensiveness in her rising voice. "Rob asked if we would let the Fellowship know. Ask Joya to call everyone to pray?" It was too windy to stay out in the yard with Simon, and she didn't want to call Joya while she was in the house where the kids could hear. Honestly, she just didn't want to call Joya at all.

"And, Nathan," she added, forcefully lowering her voice into her asking-a-favor tone, "could you stop by the hospital on your way home? Rob was crying. He's scared. Could you see how he's doing?"

Back in the house Caye realized she didn't have Jill's mom's number. With Simon still on her hip, she pulled the phone book off the shelf with one hand and flung it onto the nook table, thumbing through it until she located the area codes. She scanned down to L.A., memorized the area code that was closest to the city of Whittier, and dialed directory assistance. Linsey, Marion Linsey. There was no Marion Linsey. She asked for Linsey, M. No M. Linsey either. She thought again, remembering that Liam's first name was William, after his maternal grandfather. "How about Linsey, William."

Bingo.

She dialed the number, wondering if it would be the right one.

It was. Marion's voice came on, unnaturally friendly: "We're not available to take your call, but if you care to leave a message, please do so after the beep." She sounded as if she and William were out to lunch together, as if they would be back any moment from their happy outing. She did not sound like a widow who had lived alone since Jill left home nearly fifteen years before.

Suddenly Caye felt rattled. What was she going to say?

*Beep.*

"Hello, Marion. This is Caye Beck, Jill's friend. There's no need to be alarmed, but I wanted you to know that Jill is in the hospital for—for some tests. Could just be that she's overtired. Rob asked me to pass the message on to you."

She left her phone number and then added, "Hope everything is fine. Take care. Bye now." She hung up, feeling unsettled.

She hoped that Marion wouldn't call her back.

She thought again of Jill's father. Jill was young when he died. Maybe six. Caye couldn't remember what he'd died from. Maybe cancer. Had Jill ever said? Had Caye ever asked?

Caye remembered when she first found out that Jill's father was dead. She'd asked if that made Jill worry that Rob might die, that her children would be left without a father also.

Jill had laughed. "That's never even entered my head," she replied.

Jill felt the pressure of the automatically inflating cuff against her right arm. The beep of the monitor signaled that her blood pressure had been recorded. The sheets felt clean and smooth and slick against her bare legs. The hospital gown was twisted around her thighs.

She still clung to the thought of a baby. Just think of the unbelievable story she could tell the little one someday.

She lay completely still and listened to the soft whirs of the hospital monitors. She heard muffled voices at the nurses' station. But there was no shouting, no crying, no children pulling on her, clinging to her.

The door swung open slowly. It was Rob carrying a silver Mylar balloon with "Get Well Soon" scrawled across it in neon pink lettering.

"Thanks," she whispered, although she wished he'd bought flowers—late tulips, a bouquet of irises, orchids, even roses.

She could tell he was worried. The rims of his gray eyes were red.

"I asked Caye to call your mom," he said.

"Really? Why?"

"I thought she should know."

"I thought we should wait until we know what's going on," Jill responded.

She reached for his hand and found a wadded tissue in his fist.

"Sit down," she said. *It's time.* "I have something to tell you." *Better he hear it from me than from Marion.*

The kids paused the video and bumped restlessly from Andrew's bedroom to the living room. Caye carried Simon, who had fallen asleep, into Audrey's room. She rolled the baby onto the quilt that was still on the floor from his first nap. He scrunched his knees under his tummy. She pulled half of the blanket over his back. She looked out the window. The rain, which had been coming down in sheets, had turned to hail.

Hail. She hated it.

She'd grown up on a ranch east of the Cascade Mountains, in eastern Oregon, where her father was the crew boss. The closest town was Burns—twenty miles away. On an afternoon like this, they'd all run out and stare at the alfalfa being beaten by the hail. As a child she used to shut her eyes and raise her mouth to the spheres of ice. Later, she'd stand with her family and stare at the fields, as the green plants were shredded like paper, like currency. She hated the uncertainty of it—the lack of control.

"At least I don't own it," her father would say as he stood on the porch glaring across the field.

Jill looked around the hospital room. She had dozed. Had she heard Nathan's voice? Rob was gone. The door was closed.

Had she brought her purse? She wanted her cell phone. She looked around—at the counter by the sink, on the chair where Rob had sat. No purse. The cell was probably in Simon's diaper bag anyway.

She looked at the hospital phone on the bedside table. It had been pushed out of reach. If the phone were closer, Jill would call Caye. She would say, "Can you believe it?" She would tell Caye, "Well, I should be out tomorrow, after the tests. I'm feeling better already." She would ask, "Can you come over tonight? Leave the kids with Nathan. Bring me some flowers—and some chocolate. I need something to perk up this place—and me."

Jill wondered if Caye thought up conversations between the two of them. Sometimes Jill would make a mental list of the things to talk with Caye about. *Simon's tooth. Rob's new account. The olive bread recipe Caye asked for.*

The balloon came untied from the chair and bumped against the ceiling, caught in an upward air current from the heater under the window, and bobbed like a neckless head.

The heater, with its institutional look, made Jill think of elementary school. She shivered. Rain began to splatter against the window, hard and forceful. Jill could see it through the half-open blinds. Big drops raced down the window against the dark sky. Jill thought of her father, of the daybed in the living room. She'd been six, home from first grade to sit in the chair at the end of his bed. It was December, before they came and took her father away while Jill slept.

She could hear Rob and Nathan talking in the hall. She closed her eyes. The door opened. "I'll see you soon," Nathan said. "Let us know if you need anything, anything at all."

She heard the good-byes. She wanted to ask Nathan to have Caye call, but she didn't want them to know she was awake. Rob came back and sat beside her. She knew he wanted to talk about what she'd told him before she fell asleep, before Nathan arrived.

Jill kept her eyes closed.

The rain turned to hail. She could hear it against the window.

The children settled back down in the living room. Andrew sat on the floor against the couch. Fingerprints smudged his glasses. He draped one arm across Hudson's shoulder. Liam curled up on a blanket on the floor next to Audrey, his thumb in his mouth. Caye hadn't changed his Pull-Ups all day, and she hadn't reminded him to use the toilet either. She wasn't going to interrupt him now. She'd wait until the video was over.

She wished that she'd asked Nathan to pick up a pizza. She opened the pantry door and pulled out two boxes of macaroni and cheese. Jill's boys loved macaroni and cheese—they never got it at home.

The bag of dried Echinacea on the window sill caught Caye's attention. Jill had given it to her day before yesterday. It had come from Jill's garden last fall—she'd been drying several cuttings of it in her basement all winter because she wanted to do a painting of it. Suddenly she decided to turn it all into tea, saying she planned to do a painting of tulips instead.

Jill was an art major with an emphasis in art history. Caye had been sure that Jill had aspirations to teach, sure that was the real reason they'd chosen Ashland.

"No," Jill had said when Caye had asked. "We chose Ashland because of Rob's consulting job. I want him to make a ton of money."

Caye's eyes grew wide. Jill smiled.

"I'm serious," Jill laughed. "I want him to make enough money so that I never have to work—besides at home. I want to have five babies, garden, and do my art. Maybe someday, when the kids are grown, I'll open a gallery. Or a bed-and-breakfast. That's my plan."

Hudson was just learning to walk when Jill revealed her plan to Caye. Jill was already trying to get pregnant again.

Caye found Jill's ideas refreshing. No one else she knew talked so frankly about wanting to make a ton of money. And all the other stay-at-home moms she knew wanted to have some sort of career again, someday.

That was certainly Caye's plan.

But Jill made her plan sound so convincing that it was obvious, as long as the money was there, that she could pull it off. She made it sound so convincing that Caye became jealous. And then she realized that part of the reason Jill's plan sounded so convincing was because of what her friend had already experienced—and Caye found herself envious of that, too, of Jill's art major at USC, her time in Argentina, her wedding in a field of tulips south of Portland. Everything Jill did had purpose and meaning. She had a California way of owning everyone and everything.

For the first year of their friendship, Caye admired Jill without hesitation. Caye absolutely admired her longer than she'd admired anyone else—except for her children, but that was a different sort of veneration.

It was when Jill and Rob seriously started looking for a house to buy, when Liam was a newborn, that Caye began to suspect Jill wasn't entirely genuine. When Caye would mention a house nearby that was for sale, Jill would say in her characteristically cheerful voice, "Oh, that house is so cute."

Caye continued to imagine Jill living a few blocks away: the two of them sending kids back and forth, all the children attending the same elementary school.

When Jill and Rob found the house above the Boulevard, the thirty-two-hundred-square-foot Victorian house on two lots, Jill was ecstatic. Still Caye knew that Jill was holding back, not letting Caye know how absolutely overjoyed she was.

When they walked up the front steps of the house with their Realtor the first time, Jill said she knew they'd never be able to afford it. "We only went on a whim," she explained. "On a 'what if?'"

Caye imagined them walking through the door. Liam in Jill's arms. Hudson on Rob's shoulders.

The house needed work: a new roof, new paint on the outside and throughout the interior, and a new kitchen. The garden was horribly overgrown; the picket fence was practically dismantled.

It turned out that Jill had some money from her father that she and Rob used as a down payment, or that was what she said. Caye knew Jill's father had left money for college, but she was under the impression that was all he had left. Now it seemed it wasn't.

It was so unlike Jill to be vague. She was usually so forthright, too forthright at times. But when it came to money, or her mother, she was reticent. Caye had the idea that, even though Jill said the money was from her father, perhaps it had come from Marion. Jill portrayed

her mother as a miser with both money and secrets. "I really know
nothing about my parents," Jill told Caye. "My mother never wants
to talk about anything."

Although Jill visited her mother once a year, and her mother visited them in Ashland occasionally, Jill never elaborated on the visits.

"Oh, it was fine," she'd usually say when Caye asked. Once she
said, "Oh, my mother. She gave up too easily on life. On everything."

Jill and Rob made an offer on the house, and it was accepted.
Caye knew from the advertisement in the newspaper that the asking
price was $495,000.

It was the first time Caye felt truly jealous of Jill. First, she felt
betrayed that Jill hadn't told her right away that she didn't want a
house in the Railroad District, that she let Caye go on with her fantasy. And then Caye felt jealous—out-and-out jealousy. Not the fleet-
ing envy that was part of appreciating Jill—the way she dressed, her
beautiful paintings, and her photography that was embarrassingly
better than Caye's.

No, this was jealousy.

From the jealousy, she feared meanness. Feared that she would
turn on Jill. That she would somehow slip into making cutting
remarks, that she would grow more suspicious, that she would grow
to distrust Jill about things more important than a house, like their
friendship. *Why does she want to be my friend? I live in a box; she lives
in a mansion. I take second-rate photographs; she truly is an artist.*

Nathan told Caye to get over it.

He was right. Caye had never had a friend like Jill before. "So
she's been a little secretive about the house, but probably because she
didn't want to hurt your feelings," Nathan said. "Ditto with why she
never talks about money."

But Jill had never been petty with Caye, and her finances really
weren't anyone else's business. Caye would never have a house like
Jill's; Nathan would never make as much money as Rob, and Caye
would never have five babies—in fact, she'd accepted the fact that
she'd never have another baby. She'd said good-bye to those two fantasy children who played so quietly in the backyard.

And so Caye sat on the jealousy, hoping to control it. And mostly she had. The realization brought her some relief as it collided with the present. What if she'd walked away from Jill about something so trivial only to have her get this sick?

As she stirred the margarine into the macaroni, Caye thought about how much easier it was to deal with a friend's misfortunes than her good fortunes. *Is it because we filter what happens to a friend through our own lives? If it's good, it makes us look worse? If it's bad, it makes us look better? And therefore act better?*

As she scooped the mac and cheese into five little red Tupperware bowls, Nathan came through the back door, interrupting her thoughts. His dark, wavy hair stuck out from under his black Baltimore Orioles baseball cap, which he wore backwards. He moved his stocky frame quickly into the kitchen.

"How is she?" Caye asked softly, not wanting the kids to hear.

"It's bad, Caye," he said, his brown eyes heavy. "Rob thinks they're testing for pancreatic cancer. He's going to spend the night. He's upset—and not just about how sick Jill is. It seems she hasn't been totally honest with him."

Simon began to cry in Audrey's room as Nathan took off his cap and started telling her what Rob had said. Caye hurried down the hall to the baby. Nathan followed, waving his cap as he talked. "Her father died from it, and so did her grandfather and her aunt, and she never told Rob—not until today." She knew that was what bothered Nathan the most. In his world there were no secrets. "And she's been jaundiced all week. The whites of her eyes are yellow."

Caye answered, like a defensive child, "So?"

Holding red-faced Simon, she hurried back into the kitchen.

"This is bad," Nathan said, following her again. "Hardly anyone survives pancreatic cancer."

"How do you know?" Caye demanded.

"I read about it—in *Reader's Digest* or somewhere like that."

Caye rolled her eyes.

"What's wrong with my mommy?" Hudson asked.

Caye realized that all four of the bigger kids had grouped around their legs, that in one collective swoop they might all crash down onto the kitchen's yellow-and-green plaid linoleum. Andrew looked at her intensely, his big brown eyes concerned. *How much have they heard?*

"Here," she said loudly, pushed to the edge, unable to balance any longer. She teetered as if on stilts, as if she were in some macabre parade high above the floor, above the children, stamping out a circle to collapse upon. "Take Simon. I've got to go. You stay with the kids. I'll get the crib and diapers. And Pull-Ups."

She grabbed her keys off the hook by the back door. "And change Liam, would you?" she asked, rushing down the wooden steps of the back porch. "Put him in a pair of Andrew's underwear."

4

Caye unlocked the kitchen door to Jill's house. Scout met her at the door, whining and whimpering. They'd all forgotten about the dog.

"Out you go," Caye said, opening the door wide. She'd have to take Scout home for the night.

She wondered if Jill's mother would call and talk to Nathan while she was gone. What would Nathan say?

Caye started in the kitchen, in Jill's *Home Beautiful* kitchen with the stainless steel appliances and vineyard mural painted on the far wall. She threw the corn dogs away, scrubbed the dried mustard and ketchup off the plates, loaded the European dishwasher, and started it. She pulled out the full garbage bag from under the sink and headed to the backyard. She walked along the brick path to the side of the property and slung the bag into the plastic can against the garage. The sky was cloudy, but it had stopped raining—and hailing. She looked up at the hills to the west. The evening light filtered through the clouds, but there were no shades of color from the soon-to-be-setting sun. Scout sniffed along the pathway.

Caye walked slowly back through the garden. Weeds were scattered around the emerging sweet pea seedlings under the cherry tree. Jill's dahlia bed hadn't been tilled. The irises were starting to bud. The old-fashioned variegated tulips that faded from striking ruby red on the outside to a pale pink on the inside, the ones that Jill especially loved, were ragged, pelted by the hail. Jill had promised to divide the bulbs this year, to give some to Caye.

Caye had never been fond of pink—but these tulips looked like ruffled peonies. She would accept them regardless of the color. The forget-me-nots crowded around the tulips.

Climbing up the steps to the back door, with Scout on her heels, Caye noticed the indigo-colored paint peeling on the siding. It seemed too early for the paint to peel—it had only been two years since Jill had hired painters to do the work.

Caye felt nearly as comfortable in Jill's house as in her own, but tonight, to be in it without Jill, felt strangely intimate.

She grabbed two unused garbage bags from the box under the sink and headed to the basement, flinging the bags open as she hurried down the stairs. Fisher-Price pirates and knights were scattered across the playroom. Jill's worktable was covered with the remaining Echinacea ready to be bagged for tea. In the laundry room, Caye found the dirty clothes tubs overflowing; she stuffed clothes into both bags and clutched them with one hand.

She picked up Scout's nearly empty bag of dog food and lugged everything up the steep carpeted stairs and left it by the back door; she grabbed two more bags and headed up to the boys' bedroom. She dumped the contents of their laundry hamper into one bag and then grabbed diapers and Pull-Ups and the wipes from the changing table drawers and put them in the other. She pulled the portable crib, folded in its duffel bag, out of the closet and carefully made her way down the stairs, balancing her load, coaching herself not to trip.

She carried the load out to the car, went back to retrieve the additional bags of laundry and the dog food, and put them in the back too.

Caye should have left then, taken Scout, and gone home to help Nathan get the five children to bed. They all needed baths; they all needed hugs and a story. But she went back into the house and wandered from room to room, down the hall to the back of the house; Scout shadowed her every step.

She opened the door to Jill and Rob's bedroom and turned on the light. The sea-green walls were covered with framed botanical prints—columbine, trillium, and lupine—and Jill's paintings. Black-and-white photos covered the dressing table. The violet-print duvet was pulled back, the sheets were twisted in a lump in the middle. A plate of dried toast sat on the dresser next to a cup of cold tea.

Caye wondered if Jill had called Rob to come home early the

night before. She wondered if Jill had thought about phoning her, or if the irritation in her voice yesterday afternoon kept Jill from calling back.

The phone rang. Perhaps it was Nathan. She would tell him she was bringing the dog.

"Rhone residence."

"Hello, this is Marion. With whom am I speaking?"

"Caye," she said. "Jill's friend Caye."

"Cancer," Marion said calmly. "It's pancreatic cancer, isn't it?"

Rob began to sing.

*"My hope is built on nothing less…"* He had hymns from his childhood burned in his brain. Jill hoped for all four verses.

She opened her eyes. Her husband didn't understand that his doubts ultimately made his faith stronger. That his questions, his desire for indisputable answers, made him dig deeper. She knew he was scared. She knew his faith—which he wrestled with constantly—was at the moment the top contender against his intellectual doubts.

He hadn't opened his laptop since she'd told him about her family history of pancreatic cancer. It had been easier than she thought. One sentence: "My father, my aunt, and my grandfather all died from pancreatic cancer." She didn't add that, according to Marion, her aunt died just months after her baby had been born.

"Why didn't you tell me before?" Rob had asked.

*Like on our second date?* "I was told that it wasn't genetic," she said quietly. "That it was probably environmental—like from diet or pollution, something they all had in common. Something in Pennsylvania. Like the coal mines or all the animal fat they ate. Or because they all smoked."

*"On Christ, the Solid Rock, I stand,"* Rob sang, his deep voice clear but soft.

Jill needed to talk to Caye. She felt listened to when she talked to Caye. As much as she loved Rob, there were times she felt they were stuck in the mud, like her SUV on Mount Ashland last spring.

Sometimes it took weeks to talk a subject through with him, to rock and spin and inch forward, fall back, sink deeper. Half a conversation one day, continued nine days later, with a phrase thrown in late at night when one of them was half-asleep. With Caye it would take a few minutes, maybe an hour at the most.

*"All other ground is sinking sand,"* Rob finished.

"You don't have to stay," Jill said. "You should go home and get some sleep. Then come back in the morning after the tests."

"No," he said. "I'll stay."

❧

"Pancreatic cancer," Marion repeated over the phone. Caye envisioned the two words speeding from L.A. and then north through the telephone wires, charged with emotion, sending sparks over the mountains and through the valleys along the way. She wanted to hang up. She'd wanted to flee when Nathan told her that pancreatic cancer was one of the things they were testing for, to flee far away from Nathan and the children, to sneak into the hospital without Rob knowing and find Jill. She wanted to discover that it was all a nightmare, that none of it was true. Not Jill who ate brewer's yeast and wheat germ, who didn't even drink coffee, who walked every morning—or used to—and did yoga three times a week.

"Caye," Marion said, "are you there?"

"Did you talk to Nathan?" Caye asked. "My husband. Did you call my house?"

"No. No, I didn't."

"They don't know that it's cancer," Caye said, again surprised at her defensiveness and the adrenaline rushing through her body, suddenly aware of the scent of Jill's Fleurissimo perfume, the oils of flowers blended to perfection. "They don't know that it's pancreatic cancer. They're doing tests. Tomorrow. Tomorrow morning."

"It came sooner than I thought it would."

"You can call Rob at the hospital," Caye said, aware of how shrill her voice was growing.

"I won't bother him," Jill's mother responded. "I'm sure he has enough to deal with right now. I just wanted to leave a message. I had no idea you would be in Jill's house. Please just call, or have Rob call—or even Jill—when the tests come back. Good-bye."

Caye clicked the Off button. She felt furious. *That woman! How dare she?* And then, *How dare she what? Think it's cancer?*

"God, don't let it be true," she pleaded. An image of Jill drinking herbal tea at The Beanery while Caye downed a double espresso slipped through her head. The memory of Jill power walking in upper Lithia Park, five months pregnant with Simon, her frosted breath hanging in the February cold, hurried through Caye's mind. That was over a year ago. When was the last time Jill had been on a walk at all, let alone a power walk?

Caye sat down on Jill's bed. She rubbed her forehead with the heel of her hand, and then ran her fingers through her short hair. She undid her clippies, one at a time, and slid them back into place with a snap against her head. Her hair felt dirty. She felt shaky. Had she had lunch? Had she not eaten since breakfast?

What was the use of thinking it was cancer until they knew for sure? But what if it was? And one that was as hopeless—or so everyone seemed to think—as pancreatic cancer? All the days that she thought life was predictable marched by in a row, stretched out mercifully, day after day of taking care of the kids, doing housework, gardening, hanging out with Jill, waiting for Nathan to come home from work. She'd been fooled. Nothing was certain, nothing was sure.

Just like the hail.

Not even Jill, with her perfect life, could control this. They all, in an instant, could be shredded like the tulips.

## 5

Nathan hadn't started the kids' baths by the time Caye arrived home. "We just got back from the park," he said. "Simon was so happy in the swing that I didn't want to leave. We probably would have stayed longer if Liam hadn't wet his pants."

Caye imagined the two-block walk home, Liam walking bow-legged, Audrey keeping ten steps ahead of him, Hudson leading the pack, Simon on Nathan's shoulders, Andrew running back and forth, making sure everyone was all right.

She cleared the table while Scout rushed around the house, sniffing every corner. The cat darted under the table and then to the back door.

"Did you have to bring that dog?" Nathan asked as he let Abra out. He was upset that Caye was upset that he didn't have the kids in bed. She knew how this worked. It was his little jab. His move to put the ball back in her court. She gave him a wilting look and headed into the bathroom to fill the tub.

Caye knew that Nathan thought Rob and Jill were crazy to get the dog. "They don't know anything about training a puppy," he'd told Caye when they first got it. "It's harder than raising kids, and they hardly know how to do that." Now Andrew and Audrey, to Nathan's irritation, were begging for a dog of their own.

Caye piled the three little kids into the tub and bathed them in five minutes. "No time to play," she said to Audrey. "Daddy kept you at the park too long."

She drained the bath and then started new water for Andrew and Hudson while she got the little ones ready for bed. Caye kneeled on the floor, now puddled with water, as she toweled Audrey off. "Go get your Barbie nightgown from under your pillow," she said. Jill had bought it for Audrey a month ago.

Liam ran through the hall naked, flapping his arms. "I fly," he yelled, as he jumped over Simon, who was on his hands and knees on the hallway throw rug. Simon laughed—a loud, raucous laugh—the first Caye had heard all day.

Caye frowned at Nathan, scooped up Simon, and handed the fleshy, slippery baby to her husband. "You got them all wound up." She pulled a cotton sleeper and a diaper out of the bag of clean clothes that sat in the hallway and tossed the baby's things to Nathan too.

She tackled Liam on his next flyby and wrestled him into his Pull-Ups and Superman pajamas. "No story tonight," she said sharply, feeling like a mean mom, as she tucked Liam and Audrey into Audrey's twin bed. *Better to be a mean mom than snap.*

Nathan, still holding Simon, got the big boys settled in Andrew's room while Caye assembled the crib upstairs next to the pole-frame bed in their room. She heard Nathan's footsteps on the stairs, heavier than normal with the baby in his arms. The baby. They all referred to Simon as "the baby," as if he belonged to all of them.

She pulled back as Nathan put his hand on her shoulder. Her nerves seemed to be working their way up through her skin, ready to pop through in an instant.

"How are you doing?" he asked. "Are you okay?"

"I'm fried. And hungry. I don't think I've eaten since breakfast."

*Did they all—Rob, Nathan, and Marion—truly believe it was a done deal? That Jill had pancreatic cancer?*

She took Simon from Nathan—the baby felt as heavy as the world—and slipped him into the crib. She patted his back. He squirmed, wiggled his legs, snorted, sighed, and then was silent. Caye realized she'd been holding her breath. She let it out.

All the kids were in bed. Scout had settled on the floor beside the crib.

She turned and kissed Nathan on the forehead. "I'm going to get some food," she said, kicking her tennis shoes under the bed.

She cut an apple, dipped the slices in peanut butter, and stood at the counter to eat. The saucepan, with an inch of macaroni on the bottom, sat in the sink, the orange cheese sauce dry around the edges. The counter was sticky from spilled apple juice.

Did Nathan remember correctly that pancreatic cancer was so horrible? Maybe his information was outdated. She remembered reading recently that medical information doubled every year. Maybe there was a new treatment, a breakthrough since Jill's dad had died.

She washed the peanut butter down with a glass of water.

She was too wound up to sleep.

She carried the bags of dirty laundry, dumped in heaps at the back door, down the wooden basement stairs. She pulled a clean nightshirt from the dryer and changed out of her clothes.

She started a load of Jill's colors. She'd fold the clothes in the dryer in the morning.

Tonight she wanted to find out more about pancreatic cancer. It was a place to start. She headed back upstairs.

*Researching pancreatic cancer doesn't mean that I think Jill has it, not like Nathan, Rob, and Marion seem to think.* She reached down to turn on the computer in the alcove at the top of the stairs. She stared at the screen as it flickered to life.

She clicked on to the Internet and typed in "pancreatic cancer."

In the first paragraph of the first site Caye read, "We know how quick and deadly this disease is and how little hope conventional medicine currently offers."

She clicked to the next site. Under "key statistics" she skimmed down and read that "28,300 Americans will be diagnosed with cancer of the pancreas this year," and then, "an estimated 28,200 will die."

"Only a hundred will live," she whispered. Nathan was right. She should have known he was right.

She felt as if she'd just entered a foreign country with no map, no guide. Next was an illustration of the pancreas. "Located in the abdomen," read the accompanying text, "surrounded by the stomach, the pancreas is six inches long and shaped like a flattened pear. It is a gland that produces enzymes and hormones, including insulin."

The next page included a photo. It didn't look like a flattened pear—it looked like a salted slug.

Caye clicked to the next site. Bold letters spelled out "Risk Factors." Over fifty years old, male, cigarette smoker, diet high in meats and fat, diabetes, stomach surgery. None of those applied to Jill. Occupational hazards included exposures to pesticides. Jill gardened organically—she wouldn't have had more exposure than the average American, maybe less.

Family history was the last item on the list. Caye winced. *Why hadn't Jill told her? Or told Rob before today?* The explanation read: "Current research shows that an inherited tendency may be a factor in five percent to ten percent of cases."

"May be," Caye said aloud, highlighting the uncertainty, skimming on down to the details about mutated DNA—she'd have to reread that section in the morning. There was evidence that pancreatic cancer and breast cancer shared a gene. Next, the site listed information on treatment, detailing surgery, chemotherapy, and radiation. Caye hit Print.

Could life really be so fragile?

She'd read recently that the reason the Jewish groom stomps on the wineglass is to remind the couple that life is fragile—even in times of blessing.

It had been such a time of blessing in her life. Home with her kids, her friendship with Jill, the Fellowship.

The cursor stopped. Caye jerked the mouse back and forth. The computer froze. She reached down to the console and turned it off, then rebooted.

*Why has Jill been deceptive? For all the things we've told each other, why didn't she tell me about her father, grandfather, and aunt?* The screen came back on. Caye clicked back to her search and on to "survivors." Up popped a picture of a forty-five-year-old woman and the words "no evidence of disease for over eleven years." She'd been Jill's age when she contracted it. Something encouraging at last. Next was a fifteen-year-old boy—he'd survived for three years. The last photo was of a fifty-two-year-old man who had been without evidence of the disease for five years.

She heard Simon whimper.

"Talking with the patient," caught Caye's eyes. "Accept him or her as the person they were and still are."

Simon was quiet.

Caye continued to read, scrolling down the screen.

"Help them maintain hope."

"Honey," Nathan said.

Caye startled and jerked the mouse off the pad, scraping it against the desk.

"When are you coming to bed?" Nathan, Simon, and Scout were all staring at her.

The baby leaned his body down to her, his arms outstretched. She took him from Nathan with one arm, landed the mouse back on the pad and clicked the Print icon. She turned Simon toward her with the crown of his head tucked under her chin. Scout nuzzled her bare knee.

"I'll be right in," she said to Nathan. "Go back to bed."

She shut the program down, turned off the computer, and shuffled into the bedroom over the pine floor. Scout followed, this time settling in the doorway of the room. She rolled Simon next to Nathan and then crawled into bed between the white flannel sheets. Simon rolled toward her. She drew the baby in, half draping him over her chest, and patted his back. She felt her heart pounding against his body.

Sleep would not come.

Caye had been reluctant, in the past, to admit Jill's influence over her life. Now, terrified that something might happen to Jill, Caye began to count the ways she'd identified with Jill, emulated her, took her advice, as if that would make Jill stronger, more powerful.

Caye's hair was short and streaked with red and gold highlights because of Jill—because of one sweet "You'd look great in a sassy cut with some color" comment.

Caye had yellow sun roses, wood sorrel, tree peonies, tulips, balloon flowers, and snow in summer in her yard because of Jill. She loved van Gogh's paintings because of Jill. She read Jane Austen because of Jill. Caye's family ate mangos and papayas and used handmade soap imported from France because of Jill.

Rob, Jill, Nathan, and Caye had all attended the Fellowship together, since that Sunday when Caye and Nathan tagged along. They'd been meeting, twelve adults and now six children, at Rob and Jill's since they bought their house. Before that the members took turns hosting the gatherings.

Nathan reluctantly joined the Fellowship—he would have preferred a traditional church. He'd attended a community church in Sweet Home, where he grew up as an only child living with his father. His mother had left the home when he was nine. Nathan was determined to create the family he had wanted as a boy. A house full of children. A wife and mother who stuck around. An entire family that went to church together.

It was Caye who wanted Sundays, when she was working full-time, to catch up on errands and chores. That was part of the bargain when she said she wanted to take a few years off work. They'd find a church and stick with it.

Caye knew that Nathan had agreed to try the Fellowship to humor her. And then he decided to stick with it because he knew that Caye would keep going—as long as Jill was there.

The Fellowship seemed to be exactly what Caye needed. The members were friendly and at first seemed accepting. The teaching was fascinating.

After six months in the group, Joya had invited Caye over for coffee. Joya spent most of the visit talking about the new Christian school where she and Thomas had enrolled their daughter Louise.

"There's a group of parents at this school who have remarkable faith," Joya said, pulling her light brown hair away from her face and slinging it through a pony tail fastener into a bun on the back of her head. "I'm learning so much."

Caye needed to leave to pick up Andrew from kindergarten.

"Tell me your testimony," Joya said as Caye slipped Audrey into her infant car seat.

"Testimony?" Caye asked, looking at her watch.

Joya stood with a commanding presence and looked at Caye incredulously. Joya was actually a couple of inches shorter than Caye—but she looked imposing.

"The revelation of your faith," Joya stated.

"I know what testimony means," Caye said, trying to sort through Joya's definition. At least she'd thought she knew what it meant. The same feeling of isolation that she'd often felt in church and even sometimes in the Fellowship overcame her. When she was alone and talked to God, or read the Bible that Nathan had given her, she felt cared for by God. But in a group, she didn't feel that same love. She knew God loved the other members, but she couldn't, in their presence, always feel God's love for her.

"I became a Christian in college," she told Joya. "We've tried several different churches over the years. I didn't really grow up in a church, and it's been hard for me to find one that I feel comfortable with." She paused. "We're happy to be part of the Fellowship." Caye smiled.

"So basically," Joya said as Caye stood, "you're a baby Christian."

Over the years the Fellowship members mostly studied Scripture, but they also discussed theological and philosophical questions. Rob instigated most of the discussions. He would bring up questions such as: Is the Old Testament relevant to us, or was it written for an ancient civilization? Why is there no secular record of the Roman census that drew Mary and Joseph to Bethlehem in the first place? Is it mass hysteria that drives Christians to gather on Sunday mornings?

Jill seldom responded to his questions, but every once in a while she would. One time she smiled and said, "This is what happened to Rob from growing up in a Christian home. It really worries me for our boys. Maybe we should pretend not to be Christians. Maybe our boys would have a better chance at faith."

Another time, without a smile, she said sternly, "Rob, it all goes back to your relationship with Christ. Can't you feel truth when you read the Word and pray? The truth is there—you have to feel it."

Jill hadn't grown up in a Christian home.

Jill's best friend in junior high, Amy, was a Christian. Amy was the oldest of five kids. She lived in a big house with a swimming pool. One summer afternoon Jill and Amy were floating on air mattresses in the pool, working on their tans and talking about the fifteen-year-old twin boys down the street.

Suddenly Amy's voice went squeaky, and she told Jill she needed to tell her something, something important.

"I thought she was going to tell me she was dying," Jill told Caye with a chuckle when she related the story. They sat on a blanket in Lithia Park, under the green canopy of towering Douglas fir, ponderosa pine, and beech trees; ducks and geese and two white swans quacked and honked in the Lower Pond. The backs of the Tudor-style Shakespeare Festival buildings framed the edge of the park.

"And instantly—oh, I was horrible—I wondered if her family would still let me come over after Amy was dead," Jill laughed.

It turned out that Amy wasn't dying. She wanted to tell Jill about Christ—and she was nervous.

"I had never understood it before," Jill said, "even though I'd gone to church several times with Amy."

Under the hot California sun, Jill asked Christ to forgive her sins and to guide her life. She went home and told Marion her happy news.

"It will get you nowhere in this life," her mother responded and went into the kitchen to call Amy's mother. She told her to tell her daughter to stop proselytizing and ended the conversation by saying, "I know about Christianity; I gave up on it years ago."

Jill laughed. "'Gave up on it.' That was my mother's motto. I did learn a new word though—proselytizing. I looked it up."

Jill and Caye ate whole-wheat bagels with cream cheese and pineapple salsa and the first strawberries of the season and watched Hudson toddle after Andrew in the grass. It was five weeks until Audrey was due but only two days before she was born. Caye was big and uncomfortable, her back hurt, and her legs were cramping. She wore a pair of denim maternity overalls that pulled tightly against her belly.

Hudson came staggering over the thick, spongy grass to the blanket and collapsed in Jill's lap. Jill scooped him up and kissed his fat, round stomach, pulling up his tie-dyed T-shirt. Hudson belly laughed and they all joined him. Caye tickled Andrew as he tried to sit on her lap.

"Isn't this wonderful?" Jill asked. "What could be better than this? A perfect little town, a beautiful park, and new friends."

They toasted each other with bottles of Evian.

Simon raised his head, plopping it down against Caye's collarbone. She winced in the darkness of her room. Nathan flopped over on his side, away from her. The spring leaves of the maple tree fluttered against the window. Caye pulled Simon down from her neck. It had been so long since she'd slept with a baby sprawled across her. She gave in to the softness of Simon's breathing and drifted off to sleep.

Rob shifted in the hospital guest bed. Jill looked toward him, hoping he wouldn't wake.

Jill thought about Simon. This was the first night she had ever been away from him. Her sweet baby. She felt the sensation of her milk let down at the thought of him, but she knew there was nothing there. Her breasts were dry.

At first she'd been pleased when the weight started coming off. But when her milk started to dry up, she became alarmed. Something wasn't right. And then the nausea started. She hadn't resumed menstruating; at first she thought she was pregnant. It wouldn't explain the weight loss—but still it was an explanation. It would be crazy to have a fourth child in just five years, especially when she felt so tired as it was. It wasn't the baby alone who exhausted her. It was Liam; he was her wild man.

A month ago she'd put him on a time-out in the dining room. He pushed the chair from the corner to the window, wrapped the drape cord around his neck, and then jumped off the chair just as Jill walked down the hall to the kitchen. She screamed, "Liam!" and rushed in and grabbed him. The cord wouldn't have held, wouldn't have hanged him, at least that's what she told herself at the time, but still he had a rope burn around his neck.

Last week she was on the phone with Caye while Liam was in the tub. She ran into the kitchen to start the dishwasher after the bath was drawn and returned to find Liam's face submerged, his eyes wide open, a faint smile spread across his face. Without screaming, without saying a word, she reached into the water and yanked him out, her heart racing, afraid he was dead.

"Hi, Mommy," he responded, water flowing from his mouth.

She let go of him and sat down on the toilet lid. Liam began to laugh.

"Caye, gotta go," she said without missing a beat. She didn't tell Caye what had happened—she felt like such a bad mom when it came to Liam. She was sure Caye would never put a child on a time-out near a drape cord or leave a two-year-old unattended in the tub.

Jill heard voices in the hospital hallway. She listened for a moment, expecting a nurse to come in and take her temperature or blood pressure. Laughter followed the talking. A nearby door opened and closed. Jill stretched out her legs.

Liam was the child she had longed for most and then didn't know what to do with. As a baby, he cried and couldn't be consoled. He didn't want to be held unless he was nursing. He wouldn't take a cup until he was weaned.

When she met Caye, she already wanted to get pregnant again, but when Audrey was born, Jill became desperate for another baby, lusted after another baby. When she held five-pound Audrey in the hospital during the first minutes of life, Jill, for the first time, even thought a little girl would be wonderful.

Hudson had been napping when Caye called that afternoon of Audrey's birth. It was a gorgeous April Saturday in a long stretch of sunny, warm days. Caye, Jill, Hudson, and Andrew had gone to the mall in Medford in the morning. Rob was out of town on business. Nathan was coaching the eighth-grade baseball team at a game in Roseburg.

"Do you want to do lunch?" Jill had asked Caye. "We could get food from the deli and take it to the park."

"We'd better not," Caye responded. "I need to get some things done before Nathan gets home."

"Are you feeling okay?" Jill noticed that Caye's face looked flushed.

"Just tired."

"I'm sorry to bother you," Caye said two hours later when Jill picked up the phone.

Jill hated it when people started a conversation that way. "Bother me?" she wanted to scream. "Please, bother me."

"But I think I'm in labor, and Nathan isn't home yet."

"I'll be right over," Jill said, grabbing her keys before she hung up the phone. She ran down the hall of her split-level house and scooped Hudson out of his crib.

"Gonna go see Andrew," she chirped at her startled son.

As Jill backed her Jeep Cherokee out of the garage, she tried to remember exactly how early the baby would be—five weeks, maybe five and a half. Definitely early.

Caye's doctor was in Medford, so unless labor was really slow and Nathan got back, Jill would need to drive her over and stay with Andrew. Jill accelerated as she turned onto the Boulevard. She felt anxious. Why hadn't she asked how far apart Caye's contractions were?

"It's bad," Caye croaked as Jill hurried through the front door.

"How far apart are they?"

"Three minutes."

"Three minutes! Did you call your doctor?"

"The answering service lady is paging her."

"Where's Andrew?"

"Playing his new Fisher-Price computer game."

Jill rushed to the staircase, "Hey, you!" she called up to Andrew. "We're going to Medford. We're leaving now!"

"Just a minute."

"No. Now!" Jill commanded.

Andrew came running down the stairs. "What's the matter?"

"The baby's coming. Everyone out to the car. Do you have a bag?" Jill asked, turning toward Caye.

Caye pointed to the Reebok sports bag by the door and then leaned back against the living room wall, her breath quickening, her eyes and face scrunched.

Jill looked at her watch.

Caye shivered when the contraction ended.

"Sixty seconds," Jill said. "And strong. Maybe we should call 911. I'll call and then go get Hudson out of the car."

"No. Let's just go."

By the time they'd all made their way to the Jeep parked on the street, Caye had stopped for another contraction. Jill opened the back door for Andrew and then, when the contraction had ended, helped her friend up into the vehicle, pushing from behind. They both started to laugh.

"This is crazy," said Caye as she buckled her seat belt. "It wasn't like this at all with Andrew. It took—" Caye gasped.

"Not another one," Jill said, glancing at her watch. "Just over a minute apart. I'm taking you to the Ashland hospital. If they say it's okay, I'll take you on to Medford."

When the contraction was over, Caye answered firmly, "No. Just take me to Medford. Please. I don't know if our insurance will cover the hospital here."

"Who cares?" Jill retorted. "Do you want to have the baby in my car?" It was her first glimpse into Caye and Nathan's money issues.

"Medford," Caye repeated, unfastening her seat belt. She put the seat back, against Andrew's feet, and positioned herself on her knees, face to face with her son.

"You're not thinking clearly," Jill said. "You're five weeks early, your contractions are just over a minute apart, and you're fifteen minutes from your hospital. You have a choice. I'm either taking you to the Ashland hospital or calling 911 with my cell phone."

Jill pulled onto the Boulevard.

"Are you okay?" Andrew asked softly from the backseat, straining his neck, his big brown eyes wide.

"She'll be okay," Jill said, glancing at Andrew in the rearview mirror and then looking quickly at Caye, who had her eyes squeezed shut.

Jill pulled up by the emergency room door and rushed into the hospital. "My friend's about to have a baby," she called out as she flew through the door.

"Grab a gurney," the nurse at the desk yelled to the nurse behind her.

Jill ran back through the automatic doors and flung open Caye's door.

Caye grabbed Jill's arm, yanked it to her chest, and squeezed. She pushed her lips downward, the tendons in her neck bulged.

"Is it the baby?" Jill stammered.

The nurses arrived with the gurney.

"Yes!" Caye exploded as she came out of the contraction.

The nurses pulled Caye onto the gurney, her peach-colored T-shirt riding up over her white belly.

Jill was tempted to leave the boys in the car, but Andrew's frantic look convinced her to let them out. She quickly unbuckled Hudson from his car seat and motioned for Andrew to undo his seat belt.

"Come on, guys," she said. "Let's run."

Jill could see Caye in the hallway, the back of her head and half-exposed belly visible. The nurse grabbed the just-born baby.

"Hold on to Hudson," Jill commanded Andrew, rushing to Caye's side.

Caye grabbed her hand. "Is the baby okay?"

Jill looked at the gray blob of flesh in the nurse's hand.

"Get me a suction," the nurse yelled.

"The baby's okay," Jill answered, hoping that she wasn't lying.

"Is it a girl?" Caye asked.

Jill looked again. "Yes."

"I thought so," Caye said. She squeezed Jill's hand.

Jill began to cry. She'd never wanted a little girl—never wanted a daughter who might feel toward Jill the way she felt toward her mother. But in that moment, a little girl looked like the most wonderful thing in the world.

In a second, after being suctioned, Audrey screamed and pinked up. Jill held her tightly in the wad of bloody towels while the nurses checked Caye. An arm grabbed on to Jill's leg. It was Andrew.

"Oh, Andrew," she said, "here's your sister." She squatted down and, holding Audrey with one arm, drew both boys into the fold with the other. Andrew patted the baby's head. Jill looked up at Caye. "This is so galactic," Jill said as she began to laugh. "Totally amazing!"

Audrey was okay, but two weeks later Caye hemorrhaged and

then came down with a uterine infection. She ended up over in
Medford, in Rogue Valley Medical Center, after all, with a high fever.
The next day she had a D and C. The doctor said it was a good thing
that Caye already had her two babies. "There was a lot of scar tissue,"
she told Caye. "You might not be able to have another baby."

"Might not," Jill responded, as Caye told her what the doctor had
said. "I'm going to pray that you will."

Nathan had already used up his paternity leave and was back at
school. Over the next several weeks, Jill spent nearly every day at
Caye's.

It wasn't until late June that Jill realized she was pregnant.

Rob rolled over again, this time toward Jill.

*Life is like that.* She envisioned Caye's loss, joy, and pain all
wrapped together like a baby in a wad of bloody towels. The miracle
of Audrey—the loss of more babies.

And then the baby that Jill carried, that she had conceived at
about the time of Audrey's birth, left her too. Miscarried the middle
of July. She always thought of that baby as a girl, even though she
always said she only wanted boys.

Rob opened his eyes.

"How are you, baby?"

"Okay," she said. Funny, she thought, that she was dwelling on
Audrey's birth at a time like this. Then she remembered, looking
toward the window covered with the venetian blinds, illuminated by
the morning light, that it was Audrey's birthday—her fourth.

*Jill was standing in her garden.*

*Caye watched her friend walk gracefully away from her, toward the
back of the garden where the wisteria wound its way over the brick wall.*

*"Come back!" Caye called.*

*But Jill didn't hear. The breeze caught her long dark hair. A shadow fell across the garden. Color drained from the image. Caye felt a chill.*

"Happy birthday to me, happy birthday to me," Audrey sang. She lifted the covers, letting in the cool morning air, and climbed in beside Caye. Liam threw his body over the top of them into the middle of the bed, landing on Simon. Caye pulled the baby out from under his brother. Scout began to bark.

Nathan groaned.

The phone rang.

Caye looked at the clock: 6:40 A.M.

Nathan answered it and passed it on to Audrey, who looked at Caye as she listened.

"Thanks, Jill," Audrey said. "I knew you'd call."

## 6

Audrey handed Caye the phone. This was exactly how Audrey's other birthdays had begun—with a wake-up call from Jill.

"Hey, you! What were you doing four years ago today?" Jill asked.

Caye acutely felt the dissonance of the moment. Leave it to Jill to focus on the day rather than the issue at hand. Still, Caye smiled at the memory of Audrey's birth and the weeks after. She'd never had a friend care for her the way Jill had.

"How are you?" Caye asked.

"Okay."

"Did you sleep?"

"Some. They gave me meds. I'm not nauseated. That's a relief. Our girl sounds a year older already."

"Going on ten years older," Caye answered.

"How are my boys?"

Liam somersaulted across the bed and hit Nathan in the chin with his foot.

"I'm late," Nathan muttered, rolling out of bed in his T-shirt and boxers and rubbing his jaw. "And I've just been attacked."

Liam squealed and spread his arms and legs wide, flailing them over and over as if he were making a snow angel in the bed. The dog began to bark.

"What's going on?" Jill asked with a laugh.

"Audrey, let me get up," Caye commanded, climbing over her daughter and out of the bed with Simon in one hand and the phone in the other.

"I'm sorry it's crazy there," Jill said. "Are you doing okay?"

Liam somersaulted again, this time off the bed, catching the back of his head on the nightstand.

"I've got to go," Caye said quickly before Liam caught his breath and let out a howling screech.

"What's going on?"

"I'll call you right back," Caye answered.

"What? I can't hear you," Jill said.

Liam screamed, loud piercing cries, one right after the other. Scout barked frantically.

❦

"I'll call you. Liam, are you…" came across the line and then a click.

"What's up?" Rob asked.

"Liam just hurt himself—I think. Call Caye back, okay?" Jill said to Rob, handing him the phone.

Rob sat up, took the receiver, and hit the redial button. "Nathan? It's Rob."

Rob listened as he looked at Jill. He nodded and then touched the back of his head as he raised his eyebrows.

"Okay," he said to Nathan. "Call us back ASAP. Let me know if you need me."

"Is he okay?" Jill asked.

"He cut the back of his head on the corner of the nightstand."

Tears filled Jill's eyes.

"Baby, he's okay," Rob added quickly. "He's screaming. I could hear him. That's a good thing."

Jill nodded her head.

"They're just trying to calm him down so they can tell how bad it is." Rob grabbed a tissue from the table and handed it to her. He put his arm around her shoulder, sat on the edge of the bed, and pulled her to him.

Jill blew her nose, wiped her eyes, and tried to smile. Rob ran his fingers through her hair with one hand, pulling it away from her face, still holding her with his other arm.

She looked into his eyes. After eight years together, she still wasn't a hundred percent sure that he was happy he'd chosen her and the domestic path she'd led them down. She'd always been a hundred percent sure that he was what she wanted. Unintimidated. Impulsive. Full of questions. Surfer. Snowboarder. Computer geek.

She felt his biceps bulge against her under yesterday's wrinkled white T-shirt.

Often, when she thought of Rob, it was the image of him in midair against a snow-white mountain. Or the way the ropy muscles of his legs flexed when he ran.

Caye once asked if Rob ever planned to grow up.

"I hope not," Jill had answered. She hadn't been completely honest; still, she was hurt that Caye had asked.

Jill had pulled Rob in, domesticated him. Slung a mortgage, car payments, and charge debts around his neck. He hadn't balked, but sometimes she saw in his eyes the waves crashing on an Argentine beach, saw him wanting to tip a kayak, take a chance, live a little more.

He'd grown up in Ecuador where his parents were missionaries. His freshman year of high school he moved to Portland to live with his grandparents. "My parents were afraid that if I didn't live in the States soon, I'd never want to," he had explained.

She wondered how he would have responded if she'd told him about the cancer in her family. Would it have been too much—the whole domestic package wrapped with the threat of being a single parent? Or would he have never given it another thought? Assumed it would never happen?

"It'll be okay," he said, letting go of her.

She smiled. What would be okay? Liam? Her? Their life together?

The nurse walked in. Dark blue scrubs swished with each step; white clogs treaded across the linoleum. Her short dark hair curled around her ears.

"I'm Bea," she said, opening Jill's chart, "your day nurse."

She took a thermometer out of her pocket and slipped it into a plastic sleeve.

"Are you okay?" she asked, peering into Jill's face.

"Our son—he's at a friend's house—just hurt himself," Jill explained. "We're waiting for an update call." She opened her mouth wide.

Jill played with the metal tip of the thermometer through the plastic with her tongue. The telephone rang. Rob picked up the receiver.

"Okay. No, that sounds cool. No, stitches would just leave more scar tissue."

Jill listened, aware of Rob's split-second decision not to have Liam stitched, as he agreed with Nathan and Caye.

"No, we trust you. Thanks a million. We couldn't ask for better friends."

It was out of her control. They'd made the decision without her.

"He's okay," Rob said. "They got the bleeding to stop. The cut is only about half an inch long and not very deep."

Jill nodded. The thermometer began to beep, and the nurse took it from Jill's mouth.

"A little bit high—100.1. Now, I need you to drink this." Bea held a bottle of barium.

"Oh no," Jill answered. "I drank that last night."

"You have to drink it again—one hour before the CAT scan."

Jill frowned.

Rob walked into the bathroom.

The nurse handed Jill the barium. "Drink up."

Jill could hear Rob using her hospital toothbrush. She was aware of the antiseptic smell of the room, the clanging of the breakfast trays through the open door to the hall, the soft cotton of her worn gown. She could feel Rob drifting as she listened to him splash water on his face. Cold, cold, water, she knew. Just as he did every morning.

He was restless. It was quite the personality combination he possessed. The restless extrovert, she called him. Even when they had company he'd begin to wander—go downstairs to check the ball game score on the TV, upstairs to his office to add an item to his work to-do list, down to the kitchen to sort through a pile of mail.

She knew he needed a break. Sometime soon. He couldn't sustain his emotional focus much longer. And he really should get back to work.

Besides, she needed Caye.

❧

"Go," Caye pleaded. "Just go."

"I feel bad leaving you with all the kids," Nathan said.

She stood at the refrigerator, Liam on her hip, Simon clinging to her leg with one hand and holding half a banana in the other.

What was she getting? Right. Milk for the cereal.

Liam wiped his snotty nose on the shoulder of her nightshirt, right next to the blood-soaked neckline.

"Go," she said again. "Or you'll be really late."

Nathan stepped toward Caye and kissed her on the lips. Liam pushed at him, wiping blood on the collar of Nathan's blue oxford.

Caye frowned.

"What?" Nathan asked.

"Nothing," Caye lied. "Just go." It wasn't worth the hassle of finding a new shirt, an ironed shirt. He wouldn't notice—everyone else would just think he cut himself shaving.

As Nathan hurried out the door, she looked at the clock above the stove: 7:30 A.M. Andrew needed to get ready for school.

"Mommy, when are you going to make my cake?" Audrey asked.

"Soon. Honey, would you tell the big boys to come eat? Please?"

Caye put Liam at the table in the eating nook and poured Cheerios into a bowl. He hiccuped and picked up his spoon as Caye poured the milk. Immediately Simon, seeing his chance to be held, began to cry. Caye picked him up. He wiped his mushy banana-covered mouth on her sleeve. Scout settled on the floor next to Liam's chair and kept an eye on the cat sitting by the back door.

"They're playing LEGOs," Audrey yelled.

"Tell them to get dressed," Caye called out.

"Get out of here!" Andrew shouted at his sister.

"I'm telling!" Audrey screamed.

Caye ignored them. *If it comes to blows or blood, I'll intervene.* She wished Nathan had started the coffee. She let Abra outside.

"They're not getting dressed," Audrey announced, stomping into the kitchen. She wore the black rubber boots with her Barbie nightgown. She sat down beside Liam. "Did you know it's my birthday?"

Liam hiccuped again and took a bite of Cheerios.

Caye walked down the hall. "Come on, Andrew," she called out. No answer.

She looked into the room. Both boys were sitting in the middle of the floor surrounded by a red, yellow, blue, black, and white pool of LEGOs.

It was Thursday. Hudson had preschool. He went on Tuesday, Wednesday, and Thursday. He didn't have to be there until nine—and maybe wouldn't get there at all today. A third of the time, at least, Jill kept him home.

Andrew was in the second grade—he shouldn't skip.

"Here's the propeller," Andrew said to Hudson, tossing the red plastic set of miniature blades across the room.

The image of forcing all five kids into the station wagon again jolted through her head. *Oh, well. He'll just have to miss.*

The CAT scan was behind her. A young man from transportation had pushed her down to radiology. *My trip through the donut hole.* She'd held her breath, flat on her back, while the bizarre machine whirled around her and clicked the images. Then an older woman with long gray hair wheeled her back.

Jill reached for the phone. Rob had gone out to the nurses' station to see when Dr. Miles would make his rounds. She knew the number by heart. Stephanie had been baby-sitting for the kids since she was a sophomore at the college. She was a senior this year but took the term off to earn money. She waited tables in the evenings at a restaurant in town and baby-sat the boys two mornings a week. She lived with her aunt and uncle on the Greensprings Highway, east of town.

"Hi, Stephanie. It's Jill. Can you sit this morning?

"Great. Not at my house—at Caye's. For her daughter, too. Do you remember where they live?

"Good. At 10:30?

"Perfect."

The nurse brought in breakfast. Jill hadn't eaten since the broth last night, but she wasn't hungry. She reached for the juice. She'd try to get a little down.

Rob stuck his head in the room.

"Hey, you," she said. "You can go to work. Caye's coming around eleven."

"Look who's here," Rob said as he came all the way through the door, followed by Joya and Thomas.

❦

Caye looked at all five kids with satisfaction. Each was dressed and fed. Keeping up her hurried pace, she ran down to the basement, pulled the wrinkled clothes out of the dryer and stuffed them into a basket, and then threw the load of wet wash into the dryer. Back up the stairs she ran. She would put Simon on the bathroom floor to play while she showered. She would instruct Audrey to stay next to Liam for the next fifteen minutes and not let him out of her sight.

The phone rang.

It was Rita from the Fellowship. She was in her early fifties, divorced, with a grown son and daughter. She worked as a loan officer at a Medford bank.

"What's going on with Jill?" she asked.

"She's having tests—over at Rogue Valley."

"Joya left a message last night. She said they were testing for cancer."

*Did Joya, from hearing that a CAT scan was scheduled, know they were checking for cancer?* Caye wondered. *Joya was a nurse. Or had been a nurse.*

"I think it's just the usual tests," Caye answered.

After a quick good-bye and an "I'll let you know when I hear anything," Caye scooped up Simon, grabbed the plastic bucket of rattles she kept for him to play with, and rushed into the bathroom with the phone still in her hand.

It rang again. It was Lonnie, another Fellowship member. He was married to Summer and after six years at the college still hadn't finished his computer science degree. Summer worked as a secretary in the English department.

"Is it true?" he asked.

"Is what true?" Caye responded.

"Does Jill have cancer?"

"Who told you that?"

"That's what Joya's message sounded like."

"They're testing for it," Caye answered Lonnie impatiently, aware that she had just lied to Rita.

"Unbelievable," he sighed.

"I know," Caye answered. Her impatience melted away. Unbelievable was right.

"But I don't think it's that," Caye said. "I think she's exhausted and has a bad virus."

The doorbell rang. The dog began to bark.

"Gotta go, Lonnie," she said. "Ask Summer to pray. I'll keep you posted."

*Perhaps Rob talked to Thomas last night. Or this morning. Maybe Rob already knows the CAT scan results and called Joya first.*

She glanced at her watch—it was 10:35. She was still in her nightshirt—her bloodstained, snot-covered, banana-splattered nightshirt. The doorbell rang again. She peered out the window.

Stephanie, Jill's baby-sitter, stood on the porch.

❦

"We're praying that above all else you will have faith," Joya said. She kissed Jill good-bye, straining to reach her forehead, and added, "I talked to Gwen this morning. She said to tell you she's praying too."

"Tell her thanks," Jill said, thinking of all the members of the Fellowship. She knew they'd be concerned.

"God bless," Thomas added, patting Jill's shoulder.

Rob stood and shook Thomas's hand. "Thanks for coming," he said. "We'll give you a call as soon as we know anything."

"That was weird," Rob said to Jill as the door swung shut.

"Shh," she answered, looking at the clock across the room. "Oh no—I forgot to call Caye to tell her to come over. Would you hand me the phone?"

## 7

*C*aye quickly washed her hair in the bathroom sink, toweled it dry, and slipped on her jeans and T-shirt. She gave each of the kids a quick good-bye and ran to her station wagon. Stephanie stood on the front porch, holding Simon in her arms. Caye waved as she backed the car onto the street and headed north.

Joya had already been to see Jill. Caye wasn't surprised.

Had Jill asked Joya and Thomas to go see her? Was that why Jill called Stephanie to baby-sit? So that Caye wouldn't feel left out?

*Don't be petty.* She heard the words in Nathan's voice. *You're reacting to the way you're feeling right now—not to what you know.*

Caye had felt embarrassed as she stuck her head out the door to Stephanie. It felt like a comedy of errors as Stephanie stammered out why she was there, that Jill had asked her to come.

"But Jill's not here," Caye declared, confused. "She's in the hospital."

"The hospital?" And so it went, both trying to figure out what was going on until the phone rang.

"Caye!" Jill had said. "Can you come over?"

❧

"Really, really," Jill said to Rob. "Go. I'm feeling much better. My eyes are even back to normal—I just checked. I really think this was just a fluke."

Rob reached for his computer.

"Have some faith," she said with a smile.

"Faith? Or denial?"

She ignored the comment.

"I'll call when I get to work," Rob said. "Page me if you need me sooner. I forgot my cell at the house." He bent over and kissed her.

She felt relief when he left. A few minutes alone before Caye arrived would provide a needed break. Joya and Thomas had drained her.

Jill and Rob had been tight with Thomas and Joya when they'd all lived in Argentina. Thomas translated the Bible, and Joya worked as a nurse. They had two children when Jill first met them—a three-year-old boy named David and baby Louise. Rob was in charge of the computer system for the translating mission, until he took a job setting up a network for an international import business.

Thomas and Joya were quite offended by Rob's change of priorities.

Jill went to Argentina to work as a governess, a glorified nanny, for a diplomat's family of six kids. The children's grandparents had paid for her services to teach the three preschool children; the older kids went to the embassy school.

Two months after Rob and Jill met they became engaged. Soon after, Thomas and Joya's son, David, fell ill one night with a fever while Joya was at work. Thomas called her; Joya said to give him Tylenol.

The next morning, when Joya came home from the hospital, she found David burning hot, limp, and whimpering in his bed beside Louise's crib. Joya rushed out into the street with her son dangling in her arms, hailed a taxi, and yelled up to Thomas, who was leaning out their fourth-floor window, that she would call him, that he must check Louise and bring her to the hospital if she was feverish too.

Two hours later David was dead from meningitis.

Joya quit her job and stayed in the apartment. She hardly ate.

Rob and Jill would stop by in the evenings to try to cheer them up. They'd bring fruit and flowers, suggest they all go to the beach. Joya would just shake her head. Jill remembered Joya's long, light brown hair uncombed, her clothes wrinkled, her lips tight with grief.

Thomas was, with good reason, worried about his wife and their marriage. He felt that she blamed him—at least that's what Thomas told Rob. Thomas suggested that the two couples meet to pray and study the Bible together.

Jill found Joya fascinating, the whole incident macabre and heart wrenching. She wondered how she and Rob would deal with such a tragedy. Would one blame the other, pull away, turn inward? One summer night the four of them sat in Thomas and Joya's home. The balcony doors were open to let in a hot breeze. The fans whirred out a comforting harmony.

Joya sipped the peach smoothie that Jill had brought for her. Louise was asleep in her bamboo crib in her parents' room, where she'd been moved after David's death. The door was halfway open.

"I think Joya's better," Thomas reported with a smile.

Joya pushed her hair from her face with a frown and said, "Thanks for the smoothie, Jill."

The next week Jill brought a chocolate milkshake from the new McDonald's down the street and a couture scarf she had purchased at Saks in New York the year before. Joya led an austere life, seldom spending money on herself. Joya fingered the fuchsia-colored silk, held it to her cheek, wadded it into a ball, and put it in her lap.

The topic that evening was faith.

"God is impressed with faith," Thomas said, following his usual teaching style of starting out with a simple statement. "He asks us to live each moment of our lives in faith."

At that moment Jill imagined Joya clutching David, hailing a taxi outside the apartment building.

"That's why bad things happen," Joya said. "Because we don't have enough faith."

"Oh, Joya," Jill said. "Do you really think so?" Jill leaned forward, reaching across the hot room with her words.

"I was discontent here in Argentina. God wanted to point out my sin." Joya took a deep, quivering breath. "When I knew David was sick that night, I didn't pray. And at the hospital the next day, while he was dying, I prayed, but my faith was weak."

Joya shifted her legs; the scarf fell to the floor. She continued, "It wasn't God's will for David to die. God brought us here—I would have been perfectly happy staying in New Mexico. How could it have been his will to bring us here and then have David die?"

Thomas went over, took Joya's hand, and sat beside her on the couch. The image seared itself into Jill's mind—Thomas, at six feet four inches with his strawberry-blond hair and beard, bending over his tiny wife. He looked like a fair-haired Abraham Lincoln. The fans whirred.

Joya stood and pulled her hand away from Thomas, leaving the scarf on the floor. She walked into the bedroom.

Jill and Rob left soon after, dumbfounded.

After that, Joya did start to get better, but a few weeks later when Jill tried to bring the subject up, when she said, "Joya, I want to talk with you about what you said about faith—"

Joya put her hand up and said, "Stop. Please. I can't talk about it anymore."

Thomas seemed relieved that Joya no longer blamed him. Six months later, just after Rob and Jill returned to Argentina after their wedding, Thomas and Joya moved back to the States and settled in Medford. Thomas took a job teaching Latin-American studies at the college in Ashland. Joya had wanted to return to New Mexico. Thomas wanted more intellectual challenge.

Rob told Jill he thought it was easier for Joya to blame herself than to blame God—or keep blaming Thomas. Rob surmised that she couldn't accept that God would allow David to die—so it was easier to blame it on her "lack of faith" than to deal with her anger toward God.

By the time Jill and Rob had hooked back up with Thomas and Joya, bringing Caye and Nathan with them, the Fellowship had been in existence for just over a year. Joya and Thomas started it out of frustration. "The whole culture shock thing," Joya had explained. "It's so hard to get used to the pretensions of the American church after having been away."

Gwen and John, a childless couple in their midforties, had first joined Joya and Thomas for a Bible study. Summer and Lonnie were in their late twenties and had joined next. By then the members were referring to it as "the Fellowship." Rita was a neighbor of Thomas and Joya. She'd joined a year before the Rhones and Becks.

Most of the members had grown up attending church. "We have a lot of depth," Thomas had told Rob. "I think you'll be pleased."

Jill noted the stark surroundings of Thomas and Joya's ranch-style house that first Sunday that they attended the Fellowship. Joya had furnished it simply. One cream-colored sofa, circa 1980, eight straight-back chairs, an oak dining room table, a roll-top desk in the corner of the living room. All the walls were painted eggshell. Two framed travel prints of Argentina hung vertically over the couch. There was no TV in their home. The computer was in the back bedroom, the room Thomas used as a study.

Jill was pleased to meet the other people and to study the first chapter of John together. Light and darkness. The Word. Thomas was a good teacher, bringing in history, culture, literature, explaining it all concisely. Louise had grown into a beautiful girl with Thomas's strawberry-blond hair and Joya's greenish eyes. She colored quietly at her child-size table with the white Formica top in the corner of the dining room. She seemed obedient but sullen. Watching her made Jill sad.

After the teaching, they all shared a potluck meal. The entire event felt satisfying, mostly. Jill had a flash of hesitation when Joya sent Louise to her room for a time-out after she spilled her milk.

"We'll need to figure out a program for the kids—if you, Rob, Caye, and Nathan commit," Joya said, standing at the door in a denim skirt and a pink blouse as they left. "Hudson and Andrew are too active to be near the adults."

Jill tried to shoo away her defensive feelings toward Joya's comment. She held Hudson close as they walked out the door. She felt a pang of guilt—false guilt, she knew—for having a beautiful little boy in her arms. She thought of Joya sitting on the couch in her Argentine apartment wadding the silk scarf into a ball.

The boys, who had played with wooden alphabet blocks in the hall for most of the time, hadn't bothered her. When Hudson got fussy, Jill sat in the hallway and nursed him. She thought the boys had behaved quite well.

Months later, Joya had chastised Summer for complaining that Lonnie wasn't finishing up his degree. It had happened during a

Sunday morning group while the men and women were separated into groups. "We're not here to gripe about our husbands," Joya had stated.

Caye commented about the incident the next day to Jill. "She's right," Jill said, coming to Joya's defense. "It would be horrible to let it turn into a free-for-all."

"I think God's given you a special grace when it comes to Joya," Caye told Jill.

It was the snippiest that Caye had ever been with Jill.

After that, Caye started a program for the kids, writing the curriculum, coming up with crafts, developing a story to tell each week. She worked with the children two Sundays a month and the other members took turns the other Sundays under Caye's direction.

"I like it," Caye insisted. "I didn't get all those stories as a child. I'm learning right along with the kids."

Jill was impressed with Caye's dedication. It would have driven her crazy to be locked in a room with the kids and a flannelboard two mornings a month. The one thing she learned from her days as a "governess" was that she didn't want to be a teacher. She was the happiest, while living in the diplomat's house, hanging out with the cook and the gardener.

The nurse swished through the door. "Message from Dr. Miles," she said. "He won't be in this morning after all. He'll touch base this afternoon. I'll have your lunch here in a few minutes."

*Lunch? So soon?*

Driving over to the hospital, shifting her tired old station wagon into fifth gear, Caye felt the snake of jealousy rear its ugly head higher. She was fascinated with Joya, but also intimidated.

Jill, always generous with her friends, was especially giving toward Joya. Caye felt that Jill babied Joya. She knew Jill's motivation went back to their time together in Argentina, when Thomas and Joya's little boy died. Jill had told Caye about it—Thomas and Joya had never mentioned it. She knew that Jill saw Joya as fragile and vulnerable. But Caye had never seen that side, except through the one story. To her, Joya was rigid and unsympathetic.

She pulled into the hospital parking lot. Her jealousy gave way to expectation. Finally she would see Jill.

Caye felt anxious walking into Jill's room. She'd stopped at a florist on Barnes Road and picked up a bouquet of Japanese irises with baby calla lilies, and a chocolate truffle for good measure.

"Oh, thank you," Jill had said in relief. "I needed flowers. And chocolate."

Caye pulled the Mylar balloon from the ceiling. "Can you prick it," Jill asked, "and stuff it in the garbage?"

They spent the time chatting, sharing Jill's lunch of grilled chicken and mashed potatoes, going over the details of the morning—Liam's injury, Stephanie at the door.

"I really was miffed," Caye said in a joking voice, as if admitting her annoyance might normalize the day, hide how worried she was. "Not only did you leave me alone with all the kids, you arranged for someone to knock on my door while I was still in my nightshirt."

"I am so sorry. I had no idea Joya and Thomas were coming by."

Changing the subject, Caye asked if Rob had to go in to work, if he had a deadline. "No, I insisted he go in," Jill said. "He needed a break from me."

"Are you worried?" Caye asked, changing her tone to sympathy, concern.

"I really do feel better today. Better than I have in weeks, maybe months. I think I'm fine."

"I'd be worried," Caye said. "I am worried."

"Well, you're a worrier. I'm not." Jill stretched her arms over her head. "Remember, you're the one who thinks Nathan is dead on the freeway if he's fifteen minutes late."

Caye remembered a verse Jill had shared with her not long after they first met. It was from Psalms: "Wait for the LORD, be strong and take heart and wait for the LORD."

"I don't worry much," Jill had said. "But when I do, I recite that verse."

Caye looked at the clock. It was 1:30. "I'd better go. You should rest."

"Oh, right. You need to get Andrew."

"No," Caye laughed. "He stayed home today."

"You're kidding. Your morning was even worse than I thought."

Caye shrugged her shoulders. She didn't want Jill to think it was too much to have her boys.

"Stay then. Stephanie will be okay until 3:00 or 3:30."

Caye smiled.

Jill shifted her thoughts. "Did you call my mother?" she asked, hesitantly. "Like Rob asked you to?"

Caye nodded.

"What did she say?"

"To call back when the doctor made a diagnosis. To have you call back then," Caye answered.

Jill was silent.

"I'm going to dash down to the cafeteria for a cup of coffee," Caye said. "Want anything?"

Jill shook her head.

"I'll be right back." Caye swung through the door.

Jill felt Marion reaching across all those miles, reaching up to pull Jill down, to choke her. She thought of their last phone conversation, week before last.

"Rob says you're overtired," Marion had said in her cool, detached voice. Jill was loading the dishwasher, the phone tucked under her chin. She wore navy sweatpants and a green long-sleeve Rugby shirt of Rob's.

"Tired, yes. Overtired? No." Jill was surprised that Rob had noticed.

"You're not pregnant again, are you?"

"No, Mother, I'm not." She couldn't keep the defensive tone from her voice.

"I was hoping you could come down. Bring the kids. My treat."

"Do you need us to come down?"

"No. Of course I don't need you to."

"Do you want us to come down?"

"I thought it would be nice for the kids. You could take them to that LEGO theme park."

"Would you go with us?"

"I'd have to see."

Jill felt the coils around her neck.

"You might as well fly up here and strangle me," Jill said, her throat tightening. Rob, taking a Diet Coke from the refrigerator, closed the door firmly and looked at Jill in disbelief.

"What do you mean?" Marion asked.

"You won't tell me what you need or want, but then you try to manipulate me, buy me, and I keep falling for it."

*Why do I fall for it?* She considered the question through Marion's silence. *Because I'm greedy. Because for some reason I feel I deserve it—as if she owes me.*

And then it came to Jill, the truth, in one sentence, in one statement. She blurted it out. "You can't believe I want to have a relationship with you. Can you? That I would come down just because you wanted me to?"

The phone went dead.

*Marion has crossed the line.* Jill slammed the dishwasher door.

"You should apologize," Rob had said the next day. He hadn't actually said it. He'd sent her an e-mail and then left a message, while she was picking up Hudson from preschool, to tell her to check her e-mail.

It was the money—the gifts, all the extras Marion paid for. That was what Rob worried about, Jill was sure. She didn't call. She wasn't the one who slammed down the phone.

Caye walked into Jill's room with a cup of coffee in her hand. A soft *tap, tap* drew Caye's attention back to the door.

"Come in," Jill said.

"Excuse me." The man standing before them wore rectangle aviator glasses; dark bushy hair fanned around his smooth, wrinkle-free face. He wore long sideburns and sported a goatee on the very tip of his chin. He was short with broad shoulders.

"I'm Dr. Scott," he said, looking at Jill. "How are you today?" He didn't look old enough to be a doctor. "Dr. Miles referred your case to me. I'm an oncologist. I wanted to talk with you about your tests."

After introducing herself, Caye asked Jill if she wanted her to wait in the hall.

"No," Jill answered in an unconvincing tone.

The doctor pulled the chair close to Jill's bed. "Your CAT scan shows something going on inside you. To be specific, in your pancreas."

*That word.*

"We can't tell for sure, from the scan, what it is. It could be benign—or it might not be."

"And?" Jill asked.

"And we need to do more tests tomorrow to find out exactly what it is."

"What tests?"

"An endoscopic retrograde cholangiopancreatography—or ERCP." The doctor chuckled as he handed Jill a fact sheet. "We'll most likely do a biopsy at the same time."

"A biopsy?" Jill placed the piece of paper on the bedside table.

"Yes. A biopsy. Basically, we need to do more diagnostic tests to know what we're dealing with," the doctor said slowly. "I've scheduled the ERCP for tomorrow at 8:30. You'll be able to go home by noon."

"When will the tests come back?"

"By Monday morning. We'll schedule an appointment in my office."

They were silent. Jill stared at the doctor; Caye stared at Jill.

"Do you have any other questions?" he finally asked.

"I can't think of any," Jill answered.

He reached into his lab coat pocket and pulled out a card. "Call me when you do."

"Thanks." Jill took the card. She flipped it over and over in her hand—the blank side, the printed side, the blank side, the printed side—as the doctor left the room.

Caye sat down in the chair beside Jill's bed.

"Don't look so worried," Jill said. "At least not until we know." Jill dropped the card on the bedside table and smiled. "What did you bake for our girl's birthday?" Jill asked.

The cake! Caye had forgotten all about the cake. Every year, Caye made the kids a cake on their birthdays—her kids and Jill's. Winnie the Poohs, castles, soccer balls, cowboys. This year Audrey had asked for a daisy cake. Audrey's April birthday launched the birthdays; Liam's was in May; Simon and Hudson followed in June; and Andrew ended the season in August.

"Oh no," Caye said, spitting the word *no* out in disbelief. "I was going to make her a daisy. I forgot all about it."

At least Nathan had put together the pink bike with training wheels last weekend. It was hidden in the toolshed. All it needed was a bow.

"I'll call the bakery," Jill said. "I'll tell them it's a rush job. I'll ask them to decorate one of their white chocolate cakes like a daisy."

"No—it's okay. I'll just stop by Safeway on the way home."

"I insist," Jill answered.

❧

The cake was ready when Caye stopped by the bakery. A perfect round white daisy cake with petals carved out of the thick icing and a round of yellow dots for the center. "Happy Birthday, Audrey" was written elegantly and delicately in small green cursive on one of the petals.

It was perfect.

And already paid for. "Over the phone," the clerk said. "All taken care of." Caye imagined Jill rattling off her MasterCard number and expiration date from memory, thinking nothing of it.

## 8

When Jill started the fifth grade, her favorite pastime was riding her bike until she got lost. She'd let herself in the back door of the duplex, toss her homework on the kitchen counter, and grab an apple. Steering her Popsicle-purple Stingray bike with one hand, she'd eat the apple with the other. The September heat would waft up from the concrete sidewalks, the smoggy sky closed in from above. She'd ride as fast as she could for the first few blocks, hurtling the apple core into a corner storm drain as she sped through an intersection. She'd toss her long hair behind her and feel the wind dart along the back of her neck. She'd pedal faster and harder until she'd passed beyond her neighborhood. When she was tired, she'd slow and ride no-handed— her arms stretched wide.

Marion had found the bike at a yard sale. It had a lime-green banana seat. Jill wanted a ten-speed.

When she was younger, she pretended that her bike was a horse and that she was galloping over fields, through forests, along the beach. She'd be a medieval princess one day, an aristocrat on a fox hunt the next.

As a ten-year-old, she rode for the thrill of getting lost. She'd ride, crossing commercial streets, rolling through neighborhoods. When she didn't feel safe, she'd turn back and then take a left or a right. When she was lost, really lost, when she felt the rush of adrenaline, the panic in the back of her throat, she'd turn back, weaving left and right, making her way home. A familiar store would bring a smile. The name of a street. Finally her school, or the 7-Eleven five blocks from the duplex, would put an end to the daring adventure. Then she'd coast on home.

Marion collected duplexes. Bought them here and there all over the East L.A. area. She'd buy one. They'd move into one side of it, clean and paint the whole thing, and plant cheap shrubs in the flower beds. Then Marion would put it up for rent and look for another one to buy.

Marion worked in the afternoons. Checked on properties. Knocked on doors to collect past-due rent. Most days Jill would beat Marion home, but on the days she didn't, Marion would ask where she'd been, what she'd been doing. "I've asked you to stay in the house," Marion would say. "I've told you to stay in the house."

"I was just outside," Jill would answer, picking up her homework off the counter, heading down the hall to her bedroom.

She felt the power of her secret. She'd been miles away, alone. Away from her mother, away from the duplex. She could have secrets too.

"Turn. Over. On. Your. Side." The words floated toward her, one at a time. She was sedated enough not to object to the thin tube down her throat, winding through her body. The radiologist was navigating the tube, the endoscope, through her esophagus, stomach, and small intestine into the pancreas. X-rays would be taken and then cell samples removed for the biopsy.

The endoscope was probably down there right now. This morning the radiologist said she might insert a catheter into the bile duct to relieve the jaundice. Rob was with her then.

"Have you read the possible complications?" the radiologist asked. Jill nodded; Rob shook his head.

"Serious pancreatitis, infections, bowel perforation, and bleeding," the doctor recited. "They're all uncommon."

Jill had signed the release. Life was full of risks.

She thought of the little boy snatched off the beach at Florence last summer. They'd gone over for a weekend—Simon was a newborn. It was their first trip with all three kids. They heard about the boy at breakfast. "Watch your little ones out there today," the waitress had said. "A sneaker wave took a boy last night. His parents were twenty yards away and off he went."

Jill had imagined the horror. If it were Liam or Hudson, or someday Simon, would she run in after him, wrestle her child out of the sea, pull arms and legs and head out of the deep? Shout at the ocean, shout at God, until her child was returned? On sheer will alone, could she bring him back?

No, she couldn't bear to lose a child like that.

She thought of Joya. No wonder she still stared at the floor, gone far away from the rest of them, with her poker face tightly drawn.

She thought of the date with Caye and Nathan almost two years ago. Jill had arranged it, bought the tickets, set up the baby-sitting. They'd gone to see *A Midsummer Night's Dream*—not in the outdoor Elizabethan Theatre but inside, in the Bowmer. It was Jill's favorite Shakespearean play.

Afterward, over a late dinner of Thai food, the four talked about the fairies and the forest. "Heaven is like that," Jill said.

"Full of fairies?" Rob asked, slurping pad Thai with chopsticks, the noodles dangling from his mouth.

"They're angels there," Jill corrected. "It doesn't have the bad— the foolery. It does have the goodness, truth, and beauty."

"I think heaven is like the Internet," Rob said. "It's in inner space instead of outer space. All connected by electricity and sound waves. That's how angels fly. That's how we'll travel—but inside space, from one dimension to another."

"I don't get it," Caye said.

"Like from Web site to Web site." Rob took a long drink of his Thai iced tea.

"So you're saying we'll speed along, by electricity, from site to site, from mansion to mansion to God's throne? Does that mean the electrical currents are paved with gold?" Jill asked, pouring more green tea into her cup.

"That's a thought," Rob said. "Gold, pure gold, is an excellent conductor of electricity."

"What do you think, Nathan?"

"I've always taken a literal view. Golden streets, many mansions, God on the throne. That whole scene."

"Somewhere up in the sky?" Rob interjected.

Nathan nodded.

"On the heaven planet?"

Nathan shrugged. Jill hated it when Rob sounded so superior. "It's a natural garden, a beautiful, unbelievable, gargantuan garden," Jill said with a laugh.

"Maybe it's whatever we want it to be," Caye responded.

"But then how would we have a common reality?" Rob challenged. "We can't be isolated. That's exactly what heaven isn't."

The waitress came with another order of salad rolls, and the conversation shifted.

"Almost done," the radiologist said. "You're doing great. I'm going to take the tube out."

Jill opened her eyes. Her throat was thick from the tube and numb from the medication. It hurt to swallow.

She thought of them repacking the Suburban that morning at the beach. "This is ridiculous," Rob had said.

"I want to go home," Jill had answered. "I don't want them near the water."

"Play! Sand!" Liam howled between sobs in his car seat.

Hudson threw an orange plastic sandcastle form against the back window.

"Is this some postpartum paranoia?" Rob asked.

Jill climbed into the front of the SUV and thought, *If you don't take us home, you'll see postpartum psychosis.*

A day later, though, she came to her senses and agreed with Rob. They even laughed about it. She really had been ridiculous. And it was so unlike her to worry. It became the remember-when-we-didn't-go-to-the-beach story.

"Hi, baby." Rob walked alongside the gurney. She realized she was in the hall on the way back to her room.

"Are you okay?" he asked.

All she could manage was a nod.

*Okay? Am I okay?*

Caye made a pledge to get Andrew to school Friday morning. And she did—just twelve minutes late. She pulled the other four kids in

with her to talk to his teacher. Simon was still in his sleeper. The green
goo from two days ago was back, crusted under his nose again. Had
it really only been two days since Jill was hospitalized?

Caye had gone to Safeway at six o'clock to buy groceries before
Nathan left for work. They were out of milk and juice; the cereal was
nearly gone.

She felt near panic.

She wanted to tell Andrew's teacher what had happened to Jill,
how Caye had almost forgotten Audrey's birthday, how hard it was to
get five kids out of the house in the morning. She didn't. "I won't be
in this afternoon to volunteer," was what she did say. "Right now, I
don't know when I'll be back in."

When they returned to the house, Caye gave each of the older
kids a piece of leftover cake. She dressed Simon while they ate. Only
Liam finished his piece. Hudson and Audrey headed down to
Andrew's room to play with his LEGOs.

*Biopsy. Jill's having a biopsy.* She walked back into the kitchen and
picked up the phone and then followed Simon as he crawled down
the hall to Audrey's room. She sat on the floor by the bathroom door
where she could keep an eye on the baby and dialed. The dog nuzzled
against her free hand. On the fourth ring her mother picked up.

"Jill might have cancer," Caye said without a hello.

"Oh, honey," her mother said. "Oh, dear."

At the end of their two-minute conversation, Caye's mother said,
"I'll pray for Jill," right before she pointed out that it was the middle
of the day, the rates were high, and they shouldn't stay on the phone.

Caye felt frustrated as she scooped up Simon and plopped him
down in the living room next to the laundry basket full of little boys'
T-shirts, onesies, sleepers, and miniature sweatpants. She dug in and
started to fold. The cotton—Jill only bought natural fabrics for her
children, not a thread of synthetic material ever touched their skin—
was soft and comforting: Hanna Andersson, Baby Gap, Old Navy.

Caye thought about the conversation with her mother. What had
she expected? That there was some right thing her mother could say
to make everything better?

Part of the corporate ranch Caye grew up on had belonged to her great-grandparents. Her dad had grown up on his family's ranch, running cattle through Harney County with his dad and grandpa. But the family sold the spread to a corporation in 1950, when Caye's father was twenty-two. He started as a cowhand for the conglomerate that same year.

"It was sell it or lose it," her father said. "We were good ranchers, just didn't have the cash or luck to make it last."

But ranching was what he knew. Fifty years later he had an artificial knee and a hip replacement. He'd broken his collarbone twice and his back once. He'd retired, but the corporation kept him on to look after the old farmhouse he'd been born in. Caye's mother had retired at the same time from her job in the housekeeping department of the Burns Hospital. Together, they raised a few cows and chickens and tended their vegetable garden.

Leather gloves, the smell of burning hair, the sight of a branding iron, and scuffed boots all made Caye think of her dad. As a child, she watched his every move. She'd stand on the green poles of the corral and stare as he strode across the dirt, his brown boots kicking up the dust, his felt cowboy hat scraping the sky. When he swung her up onto a horse, she felt as if the whole world was in balance and nothing could harm her.

In his prime, he could wrestle a calf to the ground in a second or two and hold it while one of his crew branded the beast. When he herded the cattle through the high desert, he knew the best grazing, the best routes, the best watering holes. He knew how to pull a breech calf, how to calm the cow, when to walk away from a water dispute, when to call the sheriff.

His own daddy used to ride his herds to Boise to the slaughter yards, but Caye's dad loaded the steers onto trucks.

"The last of a dying breed," he'd say. "That's me."

Caye was the third child. Her older brothers, five and six years her senior, left Burns after high school. One sold insurance in Twin Falls, Idaho; the other joined the navy and made a career of it. Caye was the first in her family to go to college.

Her parents were poor; they'd always been poor. No thoughts of wintering in Arizona or taking the grandkids to Disneyland.

They'd only come to Ashland twice: when Caye and Nathan married and after Andrew was born.

Not many people could say their father was a cowboy. "You're kidding," Jill had said when Caye first talked about what her parents did. "A real-life cowboy?" Caye imagined Jill stepping back in time, putting a pinafore on Caye, tying her bonnet under her chin.

"This *is* Oregon," Caye answered with a laugh.

Caye went to Burns twice a year—at the end of summer and then at Thanksgiving or Christmas.

Caye and her mother were close, although they never went shopping as other mothers and daughters did, nor did they take trips together. Caye had never told her mother everything, and she seldom asked for her mom's advice. On the other hand, her mother rejoiced when Caye graduated from college. She was thrilled with what a nice young man Nathan was, and beside herself when Andrew was born. She was moved to tears the first time she held Audrey in her arms.

Caye's mother had taken her to church every Christmas and Easter. "We really should go more often," her mother sometimes said. But they didn't.

"Why doesn't Daddy go to church?" Caye asked one Christmas.

"Daddy's church is the open range," her mother explained. Her brothers never went with them either.

"Women's stuff," Caye's dad would mutter.

In reaction to her parents' poverty, she'd been determined to control her life. Not that she strove for wealth—she and Nathan would never be rich. But Caye was determined that they would be comfortable. She insisted they wait a year after she'd graduated before they married so that she was established in her job. She wouldn't agree to start a family until they'd gotten into a house and had a savings account. She waited to get pregnant the second time until they'd saved enough money for her to stay home for at least a year. She didn't want to be shuttling two little kids to day care; it was hard enough with one. Her original plan was to have another child when Audrey was three, and the fourth two years later.

After Audrey was born, that one year stretched into four. Caye pinched pennies to make it work, tried to make their money stretch.

Now she either needed to go back to work or start dipping into savings.

The phone rang, interrupting Caye's thoughts. She dropped the pale blue onesie back into the laundry basket and snatched the phone off the end table, willing it to be Rob with good news, even though she knew it was too early for any news at all.

It was Joya.

"Jill is going to be okay," she said. "I'm sure of it. I've been praying all morning. God's given me a vision."

## 9

Jill opened her eyes as they passed under the train trestle. The sun was shining; she pulled her sunglasses out of the pocket of her fleece.

"Caye will bring the boys over after we call," Rob reported, turning up the hill by the school. "She said to take our time, to get you settled."

Jill nodded her head so Rob would know she heard him.

When they got home, he tucked her in, pulling the sheet and comforter up to her chin. Her throat was sore from the tube. Her belly felt as if she were weighted down, as if gravity had just increased its pull on her. She hadn't had anything to eat since dinner the night before. The cranberry juice she tried to drink in the hospital after the sedative wore off was too hard to swallow. The acid burned her throat.

The tears started slowly. *I have faith, God, faith that it's not cancer. I do. I really do,* she prayed, wiggling her feet out of her socks.

After the doctor's appointment in L.A. almost five years before, Jill returned to the duplex they were living in, one of Marion's. Their crates of boxes were stacked in the garage until they made a decision on where they were going to move. Rob, she knew, was hoping to go back to Argentina, maybe Spain. Jill was looking away from California—but not that far away.

She knew which crate her art supplies were in—Rob had pulled it out the week before and suggested she try some sublimation to get out of the funk she'd fallen into. "It's so unlike you," he'd said. "What's happened to my cheerful Jill?'

She pulled out the roll of canvas, slats for frames, the jar of white gesso, her wooden box of brushes, and her plastic container of acrylics. Rob had taken Hudson to the park, and she had just enough time to get started. She found a hammer hanging on the garage wall—Marion's hammer—and found nails in a Baggie in her brush box. She hammered the frame and stretched the canvas.

She had no idea what she would paint, only that she had to.

*What do I want out of life?* She took up her pencil, ready to sketch out the beginning of the piece. The painting that emerged over the next couple of days was of a Victorian house surrounded by a garden. Wisteria grew over an arbor. Red and pink tulips bloomed in the front. A rope swing hung from an oak tree. Two women, friends, sat on the porch; children played in the yard. Hills covered with trees framed the background.

"It's Ashland," Rob said when she'd nearly finished.

She remembered their stop on their way south after their wedding.

"You're right," she marveled. "That's where I want to live."

She felt stronger, more herself, each step of the way as she painted. And then even more so after they moved, as she lived out the painting. She found the friend, found the house, planted the tulips, restored the garden. Step by step she'd built her life.

She was so sure this was what God had for her. That's why it couldn't be cancer. *Why would you bring me this far?* she prayed. And then she stopped. Not wanting to finish the thought. Refusing to think about her boys without a mother.

*I have faith,* she prayed, *that it's not cancer.*

Still the tears, hot like the sting of the jellyfish she'd touched on the Argentine beach, kept coming. One after the other, fiercely, down her face. She pulled a tissue from the box on the nightstand and wadded it in her hand.

She didn't think she was afraid, no, not really, because she did have faith, faith that it wasn't cancer. No reason to think past that until the biopsy results came back.

So why the tears? Was it the tension with Rob? She knew they needed to talk things through, knew they were stuck in the mud, knew he was upset she hadn't been clear about her medical history.

That was it. They were stuck in the mud until the biopsy came back. No reason to hash through things yet.

She could hear Rob talking on the phone, walking down the hall toward their room. The door creaked.

Jill opened her eyes. "I'm awake."

"Caye's going to bring the boys in half an hour. And the dog."

"Okay."

He softly shut the door.

Caye filled so many roles in Jill's life—friend, colleague in parenting, chief resource, role model as a mom and wife. What Caye would never guess was that she also filled Jill's need to be mothered. Caye remembered every birthday with a gift. And not only did she bake birthday cakes for the kids, but she also baked one each year for Jill. Jill had had birthdays, many of them, when she hadn't heard from Marion at all. Others when Marion would go overboard, sending as much as a thousand dollars.

So many times Jill wished that Marion were someone else, some other kind of mother.

Before Jill miscarried, Marion came to visit. Jill hadn't told her mother she was pregnant—no need to do that until it was necessary. Rob was away on business in Chicago for two weeks, and Marion had wanted to come up to Ashland. It was her first visit.

Jill stood at the gate of the airport, holding squirmy Hudson, waiting for Marion. What stuck in her memory was the heavyset woman, wearing a wrinkled white cotton skirt and a royal blue polyester blouse, who came off right before Marion. The woman was greeted by, Jill assumed, her daughter and newborn grandbaby. The two women hugged, tightly, the infant between them. The older woman quickly wiped away tears. "Oh, honey," she gushed, dropping her bags, taking the baby, and tucking the little one between her arm and ample breast, "she's so beautiful."

Jill forced her eyes away from the threesome as Marion, wearing her trademark beige suit, white blouse, and quality brown shoes, walked toward her. "How are you, Jill?" she asked, as she pecked her daughter's cheek, her right arm loosely on Jill's shoulder.

"Fine. Just fine."

"Hi, hi," Hudson said.

"We had turbulence," Marion said, her craggy, deeply lined face turned down toward her jutting chin.

"Hi, hi," Hudson called out again.

"Mother, he's talking to you," Jill interjected.

"Oh."

"Hi, hi," Hudson said again.

"Well, hello," Marion said. "Hello, Hudson."

It was during that visit that Jill miscarried, on the last day of three that Marion stayed with her in the split-level house south of town. She called the doctor the day before when she started to spot. "Put your feet up, rest," the nurse had said.

She told her mother she was having a hard period. "I can call a cab," Marion offered.

Jill said she thought that would be a good idea. She could tell Marion was offended.

She felt the bleeding increase and went into the bathroom. There it was, the little fetus. She reached over and put it on a tissue on the counter.

She couldn't tell Marion.

She opened the medicine cabinet and took out the Band-Aid box, pulled out the three remaining bandage strips and put them on the shelf. She picked up the fetus again, ran her finger down its bony back, focused on its fishlike head. It was only an inch and a half long.

*So much in so little.*

She slipped it into the box and washed her hands.

The taxi honked. Jill walked into the living room. Hudson was down for a nap. There was Marion standing by the door, leather satchel in one hand, briefcase in the other.

"Good-bye," she said.

Jill put one arm around her mother and gave a gentle squeeze. "Thanks for coming."

When the taxi had turned the corner, Jill called Caye. "Can you come over?" she asked. "I need you."

Caye hurried in the door, carrying sleeping Audrey in her car seat, herding Andrew along.

"What's the matter?" Caye asked softly.

"The baby. I lost the baby."

"Oh, Jill," Caye whispered, putting Audrey's seat on the floor of the living room and reaching for her friend.

"I put it in a Band-Aid box. I didn't know what to do." Jill began to cry.

"What?"

"The little baby. It's in the bathroom."

"Really?" Caye asked.

"Is that gross?"

Caye shook her head. "What do you want to do with it?"

"Bury it."

"Where?"

Jill decided on the little space along the parking strip. Volunteer cosmos were blooming among the garden roses. "Not in the yard," she said. "I don't plan to live in this house much longer. I want it where I can drive by and look at the flowers."

Caye found a cardboard jewelry box, with the cotton wadding still in it, in the hall closet where Jill kept the wrapping paper. Caye opened the Band-Aid box and slid the fetus onto the cotton.

"I'm so sorry, so sorry," Caye said.

Jill started to cry. Caye hugged her, patting her back, saying, "It'll be okay; it'll be okay."

Caye went through the garage and picked up Jill's green-handled trowel off the gardening bench and then triggered the garage-door opener.

Jill watched from the picture window as Caye dug in the dirt beside a blooming yellow rosebush.

The hot July sun turned Caye's face red. She came back into the house with the trowel. Jill sat down on the couch and ran her fingers down Audrey's spine.

"Where's Andrew?" Caye asked.

"Waking up Hudson. I told him he could."

"How do you feel?"

"Empty."

They sat at the kitchen table while the boys played in the backyard. Audrey practiced rolling over on a blanket on the floor.

"I keep thinking about the abortion I had in college," Jill said.

"Really?" Caye asked. Just that one word: *Really?* No judgment. No sickening fall to her voice. No questions about how Jill could have done such a thing.

"Yeah. Now I have two little babies who didn't make it."

She'd been nineteen. In college. Lonelier than she'd ever been in her life. Finally, thirteen years after his death, she began to grieve for her father. She lost her balance, forgot who she was to her heavenly Father, never acknowledged who the baby was in God's eyes. That one time she trusted her mother—a decision she immediately regretted. A mistake she immediately vowed never to repeat.

Caye poured Jill another cup of tea.

*How many years ago was that now?* Jill drifted toward sleep. *Almost four?* She heard the stampede coming down the hall. Her door flew open.

"Mommy!" Hudson yelled. Scout barked.

"Be gentle," Caye said, hurrying in after the big boys, carrying Simon.

The room was dark. Simon began to whimper.

Jill sat up, bracing herself for the force of the boys.

"Hey, all," she whispered hoarsely.

In an instant, Liam and Hudson were on the bed, hugging her with warm arms and sticky hands. She sucked in their sweaty, loamy scent that made her think of endless, sunny days, working in the garden while they played.

"Ma-ma-ma," Simon chirped.

"Come here, baby," she said, as he leaned out of Caye's arms and into Jill's.

Caye sat down on the end of the bed and smiled. Audrey and Andrew stood at the door.

"Come on, Audrey," Jill said. "Let me look at our four-year-old girl. Hey, you," she said to Andrew. "Turn on the light, would you?"

In another minute they were all on the bed, all seven of them.

"Don't jump," Caye commanded as Liam started to gear up. He looked at his mother.

"Auntie Caye is right," Jill said with a wince. "Don't jump. Mommy might get sick."

Liam began to cry. "They're tired," Caye said. "If they melt down now it's because they were so good for me. I'll stay and get dinner started—help get them settled."

"It's okay. You've done enough," Jill said.

"No," Caye responded. "I insist."

Part Two

The only thing that counts is faith
expressing itself through love.

GALATIANS 5:6

## 10

Caye looked around the room. It was half past ten Sunday morning. They were in Jill's living room for Fellowship. It was Rita's turn to be down in the basement with the kids. Caye wondered how it was going, knew Jill's kids were out of sorts. So were her own kids. They could feel the tension, the waiting.

Louise was often out of sorts anyway. She was a child who, each year, seemed more uncomfortable with herself and others.

Thomas started the meeting the same as any other. There was no hint of a possible catastrophe, of impending doom. Jill and Rob sat on the sofa. Caye knew that Jill's long hair was pulled back in an oversize barrette, and that she was wearing jeans and a gray sweatshirt, but she could not see her friend. Rob was blocking her from sight. Caye sat on one of the mahogany dining room chairs. Nathan sat beside her.

Caye had volunteered to have the Fellowship at their house, even though she really didn't want to. It wasn't easy for her, the way it was for Jill, to have people over. At first glance, she told herself it was a matter of space. Their basement was unfinished, so the kids would have to be crammed into Andrew's room. But it was more than that. Entertaining made her nervous and self-conscious. All the flaws of their house, flaws that she lived with daily and did not notice, leaped out at her. The yellow-and-green plaid kitchen linoleum, the water spots on the dining room ceiling, the chipped counter in the bathroom.

But for Jill's sake she was willing to host the Fellowship.

"Oh no," Jill said when Caye called to volunteer. "I want everyone here. Rob said he'd help get everything ready, and it will be easier for me if we have it here—I won't have to go out."

Caye even admitted, when she arrived, that Jill looked better. "Muscle relaxants and Ativan work wonders," Rob responded.

Jill gave him a "don't contradict my optimism" look.

Each member asked how she was feeling as they came in the door. Jill stayed on the couch and answered each one, "Better. Really. I'm much better."

"Well, good, you really had us worried," Rita boomed as she gave Jill a hug. Then she headed down to the basement with the kids.

Caye marveled at Jill's warmth, how she connected with each member—even when she was sick.

Thomas started the lesson on time. The teaching was on the Ten Commandments. He discussed the background, and then the group read through Exodus 20 together. Next came the discussion. The first question was, "Have you broken one of the commandments and not regretted it? Not seen consequences in your own life?" When Jill started to speak, Caye was alarmed—she was certain Jill was going to confess to not having told Rob about her father dying of pancreatic cancer.

But that wasn't Jill's subject at all.

"I stole something once," she said, "and I've never regretted it."

Everyone sat quietly.

"I stole tulip bulbs from an old lady in Pennsylvania, dug them right out of her yard, right from under her nose."

"And you've never regretted it?" Thomas asked.

"Never."

"Why?"

"Because they belonged to me."

Another pause.

"Well, they were on her property. But she wouldn't share. So I took them."

"The old entitlement-justification story," Rob chuckled, shifting his head and giving Caye a view of Jill. Rob often joked about Jill's poor logic. "She lives by her feelings," he once said. "That's why she's so optimistic."

Jill had a knack for saying whatever came to mind. It was one of the appealing things about her. Most of the thoughts she blurted out were self-effacing stories. But they weren't designed to be "oh, I'm so stupid" stories. They were just funny stories, stories that she wanted other people to laugh at too.

Caye was surprised that she'd never heard this story of Jill's before—another new Jill story. How many stories had they told each other? How many stories were left to tell?

"Thanks, Jill," Thomas said with a laugh. "Only you could discredit my point in such a cheery way."

At the opening of prayer time, Thomas looked at Rob and asked, "How can we pray for your family?"

"We find out the results of the biopsy tomorrow. Please pray that it will be negative."

"May I add something before we pray?" Joya was sitting on the edge of her chair, her feet perpendicular to the floor, toes pointed downward. She was wearing a blue-and-yellow checked jumper with a white T-shirt and white Keds.

"I had a revelation," she said. "On Friday morning. I already shared it with Caye—but I want to tell all of you." She looked directly at Jill. "I was praying during the biopsy, and God told me..." She paused. Caye felt uncomfortable, just as she had when Joya had talked with her on the phone.

Nathan reached over and took Caye's hand.

Why had Joya said that she'd told Caye? Caye hadn't said anything to Jill, hadn't told her about Joya's phone call or the revelation.

"God told me," she said again. And then, "This is hard for me, Jill." Joya began to cry and took a deep breath. Caye realized that in the four years she'd known Joya she'd never seen Joya shed a tear. "He told me that you have pancreatic cancer but that he is going to heal you."

Rob folded his arms across his chest.

Nathan squeezed Caye's hand.

"Oh, God," Summer moaned from the platform rocker. Caye thought the words sounded like disgust, not a cry for mercy.

Jill was still out of sight, but her voice rose, a little shaky yet still cheery. "Well," she said, as if Joya were a pop-up doll who had just surprised her.

"Joya, are you serious?" Summer asked.

"I've never been more serious in my life," Joya said, her voice deep.

"Well, what else do we need to pray about?" Jill asked quickly. "Enough about me. Let's move on." She looked around the room. Caye avoided her eyes, but shot a glance at Rob. He sat with his arms crossed, his chin down.

*I should have told Jill. I should have told her what Joya said.*

The group was silent for a few long moments.

Finally Lonnie asked for prayer for his computer programming class; he had a midterm the next day.

Thomas read from Psalms and then led the group in prayer. Caye wanted to pray aloud, wanted to pray for Jill, but didn't. She felt self-conscious praying in the Fellowship. She was afraid of praying the wrong thing, or showing how little she knew about the Bible and God. She was afraid of sounding unsure.

What would she have prayed?

She would have said, "God, I'm so scared. Jill is sick; something is wrong, and we don't know what. We're helpless. We ask for your healing—whether it's cancer or something else. You know we need her—her kids, Rob, and all of us. Keep her safe. Amen."

That's what she would have prayed. Instead, led by Simon's fussing, she left the room and went down the basement stairs to help Rita with the kids.

❧

"I shouldn't have blurted out my tulip-stealing story," Jill said to Caye over the phone that afternoon. The boys were all down napping, even Hudson, and Rob had run into the office for a few minutes.

"What's the story behind the tulip bulbs?" Caye asked.

It felt good to be talking to Caye on the phone—almost normal.

"I stole the tulips when I was twenty-three, a few months before I moved to Argentina. I'd gone to New Jersey to visit my friend Karen—we went to USC together. She's the one who hooked me up with the diplomat job; it was a connection through her husband's family. She and I went into New York every day for a week—went to the galleries, a few shows, the museums, did the shopping thing."

Jill had rented a car and driven to Pennsylvania on the last day of her trip to see the town her father had grown up in.

"I visited my dad's cousin, asked for some of my great-grandmother's tulips, which grew in the woman's yard. She wouldn't give me even one. So I went back and stole them after dark."

"And never felt guilty?" Caye asked.

"Never," Jill laughed. "Although I do feel guilty for confessing to not feeling guilty in front of Joya. I'm sure it will come back to bite me."

"Are they the tulips in your garden?" Caye asked.

"Yep. You wouldn't believe how I've babied them through the years. I'll divide them in the fall, really." It was a joke between them—Jill had meant to give Caye some of the bulbs for two years now, but hadn't. "If you still want them now that you know they're contraband."

"You'd better get a nap," Caye said with a laugh. "While the boys are down."

"I'll see you in the morning when we drop the boys off. And, Caye," she added, right before she said good-bye, "thanks for being such a good friend."

As she settled under the comforter, Jill thought about her trip to Mount Llewellyn, Pennsylvania. Marion never talked about the past but had mentioned one time the name of the town her father came from. When Jill asked Marion where she was from, her mother simply answered, "Close to where your father grew up." Marion also revealed that Jill's father was raised by his grandmother. "A very creative woman," Marion had said, "but not very nice."

Jill stopped at a phone booth and looked up "Linsey." She found Ada Linsey first and dialed the number. She explained that she was looking for relatives of William Linsey.

"He's dead," the woman said. "Died a few years ago—out in California."

"Yes, I know," Jill said politely. "I'm his daughter."

"Out snoopin' around," Ada said. "Wantin' to see the old home place, huh?"

"No," Jill said. "I just wanted to meet a relative or two. I didn't know there was an old home place."

"Not much left."

"Could I come by?" Jill asked. "Bring some supper? I could pick it up at the diner."

"Not a good day. I'm here all alone."

"Could I stop by? Just to meet you?"

"William was my cousin," Ada said, not answering Jill's questions. "I'm sorry he's dead. Didn't surprise me though."

"I could be over in just a few minutes," Jill said.

"No, no, no," Ada said. "Not today." And she hung up.

Jill looked at the address in the book. The house was on Third Street. She looked up at the sign across the street from the phone booth. She was on Fifth.

It was 4:30 on a weekday afternoon. The town was nearly deserted. The trees lining the street blew slightly in the breeze. As she drove, Jill imagined her father walking along the sidewalk, kicking a can. She passed a box-shaped house with new lemon-colored vinyl siding, the Methodist church topped with a traditional steeple, a park with a grove of elm in the middle. She turned on Third Street and stopped at the next corner, searching for the address on the brick house in front of her. She parked and climbed out of the car and stood looking at the front of the house. Behind the overgrown wisteria spreading from the porch to the side of the house, she made out three tiles with the numbers.

The wooden front steps were gray, with strips of paint pulled off, exposing white primer and bare wood. The screen was open and revealed a heavy old wooden door. The house had two stories.

Jill walked around to the side. The flower bed was overgrown with weeds and grass. An old oak tree towered in the yard; the large back area was unfenced. Three apple trees grew along the alley. An old shed leaned toward a garden plot that looked as if it hadn't been tilled in years.

Walking back toward the car, Jill noticed a lace curtain flutter against a six-on-six paned window. By the time she reached the corner of the property, the front door was open, and a tall, elderly woman, wearing a brown dress with a tan sweater held closed by tightly crossed arms, stood on the porch. Her short white hair was uncombed. Her legs were thin and bare, and Jill could see veins snaking their way down toward white shoes with rounded toes. "What do you want?" the woman asked in a husky voice.

"Just to see the outside of the house—that's all."

The woman frowned.

"I just talked to you on the phone," Jill said.

"And didn't even say who you were."

"Oh I'm sorry. I was sure I did. Jill Linsey. William's daughter."

Ada scowled. "How's your mother?"

"Fine."

"I liked her. Only saw her once. Scandal that it was."

Jill wondered what the old woman was talking about, thinking that Ada reminded her more of her mother than her father. It made her imagine what Marion might be like in twenty years.

"Well, you've looked around," Ada said. "Be on your way."

Jill let her eyes take in the property again, from the oak tree's new leaves against the roof to the azalea bushes along the foundation. That was when she saw the double tulips, the beautiful red tulips with the pink centers and ruffled edges on the other side of the porch.

"Those were your great-grandmother's," Ada said, following Jill's eyes. "Her best friend gave them to her. They keep coming up year after year."

"They're lovely," Jill said, enthralled with the ruffled petals, the contrast of the ruby red and soft pink.

*Why not ask for some of the bulbs?* She had nothing from her father's past, nothing at all. The flowers would mean so much to her. And the bulbs should be divided—although not this early. Still, she wanted the bulbs. It was worth the risk to take them too soon.

Before she could get the words out, Ada frowned more deeply, the lines around her mouth turning downward, her lips pulling into her mouth.

"Go on now," the old woman said. "It's time for you to leave."

"I was wondering—," Jill started.

"Now, get. Get off my property."

Jill felt humiliated. She made her way backward, retreating like a naughty child, feeling the unnamed shame of her family. She walked to the rental car while Ada squared her shoulders and pursed her lips more tightly.

"Good-bye, then," Jill said, embarrassed.

She took short steps around the car and opened the driver's door, afraid that if she took large steps or moved too quickly, Ada might rush in and call the police. She held up her hand in a fluttery wave and sank into the seat.

In the four minutes it took to reach the edge of town she had a plan. She drove back to the gas station and left a message for Karen. She'd changed her plans; she was going to spend the night in Pennsylvania and would stop by in the morning to get her things before going to the airport.

Then she went to the hardware store across the street and bought a pair of white canvas gloves and a trowel with a green rubber handle. As she left the store, she stifled a giggle.

She felt giddy as she ordered a chicken potpie at the diner out on the highway. The waitress, who was about Jill's age, avoided her eyes as she took the order. Truckers sat on red vinyl stools at the counter. The food was greasy, and her water glass felt sticky.

By half past seven, dusk was falling. Jill drove back into town, back to the house, and circled around to the alley. A solitary light illuminated the far rear corner of the house. She continued driving and parked a block away, pulled her black wool coat from the backseat, and slipped her fingers into the gardening gloves.

She laughed out loud. Why had she bought white gloves? She looked like Mickey Mouse. She picked up the trowel and took the keys out of the ignition, carefully putting them in her coat pocket. She purposely did not lock the car in case she needed to make a quick getaway.

Jill walked slowly to the house, trying her best to look nonchalant. Two boys, perhaps nine years old, rode by on bicycles, passing a tennis ball back and forth to each other as they pedaled.

"Ricky!" a woman's voice called out.

"Gotta go," the smaller boy said, sliding the ball into the pocket of his jacket.

Jill crossed the street and walked onto the lawn in front of the house. The grass was squishy under her feet. The winter snow and spring rains had soaked the sod. She knelt by the tulips and felt the dampness of the ground seep through the denim of her jeans. She plunged the trowel into the soil. She pushed and turned it against the moist loam, popping a clump of tulips out of the ground. She grabbed the stems of the clump and shook the dirt off the bulbs, then placed her treasure on the grass.

Again, she pushed the trowel into the dirt and twisted it down and around another group of bulbs.

She heard a creaking noise, and a half a second later light flooded the yard. Ada, or someone, had turned the porch light on.

Jill yanked the stems from the ground, grabbed the first clump of bulbs, and scooted, still hunched down, up against the concrete foundation of the house.

She heard the door open and footsteps on the porch, practically over her head. Was it Ada? Was she looking over the railing?

Then the steps retreated, and the screen door slammed.

Jill realized she'd been holding her breath and slowly let it out. Should she hurry off? Or was Ada standing at the window, peering through the curtains? Would she call the police?

The half-moon was rising over the house across the street. A dog barked in the alley.

Jill thought of her father. If Ada was right, if this had been her great-grandmother's home, then it was where her dad grew up. She imagined him climbing the oak tree, riding an old rickety bike down the alley, weeding this very flower bed for his grandmother. Perhaps he even divided these tulips. He liked to garden; Jill remembered that. She thought of him out pruning his roses, a cigarette dangling out of his mouth.

"I'm here, Daddy," she whispered. "I'm here thinking about you."

*And stealing from a mean old lady.* She suppressed another giggle.

She'd planned to take all of the tulips—but she wouldn't. Spite was such a nasty motivation. Two clumps were enough. She waited for several minutes and then crawled out of the flower bed; she walked quickly toward the back of the house. A dog barked and lunged toward her. Jill screamed and dropped the trowel. The dog jerked backward inches from Jill's leg—he'd come to the end of his chain. She grabbed the trowel and hurried on. She heard the back door of Ada's house slam.

Jill began to run, shoving the bulbs into the pockets of her coat. She stripped the gloves off and slipped them into the waistband of her jeans. She thought about ditching the trowel in a bush but then decided to keep it. If the tulips didn't survive, she'd still have a memento of the evening.

She turned left at the next block, circling back to the rental car, stumbling several times on the broken sidewalk.

As she reached the car, she saw a state patrol cruiser slow to a stop right in front of the old place. She opened the car door, dug through the dirt and bulbs for the keys, quickly started the motor, and pulled away from the curb toward the highway.

Would the state patrolman stop her? Charge her with stealing tulips?

She began to laugh.

The Great Tulip Caper.

She felt lighthearted driving east toward New Jersey in the dark. She'd seen where she'd come from. Well, where her dad came from.

She never wanted to go back.

Unless it was to steal more tulips.

She started to laugh again, tapping the steering wheel with her dirty fingernails. Why had she bothered with the gloves? She pulled them from under her sweater, rolled down her window, and flung the white canvas onto the highway.

She got a room at the Howard Johnson on the Pennsylvania side of Trenton and put it on Marion's Visa. As soon as she entered the room, she spread the bulbs on tissues on the bathroom counter to dry. The flowers had begun to wilt. She tore them off their stems and pressed them in the Gideon Bible. In the morning she took the Bible with her.

That summer, when she moved to Argentina, she wrapped the bulbs in fabric and smuggled the bundle in her carry-on bag. Later she refrigerated the bulbs, giving them the winter that they needed, and then planted them in pots and kept them in her room. They bloomed for Christmas. Jill kept the bulbs indoors in pots or in the refrigerator until she planted them in the garden of her Victorian house in Ashland on the day they moved in.

Jill woke to Simon's cries. Hudson was at the bedroom door. "We're up," he said.

The pain was back. She'd forgotten to take another pill before she fell asleep.

"Where's Daddy?" she asked.

Hudson shrugged his shoulders.

Jill swung her feet over the edge of the bed. What had Joya told her after Fellowship? Jill sat for a minute, not wanting to get up too quickly.

"Have faith," she'd said. "Don't go by how you feel. Believe that you are healed. Act like you are healed. Take care of your family."

She heard Rob at the front door. "Go tell Daddy to get Simon," she said to Hudson, standing to reach for the bottle of pain meds on her dresser.

## 11

Caye woke with a start. Something was wrong, terribly wrong. First she thought of the kids. *Is it Andrew? Is it Audrey?* Her heart raced. *No, they're all right.*

*Nathan?*

And then she remembered.

It was Jill.

She lifted her head to look at the clock on Nathan's nightstand: 4:50 A.M. Caye thought of her relief three months before when 1999 uneventfully turned into the year 2000. It wasn't that she anticipated a catastrophe, but still she felt her guard let down as the first of the year dawned without any repercussions. Now her guard was up again. Did calamity loom ahead?

She slipped out of bed twenty minutes later and pulled a pair of socks from the basket of clean laundry on the landing. She padded down the staircase, turned up the heat, started a pot of Monday-morning coffee, and grabbed Nathan's black sweatshirt that he'd draped over a dining room chair the evening before. She pulled it on, leaving the hood on her head, covering her short, disheveled hair.

She looked out the kitchen window while she waited for the coffee. She imagined the weeds working their way to the top of the soil in the unplanted garden. Dawn filled the backyard; the early morning light bathed the newly green trees in a golden hue.

Caye poured the coffee and wrapped her hands around the mug, hoping to draw some comfort, some solace from the warm ceramic. She picked up her Bible from the hutch as she passed through the dining room, plodded into the living room, and sat in her rocking chair.

She sipped the coffee, taking in the hot liquid; the comforting aroma filled her head. When she was growing up, her mom would start the coffee in the gallon stainless steel pot with the black plastic spigot early each morning. Caye would wake to the smell long after her father had gone off on the ranch with a thermos full of strong, black Folgers. She'd find her mother with a mug in her hand sitting at the kitchen table in her cleaning-lady uniform, ready to leave for the hospital. Both of her parents' breath always smelled of coffee from morning to night.

Nathan would be up soon. Then Audrey, and finally Andrew. Rob and Jill were going to drop Hudson, Liam, and Simon off by 10:15 on their way to Jill's appointment with Dr. Scott.

Caye shivered as she sat with her legs pulled up to her chest, her nightshirt stretched over her knees, the Bible on the cushion beside her. It was the only time she'd have to herself all day.

"God, I'm afraid," she whispered. "So afraid."

She took another sip of coffee.

It was a dream, a bad dream. Not even Caye, in her worst fit of worry, could have come up with this. Just the thought of Jill having cancer was unbelievable. But a cancer as threatening as pancreatic cancer was beyond comprehension.

She put the mug on the end table and picked up her Bible. It fell open to Galatians. There, underlined during Thomas's teachings from two years ago on the apostle Paul's letters, was the verse: "The only thing that counts is faith expressing itself through love."

❧

Jill and Rob waited in an examination room.

"What are you thinking?" Jill asked Rob.

"I'm trying not to think," he said, spinning around on the stool. "Just trying to get through this next part."

"Do you think Joya is right?"

"You don't want to know what I think of Joya right now."

The nurse, a tiny middle-aged woman with prematurely gray hair, came in and took Jill's blood pressure: 150 over 110.

"It's a little high," she said, patting Jill on the shoulder.

"I'm a little nervous," Jill replied as the nurse left the room.

"The doctor is twenty-five minutes late," Rob reported, looking at his watch, before the door completely closed behind the nurse. "Awfully inconsiderate of him, isn't it?"

"He's busy," Jill said. "He'll be in soon. I think you'll like him."

Rob spun around on the chair again.

A quick little knock on the door was immediately followed by Dr. Scott coming into the room.

He stuck out his hand to Rob. "Dr. Scott," he said.

"Rob Rhone."

"Hello, Jill. How are you?"

"Better."

The doctor sat on the vinyl seat of the straight-back metal chair.

"I'm sorry," Dr. Scott said, clearing his throat. "I have some diffi-cult news to tell you."

The room moved, shifted, began to tilt.

"The biopsy came back positive for pancreatic cancer." Dr. Scott raised his eyebrows as he spoke.

Jill's spine felt as if it were going to give, as if she were going to collapse on the table and then slide onto the floor. She folded her arms around her chest, forced herself to sit straight, to stop the fall, to brace herself against the emotional gravity that tugged so heavily, that threatened to take her down.

Rob stood and walked to the examining table; he wrapped his arms around Jill in a clumsy sideways hold, as if he were communi-cating to an unseen enemy—or maybe the doctor—that she was his, that she belonged to him, and she was not to be taken. They stayed that way for a moment, Jill hugging herself, Rob hugging Jill. Finally she grasped his forearm and held on.

"What do you know about pancreatic cancer?" Dr. Scott asked softly.

"We know it's bad," Rob answered.

"My father died from it," Jill added. *Did the doctor remember that?* He was nodding; yes, he'd read her chart.

Jill knew it was bad, but she didn't know the particulars, not exactly. She knew Marion thought it meant sure death, which made

Jill want to believe desperately that it didn't, made her want to rebel against cancer the way she'd rebelled against Marion-the-doomsayer in little ways all these years. And besides, her father had died nearly thirty years ago. Surely advances had been made since then; surely the odds weren't as bad as in the early '70s.

Jill had lived with the specter of cancer since childhood. Marion had snaked it around her life. She'd struggled to escape it, to wriggle away, to flee and leave it behind. Pan-cre-at-ic can-cer was how Marion said it, pronouncing each syllable with distinction, making it sound like one long, dirty word.

And now here it was, winding itself tighter, threatening this life she had created.

"Our course of action is to be aggressive," the doctor said. "Very aggressive. We'll start with surgery and then follow with chemotherapy to keep the cancer from spreading. And then radiation to shrink anything that's left."

"What is the prognosis?" Rob questioned.

"Have you done any research on pancreatic cancer?" The doctor asked.

Jill shook her head.

"Not really," Rob answered.

"The statistics aren't good. But Jill's young and healthy. She has a lot to live for."

"What are the statistics?" Rob asked.

"Twenty percent of patients who undergo surgery successfully have a five-year survival rate. But there's only a four percent survival rate over five years for all patients." Dr. Scott looked directly at Jill.

Jill struggled for air, for oxygen. She felt as if she were breathing fog—no, smog. Southern California smog. Buenos Aires smog. Twenty percent. Four percent. She couldn't grasp what it meant.

Jill wanted to ask about the statistics again, to have the doctor explain it slowly, but she couldn't get her mouth open to form the words. Twenty percent. Four percent. What did he mean, exactly?

"Is this the best place for Jill to be?" Rob responded. His voice sounded defensive. "I mean," he continued, "should we go to the Mayo Clinic? Or Johns Hopkins?"

"I trained at Stanford," Dr. Scott answered. "I feel fully compe-tent to handle Jill's case. Of course the decision is up to you."

"I don't want to go anywhere else," Jill said. She couldn't leave the boys. Wouldn't leave the boys. And to take them along would be so upsetting. She wanted them all together. In her house. In their house.

"I have to tell you," the doctor said as he hunched forward and leaned toward them, "I have a wife and two little girls and a third baby on the way, a family much like yours. I've thought about the two of you and your boys all weekend, wondering what the results would be."

He paused. "I'm sorry. Your case hits very close to home for me. I promise you that I'll do everything possible, everything within my power."

"Thanks," she said to the doctor.

"When is surgery scheduled?" Rob asked.

"This Thursday. Dr. Kendall will do it. I have great confidence in him. He can see you tomorrow afternoon. His receptionist will call to set up a time."

The doctor handed them two packets of papers stapled together—one on pancreatic cancer, the other on surgery.

"Please call me if you have any questions," he said as he stood to leave. After he was gone, Rob sat back down on the swivel chair and looked at Jill, stared at her, pulled her in with his gray eyes. She inched her way off the table, stood, picked her leather purse off the floor, and slung the strap over her shoulder.

"What are you thinking?" she asked.

He spread the palms of his hands, of his big, big hands, into a cup, covered his face and began to sob. Big, shaking sobs. Jill squat-ted on the floor in front of him and placed her hands on his wrists and pulled him toward her.

"It'll be okay," she said. Her strength was building. Gravity had eased its grip. "It will be okay."

"I'm sorry," he sobbed. "You should be crying, not me. I should be strong."

"It's okay," she singsonged. "We'll get through this. We'll make it. I'll make it."

"I don't want you to die," he said.

He pushed the swivel chair back and knelt on the floor beside her, taking her in his arms. He stroked her dark hair, pulled his fingers through it.

"Why didn't you tell me about your dad? About the others?"

"Would it have made a difference?"

"I would have been more prepared for this."

"And written me off years ago the way Marion has?"

"No, baby, no."

"We'd better go," she said. "They'll need the room."

"To break bad news to someone else."

Rob stood and helped Jill to her feet, held her arm as they walked out of the room. *Take care of me. Take care of me, Rob.*

Reading the literature in the car on the drive home, she realized it would take more than Rob to take care of her and the boys.

❧

The sun was warm against Caye's back, against Nathan's black sweat-shirt that she'd worn all morning.

Audrey and Hudson played in the sandbox, both singing, "Take me out to the ball game," as they lined up gritty sand cakes and cook-ies along the edge of the railroad tie box that Nathan had built three years before. Audrey's new bike was parked next to the garage. Caye had promised her a trip around the block after Simon woke from his nap.

Liam swung from the rope on the big leaf maple, back and forth, back and forth, his muddy yellow boots flying over the grass. She looked at her watch: 11:40. She should start lunch for the older kids before Simon woke.

She'd planted the white geraniums and lobelia in the window box and had begun to level the garden with the rake. The rain had formed clods of mud that needed to be broken up.

*Why hasn't Jill called?* She pulled the rake, yanking it through the lumpy soil. *Maybe everything is fine. Maybe she and Rob went out to lunch.*

She pulled the rake again.

Liam walked away from the swing over to Audrey's bike. "Get away from it!" Audrey shouted.

"Audrey," Caye said, "where are your manners?"

"Mom, he's so annoying."

*Annoying* was Audrey's new word. She'd learned it from Andrew.

"And he's copying me. He keeps wearing his boots." Audrey looked down at her own black rubber boots. Caye knew her daughter was jealous that Liam's were yellow.

"Come on, Liam," Caye said. "Do you want to help me? I'm getting ready to plant the garden."

As Caye took his hand to lead him to the back of the yard, the phone rang.

She dropped his hand. "Be right back," she told him and hurried up the deck stairs into the kitchen, snatching the phone from the table.

"Hi, sweetie," Jill said.

"How are you?" Caye blurted out, unable to control her words, never meaning the question more in her life.

"It's cancer," Jill said, the words cascading into a sob, the sob gaining momentum.

"Oh, Jill. Jill, oh, Jilly."

The sobbing continued. "I'm sor...sorry." Caye heard Jill take a raggedy breath. The sobbing stopped.

"Jill? Are you there?"

It was a man's voice. "Hi, Caye." It was Rob.

"I'm here."

"We'll call you in a few minutes, okay? I'm going to pull over. I think Jill and I both need to cry."

Caye turned the phone off, gripped it in her hand, and looked out in the backyard. It looked like a foreign land. The world had shifted. She felt as if she were standing on a steep slope, as if they were all ready to slide off the landscape. Liam flung dirt out of the garden plot onto the grass with the rake. His hands were covered with mud, and he'd smeared it across his face. Audrey sat on her bike, arms crossed. Hudson was throwing sand out of the box toward Audrey.

Caye wanted to run upstairs and fling herself across her bed. She wanted to call Nathan and say, "It's true. It's true. How can it be true?"

She stood at the window and imagined going outside and patting Hudson on the head. "Don't throw sand," she'd say. Then she'd add, "These are lovely cakes, Hudson, just lovely. I think you'll be a cook like your mommy."

Then she'd walk over to the garden. "Liam," she'd say taking his hand once more, "why don't you swing again? You looked so happy swinging."

Instead she stood and watched the scene unfold as the word CANCER reverberated through her head. *Oh, God, why would you let this happen?*

Cancer. Cancer. Not to Jill. Her heart constricted with love for her friend. Not to Jill. She thought of Jill crying, of optimistic Jill sobbing.

Tears flooded Caye's eyes. She wiped them on the sleeve of the sweatshirt.

Liam picked up a dirt clod and threw it at Hudson.

Still, Caye stood watching the children as if she were watching a movie in slow motion with the sound turned off and the color turned up. The clarity of the shifting landscape was electrifying. Her head ached.

Liam threw another dirt clod and hit Hudson's shoulder.

Caye's feet began to move. She realized the door was opening and she was moving, stepping into the foreign Technicolor world before her. The phone was still in her hand.

"No, no, Liam," she said. "We don't throw dirt clods."

Hudson threw another handful of sand at Audrey.

"Stop it, Hudson," she said, swiping her sleeve across her nose. "Please be kind."

"What's wrong, Mommy?" Audrey asked, climbing off her bike. "Have you been crying?"

Before Caye could think of an evasive answer, the phone rang again. Turning away from the children and walking back through the door, she answered.

It was Rob.

"Is she okay?"

"Yeah. We're on our way to your house. We'll be there in about ten minutes."

"You can leave the boys. Really. I'll bring them up later. You guys need some time."

"Jill wants to come to your house. She said she just wants to sit on your couch. Have a cup of tea. And then we'll take the boys."

Caye filled the kettle from the tap and turned on the stove. How could life change so drastically, so suddenly? How could she have taken it all for granted?

The phone rang again.

It was the sales manager of the magazine she'd interviewed with. "We'd like to offer you the job."

The job. She'd forgotten all about the job. No use talking to Nathan about this one. There was nothing else to do.

"I've had a family emergency," she said. "I'm sorry. I can't take it."

Jill and Rob walked up the front steps. Caye opened the door. She reached out her arms to Jill, and Jill floated into them. Caye held her, patted her back, pulled her hair away from her neck. Jill began to cry again. Soft, quiet tears.

Caye took her hand and led her to the couch.

"I'll go check on the boys," Rob said. "We heard them in the back."

Caye imagined him kneeling beside both Hudson and Liam and hugging them, holding them. She wondered if he would tell them that Jill was sick, really sick.

"Do you think Joya is right?" Jill asked, curling her feet up under her, pulling a tissue from the box on the coffee table. "Do you think I will recover?"

"Yes," Caye said.

"Not many people do."

"But some people do," Caye said, thinking of the statistics. But she meant it. If anyone could recover, Jill could. Audacious, bold, fun-loving, faithful Jill.

The sound of Simon crying came over the baby monitor that Caye had saved from Audrey's babyhood. "Tell Rob," Jill said. "He'll want to go get him."

Rob came down with Simon, who was giggling in his daddy's arms.

"Hi, sweet baby," Jill said. Rob sat beside her on the couch. Jill stroked Simon's cheek.

"I guess this means no more babies," she said.

Rob patted her knee. Caye expected him to say, "That's the least of our worries." But he didn't.

Audrey and the boys came in; Liam's boots tracked mud over the hardwood floor. Caye didn't care. Rob and Jill didn't notice.

"Hi, guys," Jill said. "Give Mommy a kiss."

Each traipsed over and kissed her, Hudson first and then Liam, two sweet kisses on the lips. Liam reached up and touched her cheek, streaking mud across it. Rob and Caye laughed.

*Rob didn't tell them.* Caye pushed her cat out of the rocker and sat down in her place of safety.

"He's marked you," Rob said to Jill, "with war paint."

"Good," she smiled. "I need it."

"We're hungry," Hudson said.

"Are you really sick? Bad sick?" Audrey asked, looking straight at Jill.

Jill looked at Caye. Caye shook her head. No, she hadn't told Audrey.

"You look like you've been crying," Audrey added.

Jill began to laugh. Caye smiled. Rob looked at Jill.

"Why are you laughing?" Audrey demanded.

"Because you're such a little woman," Jill answered, putting her arms out to Audrey. "Come here. Come give me a hug."

Audrey rushed in, gave Jill a bear hug, and sat beside her.

"We should go home," Rob said.

"The tea. You didn't have your tea." Caye stood, remembering the boiling kettle.

"We should go. I'll call you this afternoon," Jill said.

"The crib," Rob said to Caye across the backseat of the Suburban as he buckled Simon into his car seat and Caye strapped Liam in. "I forgot the crib."

"I'll bring it tomorrow," Caye said.

"Call me," she said to Jill in a pleading voice. "We can figure out meals and help."

"When's lunch?" Audrey asked, pulling on Caye's hand, pulling her away from the sidewalk.

Back in the house, Caye told Audrey, "I need to go do something. I'll get lunch in a minute." Caye rushed up the stairs two at a time and hurried down the landing, racing her tears. She flung herself across her bed; her foot kicked against the crib. She began to cry; she pulled her pillow under her head and sobbed deep, deep, belly sobs.

"Mama," Audrey whispered. "Mommy?" Audrey knelt on the bed and poked at Caye's side.

Caye rolled over.

"What's wrong?" Audrey asked.

Caye could tell her daughter was scared.

"Jill's sick," Caye said, sitting up and pulling Audrey into her arms and down on the bed next to her. "You were right. She's really sick."

"Is she going to die?" Audrey asked. "Are you going to die?"

"No. No," Caye said. *I could be lying.* She stroked Audrey's long hair. It hadn't been combed all morning. *I have no idea. Jill could live for sixty more years. Or not. I could die tomorrow. Or not.*

Caye sat up and retrieved her brush off the dresser and the two clippies she'd left beside it.

"Sit up," she said to Audrey. Gently she combed her daughter's hair. Not the normal rushed job, but soft and lovingly. Then she snapped the clippies against her daughter's head.

*Nothing in life is a given.*

"I love you, Audrey," she said as she put down the brush and hugged her daughter. The words were good words. Right words. Still they only conveyed a minuscule amount of what she felt.

## 12

"I want the Fellowship to come and pray for me," Jill said. "Tomorrow night."

It was Tuesday morning, and Caye and Audrey had come over to Jill's for the day after dropping Andrew off at school.

"I'll have Rob call Thomas—around 7:30 would probably be the best time," Jill said. "But could you call the rest?"

Caye nodded.

They were sitting in Jill's living room on the sofa, in front of the bay window. Jill yawned.

"You should go get a nap," Caye said, feeling unsettled.

"I'll wait until after lunch," Jill answered. She was wearing blue sweatpants and a long-sleeve lavender T-shirt and had her feet propped on the ottoman. Jill wrapped her legs in the variegated purple, blue, and green afghan Caye had crocheted for Jill in thanks for her help after Audrey was born.

Caye stood and picked up Jill's cold blue china teacup. The smell of peppermint hung in the air. "I'm going to go finish up the breakfast dishes," she said, heading toward the kitchen.

Caye had crocheted the afghan during the evenings while watching CNN and Nick at Nite after Andrew was in bed, between Audrey's early and late evening feedings.

Jill had been impressed that Caye could crochet. "Who taught you?" she asked incredulously, as if it were an ancient art.

"My mother," Caye answered.

It was after Jill's miscarriage that Caye finally finished the afghan and gave it to her friend. It was the first thing she'd crocheted since high school, and she'd inadvertently dropped stitches, making it wider at the bottom than at the top. Caye, fighting the urge to rip the whole thing out and start over, gave it to Jill anyway. Jill ignored her apology. "Who cares?" she exclaimed. "I love it."

Caye filled the sink with hot water. She rinsed the dishes carefully and put them in the dishwasher.

A week after Caye presented Jill with the afghan, they took Andrew, Hudson, and baby Audrey to Emigrant Lake for the afternoon. It was hot and dry, and temperatures had been in the high nineties for over two weeks. The lake was crowded with swimmers and boaters. Andrew and Hudson had wriggled out of their life jackets and were playing with Matchbox cars in the grass. Caye and Jill sat on a blanket on the grassy hillside with Audrey between them.

"What else do you know how to do?" Jill asked.

Caye looked at her friend, confused. "What are you talking about?"

"Like crocheting. What else do you know how to do?"

"Knit. Embroider. Cross-stitch."

"And your mom taught you?"

Caye nodded.

"Where did she learn to do all of that?"

"From her mom."

"How old were you when you learned?"

"Nine or ten."

"Do you sew, too?"

"I don't like to," Caye said with a laugh.

"Tell me about growing up in the Wild West," Jill said, flopping over on her stomach. Her one-piece black-and-blue striped swimsuit was cut high on the legs and low in the back. Although her dark wavy hair and blue eyes were striking, Jill wasn't a glamour girl, but she was definitely pretty with an innate gracefulness. She didn't work at being graceful—she just was. It was her confidence, her focus on others, the easy way she carried herself, the way she listened. It was how comfortable she felt with herself.

Caye couldn't help comparing herself to Jill's svelte grace, aware of her own postpartum body that was squeezed into last year's swimsuit. At least her nursing breasts filled up the top this summer.

Caye picked up Audrey, who was starting to fuss, and pulled a towel over her shoulder, sliding one strap down so the baby could nurse. Audrey latched on immediately. She was the perfect nursing age—quick and efficient, but not old enough to be distracted by her surroundings.

"What is there to tell?" Caye chuckled, thinking of the term "Wild West." She was only two generations away from the pioneers—that was true. Her great-grandparents had been part of the western migration, but it honestly had little meaning for her.

"But you did so much, learned so much. It made you so capable and independent. You're the Western ideal—the product of manifest destiny, the rugged individual."

"I think you're romanticizing the West and my life," Caye laughed. "And making me feel older than the hills."

"But you did so much more than I did. What did I do?" Jill pondered her question. "Shopped. Went to Disneyland.

"Did I tell you that Rob's decided I'm not ambitious?" she asked, changing the subject, interrupting herself. "I hope he doesn't think that I've tricked him. I've never been ambitious. It seems he just figured it out."

Caye thought about this. She saw Jill as very industrious. Jill gardened, planned meals, did the grocery shopping, seldom took a nap, kept them all busy with picnics and outings. She was definitely ambitious when it came to wanting a family.

"Did I tell you that I didn't graduate from college?" Jill asked.

"I thought you went to USC."

"I did. And all I needed to take was second-year French."

"So why didn't you take it?"

"The honest answer?"

Caye smiled and switched Audrey to the other side. The baby began to suck, but not as aggressively.

"I think I didn't finish just to spite Marion. She wouldn't pay for college unless I went to a local one. I think that was my way of getting back at her."

Caye smiled again but this time with a look of pity.

"I know what you're thinking," Jill laughed. "It hurt me more than it did her. But it hasn't really. If I open a gallery or a bed-and-breakfast, I can do that without my degree. Actually, your business degree would come in really handy. We could be partners."

Jill rolled to a sitting position. Caye took Audrey off her breast, placed the milk-drugged baby across her thighs and slipped back into her suit.

"Here," Jill said, reaching for Audrey. "Let me burp her." She flung a cloth diaper onto her shoulder and positioned the baby. "Will you teach me to crochet?" she asked.

"If you can read, you can crochet. You just follow the instructions."

Jill shook her head and chuckled as she patted the baby's back. "How about canning? Do you know how to can? Like tomatoes and peaches?"

"No one cans anymore," Caye had said. "Except my mother."

Caye walked back into the living room. Jill was asleep. Caye returned to the kitchen. She poured herself another cup of coffee and took a sip. It was too hot. She put the mug on the window sill and began wiping down the counter.

A month after the crocheting and canning discussion, late in August, they loaded the kids into the backseat of Jill's Jeep Cherokee and drove over the mountains to Kimberly, a wide spot in the road along the North Fork of the John Day River, to get peaches. Caye's mom always said the best peaches in the state came from there. "Then that's where we should go," Jill said. "It will be an adventure."

"It's ridiculous to go that far," Caye said. "We can buy peaches anywhere in the valley. The trip will take forever—with three cranky kids."

"It's a great excuse to see more of the state," Jill said. "I've never been east of the mountains."

They left at five in the morning with snacks and a lunch. The plan was to get to Kimberly by eleven, pick peaches for a few hours, and then head back. "We'll stop and spend the night somewhere if we have to," Jill had decided the day before when Caye went over the plan, the flawed plan as Caye called it, one more time.

It was Jill's idea for Caye to ask her mother to meet them in Kimberly.

Both her parents decided to go, driving from Burns, although even after several minutes of discussion Caye's mother could not understand why they would drive from Ashland to Kimberly just to pick peaches. "It has to be over three hundred miles," her mother said.

"Jill's from California," Caye answered. "She likes to drive."

All three kids fell asleep by the time they turned off I-5 onto Highway 62 on the north side of Medford. The day was beautiful as they drove into the morning sun that bathed jagged Mount Theilsen. Caye and Jill chatted away.

Caye thought about Nathan going back to work. It was his first day of the school year. He'd had only a two-week break between the end of summer school and the beginning-of-the-school-year meetings.

Caye knew he was tired. He'd barked at Andrew last night at bedtime about not brushing his teeth. "Do what your mother says," Nathan had yelled. Andrew cried and then padded down the hall to the bathroom. Caye wondered if the pressure of being the sole provider was weighing Nathan down. He'd be helping with the football team in the fall too, doing everything he could so she could stay home with the kids.

But Caye didn't tell Jill the whole story, just that Nathan was tired. It wasn't that she was worried Jill would think badly of Nathan. Jill told story after story on herself and Rob. It was more that Caye wasn't used to sharing about her family life.

Even in high school she held back. She'd been the honor society president and the student body treasurer her senior year. Her friends were the other brainy girls who studied every night and seldom went to each other's houses. She talked with them about classes and tests, about colleges and entrance exams, but seldom about her family or even her dreams.

When it came time for college, even with scholarships, there wasn't enough money. She stayed out for a year and worked with her mom in the housekeeping department at the Burns hospital. That year she decided Southern Oregon State would be the most economical. With work-study and loans she could pull it off on her own. She'd major in business.

Her mother had frowned at the plan. She wouldn't say she thought it was a bad idea; she'd never volunteer advice. She'd barely say what she thought if Caye asked for her opinion. Her mother had always wanted to be a teacher, and Caye suspected she wanted that for her daughter, too.

"Your mom was right," Jill said when Caye relayed the story. "I think you'd make a great teacher."

"It would drive me nuts," Caye laughed.

"But you're so good with the kids. It never seems like they drive you crazy. And you teach them without effort."

Jill went on. "It doesn't come naturally to everyone. I have to remind myself to teach Hudson not to run out in the street, how to hold his spoon, how to pet a cat. It's so much easier for me to just shout 'no' than to teach him the right way. But it comes naturally to you. I see what you do."

"You think I should teach preschool?" Caye asked incredulously, thinking of the low pay.

"Not necessarily preschool," Jill clarified. "How about elementary school?"

Caye thought of the long hours Nathan put in teaching high school. Grade school would be just as bad—or worse.

They stopped at the picnic area at Beaver Marsh, just past the Highway 97 junction, and changed the babies' diapers. Jill fed Hudson bites of a banana while Caye nursed Audrey. It was only eight o'clock, and the traffic was light. The day was already growing warm as they sat at the dark green table. Andrew chased a grasshopper through the tall grass.

"It's so peaceful here," Jill said.

"It's because we're in the middle of nowhere," Caye answered, thinking of the highway stretching north and south for hundreds of miles.

They reached Bend by half past ten and turned toward Prineville, where they stopped at the park next to the stone courthouse to eat lunch. Jill had packed enough for all of them—tofu "egg" salad on whole wheat bread, grapes, celery sticks, and trail mix. Andrew frowned at his sandwich, pulled the bread apart to lick the spread, and made his yuckiest face. Caye gave him a fruit snack from the bag of treats she'd brought along.

Hudson screamed when Jill put him in the car seat.

"I like it over here," she said, ignoring Hudson. He continued to scream.

"I like the park," Andrew said. "Why can't we stay longer?"

"We're going to go see Grandma and Grandpa," Caye answered, looping the belt through Audrey's seat. "Go to sleep, and when you wake up we'll be there."

"I don't want to be there. I want to stay at the park."

"Stop it, now," Caye commanded.

They arrived in Kimberly, just a junction in the road with a store, at one o'clock. Caye directed Jill to the orchard. They checked in with the owner and then drove down a dirt road overlooking the John Day River.

She saw her dad's old white Chevy pickup pulled off to the side. Wooden boxes of peaches were stacked beside it. Caye quickly counted fifteen boxes. Her parents were stretched out on a blanket in the shade.

"There they are," Caye said, pointing under the tree.

"The weary travelers," her mother called out as she sat up and watched Jill and Caye climb out of the Jeep. They unbuckled the kids and walked over to the shade. Caye introduced her parents, Bev and Hank Johnson, to Jill. Her father stood to shake Jill's hand. He looked taller than six feet three inches with his cowboy hat and boots on. His gray mustache was neatly trimmed. Under his hat he had a full head of gray hair, cut short by Caye's mom.

Hank turned to Andrew. "How's my boy genius?" he asked, hunkering down in front of his grandson, balancing on his boots.

Bev reached for Audrey. It was only the second time she'd seen

her. Nathan and Caye had driven over to Burns in June after school
had ended and before summer school had started.

Caye's mom's hair was permed in tight little poodle curls. It was
nearly snow white. She was short, shorter than Caye, and solidly
plump. She tucked Audrey into the fold of her body and began to
sway.

Caye looked at Jill, who sadly watched Bev and the baby.

"Well," Hank said. "You're late, so we went ahead and picked for
you, too."

"You didn't need to do that," Caye said.

"Sure we did."

"But I want to pick!" Jill exclaimed. The usual sparkle quickly
replaced the sadness in her eyes. "I've never picked peaches before."

"She wants to pick," Hank said in disbelief. "Not only do you
drive three hundred miles for fruit you could buy down the street
from where you live, but you want to pick it." He chuckled.

Jill smiled, her big, embracing smile.

"Hey, I like you Hank," she said. "Funny thing. You sound just
like Nathan. Don't you think, Caye? Logic, logic." Nathan also
thought it was ridiculous for them to drive to Kimberly. And he
wasn't thrilled to have Caye and the kids gone when he got home
from work.

"And what about your husband?" Hank asked Jill. "Does he think
it's logical for you two to traipse across the state with a rig full of kids
to pick peaches?"

"Rob? He doesn't care about the peaches. He's just happy to have
us off on an adventure."

Caye and Bev sat on the blanket with the kids while Hank set up
a ladder for Jill a few trees away. It was hot and dry. The green leaves
above them murmured in the slight breeze. Caye nursed Audrey while
Andrew showed Bev his Fisher-Price cowboy and horse. Hudson sat
on his haunches and clapped his hands until he fell over backward
and startled himself.

"I'll show them the river," Bev told Caye, quickly righting
Hudson and then taking his hand before he had a chance to decide
whether to cry.

Caye burped Audrey and watched Jill awkwardly climb the ladder. She heard her laugh at something Hank said. Caye could tell her father was enjoying Jill.

Jill sauntered back, carrying one box while Hank carried the other. "Look what I did," she called out to Caye.

Caye stood, leaving Audrey kicking on the blanket. Bev came back with the boys. "I'm hungry, Mama," Andrew said.

"How about some fried chicken?" Bev asked, opening her cold box. She pulled out a plastic container.

"Did you make that?" Jill asked.

"Sure," Bev answered.

"When?"

Caye's mom always made fried chicken when they went on an outing. Caye knew she'd fried it that morning. She also had potato salad, baking powder biscuits, and rhubarb pie.

"Yum!" Jill exclaimed.

They all crowded on the blanket and loaded the paper plates Bev pulled from her picnic basket.

"Caye," Hank said, wiping his mouth with his bandana, "why don't you and Jill and the kids come back home to Burns with us tonight? Spend the night. You can start on your way in the morning."

Caye smiled. She thought of her parents' tiny farmhouse. The third bedroom was now Hank's workroom. They'd be crowded.

"That way you won't have to be traveling with these little ones after dark."

Jill put down her plate. "Are you sure? Sure it wouldn't be too much trouble?"

Bev patted Jill on the knee. "We'd love to have you, all of you."

It was decided. They'd caravan the two hours to Burns and call Nathan and Rob, let them know they'd be home the next day.

Caye rode in the Chevy with her father; her mother rode with Jill and the children. That night Bev barbecued hamburgers. It was the first time Caye had seen Jill eat red meat.

After bathing the kids, Caye and Jill collapsed onto the double bed in the spare room, Caye's old room. Audrey was stretched out on a blanket on the floor, and the boys were feet to feet on the old mauve couch with the rickety dining room chairs pushed up against Hudson's end.

"You are your parents' best thing," Jill said, flinging her leg out from under the sheet. The fan in the window blew warm air across the room. "Your mother is so proud of you. Of your going to school. That you married a good man like Nathan. Your kids. She couldn't stop talking about you."

"Well, that's embarrassing," Caye grimaced.

"No. It's great. It's absolutely epical," Jill said. "I'd give anything to have a mom who talked that way about me."

They'd gone back to Kimberly each year. The end of August, they'd load up the kids, visit Burns for several days, and then drive on to Kimberly the last day before the long trip home. Last year they'd stayed nearly a week at the ranch. They joked that they'd stay all of August this year. The four-time tradition had become the highlight of Caye's parents' year.

Caye dumped the rest of her coffee and put the mug in the dishwasher. She hung the dishrag on the faucet and opened Jill's refrigerator. It was nearly empty. She pulled open the vegetable drawer. The carrots and celery were fresh. She would make soup for lunch.

The phone rang. She picked up the cordless off Jill's desk tucked in the corner under the vineyard mural.

"Rhone residence," she answered.

"This is Dr. Kendall's office," a voice said. *Jill's surgeon.* Caye found herself fully resituated in the uncertain present. "Is Mrs. Rhone available?"

❧

Jill woke to Caye patting her arm. She must have dozed, she thought, wriggling the afghan up over her arms. "Hey, you," she said sheepishly.

"The phone's for you. It's the surgeon's office."

Jill took the phone and said "hello" in a quiet voice.

After a moment she answered, "Okay. We'll be there at 4:30. This afternoon." Jill pressed the Off button and smiled at Caye.

"Did I just fall asleep? Like an old lady?" Jill asked

"Yep. Just like an old lady. Must be the afghan. Ready for lunch?"

Jill stood, wrapping the afghan around her shoulders, and waddled to the kitchen table. "Is Simon still asleep?"

"Haven't heard a peep. And the other three are in the basement playing."

"After the surgery," Jill said, sitting down on the window seat and staring into the backyard, "I might be diabetic. I might have to take insulin. No matter what, I'll have to take enzymes every time I eat."

"I know," Caye said.

Jill sighed. "Do you believe in 'name it and claim it'?"

"In what?"

"That if you claim something in Christ's name, he'll do it."

"Like boss him around?"

Jill smiled. "Not really." Caye was so refreshing.

"I think," Caye said, "that praying isn't just telling God what we want. It helps us to trust him with our lives, with the life of the person we're praying for." She paused. "Easier said than done, huh?" Caye hesitated again and then continued, "I know you don't want to hear this, but have you called your mom?"

"I should, shouldn't I?"

"You should."

Caye dumped carrots and celery into chicken broth and then added a jar of tomatoes, tomatoes they had canned last September, to make soup. Then she pulled a jar of peaches from Jill's pantry.

"When I was growing up," Jill said, speaking quietly, "Marion would freak if I got sick. She was always taking my temperature. It was the only time she paid any attention to me. If it was over ninety-nine, she'd take me to the doctor. She hardly ever went to my games and art shows, but she could always take time off to take me to the doctor.

"She reminded me every chance she got that my father had died from pancreatic cancer," she said. "And his father. And some aunt no one talked about.

"I wish it was a different cancer. A more glamorous cancer. Like breast cancer."

"Breast cancer is glamorous?" Caye asked, forcing a laugh.

"More than what I have. Pancreatic cancer just makes Marion right."

"Still, you really should call her."

"I'll call her after lunch," Jill said, "before you pick up Andrew."

## 13

Jill didn't call her mother after lunch. Instead she called Rob and asked him to call Thomas about the prayer meeting. Then she took a nap while Caye, holding Simon on her hip, called the rest of the members of the Fellowship.

"I think Simon needs a bottle," Caye had told Jill the day before. "I think he's too young to go straight to a cup."

What Caye really thought was that he needed extra comforting. She'd stopped by the store yesterday and bought more formula and a bottle. After the phone calls she mixed a batch of formula and sat down in Jill's antique platform rocker with Simon, holding him close, tipping his head back.

He grabbed the nipple with both hands, his chubby fingers poking at the rubber. Caye wiggled it into his mouth. He bit the nipple, pulled his mouth away, smiled at Caye.

"Come on, baby," she cooed. "You'll like this."

He spit out some of the formula that pooled in his mouth, then swallowed the rest. He began to suck.

Gradually her hunger for another child of her own had eased. Now, holding Simon, she realized it had disappeared. She felt as if she had another baby.

Caye's plan was to put Liam and Simon down for their afternoon naps before going to get Andrew. She would take Audrey and Hudson with her and then hurry back to Jill's. But neither of the younger boys would settle down. Simon stood in his crib and wailed while Liam sat on the top bunk and stripped off his clothes, one item at a time, throwing them over the edge. Then he put on his superhero cape and yellow rubber boots. "Guess you guys are going with me," Caye finally said, looking at her watch. Andrew would be out in ten minutes.

She took the cape off Liam and pulled off the boots; she slipped a T-shirt over his head, and held his shorts for him to step into. Thankfully, he'd left his Pull-Ups alone.

She tiptoed into Jill's bedroom before pulling Simon out of his crib. "We're going to pick up Andrew," she whispered.

"All of you?"

"Yep."

"Take the Suburban."

"Okay." It was the easiest plan. She'd be back before Rob came to take Jill to the appointment with the surgeon. And if not, Rob could drive the Jeep.

"Wait a minute," Jill said. "I keep meaning to ask you. Did you get that job?"

"It didn't work out," Caye answered matter-of-factly, hoping Jill wouldn't pry.

❧

After the boys were in bed, Rob accused her of being in denial. She'd known ever since the doctor had relayed the diagnosis that they'd have this conversation sooner or later, was even more certain of it after talking with the surgeon in front of Rob and going over her family history in detail.

She was already in bed, ready to sleep. Rob left the lamp on as he crawled in.

"I wasn't in denial," Jill said. "If I'd been in denial, I would have taken up smoking and drinking, eaten a pound of butter each day, stayed in Argentina, moved next door to a factory, used chemicals in the garden. That's what I would have done if I'd been in denial."

"No. Your logic is off. You're implying you wanted to do all those things. You didn't. Denial is that you didn't tell me. That you didn't get tested like you could have. What if this had been diagnosed a couple of months ago?"

"Who's to say it could have been diagnosed a couple of months ago?"

He was silent.

"Rob, look at the risks you've taken." *Was it fair to bring him into it?* "Have you been in denial? The surfing. Snowboarding the backside of Mount Ashland. Scuba diving. The chances of your being injured or dying were probably greater than my getting cancer." *Maybe greater. Or maybe not. Who could know?*

"But the difference," Rob said, "is that if I died, the boys would still have you. If you die, they'll only have me."

Jill reached for his hand.

She thought about their conversation as she fell asleep. Rob had no common sense when it came to the children. He'd forget to feed them lunch if she wasn't home. He said their immunization schedule was too complicated. This from a man who could set up an entire office computer system and train the staff in a matter of days. Who chastised her when she failed to screw the mustard jar lid on all the way.

He accused her of getting easily distracted, but he would forget about changing a diaper for an entire day unless the smell was bad enough to demand his attention. He still couldn't seem to comprehend that early bedtimes made for happy children and junk food made them cranky.

"God, my boys need two parents," Jill prayed as she fell asleep. "Please, God. They need us both."

The next day, Jill planned to call Marion before Caye arrived so she could answer a resounding "yes" when her friend asked. But she was still asleep when Caye got to the house at 8:45.

"I'm off," Rob said, pecking her on the cheek. "Caye's here."

Jill dozed again and woke at ten o'clock disgusted with herself. She pulled on her robe and headed down the hall. Caye was folding laundry in the living room. "I'm sorry," Jill declared. "I'm turning into such a bum."

"No," Caye answered, "you need your rest. You need to be as healthy as possible for the surgery."

"Still," Jill said, "I think I just got a record-breaking thirteen hours of sleep."

"Mommy!" Liam shouted, running down the stairs. "Makin' fort. Upstairs."

"Oh, good," Jill said, bending down, running her hand through his curls, and pulling him to her.

"They got into the linen closet and have sheets draped all over everything," Caye said with a shrug. "It's keeping them busy."

Hudson was taking another day off from preschool. He'd only gone on Tuesday this week. Jill decided it was better for him to be home—in fact she was contemplating not having him go back at all. She wanted him nearby—not off at school. He'd be off to kindergarten soon enough.

"But he needs a schedule," Caye had responded when Jill told her what she was thinking. "And I don't mind driving him."

Jill didn't answer. She didn't want to argue with Caye—but she'd go with her instincts on this one.

"Did Simon have a bottle?" Jill asked. The baby was crawling toward her.

"No," Caye said, "I was going to give him one and then put him down for a nap in a few minutes."

"I'll get it," Jill said, bending down to pick Simon up. She felt a stab of pain.

He felt so heavy, so incredibly heavy. She pulled the sash of her jade green robe with her free hand. The fabric was too light; she was cold. She swung Simon into the highchair and gave him a whole-wheat cracker to chew on while she poured the formula into the bottle and microwaved it for forty seconds. While she waited, she added "bottles" to the list attached to the refrigerator by a magnet. Someone would need to do the grocery shopping soon.

Jill settled into the rocker with Simon. He wiggled to sit up.

"Does he really take this?" Jill asked Caye.

"Once he settles down."

Simon grabbed at Jill's mouth, poking at her teeth. Then he yanked her hair.

"I should wash it, huh, baby?" Jill said. "Mommy needs to take a shower and get dressed. Mommy's being lazy."

He pulled at the opening of her robe. She tried to give him the bottle again. He pushed it away.

"Do you want me to try?" Caye asked, walking over to the rocker.

Caye took the baby and settled down on the sofa with a pillow propped under her arm. Simon started to suck and closed his eyes after a few minutes.

Jill watched, rocking slowly.

It wasn't until Caye stood to walk upstairs, shoo the other kids out of the bedroom, and put Simon in his crib that Jill started to cry. There was no reason not to be optimistic, not to believe she would be healed. Being positive could only make her chances better. No amount of being upbeat could make it worse. Still she felt a dark cloud building. She was so sad, incredibly, painfully sad. And scared.

And Simon wouldn't take a bottle from her.

She couldn't force herself to think any further than the surgery. She would get through the surgery. That's what she would do.

She pulled a tissue out of the pocket of her robe and went into the bathroom to shower. She'd help Caye fix lunch. That would make her feel better. Maybe Simon would take a bottle from her in the afternoon.

❧

Caye felt uneasy as the Fellowship members gathered to pray for Jill. The older kids were playing in the boys' bedroom. Caye had scooped up Simon and stood holding him. He comforted her. Protected her. From what, she wasn't sure.

Rita had just arrived and was hugging Jill. Summer brought an aluminum pan of vegetarian lasagna to put in Jill's freezer. Joya sat beside Jill.

Jill wore overalls. Comfort clothes. Soft and worn. Her hair hung loosely around her face.

"Let's get started," Thomas said.

Caye sat down in the rocker with Simon. Nathan sat beside her on one of the mahogany dining room chairs.

"Jill, tell us how you want us to pray," Joya said. *Was Joya being smug? Her vision had been right.*

"For healing," Jill said. "It is cancer. Surgery is tomorrow. I'm asking God to heal me. Completely."

"We're asking that too," Joya said. "And he will."

"I want you to kneel in the middle of the room," Thomas said, "and we'll gather around you."

Then Thomas took out a glass bottle from a purple cloth bag with a gold drawstring. "And I'd like to anoint you with oil before we pray."

Caye looked at Nathan. He shrugged his shoulders. Caye had heard of anointing but had never seen it done.

"Okay," Jill said, kneeling down on the carpet.

The others gathered around her, except for Caye, who stayed in the rocker with Simon. Thomas poured oil on his fingertips; he knelt in front of Jill and made the sign of the cross on her forehead as he said, "I anoint you in the name of the Father, the Son, and the Holy Spirit."

One by one members prayed, but Caye stayed silent. She was relieved to hear Nathan's simple prayer asking God to comfort Rob, the boys, and Jill, to give them strength, and to show each member of the Fellowship what they could do to help.

Summer prayed next. "God," she said, "if it is your will, we ask you to heal Jill."

Joya followed, thanking God for the healing of Jill. "We don't know when," Joya prayed, "but we know that you will heal her."

Thomas closed by leading the group in the Lord's Prayer.

The words "Thy will be done" hung in Caye's head as they finished.

Jill stood, wiping her eyes with the back of her hand. Joya handed her a tissue. Simon had fallen asleep in Caye's arms.

"Thanks," Jill said. "Thank you—all of you."

Summer started down the hallway to the bathroom. Rita hugged Jill. Caye was aware of Joya positioning herself in the hall's entryway.

Nathan stood to talk to John. Rita sat down beside Caye and rubbed her hand over Simon's soft hair. "Poor baby," she said. "How are the boys doing?" she asked Caye.

"All right, I think."

Summer walked up the hall. Caye turned her head toward the doorway, straining to hear Joya as she began to speak.

"It *is* God's will that Jill be healed," Joya said to Summer.

"How do you know that?"

"Because he is a God of life, not death," Joya said. "How could it be his will for these boys to lose their mom? For Rob to lose his wife?"

"I think God allows death," Summer said.

"I think," Joya said, taking a deep breath, "that you're being fatalistic. Jill doesn't need that. You should keep your doubts to yourself."

Rita put her hand on Caye's shoulder, pulling her focus away from Joya and Summer, and asked, "How are you doing? I know this is terribly hard for you, too."

Caye half smiled, knowing she'd just missed Summer's response. "Thanks, Rita," she said, holding back. She didn't want to talk with Rita about how she was doing in front of everyone. She didn't want to say how scared she was, to say she knew God could heal Jill but might not. Would he? That was the question. He *could* heal all 28,300 people who came down with pancreatic cancer each year—but he didn't.

And she felt confused by Joya's insistence that healing was a faith issue. Who had to have enough faith? Jill? Rob? All of them? This was the sort of thing that made her feel like an outsider in the Fellowship. She could usually talk with Jill about her confusion, but not this time.

Out of the corner of her eye she saw Joya head into the kitchen.

A wail came from upstairs.

Caye stood. "I'd better go check on that," she said to Rita, "and put Simon to bed."

Louise stood at the top of the stairs, crying. "They're mean to me," she said. "They won't let me play."

Sheets covered the bedroom, tied from the crib to the bunk bed to the window. Simon stirred in her arms.

"Everybody out," Caye said quietly. "It's bedtime for the baby."

Louise was right. The other kids were mean to her. Especially Audrey, even though Louise was four years older. Most four-year-old girls looked up to older kids. Not Audrey. She wanted to be queen.

Tonight Audrey's behavior felt like the least of Caye's worries.

"Go talk to Daddy," Caye said to Audrey. "Tell him you were mean to Louise again."

With one hand she untied the sheet from the crib, imagining Simon standing up in the night and catching his head over the knot. "Baby hangs himself in crib" the headline would read.

*Not on my watch.*

❧

"Is your mother coming to stay after the surgery?" Joya asked as she told Jill good-bye.

"I'm not sure," Jill answered, aware that both Rob and Caye were staring at her.

Caye had put Liam and Hudson in their pajamas, herded them down to say good night, and then read them a bedtime story while Jill talked with the Fellowship members. Jill felt loved and cared for. She felt genuinely optimistic.

She sat down in the rocking chair as she said thank you to Joya and Thomas. To Louise she said, "You are getting so big. I can't believe you used to be that little tiny baby in Argentina. You'll be a teenager in no time." Louise beamed. Joya's face soured.

"Please call—let us know how things go, let us know what you need," Thomas said, stepping onto the porch behind his wife and daughter, pulling the door shut behind him.

Nathan reached down and hugged Jill. Rob came over from across the room.

"Nathan," he said, "can you and Caye come to the hospital tomorrow? Stay with me during the surgery?"

"What about the kids?" Caye asked.

Jill knew Caye had expected to have them. "Rob called Stephanie this afternoon. She can watch all of them here."

"Can you get off work okay?" Rob asked Nathan.

"Of course. We'll be there," Nathan said. "What time?"

"How about eight?"

"But what about Andrew and school?" Jill asked.

"It's okay," Caye said. "He can skip."

"Thanks," Jill said, reaching for Caye's hand.

Caye bent down and kissed Jill on the forehead. Jill could feel her friend's lips sliding over the oil, the olive oil.

Caye laughed nervously as she stood up. "I just anointed my lips," she said. "Oh no—I hope I didn't take away from your blessing."

"Did you call your mom today?" Rob asked after Caye, Nathan, Andrew, and Audrey left. It was 9:15.

"Bring me the phone," she said with a sigh.

She punched in memory seven and let it ring. The message came on. "Voice mail," she mouthed at Rob who was sitting on the sofa staring at her. She wished he'd go away.

"It's Jill. I'm going into surgery tomorrow. Bye," she said, quickly pushing the Off button.

Rob shook his head slowly.

"What?"

"That's it? That's all you can say to her?"

"She knows the rest." Jill stood. "Let's go to bed."

Rob followed her down the hall.

"I'd better pack," she said when she reached the bedroom.

"I'll do it," Rob responded, pulling a sports bag off the top shelf of the closet.

"Thanks." Jill changed into her pajamas.

He put in her robe, nightgown, and Bible. Her journal and pen. A handful of socks and underwear. A pair of sweatpants and a long-sleeved T-shirt.

"We can put my bathroom stuff in tomorrow," Jill said, climbing under the covers.

Rob sat down beside her. "Baby," he said, running his hand over her cheek. His fingernails were always perfectly manicured. "I don't want to fight about this—about your mom, about the cancer, about what you didn't tell me. I just want us to work together."

"I know," Jill said.

"To work together to get you well, to keep our family going."

"I know," Jill said again.

"It's just that I'm so scared."

"It's okay," Jill said. "It's okay to be scared."

"But you don't seem that scared."

"I am," she answered, cupping his face in her hands and pulling him down to her, kissing his forehead and then his nose and then his lips. She scooted over and pulled the covers back. "Get in," she whispered.

"Is it okay?"

Jill nodded.

He slid under the covers, wrapped her in his arms and tucked her head under his chin. "Do you hurt?" he asked.

She shook her head.

It wasn't just for him, as she was sure he thought. It was for her too. For the life of it. The love. The comfort.

In the middle of the night Jill woke slowly. Her back hurt. The nausea was back. It took her several minutes to remember the bottles on the nightstand and the glass of water waiting for her. As she pulled herself up, Rob asked, "How are you?"

He was sitting with his pillow propped behind his back. Just sitting.

"What's the matter?" Jill asked.

"Can't sleep," he answered. "Just can't sleep."

## 14

Caye took a roll of mints from her purse and offered one to Nathan. He shook his head. She popped one in her mouth, turned it over with her tongue, and then bit it in half with her back teeth.

"I wonder what Rob and Jill are saying to each other," Nathan said. He shifted his weight on the gray hospital couch and turned toward Caye.

She chewed the mint.

"I feel so hopeless," Nathan continued.

*Hopeless about Jill?* Caye stayed silent. She crushed the last of the mint with her back teeth, pushed the pieces around her mouth with her tongue, and then swallowed.

A huge magnifying glass hovered over the day. Caye was aware of how much Jill meant to her, but also how much she loved Nathan and the kids. It was that Technicolor reality. Everything was too bright. Too large. Too clear. She was constantly on the verge of tears.

She was even aware of an appreciation for Rob. He had risen to the occasion. She couldn't help but wonder if he could keep it up.

"You're quiet this morning," Nathan said, taking her hand. "You're usually so talkative."

Caye shrugged. She felt hopeful—and also foolish for her hope. She felt like crying. She didn't feel like talking.

"I love you," Nathan said, squeezing her hand three times. "I can't imagine this happening to us—can't even make myself imagine it."

Caye nodded again.

"Are you mad at God, Caye?" Nathan asked.

"Ask me after the surgery," she answered.

They looked up to see Rob standing in the doorway of the

waiting room, looking lost, like Liam after his nap. His eyes were red. Nathan stood and Rob walked toward them.

"I broke down," Rob said. "Again. I didn't mean to." Nathan stepped away from the couch. Rob sat down next to Caye. "Jill was strong—but I wasn't." Caye put her arm around him. He wore a white dress shirt and gray slacks. He was dressed for business. His face was freshly shaven.

Nathan sat down on the other side of Rob.

"I'm so afraid," Rob said, leaning forward with his elbows on his knees, his forearms extended. "Afraid that they'll open her up and she'll be full of cancer. Afraid it will all be over. That we won't even have a chance to fight it."

Caye patted his back, the same pat, pat, pat that she used on Simon. She felt compelled to chant, "It'll be okay, baby. It'll be okay." But she didn't. They were hollow words. The sound and cadence wouldn't soothe Rob.

"The boys seemed to be doing all right this morning when we dropped our kids off," Caye commented. Jill and Rob had already left for the hospital when Caye and Nathan swung by the house with Audrey and Andrew. Stephanie was feeding Simon breakfast.

"So far it's all an adventure to them," Rob said, looking at Caye. "Either I'm home, or they're with you guys."

Caye didn't think it was an adventure to the boys. She thought they were out of sorts and would soon be frightened.

She smiled at Rob.

He turned his face from her, cupped his palms, and put his face in his hands. His shoulders began to shake.

Caye put her hand on his shoulder again, this time as if she could stop him, stop the shaking, stop the sobs that were rising up in him, stop the fear, the question of life or death that loomed ahead.

Nathan sat down and put his hand on Rob's other shoulder.

The three of them sat while the sobs came one after another, hard body-racking sobs. Finally Rob held his head up and wiped his red-rimmed eyes on the sleeve of his shirt.

"I'm sorry," he said.

"No need to apologize," said a voice from the doorway.

It was Jill's mother. A brown leather handbag was draped over her shoulder, a brown leather attaché case in her hand. She wore a brown suit and had an ivory trench coat slung over her arm. Her short gray hair was flat on one side. Her blue eyes lacked Jill's sparkle.

Caye had only seen Marion three times. Twice at Jill's and once last year in Anaheim when Caye and Jill had taken the kids to Disneyland.

Rob was slower to turn around.

"Has she already gone into surgery?" Marion asked.

Rob nodded slowly. "I wondered if you would come."

Caye was relieved that Jill didn't have to deal with this surprise before going under.

"I'm sorry she didn't tell you years ago, Rob," Marion said, walking toward them. "She should have. I told her to. But you know Jill—she does what she wants. She doesn't listen to anyone."

"I only had that terse message from her last night. How bad is it?"

So Jill had left a message. Caye looked over at Rob. He looked ready to cry again.

"It's pancreatic cancer," Rob said. "She's in surgery. You know that. They'll see how it goes, then do radiation and chemo if they need to."

"Is the doctor hopeful?"

"He seems to feel Jill has a lot to live for."

"But is he hopeful?"

"I think so."

"Well," Marion said, walking to a chair at the end of the couch next to where Nathan sat, "I guess we'll just wait." She dropped the case to the floor and let the bag fall from her shoulder.

Caye looked at Nathan and smiled. He grimaced. She gestured her head toward the door and then said, "Rob, why don't you and Nathan go get some breakfast. You must be starving."

Rob stood. He looked befuddled, as if he'd forgotten which way the hall was. "Marion," he said, turning awkwardly toward her, "you must be hungry too."

"No, no," she said. "I can't eat. You go ahead."

Marion excused herself and went down the hall to the rest room, taking her bags with her. Caye wondered what was in the attaché case—work or clothes. It was obvious she'd taken a taxi from the airport. That was all she brought. Caye wondered how long Marion planned to stay.

Jill had said several times that Rob got along better with her mother than she did. It surprised Caye. She didn't think of Rob as sensitive, but even in the brief interaction she just witnessed he seemed tender toward Marion.

On the other hand, Jill, who was usually so patient with people, had little tolerance for her mother.

Caye couldn't imagine having such a strained relationship with a parent. Jill didn't dwell on her relationship with Marion, but she did give away little glimpses of frustration.

Every Christmas Jill would dedicate herself to pulling off the "perfect Christmas." She'd shop for the boys and Rob, decorate the house, bake, plan scrumptious Christmas meals—crab for Christmas Eve, omelets and scones for Christmas morning, Cornish game hens for Christmas afternoon. Last Christmas Caye's family stayed in town and joined the Rhones on Christmas afternoon. It was lovely, but by the time early evening rolled around, Jill was quiet, not her usual gregarious self.

The year before Marion had spent Christmas with Jill and her family. Jill spent December 26 in bed. Later she told Caye it wasn't the work of the holiday, as Marion and Rob both thought, that exhausted her. It was just that Christmas always made her sad, made her feel so empty.

Every year Jill took the decorations and tree down by December 28. "I'm just so ready to be done with all of it," she'd say. "I want my house back."

Caye stood up and walked around the waiting room. An older man and a middle-aged woman sat in the corner. Caye imagined the man's wife—the woman's mother—in surgery. Maybe she had breast cancer. The woman read *People* magazine. The man had a book in his hands, but he wasn't reading; he was staring above the pages.

Caye sat back down. Suddenly she felt compelled to pray. "Make the surgery a success," she prayed. "Heal Jill." As she prayed, she closed her eyes. She saw the image of an operating room. She could see a figure draped in blue sheets on the table and a surgeon in blue scrubs. Next to the surgeon was a man dressed in a red T-shirt and Levi's.

She opened her eyes.

The man was Jesus.

A shiver ran down Caye's spine. She thought of Joya. *I'm losing it too.*

Jesus was in the operating room, guiding the surgeon. And she had seen him!

Caye was distracted from her thoughts by Marion walking back into the waiting room.

Caye smiled at her. She would do her best to be nice to Marion. It would make the day easier for Rob. Ultimately easier for Jill.

"How are you doing?" Caye asked.

Marion sat back in her chair. She opened her purse and pulled out a tissue.

A minute passed. She waved her hand in front of her face, trying to stop crying, struggling to regain her composure.

"My last phone call with Jill wasn't good. And then she didn't even ask me to come up when she left that message last night." Marion stopped to wipe away a single tear. "I don't even know if she wants me here."

Caye put her arm around Marion and pulled her close, but she felt no warmth, no connection, only a bony shoulder.

Moments later Marion opened her attaché case. Caye couldn't help but look. On one side were white and pink floral pajamas and a toothbrush, on the other several Manila folders. Marion pulled out the stack of folders.

Caye knew that Marion was a real-estate investor. "She buys properties that she resells or rents. Sometimes she fixes them up. I used to help her. She never let me use good supplies—too much money. It was all cheap paint, dirt, and plants." Jill had explained that her father was a real-estate agent and had purchased three rentals by the time he died. Marion had sold one of those rentals, bought two more, fixed them up, and then sold them both with enough profit to buy four more houses. "She became obsessed with it," Jill said. "I practically raised myself. I joined every club and team I could because I was so social, I wanted to be with people. I even played basketball and softball just to be with people.

"I didn't even like sports that much," she added.

"That was high school. In college I spent too much time on the beach."

Nathan and Rob walked through the door. Rob had a cup of coffee in one hand.

Marion slipped the files back into the case. "That coffee looks good. Where's the cafeteria?"

"I'll get you a cup," Rob answered.

"No, thank you," Marion replied. "I need to walk around. Which way?"

Caye glanced at her watch at uneven time intervals: 9:30, 10:05, 10:46, 11:28.

The surgery was supposed to take five or six hours.

Caye's hope was real. *Is this faith? Is it faith that gives me hope? Even when I know how bad the prognosis is? What the odds are?*

Marion had been gone for two hours.

Jill was tall and thin like Marion, and their eyes were both beautiful and blue, although Marion's had faded, but that was where the similarities ended. Marion appeared classy at first glance, but she was stiff and evasive. *Jill is nothing like her—except maybe the evasive part.* Caye sighed. She stood and looked out the window.

Caye looked at her watch again: 12:10. She sat down on the couch. "Let's go for lunch," she said to Nathan and Rob.

Marion wasn't in the cafeteria. Caye sipped a bowl of minestrone soup. Nathan ate a turkey sandwich on sourdough. Rob took a few bites of a cheeseburger.

After they were done, with nothing else to do, they trudged back to the waiting room.

A half-hour later Caye stood to go get coffee. "Either of you want another?" she asked.

"I do," Rob said, digging into his pocket.

"Don't worry about it." Caye smiled. She wanted the coffee, but she also wanted to hunt around for Marion. Caye was beginning to worry.

She hadn't told the guys about her vision or that Marion had cried.

Marion wasn't in the cafeteria this time either. But on the way back to the waiting room, Caye spotted her in a side hall, sleeping, curled up on two chairs pushed together. Caye thought of Jill, who could sleep anywhere, anytime. If she was feeling stressed, Jill could simply go to bed and sleep until she felt better. Not Caye. She would go to bed only to end up feeling anxious, more and more anxious until she couldn't even stand to listen to her own breathing.

Caye could see the surgeon, still in scrubs, sitting on the edge of a chair, talking to Rob and Nathan as she hurried into the waiting room. Caye sat down next to Nathan and handed Rob his coffee. She wrapped her hands around the coffee cup, seeking comfort.

"…a good portion of her pancreas. She's strong and healthy, considering. She's in recovery now. It'll be an hour or so until you can see her."

The surgeon and Rob both stood and shook hands. "Thank you," Rob said.

The doctor nodded and left the waiting room.

"It went well?" Caye asked.

"Not really," Rob answered, pressing the heels of both hands against the sides of his head. "They got most of what they went after but not all of it. And it's already spread. It's in her lymph nodes, too."

## 15

"Your mom's here," Rob said, stroking Jill's hair.

Jill lay flat on her back with a breathing tube down her throat, an IV in her left wrist, and a blood-pressure cuff on her left biceps.

She knew she was out of recovery; she was conscious as they wheeled her down the hall, aware of the faces looming above her, floating along in the hallways, smiling at her as they transferred her onto the bed.

Her throat was sore, her lips dry and cracked.

So Marion had shown up.

Jill's body felt as if she'd been yanked from under a pile of bricks.

"Your mom's here," Rob said again. "In the waiting room with Caye. She'd like to come in. Just for a minute."

Jill shook her head. She could feel the tears well in her sand-filled eyes. The back of her throat began to itch.

"Jill, baby, she came all this way. Can't she just come in for a minute? And then Caye and Nathan will take her to the house."

Jill tried to swallow the tickle, the cough, the tears.

"I'll tell her to be nice, extra nice. She knows you can't talk, not with the tube in. She's worried." Rob pulled his fingers across Jill's ear lobe, across the empty earring hole.

*When are they going to take the tube out?* She closed her eyes.

"It hurts," Rob said. "I know it hurts."

Jill nodded her head.

"She'll just come in for a minute. I promise."

Her mother's hand brushed her cheek. She knew it was Marion by the almond scent of her hand lotion.

"It's Mama," Marion said.

How long had it been since she'd called Marion "Mama"? Twenty-five years?

Jill opened her eyes and looked into Marion's craggy face.

Jill blinked. Marion smiled, the lines curving down deeply around her mouth.

Jill felt Marion reach for her hand, take it, squeeze it. Jill's heart squeezed back. Just a little squeeze. Why? Why did she have to respond like a five-year-old?

"I'll come back tomorrow," Marion said.

Caye came forward and kissed Jill's cheek. Jill saw Nathan beside the bed standing next to Rob.

She closed her eyes again.

When she felt like a five-year-old, she wanted nothing more than to have Marion take care of her.

Jill thought of a trip to the mall to buy school clothes, a rare moment of intimacy with Marion. Jill was twelve or thirteen. She confided, as Marion drove her navy blue Buick, that she wanted to have five children someday.

"You shouldn't have any children," Marion had responded, turning the wheel with purpose, not looking at her daughter. Jill remembered Marion's head floating alongside the dashboard.

"Why?"

"The cancer. The pan-cre-at-ic can-cer." Again Marion chanted off the morbid litany. "Your father died from it. Your grandfather. Your aunt. Having kids might wear you down—make you more likely to get it. And pass it on."

It was the first of many times that Marion advised Jill not to have kids.

"The nurse is here." It was Rob. Jill opened her eyes and made out his face in the dim light.

"I'm going to go home and check on the boys. I'll come back this evening," Rob whispered. Why was he so quiet? How much time had passed? Rob bent down and kissed her cheek. She turned toward him. The tube pulled against her lips, against the corner of her mouth.

Nathan rode with Rob on the way home. They were going to get piz-zas while Caye and Marion went straight to Jill's house. As the day progressed, Marion seemed older and older to Caye. She knew Jill's mother was seventy—although she appeared much younger with her classy clothes and business demeanor. But the day had taken a toll. Rob suggested that Marion ride with Caye; Marion did not protest.

"Jill's probably told you that I didn't think she should have kids," Marion said. The sky was clear. The late afternoon was too bright. Caye felt the incongruity of the weather. It should be cloudy, even raining. The earth shouldn't be celebrating with sunshine on a day like today.

Jill had never told Caye that Marion didn't want her to have kids.

"I was worried about her health. Worried about the cancer going on to another generation."

Caye smiled, probably what looked like a knowing smile to Marion. It wasn't. But she wanted Marion to keep talking.

"But if she was going to have one and then keep having more, I kept hoping she'd have a girl. I kept thinking that if she just had a girl, maybe she'd understand me better."

Marion began to dig in her leather bag.

"Do you need a tissue?" Caye asked.

"Yes."

Caye reached behind the driver's seat and retrieved a box of tissues.

"I don't know how Jill ever turned out to be such a good parent," Marion said, blowing her nose. "I think she got it from her dad. I know she didn't get it from me. She takes after him. Confident. Artistic. Both determined to get exactly what they want."

Caye noted Marion's present tense.

"I didn't really love him," Marion said. "Not the way a wife loves a husband. There was passion at the very beginning, but it died quickly." Caye waited for her to go on, but Marion didn't elaborate.

"I won't stay long," Marion finally said. She was looking at the window now, talking to the willow trees bowing along Bear Creek.

Marion wadded up the tissue and pulled another from the box.

Caye smiled an awkward, confused smile. It didn't matter. Marion's nose was practically pressed against the passenger window.

How much should she say to Marion? She had no idea what Jill wanted her to say. If the circumstances were reversed, if Caye were in the hospital and her mother and Jill were driving along, they'd be talking about the surgery, what the doctor said, what the boys needed, tomorrow's schedule.

Caye could come up with something to chat about with any stranger. But not with Marion. Maybe they were both too stressed, too tired.

"I've never told Jill this. It's very ironic. But as much as I didn't want her to have kids, the thought of her first one, when she first told me she was pregnant—that saved my life."

Caye was confused. Was she talking about the baby Jill aborted? Or Hudson?

"Do you mean Hudson?" Caye asked.

Marion didn't answer.

"How did he save your life?"

Marion turned her head back toward the creek and the weeping willows.

*Alzheimer's.* Caye stole a glance at Marion. *She's not making any sense.*

"Mama!" Audrey screamed as Caye stepped out of the station wagon.

Marion struggled out of the car and then hurried up the steps.

Liam ran out of the house.

"The paint's peeling," Marion said. "It shouldn't be peeling. I paid too much to have this old place painted."

Caye felt her fake smile freeze on her cheeks. Her face hurt. She didn't want to deal with Marion any longer.

Stephanie was standing at the door with Simon.

"How's Jill?" Stephanie asked. "How was the surgery?"

Caye stopped smiling. "So-so. They got most of what they're after, but it's already spread."

"Oh." Stephanie frowned. "That's awful."

"Yeah."

Caye felt exhausted. She wanted to curl up on Jill's window seat that looked out over the garden. She wanted everyone to go away. She didn't want to take care of children or do laundry or wipe snotty noses or fix meals.

"I've got to go," Stephanie said, handing Simon to Caye.

"I know. I hope we haven't made you late."

Stephanie grabbed her backpack and was off. "It's okay. I called work. They understand. Call me when you need me again."

Marion stood in the living room and looked around.

"The ceiling looks good. But the walls. What is it about cold colors and Jill? All these shades of blue. I was hoping she'd have them repainted."

"Hasn't Simon grown?" Caye asked.

"Are you trying to change the subject?"

*Lady, you're wearing me out.* "When was the last time you saw him?" Caye was doing her best to keep the conversation light.

"Thanksgiving," Marion said. She reached out and touched Simon's bare foot. He pulled it away. "Jill's children aren't very fond of me. Perhaps you've noticed."

Caye wanted to collect the children in one swoop and fly away, away from Marion, away from the word *cancer,* away from Jill's house with no Jill.

No, she wanted Marion to fly away.

"I'm exhausted," Marion said. "Do you think the sheets on the spare bed are clean?"

"Clean enough," Caye said. She bent over to pick up Simon's bottle that was dripping formula onto the oak floor. Marion headed up the stairs with her two bags, her trench coat draped over her arm.

After checking on Andrew and Hudson, who were playing pirates in the basement, Caye shooed Audrey and Liam downstairs too. "Turn on PBS," she yelled down to Andrew. Who cared if they vegged in front of the TV? She didn't.

She lay down on the couch, tucked Simon between her arm and chest, and put the bottle in his mouth.

"Hey, sweet baby," she whispered. "Your grandmother is really something."

Caye's mind went back to the first months of her friendship with Jill. Caye didn't feel lonely for months, not the way she had before she met Jill. That lonely-for-a-friend feeling, that need to tell someone good news or bad news or an idea or a sad thought. It wasn't that she didn't tell Nathan, but he never wanted to talk things through the way she did, explore the possibilities, rehash it one more time. After she met Jill, Caye realized she'd been longing for a friend like Jill her entire life. Waiting to pour out her thoughts and feelings and hopes, waiting to finally have someone who would listen.

Nathan had commented that Caye was happier than he'd thought she'd be, that staying home full-time suited her better than he'd expected. She wondered if he had any idea it was because of Jill.

But one day, as she unlocked the door to the house after picking up Andrew from kindergarten, a hint of the old loneliness met her. It wasn't because she hadn't seen Jill recently—they'd been to the park just that morning. Pulling her key out of the deadbolt, she realized Jill couldn't meet all her needs any more than Nathan could. Not even Jill and Nathan together could.

"There's a part that only you can fill. Right, God?" she had prayed.

In that moment she realized that the components of her life were all tied together. Trusting God made her a better wife and friend and mother. Having Jill as a friend made her a better wife and mother. And having a good relationship with both Nathan and Jill made her more trusting of God.

Caye pulled the bottle from Simon's mouth. He'd fallen asleep.

Rob and Nathan should arrive any time with the pizzas. *Sesame Street* would end in fifteen minutes. She hoped the dads showed up before then.

Simon had been out of sorts the last couple of weeks—and with good reason—but he was usually a mellow baby. He seemed to know from the beginning that Jill had her hands full with Liam. Simon never needed to be rocked to sleep. Jill would put him down in his bassinet, and he'd simply drift off without a fuss.

He was a good nurser. Caye would laugh at Jill who, while talking with Caye and nursing Simon, would run after Liam, struggling to get a marker out of his hand before he reached the newly painted wall, or to grab the air freshener away from him before he squirted his eyes.

"I'll get it," Caye would say, running after the three of them.

Liam would scream in anger over his foiled plans. Caye saw clearly how Jill spent her days.

"Am I a bad mom?" Jill asked. "Have I done something beyond-repair wrong with him? Now be honest."

"No," Caye would say. "Liam is just Liam." But she did wonder if Jill was so overwhelmed that she didn't make Liam mind consistently and if that was why he was such a wild little man.

He was a darling child. Big blue eyes. Curly blond hair that was surprisingly thick. People would stop all of them in the park to comment on how lovely Liam was; strangers would reach out and rub his curls. Both Jill and Caye wondered how the attention made the other children feel. "Here's someone to pet Liam again," Andrew said one day on their way to the playground after a middle-aged woman said, "Look at that curly blond hair! And those blue eyes!"

Caye would never say it, but Liam was her favorite of Jill's boys. She had two theories on why. The first was that, although no one else seemed to agree, she thought Liam with his high energy was a lot like Jill. The second was that Caye had been present at his birth.

Jill had asked her to be there. At first Caye thought it was because Jill felt obligated to since she'd been with Caye when Audrey was born.

Caye, although grateful that Jill was with her and had saved the day, wouldn't have asked her to be there. At the time she only wanted Nathan with her.

But Jill was serious. "And bring your camera. I want photos."

Caye wondered how it would work out. What would she do with Audrey and Andrew if it was a weekday? What if she had to go during the middle of the night but the baby wasn't born until the next day? Would Nathan call for a sub?

"Don't worry about it," Jill had said. "If it's meant for you to be there, it will all work out."

As it turned out, Jill went into labor on a Friday afternoon. It was late May, and baseball season was over. Jill and Rob brought Hudson over to Caye and Nathan's early in the evening to spend the night.

Jill wore soft denim maternity shorts and a neon green tank top. Her hair was pulled back in a ponytail. "I'm ready for business," she announced as she walked into the house.

She didn't want to go to the hospital sooner than she needed to, so it was decided that she and Rob would hang out for a while.

Caye had thought of Audrey's birth thirteen months earlier. "Just don't stay too long," she said with a laugh.

Rob put Hudson to bed on the floor in Andrew's room while Caye put Audrey down. Jill walked in a circle from the living room, through the dining room, into the kitchen, back through the hall, over and over.

"Okay," she said when Caye closed the door to Audrey's room, "it's time to go."

"When do you want me to go up?" Caye asked.

"Now. With us. Drive yourself so you can get back home. But please come now. And don't forget your camera."

Jill was already at seven centimeters when the nurse checked her.

The labor went quickly and smoothly. Jill walked the hall when she wasn't hooked up to the heart monitor. Rob walked with her. Caye took photos and timed the contractions, writing the information down in a little notebook she'd bought for the birth.

After an hour and a half Jill knelt dramatically beside the bed and said she needed to push. But first, she said, she needed to get the sweaty hospital gown off. She peeled it over her head. Underneath she wore a camisole that rode up above her belly. Caye knew it was one she'd bought in Argentina—a strip of Italian lace was inlaid along the neckline.

It occurred to Caye that Jill looked sexy even having a baby.

"You'd better buzz the nurse," Jill said to Rob. "Do you have enough film in the camera?" she asked Caye.

Caye nodded.

The nurse came in and helped Jill onto the bed.

"Ten centimeters," the nurse announced, pulling off her glove. "The doctor's changing into scrubs. You're faster than I thought you'd be."

Jill's legs began to shake.

Caye leaned up against one. "Brace yourself," she said.

Rob squeezed her hand.

"I need to push," Jill said.

"Hold on," the nurse said.

Jill shifted in the bed, moving her leg away from Caye, rocking herself over onto her hands and knees.

She moaned louder, pulling it into a deep scream.

*Go ahead and push.* Caye thought of all the calves that she'd helped her father pull in the middle of the night in the big barn. *Just push.*

"I'm not pushing," Jill gasped. "But he's coming."

Caye posed the camera.

"He?" Rob asked. "Are you sure?"

"Yes," Jill said.

Caye knew Rob wanted a girl. They hadn't found out beforehand, hadn't had an ultrasound—Jill had just been sure all along that it was another boy.

"Let me take another look," the nurse said.

Before she could, the baby slipped from Jill's body into his mama's hands. Jill slid to a kneeling position, holding the baby against her chest.

Caye clicked the shutter of her camera. Her tears blurred the scene through the viewfinder.

"Is it a boy?" Rob asked. The tone of his voice had softened.

Jill drew the baby from her chest for a moment and then clasped him to herself again.

"It's Liam," she said.

"Well, that was an easy one," the nurse said just as the doctor walked in.

"I didn't need you." Jill smiled at the doctor, still holding the baby tight against her chest.

Liam never cried, just looked at his mama with big, admiring eyes.

Rob held the baby, swaddled in a receiving blanket, while the nurse cleaned Jill up.

"I've seen burritos bigger than you," Rob cooed down at Liam, running his finger under the baby's chin.

Caye clicked the camera again and then put it down. "My turn," she said, taking the wide-eyed baby. In that moment she fell in love with Liam, deeper in love with Jill and, at that moment, even a little bit in love with Rob. Who could not love a man who cooed at his baby so shamelessly?

"Oh, just throw that away," Jill said to the nurse who was holding up the camisole, soiled with blood from Jill clutching the baby to her chest.

"Don't throw it away," Caye said before she realized she was speaking. "I'll take it home and wash it in cold water." She couldn't bear the thought of it going to waste.

With Liam's birth they had two shared births between them. And it would remain just those two.

Simon came quickly in the middle of the night. Rob called, his voice alarmed. "Can you come stay with the boys? Jill woke up in labor. I'm going to take her to the hospital."

The next day, Caye took Hudson, Liam, and Audrey up to the hospital to see baby Simon. It was Andrew's last day of school.

"I almost told Rob to stay with the kids and have you bring me to the hospital," Jill said.

"Would've worked for me," Rob said, holding his newborn son.

*Is he joking?* Caye looked at Rob and back to Jill. *Does he know Jill was joking?*

"It really would have helped to have you here," Jill said quietly while Rob knelt with Simon so the kids could see his face. "I had really bad back labor. I thought something was wrong. I needed someone to tell me it was normal, that it was supposed to hurt like that, that I'd live through it. Thankfully it was fast—but it was furious."

Caye had had back labor with Andrew. She understood. Seven years later she remembered it clearly, much more clearly than Audrey's nearly painless birth.

Simon began to fuss. Jill opened her hospital gown and took the baby. Caye scrunched a pillow down beside her friend's arm and helped position Simon. It all seemed so natural. Seemed as if they could go on forever this way, Jill having babies, Caye helping Jill, Jill helping Caye, the kids swarming around them.

"Do you mind keeping Hudson and Liam tonight?" Jill asked. "I'm going to stay at the hospital another night. I feel like I need my rest—I know I won't get it at home. And Rob's wiped out from last night."

Caye had felt no jealousy when Liam was born. He was Jill's second, and he came after her miscarriage. Caye felt only happiness for her friend, for all of them. At the time, she was still hoping she would have another. By the time Simon was born, Audrey was over three. It was obvious that there would be no more babies for Caye and Nathan. The doctor had been right. Too much damage had been done to Caye's uterus to carry another baby. She felt the loss acutely the first time she held Simon—but in the weeks to come, as he became his own person, the pain subsided. And besides, it was time to move on. Find a job. Concentrate on raising the two kids they had. But Caye knew Nathan still pined for another child, still wanted their family to be larger, as different from the lonely home he'd grown up in as possible.

"Pizza!" Rob yelled, coming through the front door with Nathan behind him. "Who wants pizza?"

The kids stampeded up the stairs from the basement.

Caye stood with Simon and started up the stairs to the second floor to put him in his crib. She'd forgotten to ask Stephanie if he'd had an afternoon nap. Probably not. She'd let him sleep for an hour, just long enough to get the rest of the troops fed.

Right before she reached the landing, she looked up.

There was Marion, up from her nap, her gray hair completely disheveled, standing above Caye with her arms folded across her chest, waiting to descend the stairs.

Simon began to cry.

## 16

"When is my husband coming back?" Jill asked the nurse, her first words since the tube was removed. Her voice was hoarse. Her throat was sore.

"Soon," the nurse answered, checking the monitors.

Jill's back hurt. The nurse said it was from the exploratory part of the surgery. "They moved things around," she explained. "Poked here and there. It'll hurt for a few days."

Jill knew the surgeon had stopped to see her when she was still in recovery and had told the nurse he'd talk to Jill tomorrow.

She bent her legs, trying to find some relief. They ached, her back ached, her stomach was bloated. She gingerly touched the dressing, imagining the incision under her rib cage. After Rob had left, she'd had horrible dreams of snakes crawling over her belly.

The sheets were slippery against her feet. The mauve thermal blanket slid to the right. She pulled it up to her chin, brushing the IV line against it.

*Rob, where are you? Let Caye put the boys to bed. Or you put the boys to bed and send Caye over. Just someone come over.*

The nurse handed Jill a cup of ice. "Try to suck on this," she said. "It will help your mouth and throat."

❧

"Go," Caye said to Rob. "Go back over there. We don't want her to be all alone."

Rob looked from Hudson to Liam to Simon.

"They're okay," Caye said. "I'll put them to bed. Take your time. Marion's here—you don't need to rush back."

"No. I'm going to bed," Marion said.

Caye looked at her exasperated. "If the house caught on fire you'd get the boys out, right?"

"I don't know what you mean," Marion said.

Caye turned back toward Rob.

"Okay, let's do this. You drop Nathan and our kids off at home on your way to the hospital. I'll stay here until you get back." All Caye wanted to do was go home with Nathan and have him hold her while she sobbed and sobbed.

Marion kept eating her pizza.

"You're back," Jill whispered, turning her face toward Rob.

"I'm here."

"What time is it?"

"It's 7:45."

Rob sat on the edge of the bed.

"What did the doctor say?"

Rob reached out and took Jill's hand.

"Did they get the cancer?"

"They took the tumor—most of it." He paused. "The cancer has spread to your lymph nodes."

"Really?" This wasn't the way it was supposed to happen. She struggled to comprehend what it meant, but everything swirled around and around in her mind. Spread. Lymph nodes. Most of it.

"Chemotherapy," Rob said. "You definitely have to do the chemotherapy. And the radiation."

Jill felt her body sink into the bed; her head felt crushed against the pillow. Rob held on to her hand, held it tightly, as if he could pull her back, yank her up to her feet in an instant.

"Don't leave," she said.

"I'll stay for a couple of hours," he answered.

"How are the boys?"

"Caye's putting them to bed."

"What's Mother doing?"

"Bed. She's been in top form tonight. She was even driving Caye nuts."

"Poor Caye."

"How about if your mom comes over in the morning to see you? Then maybe she'll fly home tomorrow afternoon or the next day. Could you stand that? To have her visit again?"

Jill closed her eyes.

"Who's going to watch the boys tomorrow?"

"Caye—I think."

The nurse came in to take her vital signs again. Jill opened her eyes. Rob stood and walked around the room.

"Are the boys okay?" Jill asked as the nurse took the thermometer out of her pocket.

"They're fine. They miss you."

"I feel so vulnerable," Jill said and then closed her mouth over the thermometer.

"We've always been this vulnerable," Rob answered. "We just didn't know it."

❧

"I heard you need some help."

"Oh, hi, Rita. Who told you that?" Caye asked. She tucked the phone under her chin, holding Simon and forcing his hands under the faucet.

"The queen bee herself. I just talked to her on the phone."

"Jill called you?"

"No, I called her. I'm coming over. She wants you to take Marion to the hospital. I'll stay with the kids." Which would be worse? Staying with the kids or another fifteen-minute ride with Marion?

"She told me she'd be homicidal by now if she were in your shoes."

"Okay, I'll take Marion to the hospital," Caye said, thinking she'd rather kill Jill's mom than one of the kids. "See you when you get here."

Caye had just finished cleaning Liam up after he tried to use the toilet. He'd smeared poop all over the seat and floor. While she was in the bathroom, Simon had flung dirt from the ficus tree beside the kitchen mural onto the slate floor. Marion sat a few feet from him in the window seat and read the paper, oblivious to her youngest grandson.

*How can she do it? How can she waltz in here, act like she owns the place, and then not lift a hand to help?*

Caye dried Simon's hands and then walked over to Marion.

"Here," she said, extending her arms.

Marion looked over the newspaper. "The baby," Caye said. "Take the baby." For a minute she thought that Marion might refuse.

Marion meticulously folded the paper, placed it on the cushion beside her and then took Simon. She frowned. The baby turned toward Caye. She smiled at him and moved her head from side to side. *You can do it. Show your grandma what a wonderful kid you are. Show her what she's been missing.*

"I'll take you to the hospital in about half an hour," Caye said. "Our friend Rita is coming over to watch the kids."

"I'd better go get packed," Marion, said, struggling to her feet with Simon in her arms. She swayed as she stood.

"Packed? You're leaving so soon?"

"I'm going to call and see if I can get a flight out this afternoon. Here," Marion said, handing Simon back to Caye, "you take him."

Caye cleaned up Simon's chair with one hand and put him back in it. She tossed a pile of Cheerios on the tray and gathered the bowls off the kitchen table, quickly rinsing them and sliding them into the dishwasher.

She could hear the water running upstairs. Marion must be taking a shower.

Audrey and Hudson came into the kitchen. "We're hungry," Audrey said.

"You just ate."

"That was a while ago."

"Grab an apple."

"We don't want an apple."

"Where's Liam?"

"Don't know."

"Hudson, where's your brother?"

Hudson shrugged his shoulders.

"Is he still in the basement?"

"No."

"Grab an apple, and keep an eye on Simon," Caye said.

She went to the front door and looked out on the porch first, just in case he'd gone out the front door. No Liam.

She heard quick footsteps upstairs. He must have gone to his room to play.

Caye started up the stairs.

She made out Marion's voice above the shower. "Go downstairs."

Liam was standing in the recently remodeled bathroom, the door wide open.

"Go! Now!"

Caye reached in to grab his hand. "He just has to use the toilet," Caye said to the figure in the glass shower. "He's potty training."

As Caye turned to go through the door, she caught a quick glimpse of Marion through the glass. *She's flat. Her boobs have all dried up.* Then Caye realized Marion had no breasts.

Caye quickly dropped her eyes, scooped up Liam, and rushed him down the stairs. She felt the warm urine against her thigh as she reached the bottom step.

"Try to stop, Liam," she said. "Hold it."

It kept coming. By the time they reached the downstairs bathroom, their pants were soaked. Liam began to cry. "It's okay," she said. "It's okay. You tried."

She sat on the edge of the claw-foot tub and put her hands on his shoulders.

"Mommy!" Audrey yelled. "Simon wants down! I think he's poopy."

The doorbell rang.

"Come on," Caye said to Liam, "we'll get you in the tub after I get the door."

Rita began to laugh at the sight of Caye.

"What happened?"

Caye smiled, flashing her dimples.

"I peed my pants," she said.

"You and who else?" Rita replied, looking at Liam, who stood holding on to Caye's pant leg.

"Can you put him in the tub? I need to run home and shower and change."

"Just grab something of Jill's."

Caye chuckled.

"What?" Rita asked.

"Even her capris are too long for me—and still wouldn't fit in the waist."

Rita laughed. "Get going."

"If Marion comes down, tell her I'll be right back." Caye grabbed her purse and began digging for her keys.

Not only had Jill kept the secret of her dad's pancreatic cancer, but she hadn't said a thing about Marion's cancer. Caye presumed it was cancer, thinking of the blurry image in the shower. Had she seen correctly? Had Marion had a mastectomy? She felt unsettled and naughty for having seen Marion naked.

It looked as though Jill hadn't told Rob either—or Rob would have said something to Nathan on that first day Jill was in the hospital.

She climbed into her station wagon and started the engine. The day was already growing warm. She rolled down her window to ward off the smell of urine and headed down the hill toward her house. So many secrets. It felt like a sticky mess, like the warm saltwater taffy that Andrew had smeared in Audrey's hair last summer.

And they were all stuck in the goo.

❧

"Let's get you up," the nurse said. "Swing your feet out of bed onto the floor."

Jill looked at the nurse. Her big brown eyes were kind, like Caye's. Her hair was short and gray. She wore a bright Hawaiian scrub shirt and blue scrub pants. Jill had forgotten her name. She looked at the nametag dangling in front of her and read "Diane."

"How's the pain?" Diane asked.

"Better. I think I'm getting the pain thing, the pump, figured out," Jill said.

"Do you feel like you can stand?"

"I can try."

"And walk out into the hall?"

"Okay." Jill put her weight on her feet. She could feel her muscles pull, the incision tighten.

She stood.

"Good," Diane said. "How about a few steps? The IV pole will come along with us."

Rob hadn't packed her slippers. Jill hadn't thought to ask him to. Her thick socks padded against the carpet.

She was tired, overcome by that sickening feeling of exhaustion. She took a step toward the door and winced.

Rob had come by at 8:30 and then gone into work. She'd been near tears when Rita called.

"Do you and your husband have any kids?" Diane asked.

"Uh-huh," Jill answered. "Three boys."

"How old?"

"Almost five, almost three, and almost one." Jill said, reaching the hall. She stopped.

Jill raised her head. Diane's eyes looked misty. She smiled gently, pulling the IV pole even with Jill.

"This is hard work," Jill said.

"Yep," Diane answered. "And you're doing great."

"They didn't get all of the tumor." Jill paused and took a shallow breath. "And it's spread to my lymph nodes." She stopped walking. "I was so sure that it hadn't, so sure they were going to get it all. That I would do the chemotherapy as a precautionary measure, just to make sure."

Jill took another step. "I have to fight this. I have to beat it. The odds don't look good, but God will see me through."

"If there's one thing I've watched on this floor," Diane answered, "it's God seeing people through, over and over."

"Really?"

"Really. Tell me, what do you like to do?" Diane asked.

"Garden. Paint. Be a mom." Jill smiled, a quick half smile.

"What part of Ashland do you live in?"

"Up above Briscoe School."

"Nice."

"We have an old fixer-upper."

"And three kids? You must be busy."

"It's what I've always wanted." Jill stopped again and fought for a deep breath. "Why did you choose to be an oncology nurse?" she asked, leaning against the wall.

"My mom died from cancer when I was sixteen," Diane answered.

"I'm sorry."

Diane smiled. "The nurses who took care of her made me want to be a nurse." Diane paused and then continued. "You're here because you have to be. I'm here because I want to be."

"I'm counting the days, the hours, until I get out."

"Do you have help at home?"

"Yes. Good friends."

"Great. Let's head back to your room. I'll help you clean up, and then you should rest."

*17*

Marion stood on the front porch with her coat and bags. She was dressed in her suit. Her hair was still wet and streaked with comb marks. "I have a 2:30 flight," she called out to Caye. "Can you take me to the airport after we go to the hospital?"

Caye shut her car door.

"Let me check with Rita—see when she needs me back."

Marion descended the porch stairs, passed Caye, and climbed into the car.

As Caye headed up the stairs, the screen door banged. Liam came running through it. Hudson chased after him with a plastic bat.

Caye grabbed Hudson by the arm. "What's going on?"

"He broke my pirate ship. He did it on purpose."

Liam kept on running. He wore his black cape and yellow rubber boots.

"Stop, Liam!" Caye shouted. He was halfway down the steps. He stopped.

"Hudson's mean." Liam turned around. "He won't share."

"Come on, guys," Caye said. "Let's go in the house." Hudson led the way. Caye held Liam's left hand; he shoved his right thumb into his mouth. Once inside he stood in the entryway, still sucking his thumb. His almost-three-year-old belly jutted out over his orange shorts. His white T-shirt was too short and revealed a thin strip of skin. Saliva glistened on his hand. Tears brimmed over his lower lids.

Caye bent down to hug him. He turned toward her, smearing spit on her cheek.

"Are you okay, Liam?" she asked.

He shook his head. She picked him up. He put his head on her shoulder, his thumb still in his mouth. His boots kicked against her khaki skirt.

"Let me take him," Rita said, coming in from the hall. "We'll be okay. Don't hurry back. I took the rest of the day off."

Caye passed Liam to Rita and headed back out to her car. Marion sat in the passenger seat looking straight ahead.

Marion was silent for the first ten minutes of the trip to Medford, to the hospital.

"I have to be honest with you, Caye," she eventually said.

*Does she know I saw her in the shower? Is she going to tell me about her cancer?* Caye glanced behind her shoulder and changed lanes to pass a truck. Was she going to spill her guts now?

"I'm jealous of your friendship with Jill."

Caye looked over at Marion. Marion was staring at her. Their eyes met. Caye quickly returned her gaze to the freeway.

"I've always wanted to be closer to her, like we were when she was young," Marion continued. "Things were better after she came home from Argentina, before she moved up here. I know I wasn't the best mother. In fact, I know she thinks I was a horrible mother. I think she feels that I forced her to have the abortion. She'd just started college. Later she told me she was sorry she ever told me she was pregnant. Frankly, I was surprised she did."

Marion shifted in the seat and turned her head toward the passenger window. "I wanted more for her than I had. That's all I wanted. Didn't want her to be saddled with a child."

*Saddled with a child?* Marion had been in her midthirties when Jill was born.

"The hills are so pretty," Marion said, her voice trailing off, "so green."

Marion made Caye nervous, anxious, uncomfortable in her company. The feeling was similar to the way Caye felt toward Joya—but worse. Marion was hugging the passenger door again, her face against the window.

Caye thought again of Joya and then about the weekend getaway the women in the Fellowship went on two years ago. Rita had arranged the use of a friend's cabin, and all six of them piled into Jill's Suburban for the ride over.

The idea, Jill and Caye thought, was to relax, to have fun.

Joya had other ideas. First, she insisted that they sign up to do chores for the weekend.

"Let's live by faith instead," Jill joked. "Let's see who's inspired to pitch in."

"I'm happy to make up a chart," Joya said.

"If you do," Jill kidded, "I'll call you 'Sarge' for the rest of your life. Lighten up."

Joya gave up the idea. Caye marveled at how Jill could—at times—tease Joya out of an idea.

Jill didn't try to tease Joya out of leading devotions each morning and a sharing time each evening, but she did insist that they at least hold the sharing time in the hot tub under the stars.

Joya, looking uncomfortable with the water frothing around her, suggested they create an accountability group that would be ongoing. They could meet once a week, just the women in the group, to encourage each other spiritually.

"What did you say?" Jill asked.

Joya, speaking louder to be heard over the bubbles, repeated herself.

"And Thomas will watch Hudson and Liam when Rob's out of town? Right?"

"You seem to be able to get a baby-sitter for everything else," Joya replied.

It was no secret that Joya thought Jill was extravagant. On the trip to the beach she commented on the horrible gas mileage the Suburban got. Caye felt her irritation with Joya rising. Jill simply pointed out that it was better than the women taking two cars to the beach. Caye calculated the gas and mileage in her head and concluded that taking two economy cars would beat the Suburban. Then she realized that Jill meant it was a benefit to have all the women in one vehicle. Caye wasn't sure she agreed.

At the end of the hot tub time, Summer said she had something to share.

Jill turned off the bubbles.

"I've been questioning my faith," Summer said.

"Why would you question your faith?" Joya asked.

"It doesn't always make sense."

"Then you're going too much on how you feel—not what you know."

"That's it. I'm not always sure what I know."

"What does Lonnie say?" Joya asked.

"What does it matter what Lonnie says?"

"I think it's normal to question faith," Jill interjected. "That's what makes faith stronger."

"Practicing faith is what makes faith stronger," Joya rebutted.

"That's part of the problem. Lonnie doesn't practice faith with me. He's so lackadaisical—"

"Summer," Joya interrupted, "we've talked about this before."

"About what? My faith?"

"About criticizing Lonnie."

Jill put her arm around Summer. "We'll talk," she said. "Later."

"Let's pray," Joya concluded.

The next day was warm and sunny. In the afternoon the women went down to the beach to walk. Caye and Jill kicked off their sandals and ran out into the waves.

It felt so good to be there without the kids. To be carefree.

Together, holding hands, they rushed into the crashing waves.

"It's so cold!" Jill screamed.

As they ran back toward shore, Caye looked up. Joya was staring at them. Rita was taking off her sandals to join them. Gwen and Summer kept walking.

Caye recognized, from her own past, Joya's hungry look. *She's lonely.* The thought surprised Caye. *She needs a friend.*

"Come on, Joya," she shouted. "Come in with us!"

Joya was wearing cutoff jeans, a red T-shirt, and an old pair of Keds without socks.

Joya smiled.

Caye was sure she was going to join them. For a moment, Caye was optimistic. *This is what we needed, this time away.* But then Joya shook her head and started walking toward Gwen and Summer. Caye turned and ran back into the waves. She grabbed Jill's hand and then Rita's. They danced in the shockingly cold water with the salt against their skin, soaked from head to foot.

Later Caye told Jill that she couldn't help but think of God when she looked at the waves crashing in, when she heard the roar of the ocean, looked out over its seemingly endless expanse, thought of the thousands of miles of water she couldn't see.

"That's how I feel in my garden," Jill responded.

*That's so like Jill to see God in the details. And so like me to find him in a setting that is only a sliver of what goes on for thousands and thousands of miles.* Caye pulled to the side of the road as an ambulance blared by. They were only a half-mile from the hospital. If she were Marion or Joya, God forbid, she'd be jealous too.

⁕

Marion stood leaning against the wall by the door; she shifted her feet.

"Hey, you," Jill whispered to Caye. "Rob went back to work." She felt relieved Caye had come. She reached for her hand, as if she could draw physical strength from her friend.

"Did you want him to?"

"No."

"Did you tell him you wanted him to stay?"

"No."

"Why?"

"I don't want him to get behind. He has so much to do."

"You should tell him, sweetie. He'd stay."

"It doesn't look so good, does it?" Jill whispered. She wished she could talk to Caye without Marion in the room.

Caye stooped down and hugged Jill.

Jill began to cry, softly. "This is really serious. Do you still think God will heal me? Do you still think Joya is right?"

"I do," Caye said. "I really do."

"Hi, Mother," Jill said, dabbing at her eyes with the limp tissue wadded in her fist. "How long are you staying?"

"I have a 2:30 flight."

"So soon?"

Jill's hair was loose around her head. Her voice gave away her tension, her exhaustion. She honestly hadn't wanted Marion to come at all—but now that she was here, her premature departure felt like a slap.

"How are you feeling?" Caye asked.

"Like a mess. Everything hurts." Jill was grateful that Caye was sensitive enough to change the subject.

Her friend let go of her hand and reached for the chair beside the bed, pulling it forward. "What do you need?"

"More drugs," Jill said with a painful smile. "The nurse had me walk earlier. That was a trip. How are my boys?"

"The paint on your house is peeling," Marion said.

Jill inched up on her pillow to look at her mom. "I'm in the hospital, Mother. I have pan-cre-at-ic can-cer. I just had surgery. I have three little boys. A husband. I don't care if the paint on my house is peeling."

"Well, I thought you should know. I paid a lot of money for that paint."

Jill took a raggedy breath. "Are you just going to stand there the whole time? Come over here."

Marion walked across the room.

"Are you happy that you were right? All these years you were so sure I'd get it."

"I hoped you wouldn't."

"But I did."

"And for that I'm sorry."

Caye took Jill's hand again and squeezed it.

"Why did you come?" Jill asked Marion, looking up into her face.

"I'm so worried about you," Marion answered, sitting in the chair on the other side of the bed from Caye. Marion gave Jill's arm two quick pats and then turned her head toward the window.

"Why are you going home today?"

"You don't need me," Marion spoke, directed her words toward the far-off hills. "Caye has everything under control."

Jill ran her hand through her hair. "When will you come back?"

Caye held on firmly to Jill's other hand.

"When you ask me to."

"Okey-dokey," Jill said. "I'm a day out of surgery and here we are playing this stupid game again. When do you want to come back?"

❧

Caye sat in the cafeteria with Marion, silently mulling over *okey-dokey*. She had never heard Jill say *okey-dokey* before.

"She was mocking me," Marion said. "Saying 'okey-dokey.' I used to say that when she was in junior high, and she mocked me then too.

"When *should* I come back?" Marion continued, looking into Caye's eyes.

*You're asking me?* Caye pulled her shoulders back and sat up straight, stopping her soupspoon in midair. Marion took a bite of her Rueben sandwich.

"You know, Marion, I can't figure out what's going on between you and Jill. I have no idea what to tell you, no idea when you should come back." Caye put her spoon back in the bowl.

"Then tell me this," Marion said. "Do you think family secrets are best left unsaid?"

"Jill doesn't know you had cancer?" Caye blurted out, leaning forward, bumping her spoon with a clatter against the bowl. Caye felt relief that Jill hadn't been deceptive about that too, and then embarrassment for speaking out so brashly.

Marion looked puzzled. "Well, there *is* that. But there's something else. And I wonder if there's any point in telling Jill."

Caye felt anxious. She had no idea what to say to Marion.

"Secrets separate people," Caye finally said, slowly formulating her answer. "Do you think telling Jill would help? Would it make your relationship with her better?"

"I don't know," Marion said.

*Is she going to tell me?* Caye was curious but not sure that she wanted Marion to confide anything more to her. She picked up her spoon and chased a slice of carrot around the bowl.

"How did you know I had cancer?" Marion asked, breaking the silence.

*Why did I open my big mouth?* Caye paused. Took a breath. "This morning. When I was getting Liam. I saw you in the shower."

Marion blushed slightly. "Oh."

"Does Jill know about that?"

"No."

Caye concentrated on eating her soup, waiting for Marion to continue, but the older woman sat silently, focused on her sandwich.

All Caye wanted to do was go back up to Jill's room. To brush Jill's hair. To watch her sleep. To pray with her, read her a psalm, do anything she needed. Caye's throat tightened. Her eyes began to ache.

"We'd better get going," Marion said, looking up from her watch. "I don't want to miss my flight."

## 18

"I talked to Rob," Joya said as she poked her head around the door. "He said I should come on up if I wanted to."

"Hi," Jill answered.

"How are you?"

"Sore. My throat hurts. My back hurts. My whole body hurts."

Joya nodded. Jill thought of Joya's many years as a nurse. That was one of the things that impressed Jill about Joya when she first met her—that she worked in an Argentine hospital.

"Where's Louise?" Jill asked.

"With a neighbor."

Joya sat down in the chair and handed Jill an envelope.

"Thanks." Jill decided she would open it later; she put it on the table beside the dozen pink roses from Rob. When they were delivered an hour ago, Jill thought they looked more appropriate for the mother of a new baby girl than for a woman who just had her pancreas dissected.

"How is Rob doing?" Joya asked.

"I think he's okay. Shaken. Scared. Better, though. He was pretty upset I hadn't told him."

"Told him what?" Joya asked.

"About my family history."

Joya shook her head.

"You don't know? I thought everyone knew." So Thomas hadn't known when he posed the question about the Ten Commandments on Sunday. She'd chosen to tell her tulip-stealing story because she thought Thomas wanted her to confess to deceiving Rob. Why had she said anything?

"My father, grandfather, and aunt all died from pancreatic cancer."

"And you hadn't told Rob?"

Jill shook her head.

"Why not?"

"It wouldn't have made a difference."

Joya crossed her arms. "What exactly did the surgeon say?"

Jill moved her legs, bent her knees, put her feet flat on the mattress.

"It's spread to the lymph nodes. They couldn't get all of the tumor."

"And the treatment?"

"Chemotherapy. Radiation."

"How do you feel spiritually?"

"Rocked."

"What do you mean?"

"Like God is rocking me, gently, like a baby."

Joya's eyes furrowed together. "I truly believe God is going to heal you. I think he has some things for you to learn, hard lessons, in this. I think, for you to be healed, you need to be willing to learn those lessons."

Jill thought of Joya wadding the silk scarf in Argentina. She wondered if she would feel angry if it were someone else, someone besides Joya, talking to her about healing and learning lessons.

"May I pray for you?" Joya asked.

Jill nodded. Her mind wandered to the first time she saw Joya sitting in the small stucco church in Argentina on a metal chair. She was holding Louise. Three-year-old David, a red-headed child with fair skin who held the promise of freckles, sat on Rob's lap. Thomas sat beside Joya, his long legs bumping against the chair in front of him. Even though Rob was holding David, Jill knew that Joya and Thomas were married. She kept glancing at the group throughout the service. Rob was single; she could tell by the gentle way he held David. Thomas was an intellectual, totally engrossed in the teaching. She wasn't sure about Joya. She seemed matter-of-fact toward Louise. Polite toward Thomas. Attentive toward Rob. Annoyed with David, who kept talking, interrupting. She seemed tired.

After the service, Jill singled Joya out and introduced herself. The next day Joya called and invited Jill to dinner. Jill knew Rob would be there—even though Joya hadn't said he'd been invited.

Jill was aware of Joya praying, asking God to give Rob grace and the boys strength, asking for Jill's spiritual healing.

"Amen," Joya said.

"Amen," Jill echoed, relieved Joya was finished.

"God is most interested in healing you spiritually," Joya said. "The physical healing will follow."

Jill wondered what particular spiritual area Joya thought she needed healing in, but she didn't ask.

"Thanks," she said to Joya.

"I'd better go get Louise. And you should get some rest."

Jill smiled. "Thanks for coming."

Joya left the room.

She knew Caye was right. She was tolerant of Joya. The reasons why were rooted in those first few months in Argentina when Jill and Rob were falling in love. Joya and Thomas were there, offering advice, asking them over to dinner, encouraging them. Jill was enthralled with their children. David was smart and inquisitive. Louise was just learning to crawl. Jill wanted a husband and children, a home. Joya and Thomas, for those few months, were her role models for a family. As for a home, Jill's style was very different from Joya's simple, monklike approach. Joya seemed to have no interest in decorating or aesthetic comforts.

Joya said that Jill was an answer to prayer. She'd been praying for a wife for Rob. "It really is time for him to settle down," Joya told Jill, without going into detail.

Jill opened the envelope from Joya. Inside was a plain white card. Written in Joya's meticulous printing were the words: *We are praying for you.*

It was signed *Thomas, Joya, and Louise,* all in Joya's simple cursive.

Two years ago Jill and Joya had planned an Easter dinner for the Fellowship. They sat in Jill's living room. The contractors had just finished the kitchen. The painters were coming the next day to paint the interior of the house. It was two weeks before Easter.

Joya made a comment about Liam's Nike shoes. "He's not even walking yet," she'd said. "He doesn't need thirty dollar shoes. How can you throw money away so carelessly when there are so many hungry children in the world?"

Jill changed the subject back to Easter, ignoring Joya's comment. She made a mental note not to repeat Joya's criticism to Caye. Caye took Joya's off-the-cuff statements too seriously.

Jill said she thought they should have a sit-down dinner. She had a great recipe for rack of lamb with mint sauce. It was the perfect entrée for Easter.

"I didn't think you ate meat," Joya said.

"I eat meat," Jill said. "Just not very often."

"So it's not a philosophical thing?"

Jill ignored her. "I can move the breakfast table into the dining room and all fifteen of us, kids included, can sit together." Jill had just purchased the mahogany dining room set from an antique dealer; she looked forward to using it.

"That's so much work," Joya said, "so many details. Let's just do a potluck buffet and use paper plates."

"I'll do all the work," Jill said.

"Do you think God wants you to spend your time doing all that?" Joya asked.

"What do you mean?"

"It just seems like a waste of time."

"Look at nature," Jill said. "Look at all the details. Do you think that's a waste of time?"

Joya looked outside Jill's window and then back at Jill. "Are you comparing yourself to God?"

They ended up having a sit-down potluck. Jill made the rack of lamb. No paper plates. They used Jill's Royal Copenhagen china.

From time to time, Jill thought about Joya's comment. Joya was right; Jill did feel God-like in what she created—her paintings, her garden, her home. After all, God created her in his image.

But she knew that wasn't what Joya meant. She was sure that Joya saw her as controlling and extravagant, closer to Napoleon than a person simply reveling in creation and the ability to create. Jill sometimes wondered if they would have stuck with the Fellowship had they not known Thomas and Joya in Argentina. Still, she felt loyal to Joya, felt that she needed to be protected. Through it all, flaws included, she felt that the Fellowship was a good thing.

Caye pulled into the driveway with Andrew in the seat beside her. She needed a cup of coffee—she should have stopped on her way through downtown after picking Andrew up from school.

The screen door to the house stood open. Scout guarded the entryway. Caye heard screaming as she opened the car door. *Simon.* She and Andrew walked up the steps. *No, too shrill. Liam.*

"Mom, can you buy me the LEGOs cavalry set? Can we go over to the mall? Hudson saw it awhile back. Over in Medford."

"We'll talk about it later," Caye said, quickening her pace. The screams were growing louder. She hurried through the door. Rita carried Liam down the open staircase, followed by Hudson and Audrey. Simon sat at the bottom of the stairs, a slobbery leaf from the ficus tree in his hand.

Liam leaned toward Caye, willing himself out of Rita's arms, as the older woman maneuvered the bottom step, avoiding Simon. Caye took Liam carefully, securing him around the waist, avoiding his right arm that hung limply, untying his cape so she could get a closer look.

"Mommy!" Liam screamed over and over. "I want Mommy!"

"It's broken," Caye said to Rita. "We need to call Rob."

Rita stared at her. It was obvious who was going to call Rob. *Poor Rita. What a day for her to watch the kids.*

"What happened?" Caye asked Hudson and Audrey, as she patted Liam and swayed back and forth with him.

They'd been playing Batman on the bunk beds.

"He thought he could fly," Audrey explained.

"And?" Caye asked. "Did you tell him he couldn't?"

"No."

"You're in big trouble," Andrew told Audrey and Hudson. "You're really going to get it now."

"Did you try to stop him?" Caye asked Audrey and Hudson.

They shrugged in unison. "We thought maybe he could," Audrey whispered.

"Liam, don't cry so loudly, okay?" Caye said, turning away from Audrey and Hudson. "I need to call your daddy."

❧

Caye sat in the ER waiting room at Ashland Community Hospital staring at the spot where Audrey had been born.

The doctor was sure Liam's arm was broken. "Flying off the top bunk will do that," the doctor chuckled before ordering the x-ray. "But it doesn't seem to be a particularly bad break."

"I feel like Job," Rob said as he carried Liam down the hall.

Caye stretched her legs and smoothed her khaki skirt. Nathan had probably talked to Rita by now, already knew what had happened, why she wasn't there. Rob needed to go over to see Jill in Medford—too bad they were at the Ashland hospital. If they'd gone to Medford, Caye could at least be with Jill; she hated that Jill was alone so much.

Caye's mother, in response to hard times, often said, "When it rains, it pours." It was pouring. She never remembered her mother making the comment during good times.

This morning seemed like a week ago; even dropping Marion off at the airport seemed like days ago. She still hadn't had her afternoon coffee.

❧

Rob stood in the doorway holding Liam. The room was dark. Jill raised the bed partway.

"Hey, you," she said, lifting her head. "Who do you have?" she asked. "Hudson?"

"Mommy thinks you're Hudson," Rob said. "It's because you're getting so big."

"It must be Liam," Jill said.

"We had an accident," Rob explained. "Just a little one. Liam decided to be Batman; he flew off the top bunk."

"Hudson said, 'Do it.'" Liam hiccuped.

"Oh, sweetie," Jill said. "Come here."

Rob sat down beside her on the bed. He slid Liam off his lap onto the bed next to Jill.

Jill squeezed Rob's arm. "Look, Liam," she said, "you have a cast!"

Liam started to crawl onto Jill. "Wait," she said. "Let me sit up more. Then you can sit beside me."

Liam began to cry again.

"It's okay," Jill said.

He tried to crawl on top of her. Rob grabbed him by his good arm; Liam began to scream.

"Rob!" Jill said. "Be careful." Why did he come over? For Liam? For her? For himself?

Jill raised the bed and sat up straight. "Put Liam beside me. Come on, Liam. You can't sit on me, but I can still hug you."

Liam settled next to Jill and calmed down. Jill put her arm around him and drew him close, then began to stroke his hair.

Rob walked to the window and began pacing.

"Caye thought I should come over," Rob explained. "I didn't want to take Liam back to the house."

"Who's with Hudson and Simon?"

"Rita. Or maybe Caye now. I'm not sure."

"How was work?"

"Okay. No. Not okay. I was right in the middle of a conference call when Caye paged me about all this."

Liam hiccuped again.

Jill shifted her attention to him. "May I be the first to sign your cast?"

"Why?"

"That's what people do. They sign casts."

Liam nodded solemnly.

"Do you have a pen, Rob?"

Rob pulled a blue ballpoint pen out of his shirt pocket.

Jill drew a heart but not an ordinary one, a lacey, old-fashioned Valentine heart, and then figures of a little boy in knickers and a woman in a long dress in the middle of the heart. "That's us," she explained. "You and me." Liam smiled. "I'm sorry I wasn't there when you broke your arm."

Liam began to sniffle. Jill hugged him.

"I should get going," Rob said. He bent to pick Liam up, this time gently. "I'll come over tomorrow. I'll take a long lunch." He paused. "I don't know how much time to take off—how much I'll need later."

"I know," Jill said.

"Are you okay?"

Jill nodded.

He kissed her, leaning down with Liam on his hip. Jill kissed Rob on the lips and then Liam on the cheek.

"I hate this," Rob said.

"I'll be home soon," Jill said. "A week from now."

Rob frowned. "A week. It seems like forever."

"Bye, Mommy."

"Bye-bye, Liam. I love you, Rob."

"I know," he said. "I know you love me."

*Do you love me too?* she wanted to ask as he left the dark room. But she didn't want to grovel. She knew he did. She knew he was feeling overwhelmed. And angry. Was he angry with her? Angry that she hadn't warned him? Angry at the circumstances? Angry with the boys?

She hated this time of the day when darkness settled and night arrived.

When she was growing up, she'd turn on all the lights, the TV, and the radio as the day grew dark. Marion would scold her for wasting electricity, for wasting money.

Jill felt as if the emergency-broadcasting signal of her childhood were going off, as if it would not stop. The shrill tone had her attention; she was glued to the strips of color on the TV. Waiting to hear that it was just a test.

She ran her hands along her abdomen, along the bandages. Her stomach was swollen. She felt so bloated.

It wasn't a test.

❧

"When are you coming home?" Nathan asked over the phone.

"As soon as Rob and Liam get back." Caye didn't tell him they'd gone over to see Jill; he'd assume they were still at the Ashland hospital. "There's leftover spaghetti in the refrigerator."

He hadn't asked how bad Liam's break was. Or how she was doing.

"Remember I have a game tomorrow," Nathan said. "In Eugene. And Andrew has a tee ball game in the morning."

Caye hadn't remembered Andrew's game.

"I just remembered he missed practice last night," Nathan added. He sounded like Eeyore. "And he missed last week, too."

Caye felt her irritation rising as she held the phone. "I'll be home as soon as I can," she said. "See you then."

She fed the kids leftover pizza, then bathed Simon and Hudson while Andrew and Audrey colored at the kitchen table. All the kids were tired and cranky. She gave Simon his bottle and put him to bed.

She heard Rob's Jeep in the driveway. He came in carrying Liam, who was fast asleep, his casted arm draped awkwardly over Rob's shoulder.

❧

"Go get your pajamas on," Caye said to Andrew and Audrey as they hurried through the back door, the cat sneaking by their legs. Abra looked skinny, too skinny, and the long white fur under her chin was tangled.

"Daddy!" Audrey yelled.

The house was dark. Only the TV was on. Nathan was asleep on the couch.

Audrey climbed up on his lap. He put one arm around her and opened one eye.

"We're home!"

"Good," he said. "I was starting to feel like a bachelor."

"Pajamas," Caye said. "Both of you."

The phone rang. Caye picked it up. She heard crying in the background and then Rob's voice.

"I don't know what to do," Rob said. "Liam started to cry when I tried to put him down. He woke Simon. Now they're both screaming. Hudson's hiding somewhere—I can't find him."

Caye walked into the dining room, looked at Nathan on the couch with Andrew and Audrey on either side of him. All three were glued to the TV, to a PBS program on sunspots.

"I'll be right over," she said to Rob.

"Okay," Nathan said, when she told him what Rob had said, that she was running back over to Jill's. But she could tell he wasn't happy.

"What do you think I should do?" she asked defensively. She felt torn between her family and Jill's family.

"Go," he said. "There's nothing else to do."

"Put the kids to bed, okay? Have Andrew put out his tee ball uniform. Make sure he knows where his cleats are."

"Okay." Nathan turned back to the TV. "I'll be in bed when you get home," he called out as she hurried out the door.

She saw Hudson in his pajamas on the porch as she drove up, hunched under the bay window. "Come on, Hudson," she said, reaching for his hand. "Let's go inside."

"I want my mommy." Hudson inched toward Caye on his haunches.

"I know."

"I didn't mean for Liam to break his arm."

"I know."

"I want Mommy."

"I know," Caye said, grabbing his hand. "But it's not right to scare your daddy. He's frantic."

She opened the door. "Rob, it's me. And Hudson's here."

He came out of the kitchen holding both Liam and Simon. The baby clutched his bottle against his chest.

"Where was he?"

"On the porch. Under the window."

"Hudson," Rob said sternly, loudly, "don't ever do that again."

Hudson let go of Caye's hand and ran toward Rob, swinging his fist at Rob's thigh.

"He's upset about Jill," Caye said quickly to Rob. "They're all upset, Rob." *And you, too.* "Here, let me take the little guys."

Hudson backed off. Rob handed Liam and Simon to Caye both at once. Hudson lunged forward and hit Rob again.

Liam began to cry.

"Stop it," Rob commanded, reaching for Hudson, grabbing him by the arm. "And don't let Liam fly off the top bunk again either."

Caye, even with her full arms, wanted to put her head in her hands. He was doing it all wrong.

Hudson, with his free hand, hit him again.

"I said stop it."

"I want Mommy," Hudson replied, slugging Rob in the gut. Rob let out an *oof* and grabbed Hudson's other hand.

"Stop it."

Hudson began to cry. "I didn't mean for Liam to break his arm."

"I know." Rob knelt.

Hudson sank into his arms.

"When's Mommy coming home?"

"In a week." Rob held Hudson tighter. "Do you want to go see her tomorrow—like Liam did tonight?"

"Liam saw her tonight?" Hudson pulled away, shot an angry look at Liam, and struggled out of Rob's arms. He spun around and raced up the stairs.

Rob plopped backward on the floor.

"I'll put Simon to bed. You give Liam some children's Tylenol. It's in the cupboard by the sink. I'll check on Hudson." She passed Liam to Rob. She hoped he knew to read the directions.

*One more week.* Caye started up the stairs. *And then what?*

# Part Three

I can do all things through Him
who strengthens me.

PHILIPPIANS 4:13 (NASB)

## 19

Caye walked in Jill's garden. The rain had pelted the plants last night. The white bleeding hearts hung low against the ground. A flutter in the wisteria growing high against the brick wall caught Caye's attention. The tight purple flowers were just beginning to bloom. Two blue jays sat side by side, their black hoods pointed toward the gate. Caye took small, slow steps toward them. Their feathers caught the overcast light in quick shimmers; their talons curled tightly on the gnarly vine.

She inched closer. Without ever looking at her, they rose gracefully off the wisteria and flew off together. Disappointed, Caye watched them fly above and then beyond the wall, leaving the garden behind.

She turned back toward the house and stood in the pathway, surveying the ground. In the last two weeks weeds had popped up in the flower beds among the hostas, trillium, and columbine. Blades of grass were poking up between the bricks of the pathway. Caye had intended to pull them before Jill came home from the hospital, since Rob had canceled the gardening service to save money.

Caye had half an hour before Rob would arrive with Jill. She wanted to change the sheets on Jill's bed, air out the room, get the boys out of their pajamas. Jill had been adamant about Hudson not going to preschool. Not having to rush out the door with all the kids by 8:50 did make life easier, but Hudson was at loose ends.

Rita was taking another day off work to help with the kids. Maybe she would do the weeding—or watch the kids so Caye could.

"There you are," Rita called out. Scout rushed through the back door.

"Hi, Rita. I was just looking at all the chores there are to do out here. I'm planning on putting you to work this afternoon."

"Don't trust me with the kids?" Rita asked with a laugh.

"Actually, my other idea was to escape out here this afternoon while you play another round of superhero with them."

Rita laughed again. "How's Liam?"

"Fine. He's learned to use the cast as a weapon. You'll be impressed with Hudson's shiner."

"You're kidding?"

"No."

"Yikes," Rita said. "Another thing for me to feel guilty about. Jill's going to banish me."

"Hudson deserved it." Caye stopped. She didn't want to complain about Hudson, but he was testing them all, and her patience was growing thin. The only person he'd been kind to all week was Andrew. Hudson sulked around the house each day, leaving Audrey at a loss, until Andrew got out of school. Yesterday, when Hudson pinned Liam to the basement floor over a Fisher-Price pirate infraction, Liam whacked Hudson across the face with his cast.

"Come on, Scout," Caye called to the dog. He was digging against the brick wall. Scout ignored her. She called again and then, scolding him, walked toward him and grabbed his collar.

Rita pulled the sides of her sweater together and crossed her arms against the chill.

"Want a cup of coffee?" Caye asked as she dragged the dog along the pathway. "I'll start a pot. We can sit down in the kitchen and do some planning for a few minutes. Then I'd better get the kids dressed."

A few minutes later Caye and Rita pored over a yellow legal pad. "This is what community is all about," Rita said as she looked at the list before them. They'd mapped out the next week, signed up Fellowship members for meals, penciled in Caye to be with the kids each day. Rita would come over after work two nights a week to help get the boys to bed. They volunteered Gwen to do the grocery shopping. "I'll call her," Rita said.

"I haven't called Stephanie this week."

Rita looked puzzled. "Stephanie?"

"Jill's baby-sitter."

"I thought they needed to economize."

Caye had told Rita that Rob canceled the gardening service and was thinking about canceling the Wednesday morning housekeeping. He was suddenly worried about money. He didn't say so, but Caye had the feeling his worries were tied to Marion. Again Caye wondered just how much Marion had been contributing to keep Jill's household going through the years.

"Well, if I use Stephanie, it will be just for a few hours. I'll definitely keep her as a backup in case I need to take Jill to the doctor."

It was Joya who often talked about community and how it was God's design. She and Thomas based the concept of the Fellowship on the first-century church.

On Sunday Joya had thanked the group for their efforts on Jill's behalf. "This is what it's all about," she said. "Letting God use us to take care of each other."

They'd met at Jill and Rob's, although Caye felt eerie being in the house as a group without Jill. Rob was quiet. Thomas taught on Colossians 3, focusing on praising God and being thankful.

It was Gwen who suggested they pray for Jill's spiritual healing. "That if she has any unconfessed sin, she would deal with it," Gwen explained.

Caye imagined that Joya had been talking to Gwen. "Do you think that's why she's sick?" Summer asked.

"It could be," Gwen answered.

Caye thought of Jill's abortion. That sin had been definitely confessed before God and others. She'd been open with all of them about it. Gwen must be referring to Jill not telling Rob about her family history.

"Speaking of Job," Rob said.

"Pardon?" It was Joya, straining her neck to look at Rob.

"Job. His friends tried to tell him that his illness was because of sin. God rebuked them."

"But, Rob, you were upset that Jill hadn't told you about her chances of getting sick."

"Joya," Rob answered, "she didn't know what her chances were. No one did." He paused. "Do you think she sinned in not telling me?"

Joya didn't answer.

"Well, she told me she was sorry. Does that make you feel better?"

"Did she tell God she was sorry?"

"Was it a sin?"

Caye smiled at Rob's defense of Jill.

"I think so." Joya sat back and crossed her arms.

"Well, if she confessed it, God doesn't remember it. Why are you keeping track?"

Thomas intervened. "Jill is in God's hands. We must keep praying for her. Praying for her life and healing." He sounded uncomfortable. And weary. "And we need to keep praying for Rob and the boys, for strength to get through this."

"Sunday was weird, wasn't it?" Rita filled the coffee mugs from the pot.

Caye nodded. "I was just thinking about it."

"I hate it when Gwen speaks Joya's stuff. The unconfessed-sin bunk. You know she didn't come up with it on her own." Rita sat back down. "Joya's always the one talking about community, but this is where I find it."

"Jill's the one who creates it," Caye said matter-of-factly and then took a sip of the coffee. It was too hot.

"No, not just Jill. You and Jill."

Caye furrowed her brow.

"You don't believe me? Look at everything you're doing."

"What else would I do?"

"That's what makes it so communal. It's from your heart."

"I don't know about that," Caye answered. "I just think that's what makes it easy." *Except for Hudson, poor guy. And Joya and Gwen.* She wished they'd lighten up. They had no excuse, unlike four-year-old Hudson, for their bad behavior.

Rita walked to the sink and started doing the dishes.

"I'll go make Jill's bed," Caye said, looking at her watch. She had seven minutes until *Sesame Street* ended.

As she stripped the sheets, she thought again about the Fellowship women's getaway. The last evening, after they played on the beach and before their sharing time, Jill and Caye had made a run to the store for ice cream.

"Let's pull a prank," Jill said. "Spice things up a little."

"Like?"

"Something biblical."

They strolled down the grocery aisle. Caye pushed the cart.

Jill stopped at the Kool-Aid display. She stared at the packages, strumming her index finger against her chin.

"I've got it! The plagues of Egypt."

Thomas had just finished a sermon series on the Israelites' escape from slavery to freedom.

"You want Kool-Aid to be one of the plagues?"

"Yes. Red Kool-Aid in the showerhead for the water that turned to blood. Red dots—we'll buy a red pen—for the boils. Did you hear the frogs last night? Do you think we could catch some? We can buy a bag of Styrofoam packing pellets for the hail. Do you think that's enough? Do you think they'll get the idea?"

They got the idea. The fun started with a scream from Joya. None of them had ever heard her scream before.

"Where is she?" Gwen asked, jumping out of bed.

"Try the bathroom," Jill answered.

Gwen got as far as the hall when she noticed the red dots on her forearms. She was the heaviest sleeper and was therefore chosen for the boils.

"What are these?" Gwen asked in disbelief.

*Wait until she sees her face.* Caye had smiled at the thought.

Summer stumbled out of her bed, sending the Styrofoam that covered her blankets in six directions.

Rita had made her way into the kitchen. She let out a shriek. "Frogs!" she yelled. "There are frogs in the kettle!"

Gwen knocked on the bathroom door. "Joya. Are you okay?"

The door opened. Red water was streaming down Joya's face. She was wrapped in a white towel.

"What happened to your face?" Joya asked Gwen.

Gwen made her way to the mirror. Summer came stumbling down the hall with the Styrofoam stuck to her flannel pajamas. Rita poked her head out of the kitchen. She had a frog in her hand. "Look!"

Jill snickered. Joya looked at her with a straight face, not even a frown. "The plagues of Egypt. Right? Very good, Jill. And Caye, I presume. Thomas would find it very clever."

"I get dibs on the shower next," Gwen said as she came out of the bathroom. Joya firmly closed the door.

"I hate pranks," Gwen added on her way to the sleeping room.

She didn't know how much until it was her turn to use the shower. Jill had—inadvertently, she swore—picked out a red permanent marker.

Caye folded the last corner of the sheet and flung the comforter over the top. She smiled at the memory of the prank, but also because she finally felt a measure of happiness after days of turmoil.

Jill was coming home. The doctor said that she was healing well. She was gaining strength. It was obvious she was determined to beat the cancer.

Caye placed the pillows in position.

She felt such relief. The first hurdle had been crossed. Jill was coming home.

❧

Jill walked slowly up the front steps with Rob.

"She's here!" It was Rita's voice. She opened the front door; Jill could hear the children thundering down the stairs from the boys' bedroom.

"Mommy!" Hudson and Liam yelled, slamming out the screen door.

Caye came in from the kitchen carrying Simon.

"Hey, guys," Jill said, taking off her sunglasses. She walked slowly through the door, stopping to rest with one hand on the back of the couch. "Hudson, look at your eye. Daddy told me you took a hit."

Hudson smiled and then jabbed his finger into Liam's side. "He did it."

"So I heard."

Liam grabbed the leg of Jill's sweatpants and started jumping up and down.

"Careful," Rob said. "Don't hurt Mommy."

"Your bed's ready," Caye said, "if you want to go rest. Rita and I were just going to feed the troops."

"Thanks." Jill started to walk again. She reached for Simon's fat little leg, squeezed it quickly, and then took Caye's hand.

"How are you?" Caye asked.

"Okay. Just tired. I'll go nap a little and then hang out with the boys. Oh, Rita. There you are. I heard your voice but didn't see you."

Rita had taken a spot by the staircase. "Hi, doll."

"Why are you here? To see my homecoming?"

Rita smiled and nodded her head.

*And to help with my rowdy boys.* Jill's medication was wearing off. She needed to take a pill, lie down, regroup. She shivered. All week when she had thought about leaving the hospital, she imagined a gorgeous day, warm, and bright. She would go home. It would be warm and sunny. She would start to heal.

It was dreary and cold. Even with her fleece on over her sweatshirt she couldn't stay warm.

Still, she was home, and after a week in the hospital, after talking with Dr. Scott again yesterday, she was counting on being healed. "There's no way to call this," he had said. "We'll start the chemotherapy next week since your incision is healing so quickly—radiation, if all looks well, the week after. There's no reason not to be hopeful."

"We'll beat this," Rob said.

Jill had smiled at Dr. Scott. He smiled back, his gray eyes twinkling behind his smudged glasses. She thought of his pregnant wife and two children at home. He shook their hands fervently before he left, first Jill's, then Rob's, as if they'd just sealed a deal to make her well.

"It's so hard to understand," Rita said. "Why Jill? Why someone who lights up a room? Not just a room, a whole house, a whole community?"

Caye and Rita sat on the steps of the front porch and watched Hudson and Audrey ride their bikes up and down the sidewalk. Liam and Simon were down for their naps. Caye would leave to pick up Andrew in a few minutes.

Both Rita and Caye had their hands wrapped around their coffee mugs.

"It's too late in the spring for this cold weather," Caye complained.

"Every time I see someone smoking I think, why not them?" Rita said, ignoring Caye. "Isn't that awful?"

Caye leaned against Rita, giving in to the conversation. She'd wanted to distract Rita into talking about the weather. She didn't want to think about "Why Jill?" The absence of answers made her too sad.

"I even think that about myself."

"What?" Caye asked.

"Look at me. I haven't exactly taken good care of myself. I'm overweight. I don't exercise. Why would this happen to Jill instead of someone like me?"

"Rita," Caye whispered, "it doesn't work that way."

"I wish it were happening to me instead of her."

"Don't say that."

"My kids are grown. Hers are just babies. How could it be God's will for her to be so sick?"

"I don't think it is God's will."

"He's letting it happen." Rita took a sip of coffee.

Caye took a deep breath.

"I know, I know," Rita said. "It's not his perfect will, it's his allowed will. Blah-blah-blah. Whatever. He could've stopped it."

Caye put her coffee cup on the step beside her and put both arms around Rita. The older woman began to cry. They sat for a moment until Rita pulled away and retrieved a tissue from her sweater pocket. Caye rubbed one hand over her friend's back while Rita dabbed at her eyes.

They both looked up at the sound of car doors slamming. It was Joya and Thomas.

❧

The snake crawled across her stomach, up her arms, over her chin.

"Jill."

She heard Caye's voice; Caye would make the snake go away.

"Jill. Joya and Thomas are here."

Jill turned her head toward the doorway, toward Caye. It had been several days since she'd had the snake dream. She'd hoped it was gone for good, left behind at the hospital, but it had followed her home.

Caye stood next to the bed. "Do you feel up to seeing them?" she asked quietly.

"Give me a minute. I'll get up."

"Want some help?"

"Thanks." Jill sat on the edge of the bed. Caye took Jill's slippers from the closet and positioned them under her feet.

"Is Sunday Mother's Day?" Jill asked.

"Yeah."

"I thought so. It feels like May is halfway over, and I've missed it. It's my favorite time. Mother's Day. Liam's birthday. Then Simon and Hudson's birthdays in June. All the flowers."

Caye helped Jill stand.

"The warm days. But not today. It's so cold."

"It's starting to warm up," Caye said. "Audrey and Hudson are playing outside. Hudson's doing better this afternoon."

"I keep wanting to dream about flowers, about my garden. Instead I keep having nightmares about snakes."

They walked down the hall together and into the living room.

Thomas looked tired, befuddled. His eyes were cast down when they walked into the room. Jill saw a spark of interest in his eyes when he looked up.

"Jill," he said, rising to his feet. "How do you feel?" Seeing Thomas made Jill feel young and well again for a moment. He thought of her that way, she could tell, the way he'd first seen her in Argentina. Tall and tanned and healthy.

"Okay."

Rita stood and pulled the rocking chair closer to the couch.

"Sit here," she said.

"Hi, Jill," Joya said.

"I need to go get Andrew," Caye said, looking at her watch and then straight at Jill. "Will you be all right?"

Jill knew Caye was asking if she'd be all right with Joya and Thomas. Rob had told her, briefly, that Joya had insinuated on Sunday that sin was the cause of Jill's cancer. "I think she thought God would heal you through the surgery. That it would all be over."

"So did I," Jill answered.

"And when it didn't work that way, she latched on to the fact that you hadn't told me about the cancer in your family."

Jill thought about that now as she looked at Joya and Thomas. It was all coming together. Caye was concerned that Joya would corner Jill. But Jill wasn't worried. She and Joya believed the same thing—that God would heal her. She could ignore the rest.

"I'll be fine," Jill said to Caye as she sat down in her rocking chair and faced Joya and Thomas.

"I'll take Hudson and Audrey with me," Caye said. "Rita, the little boys might wake up before I get back."

Jill began to slide the platform rocker back and forth, back and forth.

Caye slipped out the front door; Rita stood by the fireplace, her arms crossed.

Jill smiled.

"I'm concerned," Joya said. "We're concerned."

Jill stopped rocking.

"Do you have any unconfessed sin? Anything that might keep God from healing you?"

Jill shook her head. The words to Psalm 139 floated through her head: *See if there is any offensive way in me, and lead me in the way everlasting.*

"Have you confessed your sins?"

Jill nodded.

"I keep thinking about when we were all in Argentina, when David died."

Jill nodded again and said, "Me, too."

"I don't want your family to go through what we went through. You have time to figure this out, to see what God wants to teach you. To grow in faith and experience his healing."

Thomas looked uncomfortable.

Rita uncrossed her arms. Jill was aware that, in all these years, Thomas and Joya had never talked about David in front of the Fellowship.

"Whose faith do you think will heal me?" Jill asked.

"Yours. Rob's. All of ours. Yours first."

"What if God doesn't heal me?" She was being contrary. God was going to heal her; she was playing the devil's advocate, talking the way Rob would talk to spice up a conversation.

"Why wouldn't he heal you? How could it be his will for you not to be healed?"

"And if God doesn't? What will that mean to you?"

"He will, Jill," Joya said, leaning forward with her hands on her knees. "He will. Let your faith grow."

"We should go," Thomas said. "You must be tired."

"Jill, I really love you," Joya continued. Joya had never told her that, never spoken of love or even friendship directly. "I consider you my closest friend."

Jill resumed rocking.

"I want more than anything for you to live. For your boys to have their mom. For Rob to have his wife."

"I know," Jill answered. "I do too."

"We need to go," Thomas said, patting Joya's knee. "Jill needs to rest."

"Who was David?" Rita asked, looking out the window. Jill heard a car door slam.

"Is that Caye?" Jill asked.

"No. Just Joya and Thomas leaving."

"Simon's crying," Jill said, pulling herself out of the rocking chair. "And Liam's up." She could hear his footsteps on the landing. "Can you take care of them? I'm exhausted."

Jill headed down the hall before Liam got to the bottom stair. She sat on her bed and cried. She was going to have to figure this out, determine what she could do for the boys. *It's only the first day. It will get better. Don't be so hard on yourself.*

Last evening, when Rob was still at the hospital, after Dr. Scott had left, they'd decided together to think positively. "We know the statistics are grim," Rob said, "but people do survive this. Why not you?"

It felt comforting to hear him talk that way. The surgery results had discouraged her, but now this optimism felt like a pact between them. It felt as if he'd forgiven her for not telling him about her father, as if they could beat the cancer together.

So why had she posed the possibility of not being healed to Joya? Why had she felt so defensive?

❧

"Who was David?" Rita asked, holding her purse with both hands across her chest, as if protecting herself. She stood at the door, ready to go.

"Did Joya talk about David?" Caye said.

"She mentioned him."

"What else did she say?"

"That faith would heal Jill. Jill's faith, Rob's, all of ours. That it was God's will for her to be healed. That she should confess her sins."

"What did Thomas say?"

"Not much," Rita answered.

"David was Thomas and Joya's little boy. He died when they were all in Argentina," Caye said with a sigh.

"No way."

Caye nodded. She felt a pained expression cross her face.

"But they've never talked about him, never mentioned him," Rita stammered.

"I know—Jill is the one who told me."

Rita rolled her eyes like a teenager disgusted with her parents. Caye wanted to laugh but realized she didn't really find any of it funny—the urge was just nervous energy.

"Joya is so strange. I feel sorry for her. That little bit of information explains so much," Rita said. "But at the same time I'm, you know, angry with her. There are times when I feel it should be me instead of Jill. And moments when I feel it should be Joya."

"Oh, Rita. Don't," Caye whispered.

"I'm leaving," Rita said, "or I'll say worse things. Or start crying again."

Rob's Cherokee turned into the driveway. Caye noticed that the magnolia tree had lost its flowers; it stood guard by the driveway completely naked of its beautiful blossoms, the large petals covering the surrounding grass. Caye remembered how Rob hated the tree. "It looks great for a week and then it's just a mess. We should cut it down." Of course, Jill wouldn't let him. "It's the prettiest tree in the garden," she said. When it was in bloom, it looked like a field of tulips all on one tree.

Caye quickly hugged Rita and said, "Give me a call tomorrow when you have a chance. I'll be here."

## 20

"Happy Mother's Day!" Caye said. With a pat on the shoulder, she greeted Jill, who sat in her rocker, wearing her faded overalls with a gray T-shirt.

Rob stood at the top of the basement stairs holding Simon. "Hudson," Rob called down the stairs, "Andrew's here. And Audrey."

It was Sunday morning. Thomas had called everyone last night and canceled Fellowship.

Rita had hung up from talking to Thomas and immediately called Caye. "What's going on?"

"I don't know. Nathan was just going to call Rob."

Rob didn't know either; he'd had a message from Thomas earlier in the day saying the meeting was canceled. Rob asked Nathan and Caye to come anyway. Nathan asked if it was okay for Rita to come too. Rob decided to call everyone, even Thomas and Joya, to see if they'd come for a potluck brunch.

"That's too much for Jill," Caye said, taking the phone from Nathan and quickly dialing in Jill's number.

"Not if I don't do anything," was Jill's answer to Caye's concern. "And I know you won't let me. I'll be fine."

It was decided that those who wanted to would come from 11:00 to 12:30 and then leave promptly. "Jill tires so quickly," Caye explained, calling each member. "She doesn't realize how little energy she has until she's suddenly exhausted."

Caye went into Jill's kitchen to scramble the eggs and set out the muffins she'd brought. What she really wanted to do was sit down by Jill. She saw her every day but missed her. Their conversations now were about Jill's pain level. If Simon was napping. What Jill thought she could eat. Whether she'd taken her medicine. The morning was overcast. A sweater day so far. Someone had left the back door open, and Scout whined at the screen. Caye kicked the door shut.

Rob, carrying the baby, followed Caye into the kitchen. Rita, Lonnie, and Summer were busy mixing juice and making coffee. Rita had brought paper plates and cups.

"Thomas called back this morning. They're not coming over," Rob said. He picked up a blueberry muffin as he talked, tore off a chunk, and handed it to Simon.

"Why?" Summer asked.

"He said he'd call me back later. Said Joya needed a rest."

"Is the Fellowship dissolving?" Lonnie asked. "'Cause I don't know where else to go."

"What do you think Joya needs a break from?" Nathan asked Rob. He pulled a plastic container of salsa out of a paper grocery bag and peeled off the lid.

"Real life," Rob answered, popping a bite of muffin into his mouth.

All her frustrations with Joya and the Fellowship aside, Caye agreed with Lonnie. Where else was there to go? What would they do if the group dissolved?

"I feel like we have all these undiscussed issues concerning faith and healing," Rita said. "Thomas should be teaching on faith right now. We should all be walking through this together."

"Faith," Summer said. "I'm questioning mine again. I can't feel it. How could God let this happen to Jill?"

Caye was aware of Jill in the living room. Gwen and John had just arrived. She heard them talking to Jill.

"I don't know if the issue is so much how our faith feels to us," Caye said, "but how we show it right now."

"What do you mean?" Lonnie asked.

"Well." Caye took a breath. She felt her neck grow warm. She knew red blotches were forming under her chin. Why did this make her nervous? "We can show our faith through love, like it says in Galatians, or we can be disappointed that God doesn't reward our faith."

"I don't get it," Summer said.

"We should focus on God and showing love to others, not on controlling God." Caye stepped back from the stove, and Nathan emptied the container of salsa into the eggs.

"Do you think Joya is trying to control God?" It was Gwen, standing in the kitchen doorway.

"She seems to be looking for a formula," Caye said and then hesitated. She wouldn't have said anything at all if she had known Gwen was listening. Too late now. She plowed ahead. "She seems to think Jill's cancer was caused by unconfessed sin and that she wasn't healed through the surgery because she didn't have enough faith."

"She's praying for Jill every day."

"I know that," Caye said. "But it feels like Joya's looking to place blame." She stirred the salsa into the eggs.

"So you must be relieved they're not here today?" Gwen said.

*Did Gwen think they were all turning on Joya and Thomas?* "No. I wish they were."

"I agree," Rob said. "I'm frustrated with Joya. And I haven't had a chance to talk this through with Thomas. But I don't want them *not* to be here. I'd like to work through this as a group, to feel some unity. I need everyone right now. Jill needs everyone."

"Don't bring this up in front of Jill," Rita ordered. "She has enough to worry about. Let's just make this a good Mother's Day."

"Did Jill get her medicine?" Caye asked, looking at Rob. "This morning?"

"She took her pain meds. I know that," Rob answered slowly.

"What about the enzymes? So she can eat? And her diabetes medication?"

"I don't know."

*Great. Jill's spaced out on pain drugs, and Rob's not keeping track of her other medicine.* So far Jill only needed the oral diabetes meds—not insulin. But if she didn't take it, she'd soon need the shots.

Caye kept having a strong urge to move her family in with Rob and Jill, to totally take over. She'd even mentioned it to Nathan last night.

"Don't you think they need their privacy?" he'd responded. No,

Caye didn't think they needed their privacy more than they needed someone to take care of them. She knew Nathan really meant that he needed his privacy.

Maybe what she needed to do was just move in with Andrew and Audrey, but the thought of Nathan all alone kept her from making the suggestion. He was an introvert, yes, but he needed his family. He hated it when they were gone.

Caye grabbed Jill's pills from the cupboard next to the sink.

"So how is Jill doing?" Gwen asked. The tone of her voice had softened.

"She starts chemotherapy tomorrow," Rob said, "because she's healing from the surgery so quickly."

"How is she doing emotionally?"

"She's hopeful. She honestly is."

"And you're not?"

"I am. I'm hopeful beyond reason."

"But."

"No buts." Rob handed Simon another piece of muffin. "This is my life. And it's a good one. Seventeen days ago I realized that I was the luckiest man in the world. I'd like to live that out now that I know it."

"Luckiest?" Gwen asked.

Rob shrugged. "Blessed. Insert whatever word fits your expectations, your spiritually correct vocabulary." He walked out of the kitchen into the living room.

"Let's get the kids eating in the kitchen first," Caye said, scraping the scrambled eggs into a serving bowl. Her stomach was in knots. "Then we can fill our plates and eat in the living room."

❧

Jill looked around the room. Gwen wasn't talking. John, who had been so chatty when they first arrived, was quiet. Summer was making small talk with Rita. Lonnie and Rob were discussing the basketball playoffs.

She could hear the kids upstairs—except for Simon. Caye sat across the room and gave him a bottle. Jill had thought it would be good to have everyone over, but just looking at all of them made her tired.

It bothered her that Joya and Thomas canceled Fellowship. She could forgive Joya her judgmental attitude, her concern that Jill had unconfessed sin, her fear that Jill didn't have enough faith. But it was hard to take them not showing up.

"Do you think one has to have a certain amount of faith to be healed?" she blurted out.

The talking stopped. Simon sat up straight on Caye's lap.

John spoke first. "Jesus healed people who had no faith at all."

"Like who?" Gwen demanded.

"Like the man who was lowered through the roof. His friends had the faith."

Jill smiled. "So it's up to all of you—"

"But we don't know he didn't have faith," Gwen interrupted. "The faith of his friends is mentioned—his isn't specified."

"Paul asked to be healed, but God never did it," John continued.

"Have you ever noticed that he only asked three times?" Rob questioned. "Can you imagine any of us only asking God three times for anything that we really, really wanted?"

"I don't think we should talk about this now," Gwen said. She stood up and walked over to John. "We should all get going. We don't want to tire Jill."

Jill's mouth twitched in an attempted smile. She felt defeated. She looked down at her plate; she'd had two bites of muffin and a strawberry. She couldn't get over the bloated, full feeling that weighed her down.

Sadness swept over her. The Fellowship suddenly felt like a burden. In these few weeks, everything had changed. Only Caye was treating her like herself. Rob was being too careful, as if she might break. Everyone else was treating her as if she'd lost her brain along with half her pancreas.

She wanted to talk this through, she wanted to know what the others thought, she wanted to know that they were praying for her, supporting her. She felt disappointed, let down. Her back was hurting. Her incision itched.

"You okay?" Caye asked.

"I need a pill. Could you help me to bed?"

Caye handed Simon to Nathan.

"I had a vision," Caye said, as she fluffed Jill's pillow, "when you were in surgery. A man wearing Levi's and a red shirt stood beside the doctor. The man had brown hair and dark eyes."

"Was it Jesus?" Jill asked.

"Yeah. I think so. Do you think that's weird?"

"No, I like it."

Rob came in. Caye could hear Simon fussing in the hall.

"Who has Simon?" Jill asked.

"Nathan. Everyone else left."

"Tell Nathan to bring the baby in," Jill said. "I want to hold him for a minute."

Nathan stepped in, patting Simon on the back. Jill reached for the baby and settled him beside her on the bed. She tickled his bare feet, making him giggle.

"I need you guys to help me," Jill said, looking up at Nathan, Caye, and Rob. "No one will talk about what I want to talk about."

"Which is?" Rob said.

"Faith and healing."

"Everyone's been talking about it," Rob said. "Just not in front of you. Except for Joya."

"Do you think that I haven't had enough faith?"

"No," Rob said.

"What do you think, Nathan?"

"I think," he said slowly, "that God wants you to believe in him more than in the healing. Don't obsess about the healing."

Caye cringed inside. What was Nathan saying? Had he just offended Jill and Rob? Don't obsess about the healing? Was it possible not to? When they only had so much time? When the cancer was so aggressive?

"Well, that's an answer," Jill said.

"I'll put the little guys down for a nap before we leave," Caye said, bending to kiss Jill on the cheek and to take Simon from her. Jill was right—they didn't want to talk about faith and healing in front of her.

As Nathan and Caye headed out the door, Jill called out, "I always knew Jesus wore Levi's."

Caye smiled.

Nathan chuckled. "What was that about?"

"I'll tell you later."

❧

Caye knelt on the railroad tie beside her raised garden bed and pulled weeds from around the tomato seedlings. She didn't wear gloves; she enjoyed the feel of the dirt against her hands, savored the smell of the soil, of the fresh baby plants.

*Mother's Day. What if it's Jill's last? No! Don't think that. Faith. Have faith.*

Caye wiped the sweat from her forehead up to her hairline with the back of her hand. The day had turned muggy. Nathan had taken Audrey and Andrew to the park to play so Caye could have an hour of peace.

Jill was sick. The Fellowship was a mess. Thomas and Joya were undependable. None of them knew, exactly, what faith was anymore. Marion was worse than no help at all.

On the way home in the car, Nathan had explained himself. "Everyone is acting like faith can heal Jill. Jill's faith. Rob's faith. Our faith. Only God can heal Jill. He's called us to trust him, to have faith, not to heal Jill through our faith."

Caye tossed another handful of weeds into her pile in the wheelbarrow. *Show your faith through love.*

Did she have enough love to care for Jill the way she needed to? To be a good wife to Nathan in the midst of all of it? To be a good mom to Andrew and Audrey? A good auntie to the boys? A good friend to Rob? Could she show her own faith through love?

She felt tired. Overwhelmed. Two weeks ago she had the

adrenaline-driven energy to take care of all of them. Now she felt exhausted.

What held her back from talking with Jill about healing? Was she afraid of saying something stupid?

If they could talk about healing and faith, could they talk about other things? Could she tell Jill that Marion had fought breast cancer?

Nathan had told her to go with her intuition. Her intuition said that Marion should tell Jill, but what were the chances of that?

*Leave well enough alone,* Caye's mother always said. *Don't put your nose in other people's business.* But Jill wasn't an "other" person. She was Jill.

Caye pinched back the new growth on the tomato plants to make the vines stronger, sturdier, able to support the tomatoes that would soon develop from the yellow buds.

She wanted to talk with Jill about so many things. The boys for starters. Had Jill and Rob sat down with Liam and Hudson and explained what was going on? Had they considered talking to a counselor or a social worker to get some ideas on what the boys needed?

The pumpkin seedlings had popped through the ground and were wearing their ivory-colored seeds like hats. Abra picked her way through the vegetable bed, just out of Caye's reach. "Here, kitty," Caye called, noticing matted fur on Abra's belly. The cat ignored her.

Caye moved off the railroad tie and sank to her knees on the grass. She wrapped her arms around her denim-covered legs. *So tired. So sad,* she thought. She rolled over to her side. The grassy earth felt good beneath her, against her bare arms.

She remembered watching the clouds as a child, calling out their shapes to her mother. Dragon! Whale! Crookneck squash!

There were no clouds today. Only the sticky overcast sky. It didn't matter. She wasn't interested in what was above her. She was interested in the earth, as if she could derive some comfort, some reassurance from the feel of the world beneath her. She closed her eyes. Took a deep breath. How long had it been since she'd felt relaxed? More than two weeks. What had Rob said today? Seventeen days. It felt like seventeen years.

"Mommy!"

Caye opened her eyes. Andrew stood over her. It had been a long time since he had called her Mommy. He was out of breath. She raised her head. Audrey and Nathan were running toward her, hurrying down the stairs of the deck.

"Caye!"

"What's the matter?" she asked. Her heart raced. What had happened?

"Are you okay?" Nathan asked.

"I'm fine," she said, sitting up, realizing that they were worried about her. Feeling foolish, she brushed her hands together and laughed. "I must have fallen asleep. It felt so good to be out in the fresh air."

Nathan offered her a hand and pulled her up. He put his arm around her shoulder and squeezed her. "You scared us," he said.

"I'm sorry," Caye answered. "I didn't mean to."

Caye took Audrey's hand. Andrew grabbed the handles of the wheelbarrow and headed to the compost bin by the shed.

"Did you call your mom?" Nathan asked.

"I will now," Caye said.

Nathan squeezed her shoulder again. She knew he was thinking about his mother, who left all those years ago. He sometimes wondered where she was, how far she'd gone. He seldom talked about her, or his disappointment, his anger that a mother—his mother—would just leave. Caye put her head against her husband's shoulder. Nathan bent toward her, and the bill of his baseball hat brushed against her hair. Audrey skipped along beside them as they walked toward the house.

## 21

Jill sat with the plastic tube stuck in the vein of her hand. She shot a quick glance at the woman beside her, stole a look at her drawn-on eyebrows. The woman across from Jill wore a turban. Thirty minutes is what the nurse had said. Jill looked at the bag hanging above her head. *Bag of toxins, poisoning me.* The nurse called it an infusion. Gemcitabine was the drug. Jill had asked the nurse to spell it. She hoped she'd be able to remember the name of it to tell Caye. She knew Caye would want to look it up.

Had her dad had chemo? Radiation? She had no idea. The question almost made her want to call Marion. She nearly called her mom on Mother's Day, out of habit, but stopped herself.

What was it going to take for things to be better with Marion? Would her mother call in a month to see if she was still alive?

Caye told her last Friday, when they were sitting on the kitchen window seat after lunch, that Marion had asked when she should come back again. "It would be nice," Caye had added, "for her to want to help with something."

"See why I like your mom so much?" Jill responded

After twenty minutes, the bag was only half empty. She would have the chemo once a week for three months and radiation for the next five weeks. The nurse unhooked the woman with the turban. "You really do look great," the nurse said, giving the woman a hug.

"Thanks," the woman laughed. "Not that I believe you—but thanks anyway."

Rob was in the waiting room with his laptop. That was good. At least he was getting work done.

Jill refused to let herself worry about Rob's job, or money, or

whether Marion would cut them off financially. She never intended
for them to become so dependent on her mother. The little and not-
so-little stuff helped—paying for the house to be painted, the house-
cleaning and gardening services, Hudson's preschool, the trip to
Disneyland last spring. Marion hadn't sent money for Hudson's preschool since the beginning of May. Jill had already decided to keep
Hudson home and use that money to help with other things—like
the mortgage. She knew Rob's travel pay would go down since he was
cutting out work trips—at least until she was better. He was going to
try to do as much as possible over the phone.

She imagined Marion all alone in her duplex on Mother's Day.
Had she hoped Jill would call? Had she thought about calling Jill?

She felt abandoned by her mother. She thought of her wedding
day, of Marion's behavior. Jill had felt incredibly lonely as the ceremony in the tulip field started. She and Rob walked down the pathway together, between the tulips. Marion had offered to walk her
down the "aisle," but Jill had declined; she was sure Marion was
relieved. It seemed to Jill that Marion saw the wedding as something
to be endured, not as a celebration. All day it seemed she was looking
forward to the end.

*Why did we include her?* Jill walked through the tulips with Rob,
catching a glimpse of Marion's glum face. *Because she's paying for it.*
That was certainly one reason to include her.

Rob's parents, grandparents, and older brother, who traveled
from Spain, stood waiting for them. Rob's dad officiated. After the
ceremony, they had a wedding luncheon at a restaurant high on a
bluff overlooking a bend in the Willamette River.

A few minutes into the meal, Marion spilled her red wine on the
linen tablecloth and then dabbed at it with her napkin. "It's okay," Jill
said, patting her mom's wrist. "It's not a big deal."

Later the photographer took pictures of Jill on the deck of the
restaurant. The wind whipped her fingertip veil around her face. After
he shot the last photo, she raised her hands over her head, catching
her veil and raising it upward. The photographer quickly snapped the
image. The look on her face was pure happiness. It was Rob's favorite
photo from the wedding.

She had been happy. Happy to marry Rob. Happy to have the ceremony in a field of tulips. Happy to have had the elegant luncheon. Happy to have been with Rob's family. Even, by the end of the day, happy to have been with Marion. But she was most happy that she'd just taken the first step to creating her own family, her life away from her mother.

Still, when Jill kissed her mother good-bye that afternoon, she felt a surge of unexpected compassion. Now Marion was truly alone.

Jill looked back over her shoulder as she and Rob drove away. The others had gone back inside the restaurant for coffee. Marion stood alone in the parking lot with the river behind her. She looked old; she touched her face quickly—Jill thought for a split second that Marion was going to blow her a kiss, then she thought perhaps Marion was wiping away a tear. But her mother turned back toward her rental car, and Rob sped down the road along the bluff.

As she watched the slow drip, drip of the medication entering her bloodstream, Jill didn't feel exactly abandoned by God. In an odd, twisted way, she felt chosen by him, as if he'd just reached down with his hand and stirred up their lives, all of their lives, in some huge, galactic way.

Her arm began to burn where the chemicals entered her body. The oncology clinic had a strange, sharp smell to it, metallic. After so many years of taking care of her body, it felt appalling to let toxins enter it.

She wanted to go home. She wanted to crawl into bed. To sleep, sleep, sleep. To wake up and have it all be a bad dream.

She looked at the bag. It was almost empty.

She'd come back in a week for her next chemo. She had an appointment with Dr. Scott on Thursday. And then sometime soon they'd do another CAT scan to see if the cancer was shrinking.

*Shrink,* she commanded. *Shrink, shrink, shrink.*

It had been an easier day for Caye. She and Jill had even sat out in the garden in the afternoon, after Caye had picked up Andrew from school, after Jill had napped.

"The nurse said my hair probably won't fall out," Jill told Caye after she'd explained the chemo procedure. "It's not a common side effect of the drug they're using."

"That's good news," Caye said as she looked at Jill's long hair.

And starting the chemo felt like good news too.

"Did Joya stop by while I was napping?" Jill asked.

"She brought a meal," Caye answered.

"Did she say anything?"

"Not really."

Caye was surprised that Joya showed up with the meal she had promised. Chicken and rice casserole. Easy to digest, she'd said. As she left, she said she'd be back on Thursday with another meal. Caye had felt awkward around Joya. She wondered if Gwen had reported back to Joya about yesterday's conversation at the brunch.

Caye left Jill's house after Rob arrived. The table was set; the boys were in their pajamas. Dinner was hot. When she got home, she threw a jar of Alfredo sauce in a pan and put water on to boil for pasta. Nathan was late.

He got home at seven o'clock. "How was baseball practice?" he asked Andrew, who was sitting at the table reading a *Star Wars* paperback.

"I forgot." Caye answered from the kitchen, poking her head through the door, her heart sinking. Andrew looked up with a sheepish expression.

"It doesn't look like Andrew did," Nathan answered. "It looks like he just didn't want to go."

After dinner Caye hustled Audrey and then Andrew through their baths. At 9:15 she was loading the dishwasher, thinking she should restart the load of laundry that had been sitting in the washer since Saturday.

"Mommy," Audrey called from the hallway, "I can't sleep."

"Go back to bed," Caye said.

"But I can't sleep."

"Nathan," Caye called into the living room. She could hear the TV. "Can you put Audrey back to bed?"

He didn't answer.

"Nathan," she called again. Drying her hands and flinging the dishtowel over her shoulder, she marched into the living room.

He was asleep on the couch.

"Come on, Audrey," Caye said, leading the way down the hall. "Get back to bed."

Andrew stood at the bathroom sink turning the tap on and off, bobbing a bar of verbena soap in the water. "Brush your teeth," Caye snapped as she hurried past the bathroom. Most nights she checked his teeth and made him brush a second time. Not tonight.

Caye tucked Audrey under the blanket. "Don't come out again— not until morning."

Andrew had brushed his teeth in his usual record time and sat on his bed in a pair of yellow thermal pajamas. Caye smelled the herbal soap as she bent to kiss him on the forehead.

"In bed," she said. "Now."

"Mom," he asked, "why don't you read to me anymore?"

Caye stopped halfway to the door and turned around.

"I do read to you." How long had it been? "It's just that it's so late. Sweet dreams," she added, turning back to the door.

"Mom." She felt her irritation rising. The dishes weren't finished. Nathan was asleep in front of the TV. Laundry was souring in the basement.

"What?"

"Is Jill going to die?"

Caye turned back toward her son. He was sitting up in bed. His brown eyes glistened behind his round glasses. His face wrinkled, twisted, contorted. She turned and walked back to his bed, sat down, and pulled him toward her.

"I don't want her to die," Andrew said, starting to cry.

"I don't either," Caye said.

"Is she going to die?"

Caye stroked her son's hair, moving his straight brown bangs away from his brown eyes. She could say "no," or "I don't know," or "maybe," or "maybe not."

"I don't know whether Jill will live or die," she answered. "I really believe she's going to live." Did she?

"Why did God let this happen?"

Caye shook her head and swallowed hard.

She was missing some chance, she was sure. A chance to impart truth, to build Andrew's faith, to do something, somehow. But she didn't know what or how.

Andrew began to sob. "I think I'm mad at God." He pulled away and put his glasses on the bedside table.

"That's okay," Caye answered. "He can take it."

"Mommy,"—Audrey stood in the doorway—"I still can't sleep."

"Come here."

"Why is Andrew crying?"

"He's sad." *He's mad. He's sad. We're all so sad,* Caye thought. *And mad.* It was all twisted together. *I'm mad at God too. Unless Jill is healed. Then I won't be mad.* She frowned.

"I'm sad too," Audrey said, and then she began to cry.

"Move over, Andrew," Caye said. She pulled Audrey along with her and squirreled under the blankets.

She woke to Audrey's soft snore in her ear. Her usual waking thought that something was wrong was followed by the image of Jill. Not of Nathan. Not of the kids. Jill.

She felt tense and tired. She'd slept but hadn't rested.

She wiggled out from between Audrey and Andrew and walked, bleary eyed, into the living room. By the light of the TV she could see that Nathan was still asleep on the couch.

"Come on, honey," she said. "It's past bedtime."

❧

"Let's go to the park today," Jill said to Caye.

Jill could tell, by the way Caye looked at her, that she thought she was joking.

"I'm serious."

"Do you feel up to it?"

"Let's take a picnic. We can go right after Simon gets up from his morning nap."

"I'll go get some laundry started first," Caye said. "I brought mine over too. I'll just mix it all together."

Jill felt better than she had in days. She'd gotten up before Rob left for work and was giving Simon his bottle when Caye arrived.

She felt mixed emotions when she fed the baby. The other two were weaned straight to a cup. This was the first time she'd had bottles in the house. She felt as if Caye had made the decision for her.

On the other hand, Simon was calm and cuddly when he took his bottle—and he had been forced to go off the breast much sooner than Hudson and Liam. Each time she gave him his bottle, she felt uneasy, as if the bottle symbolized her failure. But then, by the time they'd snuggled for ten minutes, she felt sad when he was done and ready to get off her lap and practice his crawling. Soon he'd be practicing his walking.

She realized that if Caye was around, she let her feed Simon. She decided she wasn't going to do that anymore. She would feed her baby. She needed to do everything she could for her boys—especially Simon.

"Hey, Jill." Audrey interrupted her thoughts. "We need Scotch tape."

"Hey, you," Jill answered. "Look in my desk in the kitchen."

"I already did."

"Ask your mom then. I think she's down in the laundry room. And hey, tell Hudson and Liam that we're going to the park after Simon wakes up."

"All of us? You, too?"

"Yep."

"Cool. Hey, Hudson," Audrey yelled, starting down the basement stairs, "your mom is better."

By the time they reached the park, Jill began to tire; her morning surge of energy was fading. As they walked from the Suburban, she carried Simon's diaper bag while Caye pushed the stroller loaded down with the baby, the picnic lunch, and the blanket.

Jill squinted, even with her sunglasses on, against the blue sky. As they crossed the bridge by the playground, Jill looked around at the trees, the flowers, the cobblestone pathway. It was fuzzy, soft, swimmy. The scene looked like a reflection in a buckled mirror that was gently swaying.

Hudson, Audrey, and Liam ran to the playground.

"Do you think Liam's going to be okay with his cast?" Caye asked.

Jill nodded as she watched him climb the ladder and hold on with one hand. Audrey had decorated the plaster with a pink fluorescent highlighter, just a shade brighter than the cherry tree blossoms.

Jill sat down at their regular picnic spot on the grass, just up from the creek. Caye pulled Simon out of the stroller. He crawled on the grass toward Jill. His blond wispy hair lifted from his head with each jerky motion of his body. He needed his first haircut. Hudson and Liam needed haircuts too.

Jill felt intense hope as Simon scurried toward her.

She thought of the cancer in her body. She imagined the chemicals flowing through her blood, attacking the cancer cells, destroying them.

She needed a plan, a plan to beat the cancer. More than optimism. Something concrete.

"What research have you been doing?" she asked Caye as she pulled a whole-wheat cracker out of the bag and handed it to Simon.

"Research?"

"About my cancer."

"I've gone to some Web sites, checked out a few books from the library."

*Caye must be reading the books at her house, at night,* Jill thought.

"And what are you finding out?"

Caye shrugged and looked toward the playground.

"Come on, Caye. You know I know it's bad. One of the worst cancers there is. I'm asking if you've found anything good out there—anything to pin a plan on."

Jill felt Caye's eyes meet hers. Caye shifted her body and tucked her feet beneath her legs. She sat up straight.

Jill smiled. *I knew I could count on Caye. She was waiting for me to ask, waiting for me to feel well enough to soak this in.*

"Basically," Caye started, "there are three areas worth exploring. The first is strengthening your body through vitamins, supplements, and really good nutrition. You should talk with Dr. Scott on Thursday about that approach."

"Okay."

"Next is your psyche. Granted, your case is a little different than the average cancer since it seems genetics is involved. But the stuff I've come across suggests exploring your inner person. Do you have stress you haven't dealt with? Bad relationships you need to mend?"

Jill pursed her lips and pushed her sunglasses up on the bridge of her nose.

"What?" Caye asked.

"It sounds like Joya's question: 'Do you have sin in your life?'"

"This is from a secular perspective," Caye explained. "The idea is that cancer feeds off bad vibes. But you're right, it can be looked at spiritually, too."

"Are you thinking of Marion? Is this a setup to force me to make amends with her?" Jill chuckled. "Because if it is, you're not being very subtle."

Caye moved her shoulders from side to side in a sassy comeback. "I'm not making this up, Jill. I'm just reporting the research. You interpret it as you please." Her short hair swung away from her head in little bursts.

"Joya thinks it's the way I've treated Rob." Jill, with effort, kept her voice light. "You think it's the way I've treated my mother."

"I don't think it's the way you've treated your mother."

"Do you think it's the way my mother's treated me?"

Caye shrugged her shoulders slightly. "I think your mom's been awful, but you don't have control over her. You only have control over yourself. Is there anything you can do to make things better?"

Jill raised her eyebrows. "Okay. What's the third thing?" she asked.

"Faith. Even the secular books talk about faith, about believing in a purpose in your life, that your work isn't done. There are incredible case studies of people whose cancer disappeared because they believed a placebo would work."

"So it's all in the mind?"

"No. Sometimes it's in the mind. But it's more than that. Case studies have shown that cancer patients who get angry, who aren't the model patients, who challenge their doctors and take charge are the ones more likely to get well."

"Is it time to eat?" Audrey bellowed from the play structure.

Caye motioned Audrey to come over to the blanket.

"So I need to get angry? At Dr. Scott?" Jill asked. "Then I'll get better?"

"If there's a reason to get angry at him," Caye said.

Jill watched Caye pull the sandwiches, grapes, and juice boxes out of the picnic basket and spread them on the blanket. Jill thought about the anger issue. She'd never felt mad at Dr. Scott, although Rob seemed agitated each time they met with him.

Caye was right about Marion. Jill had an underlying issue of disappointment when it came to her mother. Perhaps she was projecting anger onto Marion—as if it were Marion's fault that she had cancer.

Who would she be angry with ultimately? God? But why should she be angry with God when, ultimately, that was where her healing would come from?

Caye handed Jill the thermos of broth.

Simon pulled himself up on the stroller and began to push it backward. Jill twisted the cup off the thermos and thought again about the chemicals coursing through her blood, attacking the cancer, destroying it.

"You know what sounds good?" Jill said, her hand on the cap of the thermos. "Watermelon."

Audrey, Hudson, and Liam ran onto the grass and collapsed on the ground in a heap.

"Watch out for Liam's arm," Caye said, as Hudson and Audrey rolled off him.

"And salmon." Jill grinned. "And they're both in season—or nearly."

Simon fell against the footrest of the stroller and began to cry. Jill put the thermos down and reached for him just as Caye put down the napkins to scoop him up. Jill grabbed the baby first and dragged him along the blanket into her arms. She was aware that she had reacted too quickly; she felt the movement in her incision. Simon banged his head against her collarbone.

"Whoa, baby," she said, pulling him against her chest. "Don't hurt your mommy."

Liam plopped on the blanket beside her, slamming his cast against her thigh. Hudson put his arms around her neck. Her three little boys clung to her, needed her. They were the core of her plan. Maybe she could be angry with God, for the inconvenience of all this, and still believe that he was going to heal her.

She didn't feel the anger though. Not toward God.

She thought of her house—of the painting she'd done back in L.A. before they moved to Ashland, before they bought the house.

She needed to paint. That was what she needed to do. Paint her future.

❧

Caye watched Jill with the boys until Hudson moved back to the blanket and settled down next to Audrey with his sandwich in his hand, and Liam inched away from Jill to grab a juice box. Simon wiggled down into his mom's lap and clapped his hands. Jill handed him a cracker and then wrapped her hands around his tiny bare feet.

Audrey sighed as she took a bite of her sandwich. She only tolerated the whole-wheat bread from Jill's house. Caye knew she was wishing she had peanut butter and grape jelly on white, instead of hummus on wheat.

The muscles in Caye's stomach began to relax. She fell back on the blanket and looked at the blue, blue sky. A single white wisp of a cloud floated overhead. The dark burgundy leaves from the flowering plum trees flickered in the breeze. The sun warmed her face.

"This little piggy went to market," Jill said. Caye turned her head to watch Jill wiggling Simon's bare toes.

When Caye called her mother on Mother's Day, Bev listened as Caye talked about Jill.

"Do you want us to come down, honey, to help? Your dad and I could."

Caye hadn't even considered that. The thought was tempting.

"Wait," she said. "Let's see how things go. I might need you to come down later even more."

In the park with Jill and the kids, Caye felt as if they might not need Bev at all. Maybe Marion would come up for some sort of reconciliation, but besides that they could make it on their own. Caye, with Rita's help and meals from the Fellowship, could handle the childcare and attending to Jill.

*Jill will get better. She will recover. We will go on like this for years, surrounded by kids, someday by grandchildren. We are being tested, reminded not to take any of life for granted. We are learning our lesson. We're all being healed spiritually by Jill's illness.*

Caye's confidence deepened. *Jill wants to get better, more than anything. She is the woman with a plan, the woman who makes things happen. Today is a turning point. The chemotherapy has begun to work. Jill will tackle any issues that might hinder her healing. We will all move forward.*

Caye looked into Jill's pale, cheekbone-framed face. Caye was aware, again, of how thin her friend was, except for that puffy belly. Her blue eyes were bigger than ever.

## 22

It was Saturday afternoon, and Jill sat in the window seat, looking out over the garden. The bearded irises were blooming against the fence—purple, blue, and white. Their first spring in the house, Marion had told her that in Pennsylvania they pulled the bearded irises out because they were too prolific.

"I didn't know you gardened," Jill had said to her.

"I did in Pennsylvania. My father liked to garden. I tended it after he died."

"But you didn't like it," Jill stated.

"No, I did," Marion answered with a frown. "Especially yanking plants out."

Jill did as little pulling as possible in her garden. Dividing and replanting, yes, and selective thinning. Destruction of plants, no.

The wisteria was in full bloom. The clematis over the rock fountain in the far corner was just starting to bud. In a matter of days it would be covered with deep-purple five-petal flowers.

The garden looked like a painting. A perfect balance of shapes, colors, and textures. Her eyes teared as she looked out the window. The ceiling fan was on, and the windows were raised. She could feel the heat of the day and smell the sweet, warm scent of the flowers.

At times she'd felt guilty for all she had—her husband, three children, the house, the yard, living in Ashland, the Fellowship, her friendship with Caye. She'd felt so loved. So blessed.

She didn't know anyone as blessed as she was.

Did the cancer eradicate all that?

A tear welled over her eyelid.

No. She was still loved.

Another tear escaped.

Still blessed.

Jill wiped at her eyes with the back of her right hand.

Caye had taken the boys to Andrew's game. Rob was out for a run. It was too quiet. Too lonely.

She felt irritated and on edge when the boys were home—depressed and lonely when they were gone.

Scout whined at the back door. She stood and let the dog out.

Caye held both of Simon's hands, hovering above him, gently guiding from foot to foot, side to side, as he practiced his walking over the grass toward third base. Liam, Hudson, and Audrey ran back and forth under the bleachers.

It was midafternoon and hot. Caye felt sweat drip down the back of her knees. She'd called Jill about taking Hudson and Liam. When she got to the house, Simon had just gotten up from his nap. Rob was off on a run.

"I'll take Simon, too," Caye said. She could tell Jill wanted to have Simon stay, but it was hard for her to handle him.

"Whose baby?" one of the moms asked as Caye climbed onto the bleachers with Simon. Maybe he would let her sit for a minute or two.

"My friend Jill's," Caye answered.

"The one with cancer?"

Caye nodded. She had told some of the baseball mothers Jill's story when Jill was first diagnosed.

"Your friend the artist?" the mom sitting behind Caye asked. "The one who was pregnant last year?" Jill had done a ceramic project with Andrew's class when she was seven months along with Simon.

"That's the one," Caye answered.

"How old is she?" the first mom asked.

"She's thirty-four," Caye answered.

The women asked how many kids, what the diagnosis was, what the prognosis was.

Caye felt as if she were dramatizing the situation. Three kids turning five, three, and one. Pancreatic cancer. A 1-in-287 chance of living one year.

No, she wasn't dramatizing it.

"How's her husband doing?" the woman sitting behind Caye asked.

"He's hanging in there," Caye answered.

"Let me take the baby," the woman next to Caye said as she reached out her arms.

Simon smiled and leaned toward her.

Caye passed Simon over. She could feel her emotions shift and settle. It felt cathartic to talk about Jill's cancer. She was also aware of how altruistic she appeared. She was the good friend. She was admired for her loyalty, for her devotion.

On the surface the admiration felt good, but taken deeper, it annoyed her. What else would she have done but care for Jill and her family? There was nothing to be admired. It was simply the right thing to do.

On the other hand, the concern of the baseball moms warmed her. Their authenticity was a universal trait of mothers. But she also knew they felt relieved that some other mom, and not them, was facing such a horrible ordeal, a mother's worst nightmare.

During the last inning, Caye walked Simon up and down the edge of the field. She heard yelling and looked up to see Jason, who was playing shortstop, in right field, throwing the ball to second. The player was safe. Andrew looked befuddled.

"Oh, Andrew," Hudson yelled in disappointment and then ran back under the bleachers to where Audrey and Liam were digging in the dirt.

After the game was over, Andrew walked slowly from the outfield.

"Andrew Beck," the coach bellowed, "you didn't even try to catch that fly ball. It was coming right at you."

Andrew pushed his glasses up on his nose. Caye swung Simon up into her arms.

"It would help if you'd make it to practice." The coach yanked off his hat and ran his hand through his sweaty, thinning hair.

Caye felt her face redden.

"My fault," she said, striding quickly over to the coach with Simon bouncing on her hip.

"Was it also your fault he didn't catch the ball?" the coach demanded, looking down at her.

"Let's go, Mom," Andrew whispered, tugging on her shorts.

The coach marched away with his baseball cap still in his hand. Caye's temper surged as she watched the back of his balding head.

"Let's go," Andrew said, pulling on her wrist.

It wasn't just that the coach had yelled. It was that she regretted that Andrew had missed the baseball practices but felt helpless to make them a priority.

Caye wished Nathan weren't coaching middle school baseball. *He should be here for Andrew. For both the practices and the games. There's no way the coach would have treated Andrew that way with Nathan around.*

When they reached the house, Andrew rushed into his room and slammed the door.

Caye took a Tums and fixed hot dogs for dinner while Simon played in the Tupperware drawer and the other kids turned the backyard picnic table into a covered wagon.

When she called Andrew for dinner, he was sitting on his bed, popping the heads off his LEGOs men.

"Did you try to catch the ball?" she asked. As long as he tried, that was what mattered.

"I never saw the ball," he answered. "Not until Jason ran over me."

"I hate playing baseball. I don't want to do it anymore."

Caye thought of Jill having Hudson quit preschool. There was no way Nathan would allow Andrew to quit, not in the middle of the season, not even if he hated it, not even if it would make life significantly easier for Caye.

"We'll talk about it later," Caye said, "with Daddy."

❧

"How was your baseball game yesterday?" Jill asked Andrew.

"I got put out at first. We lost. And I missed a pop fly."

"Did you have fun?"

Andrew pushed his glasses up on his nose and looked at Nathan. "Not really."

Caye had brought chicken to barbecue for lunch for the two families. The other Fellowship members had left.

"Want to go for a walk?" Rob asked Nathan. "Scout needs some exercise. We can take the little boys, too."

Jill imagined Rob's frustration as he wrestled the double jogger stroller out of the garage and put Liam and Simon in it. "If you go by Starbucks, bring me back a latte," Jill heard Caye call after the guys as they headed down the hill. Caye stayed outside; Jill decided she was probably starting the grill.

Andrew, Hudson, and Audrey banged out the front door to play in the yard. They'd been playing Oregon Trail the last few days—a game inspired by Andrew's southern Oregon history unit at school. Jill imagined Liam falling off a wagon.

With her fingertips she felt her incision under her sweatpants. It was bumpy. It still itched.

Jill heard Caye come in the back door, open the refrigerator, and walk into the living room.

"The grill is heating up," she said, handing Jill a glass of ice water and sitting beside her on the couch.

"Fellowship was weird today," Jill said. She couldn't keep herself from talking about it. The whole meeting, under Thomas's direction, was spent in prayer and silence. "I feel like the thorn in the flesh of the whole group. Like I've changed everything. Thomas isn't teaching. Joya isn't praying. They never explained why they canceled Fellowship last week and then didn't come for the potluck either. Gwen isn't talking. Summer looks like she's going to burst out crying any minute. I just want it to be the way it was before."

"It can't be the same," Caye said as the phone rang. She went to get it.

Jill heard Caye say, "Let me see if she's up to talking," as she walked back into the living room.

"It's your mom," Caye mouthed to Jill, holding her hand over the receiver.

Jill started to shake her head and then stopped. She reached for the phone.

"Hi, Mother," she said slowly.

"How are you?"

"Okay."

"Have you started the chemo?"

Caye stood in the doorway looking uncomfortable.

"Yes."

"How are Rob and the boys?"

"Hanging in there." There was a long pause.

Jill wanted to ask Marion if her father had had chemo. She didn't even know if he'd had surgery.

"Well," Marion said, "I shouldn't keep you. I'll call in a few days."

After she put the phone down, Jill looked at Caye. "I don't get her," she said. "Not at all."

❧

By the time Caye and her family went home, it was hot, over ninety. The day turned into a spring scorcher. Audrey had the Chutes and Ladders game out on the dining room table. Caye changed into shorts and a tank top and collapsed on the couch with a book about surviving cancer while Nathan and Andrew went out to play catch. Dirty laundry was piled up in the basement, and the breakfast dishes were still in the sink. She decided to ignore both.

Caye felt sticky.

"Hold your mitt up," Nathan yelled.

Caye heard the ball bounce on the pavement—again.

Even now, feeling exhausted, she wanted to go back over to Jill's. She was obsessed with being with Jill. All day, five days a week, plus half a day on Sunday didn't feel like enough. When she was away, all she thought about was Jill and her house. What Jill might eat. What chores needed to be done.

She wanted to fix soup for Jill, help put the boys to bed, throw in a load of wash. She knew it was driving Nathan crazy.

"We still have a life, Caye," he'd said last night. They were climbing into bed—she'd just returned from Jill's after taking Hudson, Liam, and Simon home. She'd stayed and bathed them and helped Rob put them to bed. "You have your own home and kids to care for."

"What's really bugging you?" Caye had asked.

"I just told you."

Caye knew it was something more.

"Mommy," Audrey said, "would you play with me?"

"Ask Andrew."

Audrey banged out the screen door. Caye was sure Andrew would say yes just to get out of playing catch.

Nathan followed Audrey and Andrew in and sat beside Caye. She reached over and rubbed his sweaty neck with one hand, still holding the book with the other. The hair on the back of his neck was fuzzy. He took off his baseball cap and nudged her hand with the top of his head.

She tousled his hair and then went back to her book.

"Rob was pretty chatty on our walk," Nathan said, wiping his forehead with the hem of his T-shirt.

Caye glanced up. Rob was usually pretty chatty. It was Nathan who was the quiet one. Rob must have said something significant for Nathan to want to talk about it.

"What he said kind of bugged me. The timing is just hard to take, harder than it would be normally. Although normally I'm sure he never would have said a thing."

Caye put the book down. "What did he say?"

"Well, I asked him if he was still upset that Jill hadn't told him about the cancer, like he was that first night at the hospital."

"And?"

"He said he wasn't, that it made him feel better about his stuff."

"His stuff?" Caye asked. What was Nathan talking about?

"It's not like he's been unfaithful."

Caye sat up straight.

Nathan looked at her. "I can't tell you this if you're going to over-react. You can't talk to him about this. You can't say anything to Jill. I just need to talk with you about it."

Caye tried to slouch a little.

"He said that he and Jill had drifted since Simon was born. Jill was always so tired, so preoccupied with the house and the kids. He was traveling all the time. When he had that project in Raleigh, his liaison was a woman."

Caye remembered Rob traveling to Raleigh several times in the months before Jill's surgery, since Christmas.

"Late twenties. Not married. Smart. Pretty. They'd go out to lunch. Talk. They started e-mailing back and forth. Nothing heavy. Just chatty stuff. The last trip to Raleigh he stayed longer than he needed to. He justified it—said he needed a break. He took the woman golfing—a business outing, he told himself."

Caye frowned.

"He'd just gotten home the day before Jill got so sick. He'd been gone more than two weeks. He said at first he just tried to process Jill's stuff, how vulnerable she was physically.

"Still it made him angry that she'd never said anything. But then it hit him how vulnerable he was too. He said if, in fact, Jill had sinned it was a sin of omission. But what had he been doing? What if he had been unfaithful and then Jill got so sick? What if he'd thrown it all away?

"He said he felt like he'd escaped from a fire."

Caye was silent.

"Do you hate him?" Nathan asked.

"Not entirely."

"He feels like he's escaped the fire, but—"

"Jill's still in one." Caye finished Nathan's sentence.

He nodded.

"And so is he." Caye paused. "Is he going to tell Jill any of this?"

"Maybe. He doesn't know what to do," Nathan continued. "I told him to talk to Thomas."

"Do you think he will?"

"Yes."

"But what if Thomas tells Joya?" Caye asked.

Nathan wrinkled his brow. "It's all so messy," he said. "Jill and Rob. Marion. The stuff with Joya. Why does it all have to be so messy?"

"I know how much you hate messes," Caye said.

"Especially other people's messes. At least when they're your own, you can clean up."

"You cheated," Audrey yelled.

Caye heard a game piece hit the floor.

"Sometimes," Caye said. "Sometimes you can clean up. Why would Rob think about straying when he has a wife like Jill?"

"He took her for granted. Like we all do. We all take each other for granted."

"I'm never going to take all of this for granted again," Caye said. "Are you?"

"We all will. A few months will go by. A year. That's our nature."

"You were the one who wanted to play," Andrew told Audrey calmly.

"Go play baseball again. Maybe you'll actually catch the ball."

"Audrey," Caye said, "don't be rude."

"Was the game yesterday really that bad?" Nathan asked.

Caye frowned. She didn't want to talk about the game. "If Joya finds out about Rob, she'll say it's his fault Jill has cancer."

Nathan crossed his arms.

More game pieces hit the floor. Audrey laughed her high-pitched cackle.

"Put the game away!" Nathan yelled.

"Do you think Rob is telling the truth?" Caye asked.

"Audrey, I'm never playing with you again, ever!" Andrew yelled.

Nathan started to stand. Caye caught his hand. "Just ignore them. Please." She wanted to finish their conversation.

He sat back down.

"Do you think he's telling the truth?" she asked again. "Is there more?"

Nathan shook his head. "I don't think he would have said anything at all if there was."

The board hit the floor.

Nathan sprang to his feet and rushed into the dining room. "Audrey, pick up the game, or I'm taking it away for the next year."

Audrey began to wail.

Jill sat with her hand wrapped in a heating pad. The nurse had already drawn blood. After Jill's hand was warm, the nurse would insert the catheter for the chemo.

It was Monday. Thursday she'd have another dose of radiation.

"Think of the chemotherapy and radiation as power in your body," one of the books Caye had read advised. "Don't think of it as poison."

Again she thought of the chemicals rushing through her blood, tearing out the bad cells.

"Nausea does not have to occur. Tell your body not to lose its hair, not to give in to sickness. Healthcare providers set up patients for side effects by focusing on the worst-case scenarios," the same author had written.

She hadn't been nauseated, not any more than she'd been for the last six weeks.

Caye had pulled up in front of the clinic, dropped off Jill, and then taken the kids to the play structure with the little white house and the picket fence on the hospital grounds.

The woman with the turban sat down next to Jill. The nurse handed her a heating pad, and the woman wrapped it around her hand.

"Hi," she said to Jill.

"Hello."

Her name was Marguerite. "I have kidney cancer. They took the one out, then it showed up in the other," she said with a sigh. "Double jeopardy. I get chemo once a week and dialysis three times a week."

"How long have you had cancer?" Jill asked.

"Altogether? Three years. Not straight. But six months on, a couple of months off. I keep getting sick, from the chemo—every Tuesday I'm a mess."

The woman patted Jill's right arm and then let her hand rest on Jill's wrist. Jill liked the feel of the talon-like fingers against her arm, holding on, keeping her from floating away.

"You're new, aren't you?"

Jill nodded.

"What do you have, honey?"

"Pancreatic cancer."

"Really? You look so good."

"That's because I'm going to get well," Jill said with a smile.

The woman chuckled. *She's a classy lady,* Jill thought. *That's what I want. To get through this with class.*

❧

Caye put the last of the lunch dishes into the dishwasher and thought about how much she looked forward to Mondays, to Jill's chemo. It gave her hope. The little boys were down for their nap. Caye realized how relieved she felt when nap time rolled around.

Jill was sitting in the living room. Audrey and Hudson were playing in the garden with Scout.

Illness could elicit many responses, Caye had decided. Summer, with all her crying, seemed pessimistic, even fatalistic. "God already knows the outcome of all this. It's already been decided," she'd said on Sunday. Then there was Joya's dogmatic response, that all it took was enough faith.

What did Caye believe?

The phone rang.

It was Marion again.

"Is it you, Caye?" she asked.

"Yes."

"I want to talk to Jill. But tell me first, is she worse than she was?"

"No, no, she's not worse."

"Is she better?"

"She seems better, at least a little."

"Well, there's something I need to tell her. Unless you already have."

"About?" Caye responded.

"About my cancer."

"No," Caye said, "I didn't tell her."

"Oh." Marion hesitated. "I was wishing you had."

"I'll get her," Caye quickly said, feeling Marion might lose her nerve any minute.

Caye walked into the living room and handed the phone to Jill. "Guess who?" Caye mouthed.

Jill pursed her lips.

Caye started to leave the room, but Jill motioned for her to stay. Caye sat down in the rocking chair. It was hard to sit when there was so much to do.

"Hi, Mom," Jill said.

Caye listened. It sounded as though Marion jumped right into her confession.

"Before Hudson was born?" Jill asked, looking up at Caye.

Jill was silent for a couple of minutes.

"What kind of cancer?"

Jill was quiet again. Caye imagined Marion rambling on and on. She wondered if she was making sense.

The conversation continued for a few more minutes. Jill said the boys were doing fine. That Simon was practicing his walking. She didn't mention Liam's broken arm.

"Did you have chemo?" Jill asked.

Caye was sure that Marion had.

"Did Daddy have chemo?"

Caye was surprised at the question. She gathered he hadn't by the short answer.

"I'm going to go rest. Talk to you later," Jill said. "Bye."

Jill turned off the phone. "Did you know?" she asked Caye.

"By accident."

"So Mother had cancer. No wonder she didn't come down when Hudson was born. Did she tell you the thought of a grandbaby gave her the will to live?"

Caye nodded.

"Do you know about Rob, too?" Jill continued.

Caye grimaced.

"Did Nathan tell you what Rob told him? About the woman he was attracted to in Raleigh? His emotional affair?"

Caye nodded. "But Nathan didn't call it an emotional affair."

"Neither did Rob."

Jill ran both hands through her hair, a quick flick-back, off-her-neck gesture, and changed the subject back to Marion.

"She's so glacial," Jill said. "So colossally cold and monumentally slow. "

Caye smiled.

"What are you thinking?" Jill asked.

"How much you have to live for," Caye answered. If Marion could will herself to live, then surely Jill could too.

❧

That night Rob set up a laptop in the bedroom, and Jill went on the Web to look up pancreatic cancer. As she scanned the cancer sites, she thought of Caye's advice: "Remember, it's just information. Possibilities. You are the exception."

Jill found information about genetic studies on breast cancer and pancreatic cancer. Although the evidence wasn't conclusive, it seemed that there was a link between the two.

"So why not breast cancer, God?" Jill had asked aloud. "Why couldn't you have let it be breast cancer?"

She entered a cancer survivors' chat room and stared at the screen for a moment before logging off. She wasn't up to chatting with strangers about her cancer. She snapped the laptop shut.

Rob was putting the boys to bed. Scout was sprawled on the floor.

She found it ironic that Marion, who said she'd been saved by the thought of a grandchild, didn't seem to like being a grandmother.

Jill thought about when Hudson had been born and the months that followed. She'd wanted to leave Argentina because she was suddenly afraid of dying. But it had been Marion who was fighting for her life.

She wasn't angry earlier on the phone. The confession just seemed like another weird Marion thing. In fact, as Marion told her, Jill felt relieved to hear it, as if it might be a clue to why Marion was the way she was.

But now she was angry. The anger had grown thought by thought through the afternoon and evening.

She reached for the phone.

"I thought you'd call," Marion said as soon as Jill said hello.

"Why didn't you tell me about your cancer?"

"I didn't want to worry you."

"Bull."

Marion was silent.

"Why didn't you tell me?" Jill asked again.

"There's more I haven't told you," Marion finally said.

"More?"

"Yes."

"What?"

Just then Rob walked into the bedroom.

"Mother?"

"Let me call you back," Marion said. "I promise I will. In a day or two."

"Mom?"

Rob sat down on the bed.

"I'll call you," Marion said.

Jill hung up the phone.

"What's up?" Rob asked.

"I don't know."

## 23

"Let's go to Emigrant Lake today," Jill said to Caye. She was thinking of the woman in the turban at the clinic who said she was always a mess on Tuesdays. It was Tuesday. Jill refused to be a mess.

"Are you sure?" Caye asked.

Jill nodded. *Sure of what? Sure that I'm not in pain? Not nauseated? No. I'm both.* "It's supposed to be nice today," she said. " A little cooler. In the eighties. Doesn't it sound like fun to go to the lake?"

"What about Liam's cast?"

"We can wrap it in plastic. We'll tie a garbage bag around it."

Jill made a bottle for Simon and packed the diaper bag while Caye spread cream cheese on whole-wheat bagels.

"I think I'll try to garden some tomorrow," Jill said, looking out the window. "It's not too late to plant the dahlias."

"I'll help," Caye said. "I noticed the tubers in the garage."

Jill sat down on the couch to rest while Caye went upstairs to wake Simon.

Liam walked up beside his mother and stroked her hair.

"Uh-oh," he said, pulling his hand away from her head.

"What?" Jill asked, afraid the nurse had been wrong, afraid her hair was falling out after all.

Liam looked down. A circle of wetness was spreading across the front of his shorts.

She'd have to climb the stairs for clean underwear and pants. And then mop up the floor.

It was past the kids' lunchtime when they finally reached the lake.

Three college students were stretched out on blankets with unopened books by their sides.

Jill laughed when she saw the young women. "I used to go to the beach all the time in college, but I was smart enough not to take my books," she said.

Audrey ran up to the oak tree with the split trunk and stood in the center of it. "Andrew is going to be so jealous that we went to the lake today," she announced to everyone. "I can't wait to tell him."

Liam and Hudson climbed on top of the picnic table where Jill had stopped.

"Get off," Caye commanded, pulling the blue checked plastic cloth off the stroller hood. They jumped. She watched in relief as Liam landed on his feet; she flung the cloth over the table. A crow swooped down and landed on the plastic.

"Shoo!" she shouted.

After lunch Audrey and Hudson started toward the water. "Life jackets," Caye called after them. She'd dug them out of Jill's garage before they'd left. She pulled the plastic garbage bag out of the picnic basket and wrapped it around Liam's arm, tucking the bag under his cast. Then she fastened each jacket securely.

Caye carried Simon and the blanket, and Jill carried the diaper bag as they walked down with the kids to the lake.

Jill was quiet.

Caye felt sad. It was too easy to compare this day at the lake to so many others in the past. She was tired of this waiting and wondering. *Just make her better, God. We know you're going to do it. Just do it now.*

Scrubby oak trees grew in the grass above the beach area. Parasitic mistletoe, nearly hidden by the new leaves, hung high in the branches. Crows flew up from the treetops, cawing at each other, at Caye and Jill and the kids. No, at Jill. Caye felt as though everything was directed toward Jill. Nature, people's thoughts, gravity, the rotation of the earth. Some collective energy was building, growing, focusing on Jill.

Under other circumstances, Caye would have been jealous of this force, this cosmic attention on her friend. Under the present circumstances she felt comforted, hopeful—but impatient.

Caye looked out across the lake to the hills covered with trees and shades of green. The reflection of the hills rippled in the water.

Jill spread the blanket on the sand and sat down cross-legged. She wore baggy short overalls and black leather clogs. Her sunglasses slipped down her nose. She pushed them up and held her finger against the bridge for a long moment.

"What do you want to do for Liam's birthday?" Caye asked, sitting down beside her and letting Simon crawl on the blanket.

Jill smiled. "What day is today?"

"The twenty-third," Caye answered.

They were silent for a moment.

"A simple birthday at the park would be nice," Jill finally said. "How about at Railroad Park?"

"I could make a train cake."

"Perfect," Jill said.

The books and articles she'd been reading puzzled Caye. Jill didn't fit the cancer model. She wasn't a victim. She wasn't a worrier. She didn't internalize. She wasn't passive. She hadn't had a tragedy in the last year. Her life wasn't perfect—but it was closer to perfect than anyone Caye knew. Caye was sure that Jill was determined enough to beat the cancer. One of the books she read insisted that love was the most effective element of healing. Jill was loved. Not perfectly, of course, except by God. But she was loved. And she loved.

At the water's edge, Hudson splashed Audrey. Then they both splashed Liam. The plastic bag over his cast bothered Caye.

"Let's walk to the boat dock," she called out, her anxiety rising.

"I'll stay with Simon," Jill said.

"Are you sure?" Caye asked, knowing Jill shouldn't lift the baby. What if he crawled away from her?

Jill frowned. "I can take care of him, Caye. Really."

*She's annoyed with me.* Caye stood and watched the kids run ahead along the shore. She kicked at a rock with her sandal and then started walking quickly to catch up with them.

"Stop at the boat ramp!" she yelled to the kids.

She took Liam's hand as they walked out on the floating metal pier. His arm stuck out nearly straight from the life jacket. Walking the dock was the kids' favorite thing to do at the lake. In another couple of years, they'd all want to go on the water slide at the entrance to the park instead.

Liam stomped his feet on the metal grating, then looked up at Caye and smiled.

When they reached the end of the ramp, Caye glanced toward the beach. Jill was waving at them. She looked distressed.

Caye dropped Liam's hand to shade her eyes and get a better look at Jill. Liam jumped on the metal grating. Audrey stepped forward. Liam jumped again. The two collided. Caye sensed that Liam was falling backward. She reached and snatched him by his good arm, then turned her head to see Audrey falling sideways, her arm extended toward Caye, her mouth wide open in a shocked, desperate expression, her braids flying out in both directions. *At least she has on her life jacket.* Caye stretched for her daughter, knowing she couldn't reach Audrey's flailing hand.

*Is that the difference between Jill and me?* Audrey went over in a long, slow moment. Caye took the two steps to the edge of the boat ramp, dragging Liam with her. Jill would have miraculously grabbed Audrey's hand but not enforced the life jacket. *I missed the hand but made her wear the life jacket.*

Audrey splashed.

Caye fell to her knees and reached into the cold water, still holding on to Liam.

"You're okay," Caye said before Audrey could scream.

"I am not," she sputtered. "You didn't catch me."

Caye grabbed the back of Audrey's life jacket and yanked her onto the pier.

"You saved Liam," Audrey sputtered, collapsing in a heap, "and left me to drown."

Caye put Liam's hand in Hudson's and picked Audrey up and hugged her. She felt the cold water soak through her T-shirt.

"Let's go get a towel."

❧

Jill gasped as Audrey went over. In a second, Caye had her on the pier, but Jill felt shaky. If she were well, she would have been with them.

The pain stabbed at her again. It came on so quickly. Sharp, jagged, hard-to-breathe jabs. She'd taken her pain medication before they left but hadn't brought any with her.

Simon began to fuss. She pulled his bottle out of the bag. He grabbed it before she could put it in his mouth and tipped his head back.

Another stab of pain.

Tears were streaming down Jill's face by the time the others reached the blanket.

"Audrey's okay. Really," Caye said.

Jill nodded.

"What's wrong?"

"I didn't bring my pain medicine. I took a pill right before we left. I thought I'd be okay. I'm sorry."

In the car Jill couldn't get comfortable. She squirmed and wiggled. She took off her sunglasses and put them on the dashboard; then she unbuckled her seat belt and lay on her side.

"Should I take you to the hospital?" Caye asked.

"No. I'll be better as soon as I get a pill."

"This is really déjà vu," Caye said.

"How so?"

"I was thinking of when Audrey was born."

"But you got a baby out of it," Jill said. And then she began to cry again.

"I'm sorry," Caye said, patting her friend's head. "So sorry."

Jill didn't answer. Her head was pressed against the seat and Caye's leg. Her hands pressed against her belly.

❧

Caye left Jill's house with just enough time to get Andrew home before his baseball game.

She was relieved to go. Audrey falling in the lake, Jill's painful ride home—it was all wearing Caye down.

"Get your uniform," she said to Andrew as they walked in the door. "And hurry."

"Mom," Andrew called out from his room, "there's something wrong with Abra."

The cat was on Andrew's bed, moaning softly.

*Great. When will I have time to take the cat to the vet? Doesn't Abra know how busy I am right now?* She sat down on the bed and looked into Abra's eyes. The cat turned her head away. The calico was definitely sick. She howled as Caye picked her up.

Nathan stood in the doorway, baseball cap in hand.

"What's wrong?"

Caye looked up. "You're home early."

"No practice. The eighth graders are on their class trip. I thought I'd take Andrew to his game. What's wrong with the cat?" he asked again.

"She's sick."

"Should we take her to the vet?"

"No," Caye said. Abra was probably dying. There was no use even calling the vet. She had noticed over the last couple of weeks that Abra was skinny and her fur was matted. But honestly, Caye had been so busy she hadn't put much thought into the cat. Now Caye could feel Abra's hipbones and spine as she held her.

It was better this way. Abra was thirteen—an old lady for a cat.

Caye grabbed a towel from the hall closet and wrapped Abra in it. She walked into the living room and sat in her rocker.

"Audrey, would you go get me the kitty's brush?" Caye asked.

She sat and combed Abra while the cat purred. Stickers and leaves were caught in the white fur under her belly. "When did you stop washing yourself?" Caye chided.

"We went to the lake today, Daddy," Audrey said.

"Really?"

"I fell in the lake. Off the boat ramp."

Nathan shot Caye a look. Caye mouthed, "I'll tell you later."

"It's not fair that they went to the lake. They shouldn't do that when I'm in school," Andrew whined as he walked into the living room with his baseball uniform on, socks and cleats in his hands.

"How did you fall in the lake?" Nathan asked.

"Mama grabbed Liam, and I fell in."

Nathan looked at Caye with raised eyebrows.

"Why don't you take Audrey to the game too? I'll stay here with Abra," Caye said.

Caye rocked Abra. *Cancer. She probably has cancer.*

Caye had rescued Abra from the ranch right after she'd graduated from college, the year before she married Nathan. It was one of the few impulsive decisions Caye had made.

"That cat's nothing but trouble," her dad had said. "She's the runt of the litter. If you take her, you'll have a hard time getting an apartment. She's not worth it."

Caye knew Abra wouldn't last on the ranch. The kitten's mother kept dragging her away from the rest of the litter. Caye took the kitten into the ranch house and started feeding her milk with an eyedropper. She sneaked the cat into her first apartment, changing the cat box every day so the manager wouldn't suspect she was breaking the rules. When they married, Nathan insisted that they find a place that allowed pets even though it cost another hundred dollars a month.

Abra had been her baby for six years, until she had Andrew. Now, just as the cat was finally growing fond of the children—well, Andrew anyway—she was dying.

Caye had seen the dying process on the ranch with cows, dogs, and cats. Her dad would have taken Abra behind the barn by now. "No use prolonging it," he would have said.

She stroked the cat's face, running her finger along the half-orange, half-brown nose, down to the dry tip.

The cat moaned again. Caye put her on the floor and went to the basement to retrieve a cardboard box. She lined it with old white towels and put Abra in it while she fixed beans and rice with sausage for dinner. She ate, left the food on the counter for the rest of the family, then settled back in the chair with her cat.

"Dinner's in the kitchen," she told Nathan and the kids as they came in the house. Andrew went straight to his room.

"I wouldn't let him take a LEGO cowboy out to right field," Nathan explained.

Before the kids went to bed, Caye had each of them say good-bye to Abra. "She might be dead in the morning," Caye explained. Both of them frowned as they patted Abra. "Thanks for being our cat," Andrew said.

"Thanks," Audrey echoed.

It felt good to hold Abra, all wrapped up like a baby. The rocking motion soothed Caye. *Abra, old friend.* The tears started slowly. One escaped, then another.

Abra was dying. Jill was sick.

She wanted to call Jill and tell her about Abra, but the cat's dying seemed insignificant compared to what Jill was facing.

Caye felt so alone.

"When are you coming to bed?" Nathan asked, standing in the hallway in his boxers.

"Soon," Caye answered. She sat and cried, let her emotions work their way up. Abra was an excuse for what had been sitting in her gut, twisting up her insides. She cried for Jill, for the surgery, for the cancer. She cried about Marion and about Rob's attraction to the woman in North Carolina. She cried about Liam's broken arm and Audrey falling in the lake and Jill's horrible pain. She cried about Joya and Thomas and the Fellowship. She cried about Abra.

At 11:30 she put the cat in the box and went to bed. At 3:15 she tiptoed down the stairs and checked on Abra. She was still breathing.

At 6:30 she woke. Nathan wasn't in bed.

She had the usual horrible sinking feeling that she woke to every morning. *Jill,* she thought. *And Abra.*

*Abra.* She hurried downstairs. The box was gone. The back door was open.

She rushed outside.

Nathan was next to the maple tree, digging a hole. Beside him was the box.

"What are you doing?" she yelled.

"She's dead."

"I need to see her," Caye said. "The kids need to see her."

Nathan gave Caye an exasperated look. "And I need to get to work."

"I never asked you to bury her," Caye retorted, walking across the cold grass in her bare feet, her nightshirt riding against her thighs.

She lifted the box and headed back to the house. Abra was stiff. Her eyes were closed. Her hipbones were visible through her fur. *I should feel guilty that I didn't take better care of her these last few weeks. But I won't. I won't feel guilty.*

She woke the children. "Come see Abra before Daddy buries her," she whispered into their ears. They padded out into the kitchen.

"Dead," Audrey said. "All dead. When can we get a kitty?"

Caye ignored her question. Audrey headed into the living room to see what was on TV.

"Sorry," Andrew said and went back into his room.

Caye took the box back outside. Nathan had finished the hole. "She's better off," Nathan said.

"It's still hard," she said, pulling Abra out of the box and wrapping her in the towels. Gently she lowered her into the hole and took the shovel from Nathan and covered the towel with dirt.

When she finished, she sat in the living room and stared stupidly at a television news show.

She heard Nathan shaving, making coffee, sitting at the table to eat his cereal.

"Shouldn't you guys be getting ready?" he asked before heading out the door.

Caye teared up. She didn't want to get ready. She wanted to stay home. She didn't want to move.

"Are you okay?" he asked.

"No, I'm not okay."

"What do you want me to do?" He had that frustrated tone in his voice again.

"Nothing. Go to work."

She realized, as she heard his old Volvo sedan drive away, that he hadn't kissed her good-bye.

## 24

"How are you doing?" Dr. Scott asked Jill.

Rob spun back and forth on the swivel chair and stared at the doctor.

"I let my pain meds go too long the other day," Jill said. "I thought I was dying."

The doctor nodded.

"I won't do that again."

"Any side effects from the chemo?"

"I haven't been too nauseous. Not any more than before I started chemo. The antinausea meds seem to be working."

Dr. Scott asked about the boys. "Do you feel like you need more support? A social worker to arrange home health? Other services?"

Jill looked at Rob. He shrugged.

"No," she said, "I think we're okay."

"Any questions?"

"When will we get the results of the CAT scan?" Rob asked. The test had been done before the radiation treatment.

*You know that, Rob.* Jill turned from her husband toward the doctor. The radiologist had told them just an hour ago.

"Tomorrow," the doctor answered.

"What's the consensus on the blood tests?" Rob asked.

"So far the levels are holding steady."

"What about the other stuff—the supplements, the visualization? Do you think that helps?"

"Yes. And I think that having faith Jill will get well is as important as the chemo and radiation."

"I think we have that," Rob said. "It's just frustrating. I feel so helpless."

The doctor nodded. "That's very common for spouses." He smiled. "Especially husbands."

He turned to Jill. "Are you able to do things you enjoy?"

"I was thinking about working in the garden a little today."

"What else do you like to do?"

"Paint." She'd been longing to paint. She just hadn't had the energy to get started.

"I'll set up your drafting table in the living room," Rob said.

"How about the two of you?" Dr. Scott asked. "Have you been able to carve out time for yourselves? Go out to dinner? Go for a drive?"

"Not really," Jill answered.

"You should. This is stressful on a marriage," the doctor said. "It's also a good idea to plan things to look forward to. A short trip. An outing. That sort of thing."

On the way home, Jill imagined the radiation bouncing around the tumor, zapping the tissue, breaking it into pieces that floated away like escaping balloons.

One of the pieces looked like Rob. A little tiny Rob zapped by a lightning bolt, floating away. Another piece, a larger chunk, looked like Marion.

The skin on her abdomen burned from the radiation.

They were in the Jeep. Caye had the Suburban.

Jill looked at Rob, just a few inches from her.

"What?" he asked.

"Are you going to have an affair?"

He looked hurt.

"Are you going to go back to Raleigh and have an affair? Or find someone here?" She thought of her swollen abdomen. Of her three needy boys. Of their finances.

"Jill," he said, drawing her name out.

"I want to know."

"No, I'm not going to have an affair. I told you that."

"Because if you feel like you can't cope with all of this—"

"Who said I couldn't cope? I'm coping. I want you. I want you to get better. To get well."

"What if I don't get well? What if I go on like this for months, for years?"

"Then I'll have you with me."

"With a bloated stomach? In pain? Irritable? Downright mean?"

"I don't care."

She didn't believe him.

"Have you talked to your parents lately?" she asked.

"I had an e-mail from them last night. They'll be in Houston next week. They'll call from there to let us know when they're coming."

"What do they say about all of this?"

"That they're praying for you."

"Would they come and help with the boys?"

"I don't know. Do you want me to ask them to come?"

She didn't know them well enough to really want them to come, but she wanted them to be willing. She was afraid that Caye was going to burn out. A few years ago she might have asked Rob's grandparents, but his grandfather had had a stroke the year before. They were out of the question.

She wanted Bev to come help. She'd feel most comfortable with Bev taking care of her, to help Caye, because Bev was so much like Caye.

Bev, like Caye, wouldn't feel sorry for her. Wouldn't talk down to her. Wouldn't expect her to be ticked at God. Wouldn't treat her as if she were ready to break.

Jill didn't feel angry with God. It was life, not God. For some reason he had not prevented this from happening. She couldn't guess at his reasons.

"Do you want to get away? Go on a little trip?" Rob asked.

Jill looked at him. What did she want?

She wanted Rob. If she were healed tomorrow, or not for two years, she wanted him back. She wanted to feel the way she felt about him when they were in Argentina, when they first moved to Ashland, when they first got the house.

*A trip, a little trip. Hawaii? New York? Victoria? Paris?*

"I want to go to Caye's parents' with you," she said, "and Caye and Nathan and all the kids. All these years I've thought it would be fun for you to go too."

"Are you sure?"

"Yes."

"What else do you want?"

"For us to be okay."

He reached over and held her hand.

"I think," she said, "that we need to spend time together. Listen to each other." And she wanted them to pray together, but she didn't want to say it; she wanted Rob to know, to take the lead.

"What else do you want to do?"

"Paint. It might be easier now than gardening."

"What about Marion? What do you want to do about Marion?"

"What do you think I should do?"

"Try to work things out."

Jill looked out the window. They were passing the Bear Creek rest area. How many times had she stopped there on trips back from Medford when Hudson was potty training? He loved to stop there, insisted on stopping there even though they were only a few minutes from home.

"I don't know what to do about Marion," Jill said.

"We could pray about it," Rob suggested, turning to look at his wife.

Jill exhaled into a tiny smile.

"What?" Rob asked.

Jill shook her head and chuckled. "Nothing," she answered. "God's just messing with me, that's all."

That night before Jill drifted off to sleep, they prayed together— or Rob prayed. He started by asking God to heal Jill and Marion's relationship. Then he asked God to strengthen their marriage and to protect the boys. And finally he asked God to bring circumstances, medicine, and miracles to heal Jill. He prayed that the CAT scan would show that healing had begun.

"Amen," Jill said as she fell into sleep, lulled by the pain medication into a garden of gigantic leafy pumpkin plants, green beans, and sun-flowers. It wasn't her garden she dreamed of—it was Hank and Beverly's late summer half-acre of vegetables and flowers.

She'd forgotten to ask Caye about a trip to Burns.

&

"You want to go to Burns?" Caye asked incredulously. Jill sat in a chair in the kitchen and spooned oatmeal into Simon's mouth.

*Is this like some last trip?* Caye wondered. *And she wants to go to Burns? To Mom and Dad's place? All of us crammed into their tiny house?* Caye could think of a dozen, three dozen, a hundred other trips she would have assumed Jill wanted to take.

"Yes," Jill said. "Doesn't it sound like fun?" She swiped the spoon across Simon's chin just as he rubbed his mouth with his hand. "Simon, baby, don't do that," she cooed.

Simon wiped the textured mess across his eyebrow.

A trip to Burns didn't sound like fun to Caye. The summer trips with the moms and kids each summer were hard enough. It sounded like an ordeal to include the dads.

But Caye smiled. If Jill wanted to go, they'd make it happen. "It only sounds like fun if you're absolutely sure you want to go," she answered.

&

"The tumor's shrinking," Jill yelled from the bedroom.

Caye ran down the hall from the kitchen. Jill stood in the door-way wearing a black camisole and a pair of Rob's blue and green plaid boxers. She waved the cordless phone in her hand.

"It's shrinking," she yelled again.

Jill flung her arms around Caye.

Audrey and Hudson stood at the end of the hallway watching their mothers.

"Hudson, Mommy's getting better!" Jill said over Caye's shoulder.

Audrey grabbed Hudson's hand and started jumping up and

down. Audrey's pigtails flew around her face. Hudson's pirate hat flew off his head. They collided in midair and collapsed on the floor.

Jill watched them. *That's what I want to do. Collapse on the floor hugging Caye.* It was a *Splendor in the Grass* moment, like the scene when Natalie Wood's character returns home and her two best friends jump up and down with their arms around her.

She let go of Caye.

"I'd better call Rob!" she said, looking down at the phone to punch in the number as she thought of his prayer from the night before.

On Sunday, during Fellowship, everyone was upbeat. Joya prayed. Thomas laughed. Summer spoke of her lack of faith and the lesson she was learning from Jill's cancer.

Gwen asked Jill if she was making progress in dealing with the issues in her life. Jill sat on the sofa like a queen on her throne and shot a terse smile across the room to Caye. Caye scowled. *We are not amused.*

Rob beamed; he, too, ignored Gwen's question. He sat through the meeting with his arm around Jill.

On Monday, Memorial Day, they celebrated Liam's third birthday in Railroad Park. While the kids played tag on the equipment, Caye, Jill, Nathan, and Rob talked about the trip to Burns. Nathan had just finished baseball. Andrew would miss his last game, but no one except Nathan minded.

Caye had called her parents to tell them the good news about Jill's CAT scan and to ask if they could all head over to Burns the next weekend.

"Of course," Bev said. She decided that Jill and Rob would have the guest room, Caye and Nathan would bring an air mattress to sleep in the extra bedroom that Bev used as a sewing room, and the kids would sleep in the living room.

Liam's cast came off on Thursday, and on Friday afternoon, as soon as Nathan was home from work, they headed to Burns. All nine of them and Scout rode in the Suburban. Caye wedged herself between Liam and Simon in the middle seat. She wasn't looking forward to the ride home.

On Saturday afternoon, Caye sat on the grassy slope by the irrigation pond in a lawn chair. Jill and Simon were in the house napping. Rob, Nathan, and her dad had taken the all-terrain vehicles across the road to the south pasture. Her mom was making apple pies for dessert. The kids chased butterflies along the edge of the pond. Scout chased the children.

The last week had been a whirlwind. Finally they had something to celebrate. Caye looked at the garden just up from the pond. It was surrounded by a fence to keep the deer out. The seedlings were just coming through the ground.

None of the kids had asked to swim in the pond. Last year, Caye and Jill had taken the children, except for Simon, into the murky water. Audrey, Hudson, and Liam liked it. Andrew said the bottom was too muddy. He was right. As a child Caye swam in it every summer, but she didn't plan to ever go in it again. If the kids wanted to, Nathan and Rob could take them later.

The children had wandered over by the corral. Hudson and Liam wore matching red T-shirts. Liam and Audrey both wore their rubber boots. Billy, the two-year-old gelding, kicked up his heels and pranced toward the kids. "Stay away from the fence," Caye called out.

The afternoon sun beat down on her. She stretched out her legs and pushed her hair away from her eyes. A dragonfly flew around her head. She wiggled her shoulders against the sticky woven plastic of the chair.

For all the work of making the trip, Caye was flattered that her parents' place was where Jill had wanted to go. She knew Jill felt loved by Bev and Hank, and cared for. And that she'd wanted Rob to see the ranch since the first time she'd visited.

Caye closed her eyes and felt the heat of the sun on her face. She felt relaxed for the first time in nearly six weeks.

She heard Audrey say, "Let's look at the baby chicks."

She heard Andrew say, "Just look, Liam. Don't try to pick them up. You'll hurt them. We don't want to do that."

Scout barked, a soft agreeing bark. He'd been good with the live-stock, even the chickens. Much better than Caye had expected. She honestly hadn't wanted to bring him.

Scout barked again, this time an urgent, serious bark.

Caye opened her eyes. Had she dozed? She looked around for the kids.

Scout was running back and forth along the shore of the pond.

None of the kids were by the water.

She turned her head. Andrew, Hudson, and Audrey walked toward her, away from the chicken coop. The gate was closed.

"Where's Liam?" she yelled, rising from her chair. Andrew looked puzzled. Hudson looked scared.

Scout leaped into the pond.

Caye started running toward the water.

Scout had something red in his mouth. It was Liam's shirt.

Caye splashed into the water as he surfaced. She grabbed him from the dog.

"Go get Grandma!" she yelled at Andrew. "Tell her to call 911." *How long would it take for the ambulance to arrive?* They were thirty minutes from town. Maybe they could make it in twenty. Would that be soon enough?

How long had Liam been in the water? She squeezed him to her. Water flowed from his mouth. He began to sputter.

She took three big steps out of the pond and sloshed onto the shore. She laid Liam on the pasture grass and tilted his face to the side.

Scout shook his coat in a furious motion and splattered Caye's face with pond water.

"Is Liam dead?" Hudson asked. Andrew and Audrey stood side by side, their eyes wide.

Liam opened his eyes as Caye lowered her head to check for his heartbeat.

He began to cough.

"Liam?" she called out. "Liam, can you hear me?"

He began to cry.

She scooped him up and held him, falling back on her bottom, rocking him from side to side.

She began to cry.

Bev came running, carrying the phone with her.

"What happened?" she yelled.

"I think he's okay," Caye answered. She couldn't stop crying.

Bev sunk to her knees beside Caye and tugged at Liam's arm.

He let out a shaky yell, holding the sound until it wavered.

"He's screaming," Bev said. "That means he's breathing."

"Do you think he has brain damage?" Caye asked.

"No, I don't think he'd be screaming if he did."

Caye pulled Liam from her chest and looked in his eyes. He dropped his head against her neck and collarbone.

"What happened?" Bev asked again.

"I think I dozed," Caye said. "And then the dog started barking. He jumped in the pond, and I realized that Liam was in there."

Bev put her arm around Caye.

"I'm such a horrible friend," she sobbed.

"No, no," Bev said. "Things happen. He's okay—that's what counts."

"What if Liam had drowned?"

"God took care of him," Bev said in her husky, soothing voice.

"And he used a dog I don't even like to save him." Caye started to look around for Scout.

"He's behind you," Bev said, "standing guard."

Caye turned her head. Scout started to shake, again flinging a sheet of water into Caye's face.

"Andrew," Caye said, "why didn't you keep Liam with you?"

"I thought he *was* with us," Andrew said.

His face looked tense. Caye bit her lip. She didn't want to do the blame thing. It wasn't Andrew's fault. It was her fault.

"He lost a boot." Audrey pointed to Liam's bare foot. One of his yellow boots was missing. "He has one boot on and one boot off."

"Where's my boot?" Liam asked, lifting up his foot.

"I'll call 911 and tell them not to come," Bev said.

"Won't they come anyway?" Caye asked.

"Not out here, honey. They'll believe me."

Caye heard the all-terrain vehicles crossing the road.

Nathan put his hands on Audrey's shoulders as Bev explained what had happened. The bill of his baseball cap was pulled down on his forehead, shadowing his brown eyes.

"Caye?" he said, in a questioning, drawn-out tone. "It's so unlike you to let down your guard."

Rob took Liam in his arms. "It's okay," he said. "Liam's all right. I wouldn't have watched them any closer."

"Rob!" It was Jill's voice coming from the patio. "What happened?"

Rob started up the road to the house, carrying Liam. Hudson, Audrey, and Andrew followed.

Caye felt devastated.

"I didn't realize how tired I was," she said. "I dozed."

"You shouldn't volunteer to watch all the kids if you don't feel up to it," Nathan said.

"It's over," Bev interjected. "Rob is right. Everything's okay. Come up to the house."

"I'm going to get Liam's other boot first," Caye said and turned her back on Nathan. She was annoyed with him for being so critical; she was annoyed with Rob for being so gracious. Would he be acting the same way if Liam were dead right now?

Caye thrashed around in the pond waist-deep, reaching in with her arms and kicking the bottom with her foot. Her saltwater sandals slurped through the mud. She felt the bottom give. She reached down and grabbed the yellow boot.

She walked slowly up the road. Scout followed at her heels.

Nathan and Bev waited halfway to the house for her.

It was her pride that hurt, she decided.

"Caye, are you okay?" Jill's sweet voice floated down toward her.

Caye was silent until she reached Jill, and then she began to cry. Jill hugged her.

"I'm all wet," Caye said. "You'll get all dirty."

"It's okay. He's okay."

"I'm sorry," Caye said.

"No," Jill said. "It's okay."

"What if Scout hadn't pulled him out?"

"But he did."

Caye kept crying. Jill patted her back. Bev said, "Now, now."

"I'm going to go get a shower," Caye said, pulling away from Jill.

Jill sat at the kitchen table and peeled apples while Bev rolled out the dough.

"Has your mom been up to Ashland?" Bev asked.

"She came while I was in the hospital."

"She must be awfully concerned about you."

Jill sliced the apple and put it in the bowl.

"She is. But she doesn't know how to show it."

"Has she acted this way before?"

"There's always been a colossal chasm between us. And she's secretive. I just found out she had cancer five years ago. Why didn't she tell me?"

Bev washed and dried her hands.

"She's always been secretive. She'd buy a new property for us and not tell me until the day before we moved. 'Pack your bedroom,' she'd say. 'We're moving tomorrow.' The only thing she did talk about when I was growing up was my dad's cancer.

"She really wasn't a very good mother," Jill concluded.

"How did you learn to be such a good mom?" Bev asked, pulling up a chair beside Jill and taking the second paring knife.

Jill laughed and started to peel another apple. "Well, I'm not. Not really. I let them get away with way too much. Ask Caye."

Bev shook her head. "You're a great mom."

"I emulate other moms. My friend Amy's mom was wonderful. I watched what she did with her five kids, husband, big house, and garden. The diplomat's wife in Argentina taught me all sorts of things—and the cook and the gardener. And Caye's taught me how to be a good mom—and you."

Bev smiled.

"If I can't decide what the right thing to do is, I do the opposite of what Marion did."

Bev laughed.

"It's true." Jill put her paring knife down. "Caye thinks I should make amends with her—that it would help my healing process."

"Do you think you can?" Bev asked.

"I don't know. I tried when we came back from Argentina, but it felt so flat. As if she was just going through the motions."

"Maybe if you can't make amends, you can at least lighten the load."

*Lighten the load.* Jill thought of the pieces of cancer floating away.

At dinner, as they stood around in a circle on the patio, Hank asked Nathan to pray before they ate.

Jill caught Nathan's quick glance at Caye. Her friend's eyes were still red. Caye and Nathan had spent an hour in Hank's workroom with the door closed. Jill was heartbroken that Caye felt so badly about Liam falling into the pond.

Nathan cleared his throat. He thanked God for Bev and Hank and their hospitality, he asked that Jill would be healed, and then he asked God to use the food they were about to eat to help them love each other more.

As she opened her eyes, Jill saw Nathan quickly squeeze Caye's hand.

She noted that he hadn't thanked God that Liam was unharmed. No need to rub that in. They'd already said that thanks.

## 25

Something changed inside Caye after the "pond incident," as she thought of it. It was too hard to think the words "when Liam nearly drowned" or "when Liam could have drowned." She'd realized in her head, after Jill was diagnosed with cancer, that they were all vulnerable. Now she felt it in her heart.

That evening, sitting on the patio, Caye looked from person to person. Rob sat close to Jill, his arm draped around her shoulders. Hank's suspenders buckled against his chest and looked as if they weren't accustomed to him sitting down. Bev was enjoying the hubbub. They didn't often have company. She sat in her rocker lawn chair and gave Simon his bedtime bottle.

Crickets chirped in the high grass around the yard. The cows mooed in the field. Soon the toads would begin to croak.

Caye was still irritated with Nathan. He'd been so critical of her for dozing. She knew he was right; she'd been hard on herself too. That's why she was irritated. Why did he have to make it worse? She'd tried to talk things through with him after her shower. Finally she asked again what was really bugging him. He said he'd been thinking about when his mother left. Caye didn't pry. She knew before he said it that that was the issue, but she didn't have the energy to dig it out of him, to help him sort it through. His hometown, Sweet Home, was a logging community. Not only had his mother left, but the whole town knew she'd taken off for Portland, that she couldn't stand the small-town life or Nathan's father anymore. In Nathan's mind, she couldn't stand him either.

Bev asked Jill and Rob why they moved to Ashland.

"It was part of Jill's sovereign plan," Rob said with a chuckle. "She

saw the big picture for our lives very clearly, and Ashland was the setting for that plan."

*Jill and her plan.* Caye thought about her own simple plans—how
long to stay home with the kids, what kind of job to find, how to pay
the bills, what to plant in the garden. That was it. No mansions. No
trips to New York or Europe or Argentina or even Disneyland. No
thoughts of someday opening her own business.

*Jill makes the big-picture plans,* Caye thought. *I come up with the
daily details.* But that wasn't entirely true either. Jill planned the activ-
ities and adventures, the special dinners. She decorated and painted
and filled her house with bouquets of flowers.

*That's it. Jill plans the fun stuff—I do the drudgery.*

Simon's head bobbed against Bev's arm as he fell asleep. "Should
I just put him down?" she asked. "In that fancy portable crib?"

"Thanks," Jill said.

Caye couldn't stop thinking about Liam. In all her diligence, she'd
failed. She'd let her guard down. She had fallen asleep. Her hyper-
responsibility wasn't enough.

The sun was setting over the river. Hank stood. "I'm going to go
check on those calves," he said.

"I'll go with you," Jill said, rising to her feet.

"Sure you feel up to it?"

Jill nodded and followed Hank off to the ATV. The calves were
just across the road in the pasture, but with Hank's bum hip he drove
even short distances. Caye heard the motor whine as it started and the
wheels grind on the gravel as Hank pulled out.

"Can we catch toads?" Andrew asked Nathan.

"Please?" Audrey chimed in.

"What do you think?" Nathan asked Caye.

"I'm going to bed," she said. "Do what you want."

"Please," Audrey said again, grabbing Nathan's hand and jumping up and down.

Caye gathered up the pie plates and headed to the kitchen.

Bev stood at the sink and ran the hot dishwater. "I know Jill's getting better, but she sure doesn't look good. Too skinny. She hardly
eats. And that belly sticking out is just eerie."

Caye nodded. "She really is better though."

"Are you okay?" Bev asked her daughter.

"Just tired." She looked out the window. Nathan had pulled the flashlight off the shelf by the back door. He and Rob, followed by the kids, walked toward the pond in the twilight. Scout followed.

❧

"Why are you so quiet?" Jill asked Caye the next day. They stood on the patio watching Rob tie the luggage onto the Suburban's roof rack. Liam ran back and forth across the patio, plowing the air with his head pointed toward the ground.

"Just tired."

"Is it the stuff yesterday with Liam?"

Caye shook her head.

"Just look at him," Jill said. "I love him to pieces, but he's an accident waiting to happen. He's one of those kids that you just have to hope God assigned three guardian angels to."

Caye smiled.

"Don't beat yourself up about it."

"I'm not," Caye answered.

The best thing about being in Burns, Jill decided, was that Caye had stopped asking her how she felt fifteen times a day. Maybe it was because they were in a different location, away from Jill's house. Maybe it was because Jill really was feeling better, and it showed. It had been nearly six weeks since the surgery. It made sense that she was finally feeling better. And the cancer was shrinking—the thought sustained her through every minute of every day.

"I think what is really bothering me," Caye said, "is how little control we actually have over our lives."

"But don't you think that's a good thing? Think of all the extra trouble we'd get into if we really were in control."

"How can you forgive Rob so quickly?" Caye asked.

"That was a topic change."

"Not really," Caye said. "It's all related."

"How?"

"You can't control Rob, but you seem to have forgiven him. His actions could have placed you in a very vulnerable situation, but you haven't held it against him."

"He asked my forgiveness. I forgave him."

"Just like that?"

"Maybe not just like that. It's a process. I really think he was sincere. He dropped the account. He's not going back to Raleigh. It still hurts—hurts my trust, my pride. But I'm living on borrowed time. I don't have the privilege of carrying a grudge. Or of giving in to being insecure."

"What about Marion?"

"What do you mean?"

"Don't you think you should work things out with her?"

"I think she should work things out with me." Jill smiled at Caye, a cutting, conclusive smile.

"But, Dad." Both women turned their heads toward Andrew and Nathan. "I have to take the toad with me." Andrew held a half-gallon mayonnaise jar with a toad, a rock, and a quarter-inch of pond water.

"He won't live," Nathan said. "And we don't have room in the Suburban."

"I'll hold him on my lap. Grandma said I could take the jar with me."

Andrew held up the jar. The toad slid off his rock onto the glass bottom.

"He'll just die."

"I'll let him go when we get home."

"Let him go here."

"Let him take the toad," Jill said. "That's why God made toads. For little boys."

Nathan turned his baseball cap forward so the bill shaded his eyes from the sun.

Caye headed toward the house.

"It's not a big deal, Nathan," Jill said. She began to feel uncomfortable as Caye walked away.

"It is a big deal for him not to obey me."

"It's okay for him to know what he wants."

"Keep the toad," Nathan said, turning to Andrew. "But let him go as soon as we get home."

Immediately Jill regretted butting in. Nathan had probably only agreed to humor her. Six weeks ago he wouldn't have. Six weeks ago he wouldn't have had to—she wouldn't have pressed the issue, wouldn't have interfered. Jill tousled Andrew's hair. "Keep that thing in the jar. He's gargantuan, big enough to have his own seat belt, and we don't have any to spare."

Caye stood in her mother's kitchen and wished she were nineteen again. Where had this husband come from? These children?

She wished that they were all going home and she was staying. She wished she could sleep, the way she used to when she came home after finals, for a week.

Tears smarted Caye's eyes. She felt so tired.

She watched her mother dry her hands on an embroidered dish-towel. Everyone else congregated around the Suburban ready to go. Through the kitchen window, Caye could see Hank walking from the barn to the house.

"I just don't feel like I can do it all," Caye said to her mom. "I try so hard and still don't get it right."

"You can do everything you need to do," Bev said. "Maybe not to meet your standards. But you can do what needs to be done, and if you can't, ask for help."

Caye stood silently, her arms crossed.

"Ask the people in your home church. Or ask me. Remember, Daddy and I can come over for a few days."

Caye sighed.

"But don't beat yourself up. You're exhausted. Anyone would be."

"Jill's getting better, and I'm turning into a mess." Caye tried to laugh, but the sound came out like a sob. For the first time since Jill was hospitalized, Caye felt tension with her friend.

*Show your faith through love.*
*What happens when I'm too tired to love?*
"Everyone's waiting," her mother said.

❧

Caye drove Jill to her Monday morning chemo, but Joya would take her home. A message from Joya offering the ride was waiting for them Sunday evening. "So Caye doesn't have to hang out there with the kids," Joya said. "It should be easier on everyone."

"Interesting that Joya's willing to show her face now that you're getting better," Rob had commented after listening to the message and relaying the information to Jill.

Now, pulling out of the clinic parking lot, it dawned on Jill that Joya had a specific purpose in taking her home.

"I wanted to talk with you," Joya said. "Alone."

Jill rubbed the spot on the back of her hand where the catheter had been inserted. It was so like Joya to jump right into a conversation without a warmup.

"We were talking about your cancer during Fellowship yesterday." The group had met at Thomas and Joya's.

"Obviously something has changed. I wanted to ask you, in private, what it is. What has happened to you spiritually to allow the healing?"

Jill's head began to ache. A dull pain settled at the base of her skull.

What had changed? Things were better between her and Rob. She felt hopeful. She was more aware of her trust in God. It was true: The better she felt, the easier it was to trust.

There was a time when she would have said something vague to please Joya. Back when they were in Argentina.

"Let me ask you a question, Joya."

Joya nodded.

"What are you looking for? A sin I've confessed? That I'm sorry I didn't reveal my family medical history to Rob? That I'm human? Joya, I don't know what you want."

"I want you to be healed. I know God's going to do that. I want to understand the process." Joya paused and took a deep breath.

Jill sank inside.

"Rob told Thomas about a confession that he made to you. I'm wondering if Rob's confession has led to your healing."

*Why had Rob said anything to Thomas? Why had Thomas said anything to Joya?* The image of David sitting on Rob's lap back in Argentina floated into her mind, followed by Joya wringing the fuchsia scarf.

"Why don't you ever talk about David in Fellowship?" Jill asked.

"There's never been a reason to."

Jill looked intently at Joya.

"Do you feel like you've dealt with his death?"

"What is there to deal with?"

Jill looked out the window. She imagined the chemo attacking the cancer. This time the pieces floating away looked like Marion and Joya.

❧

Caye stood on the deck and watched Jill carefully select and cut roses for a bouquet. Jill wore a sundress with a long-sleeve white shirt over the top. In a few minutes Rita would come to stay with the kids so Caye and Jill could shop for Simon's and Hudson's birthdays. Rob had done the shopping for Liam's. Jill didn't want to miss out again, plus she'd said it would be good to get out of the house without the kids.

Jill straightened her back.

"What's the matter?" Caye asked.

"I just had a pain. I'm okay."

Caye watched as Jill cut another rose. A Tropicana. She held a garden bouquet in her hand—yellow, red, orange, and pink. The smell of the roses filled the courtyard.

Jill straightened up again. "Yikes."

"You okay?"

"This is a different pain. I haven't felt it before."

"Is it time for a pain pill?"

"Guess so."

❧

"What's the matter?" Rita asked as she came through the front door. Jill stood at the front window sipping a glass of water. "You're so pale."

"Just some sharp pains."

"Hi, Rita," Caye called out as she came down the stairs. "Simon and Liam are asleep. Hudson and Audrey are playing in the basement. How long can you stay?"

"Two or three hours. I need to stop by the office on my way home."

"We'll be back by then. Call Jill's cell if you need us."

"What about Andrew?"

"He's going home with a friend."

Jill stopped before she climbed into Caye's station wagon.

"Does it still hurt?" Caye asked.

"A little."

"Do you want to go? Or stay home?"

"No, let's go."

As they walked across the parking lot to the Rogue Valley Mall, Jill stopped.

"You're not okay, are you?" Caye asked.

"This is really bad pain. Sharper. Different."

"What do you want me to do?"

"Take me home."

They climbed into the car. Jill started to fasten her seat belt and then stopped. "It hurts. Really hurts."

Caye put her hand on Jill's shoulder. Jill reached up and grabbed her friend's hand.

"I changed my mind. Call Rob. See if he thinks I should go to the doctor," Jill said.

It was not like Jill to think of calling Rob before making a decision.

"Maybe we should just go to the doctor."

"No," Jill said, pulling her cell phone out of her purse. "Call him first, okay?"

❧

"It could be a pinched nerve," Dr. Scott said. "Perhaps the tumor is growing again. There could be lesions that have grown since the CAT scan."

"That fast?" Rob asked.

Dr. Scott shrugged. "We see everything. Let's hope it's a pinched nerve. We'll start with an MRI. In the meantime, we'll admit you," he said, looking at Jill. "And we'll give you more medication to ease the pain."

Jill stood by the sink in the examining room. It hurt to lie down.

"What about the boys?" she said to Rob.

"Caye will stay with them."

"But she's so tired. I think we've worn her out."

❧

Caye cried as she talked to Nathan on the phone. "Rob just called. She's going back into the hospital."

"Why?"

"Her pain was really bad. Excruciating. They're going to do an MRI."

"Where are you?" Nathan asked.

"Back at Jill and Rob's. With the boys and our kids. I picked up Andrew on my way."

"Should I come there?"

Caye sobbed.

"Are you okay?"

"No. I'm a mess."

"About Jill?"

"About everything."

*He's going to ask if it's PMS.* It probably was. Not that having Jill so sick wasn't enough to cry about, but it wasn't like Caye not to be able to cope.

"Are you pregnant?" Nathan asked.

When had her last period been? She couldn't exactly remember.

"No, I had a period just a month or so ago. Or two months ago. Maybe more."

Pregnant. It couldn't be.

"I'll pick up a test," Nathan said.

"I'm not pregnant," Caye said. "I would know if I were pregnant. I'm just a mess."

Nathan was silent.

"I'll go to the store after you get here. We need milk and cereal and a bunch of other stuff," Caye decided.

"I can stop on my way home," Nathan said.

"No. You come here and feed the kids. Get a pizza on your way. I'll go to the store."

The cart pulled to the right as Caye pushed it through Safeway's produce section. It felt too heavy to handle, as if she might have to abandon it next to the nectarines. Instead she trudged to the cereal aisle. Jill never let her boys have sugared cereal. Caye chose two boxes of Lucky Charms.

As she passed the tea and coffee, her eyes fell to a large empty space ready to be restocked at the bottom of the shelf, just below the hot chocolate. She stopped the cart, overcome by fatigue. She wanted to curl up on the shelf to rest, to sleep. She wondered if anyone would notice.

She glanced at her list. Pregnancy test. She wheeled the cart around and headed to the pharmacy.

## 26

"The cancer has spread to your liver," Dr. Scott said.

Jill leaned against the sink. Rob had spent the night at the hospital with her. She'd hardly slept.

"Liver?" Rob asked.

Dr. Scott nodded.

"How can it be shrinking one week and in her liver the next?"

*Two weeks. It's been two weeks.* Jill corrected Rob silently.

"It's unpredictable," the doctor said.

Rob kicked the end of the hospital bed. Hard.

"I'd be angry too," Dr. Scott said.

"That's right," Rob retorted. "You have a wife. And kids. And another baby on the way."

He kicked the bed again.

"Rob," Jill said, turning toward him.

Jill climbed back on the bed and sat facing the doctor. She reached for Rob's hand. "What now?" she asked.

"We keep going with the radiation and the chemo. We do more to manage your pain."

"And what are our chances?" Rob asked.

*Our chances.* The chances that their family wouldn't be set adrift. The chances that their family would remain intact.

"Once cancer reaches the liver, it's very serious. I'll be honest. The chances—from a medical perspective—don't look as good as they did two weeks ago."

Rob sat down hard on the bed. Jill winced.

"Is there still reason to be hopeful?" Rob asked.

"There's always reason for hope."

"When can I go back home?" Jill asked.

"As soon as we get your pain under control."

"Best case scenario, until the miracle occurs, what are we looking at?" Jill asked.

"As far as what?" Dr. Scott asked.

"Time."

"I don't give my patients estimated times. There are too many variables."

"What's the purpose of the chemo and radiation now?" she asked.

"To prolong your life."

Rob buried his head against Jill's neck.

"Thank you," Jill said to the doctor. "For being honest."

He sighed. "You could live for months," he said. "For years. And you could still be healed. Don't give up on that."

Jill thought he sounded sad, despondent. "Have you seen it happen?" she asked. "With pancreatic cancer?"

"I haven't seen it," he said. "But I've read about it."

"So have I," Jill answered. But what she meant was "so has Caye."

Caye stood in Jill's upstairs bathroom and looked in the mirror. She spotted a few gray hairs among the red and gold highlights. She needed a haircut and her color touched up.

She took a deep breath and let it out slowly. She felt old.

She picked up the baby stick, as Nathan called it, and then dropped it on the counter. The bubble of color really had changed to green. She was pregnant.

"Maybe it's wrong," she said to Nathan, who stood in the doorway.

"Only if it's negative, remember? They're never wrong when it's positive. Remember, that's what the doctor told us when you were first pregnant with Andrew."

Their first test, with Andrew, had registered negative. It had taken Caye a few months to realize she was pregnant that time, too. Her cycles were typically long.

Nathan did a little dance around the bathroom. Caye sat down on the toilet and cried.

"What's wrong?" he asked.

"I don't want to be pregnant." She wasn't sure, but she was probably nine weeks along. That would make for a January due date. She couldn't think that far ahead—she couldn't imagine life past next week.

She buried the stick in the bathroom garbage. She didn't want Rob or Jill to see it.

Nathan had a smile on his face all evening. He seemed to forgive Caye her negligence of the kids and overinvolvement with Jill all at once.

In the morning Nathan changed Simon's diaper and fed the older kids so Caye could sleep.

"So are you all better?" Caye asked as Nathan hurried out the door.

He squinted his eyes.

"You were out of sorts. Now you're better."

He smiled.

"Was it Jill's being sick? My being so preoccupied? Did it make you think of your mom not sticking around?"

"I've got to go," Nathan said, glancing at his watch.

"But a baby offers hope?" Caye knew she was being relentless.

Nathan shrugged again. He kissed her quickly on the lips and then hurried down the steps to unlock the car door for Andrew.

As Caye fed the baby his cereal, she thought about when Jill was five months pregnant with Simon.

Jill had left a message for Caye: "I have a great idea! Give me a call." Caye had returned late in the evening from grocery shopping. Brown paper bags lined the counter. The sink was full of dirty dishes. Audrey had thrown up the night before, and the sour laundry was still piled in the basement.

Caye picked up the phone and hit speed dial for Jill.

"How are you?" Jill had asked.

"You don't want to know," Caye moaned.

"Ready for an adventure? To get out of town?"

It was the middle of February. Both had been complaining of cabin fever.

"Disneyland," Jill boomed. "Let's take the kids to Disneyland. I made some phone calls today. We could go the last week of the month."

Jill covered the airfare and the hotel, claiming that Rob had enough frequent flier miles and she'd gotten a two-for-one deal on the rooms. It took Caye several late-night discussions to convince Nathan to let Andrew miss three days of school. "For crying out loud," she finally said, "he's only in the first grade. It will have no bearing on his long-term academic career."

They'd stayed in a suite near Disneyland. On the third day, Jill asked Caye if she would mind if Marion met them for dinner at the hotel. Of course Caye didn't mind. But she was surprised. She didn't know when Jill had called her mother or why they hadn't seen Marion sooner.

Marion sat next to Hudson during dinner. "Put your napkin in your lap," she told him. "Don't talk with your mouth full." She entirely ignored Liam, even when he knocked the metal highchair tray to the floor with a horrible clatter.

Jill was unusually quiet.

Caye tried to make small talk. "Aren't you excited about another grandbaby?" she asked Marion.

"I'd be more excited about Jill taking care of herself," Marion answered. "All these kids so close together can't be good for her."

Marion looked at Jill. "Why do you have to have more? Caye stopped at two, and she's perfectly happy."

Jill gave Caye a pained look. "Mother, stop," she said. "You don't know what you're saying."

They'd gone back to Disneyland that evening for the night show. Jill took Hudson, Audrey, and Liam to the teacups while Caye and Andrew ran to Splash Mountain for a final ride. It was glorious. Caye was so glad they'd made the trip, that she'd swallowed her pride and accepted Jill's generosity.

She and Andrew raced back to the teacups, running hand in

hand, darting around rides and people. Caye spotted Jill standing toward the front of the line holding Liam. Hudson and Audrey held each other's hands. Jill looked like a stranger for a moment. Her dark hair was back in a French braid. Her face looked clouded, uncertain. The confident look Caye was so used to was missing. She looked weathered, almost mystical.

"Jill!" Caye yelled and waved.

Jill looked around, a slow smile spreading over her face. "You don't mind," she said to the people behind her, "if my friend cuts in? I need her help with the kids."

Caye and Andrew slipped under the metal chain. "Let me take Liam," Caye said.

The phone rang. Caye slipped another spoonful of cereal into Simon's mouth and picked up the phone.

It was Nathan. "How do you feel?" he asked.

"The same. Like a mess." She tucked the phone under her chin and lifted Simon from his chair.

"I'm so happy," he said.

"I'm so shocked."

"It will be wonderful."

It was hard not to smile at his enthusiasm. "But we've wanted this for so long," he'd said last night.

"I wanted it for so long that I stopped wanting it. I moved on," Caye said. Hadn't they decided she needed to go back to work? That they could hardly afford the two kids they had?

"I'm almost done with my master's," Nathan replied when Caye posed the questions. "I'll get a job as a vice principal. I'll keep coaching. We'll make it."

Nathan said good-bye without asking about Jill.

The phone rang again. "How is she?" It was Joya.

"I haven't heard anything yet. I'll call you when I do." Caye hung up, wondering at Joya's response if the news was bad.

Minutes later the phone rang a third time.

It was Rob.

"We're going to increase the pain meds," the nurse told Jill. "This pain is too much."

Jill nodded. It was morphine now. She hated the thought of it; she hated the pain more.

*She stood in a garden holding a hoe, a big open garden with no fence. The sun was hot on her face, her neck.*

*She looked up at the house.*

*The boys were asleep. Napping.*

*How much longer did she have to hoe? She felt anxious about her work, about completing her task.*

*She heard the sound of the plane but never saw it.*

*Something pierced her—shot through her lower back into her belly.*

*She dropped the hoe and sank to her knees in the soil. The roar of the plane drifted away. Who would take care of her children? Who would be there when her baby boys woke from their naps?*

*The snakes came then, crawling across the garden, scaling the plants, scurrying onto Jill. She covered her face with her hands.*

"Jill. You're having a bad dream." She felt a hand on her shoulder.

Jill opened her eyes. It was Caye.

"Who's with the boys?"

"Rita. She left work early. Where's Rob?" Caye asked.

"He had to go into the office. It's in my liver."

"I know. Rob told me."

"I'm scared."

"I know."

"Do you think I can still be healed?"

"Yes."

Caye sat down on the bed and wrapped her arms around Jill.

Jill shivered. "So do I. But I'm worried about the boys."

Jill took a deep breath. "I'm afraid Rob will forget their immunizations. He won't think to feed them lunch on the weekends and to have them brush their teeth. I'm afraid he'll forget about swim lessons and homework."

"Shh," Caye said. "Don't talk that way."

Jill began to cry.

Caye held her without saying anything until Jill pulled away and yanked a tissue from the box.

"Is the pain better?"

Jill nodded.

"We spent the night at your house last night," Caye said. "We can again tonight, too, if that's easier."

"Is Nathan okay with the idea?"

Caye nodded.

"It might be easier. I don't know what Rob's doing—if he'll stay here or not. I should be able to go home tomorrow." Jill paused. "I'm having a hard time being positive."

"That's okay," Caye said. "You'll feel positive again."

"Did you tell Joya?" Jill asked.

"Yes. And the rest of the Fellowship."

"What did Joya say."

"Oh."

Jill began to laugh. "That hurts." She took a deep breath. "She said 'oh'?"

"Yep. Just 'oh.' Then she said she had to go pick up Louise." Caye looked toward the window. "It's hot out there. Close to ninety."

"How does my garden look?"

"Good. Well, pretty good."

As Caye sat down on the bed next to Jill, Rob walked into the room.

"Congratulations," he said to Caye, without acknowledging Jill. His voice was strained. "I stopped by the house. Nathan told me your news."

## 27

*Why did Nathan tell Rob?* Nathan seldom spoke impulsively. He usually thought things through. Why had he blurted it out? It hadn't occurred to her to ask him not to tell anyone.

"What?" Jill asked, looking from Rob to Caye.

Neither answered.

"Are you pregnant?" Jill asked, sitting up straight.

Caye nodded. She was afraid to say anything. Afraid she'd start to cry and not be able to stop.

"That's wonderful!"

Caye looked at Rob. His arms were crossed.

Caye began to cry.

"Aren't you excited?" Jill asked.

Caye nodded. She was lying.

"But it's wonderful," Jill said. "I'm so excited. It's such a reminder that life goes on. It's such an answer to our prayers."

❧

Caye sat in the parking lot with the air conditioning on. It was 5:30. She hoped that Rita had gone home—and that Nathan was feeding the kids. Why had he told Rob? If she'd had any idea he was going to do that, she would have told Jill first.

*I feel guilty. Jill's fighting for her life, and I'm growing a baby. I'd give anything not to have another child as long as Jill could live.*

She caught a glimpse of movement from the corner of her eye.

It was Rob. He was a few steps away from the car.

Caye hesitated and then reached over and unlocked the passenger door.

"I'm sorry," he said as he opened the door.

Caye shook her head.

"No, I behaved badly."

He lowered his body into the seat and shut the door.

Caye was silent.

"Nathan was right to tell me. The sooner the better. And don't think I'm not happy for you. It just feels as if God is blessing you…and not us."

Caye nodded. She knew the feeling. All the years she'd known Rob and Jill, she'd seen God's blessing on them. Now she was ashamed for how she'd felt.

"You've been such a good friend to us," Rob said. "I'd be crazy to hurt you."

Caye wondered whether Rob realized that she was hurt by his response—or if Jill had pointed it out.

"I'm scared," Rob said.

"I know. I am too."

"Jill doesn't seem to be."

"She is," Caye said.

Rob stared at the dashboard. "What do we do?"

"What we've been doing."

Rob opened the car door.

"Have you called Marion?" Caye asked.

Rob pulled the door shut. "No. I thought about it this morning. But I didn't. I'll ask Jill what she wants me to do."

Caye nodded and watched him walk back toward the hospital. He wore Levi's and a white oxford shirt. His long legs moved quickly over the asphalt. His shoulders drooped.

❧

Jill sat in her living room and stared at her tubes of paint. She had decided to do watercolors. Acrylics would take too long.

Rob had brought up her drafting table and supplies from the

basement and set them out for her. The paint, brushes, palette, sponges. He'd even wet the paper and taped it to the board.

She would start with the magnolia tree for Rob. Then do the cherry tree for Simon. For Hudson she would paint the wisteria. Liam's painting would be of the Tropicana roses that always bloomed for his birthday.

That left Caye's. Jill's grandmother's tulips with the forget-me-nots scattered around would be the subject of the painting for her friend.

Something was changing inside her body.

It was Saturday afternoon. The little boys were napping. Hudson was at Caye's playing with Andrew. Rob was out for a run.

It was a joke to give Rob the magnolia tree. She hoped he'd appreciate it. Life, even though it was messy, was beautiful. And for short periods of time it smelled like gardenias.

She drew the magnolia tree, the sturdy trunk, the tall branches, the beautiful blooms. She chuckled. Rob, too, was like the magnolia tree—beautiful but messy. She was sorry she'd taken him for granted the last year. Sorry, but not surprised. She was sure that, if she hadn't gotten sick, she would have come out of it. The passage would have been normal. An adjustment after a third child. Part of the landscape. Except for his emotional affair. That was a glitch, a tremor.

Thomas had called about Fellowship the next day. He wanted all the members to be together. Joya had mentioned Jill's baby-sitter. Did Jill think she'd come during Fellowship and watch the kids?

Jill called Stephanie. She was willing.

"What's up?" Jill asked Thomas when she called back. "What are you planning?"

"Communion. I want all of us to be together."

"Is Joya coming too?"

"Yes," Thomas answered.

Jill thought ahead to the cherry tree painting she would do for Simon, for her baby. The cherry tree was so fragile with its pale pink blooms. So new and fresh as it ushered in spring. The wisteria, for Hudson, was sturdy and strong, strong enough to tear down a building if not supported. The Tropicana rose for Liam was vibrant with its orange, pink, and yellow mix. It screamed of action and beauty.

She worried about the daily stuff for her boys—that they'd get what they needed—but she didn't worry about the lifelong picture. They were her babies—they would succeed.

She'd think more about Caye's painting later.

She picked up her paintbrush and started the background wash of the magnolia.

Stephanie stood gaping at Jill.

"It's so good to see you," Jill said, standing to give Stephanie a hug.

Caye held Simon and watched the scene unfold, seeing Jill the way Stephanie, who hadn't seen her in weeks, saw her. Elbows jutting out, skinny legs coming out of her short overalls. Her face accented by her cheekbones. It was her belly that was the most alarming—it looked as though she were six months pregnant.

"How are you?" Stephanie asked.

"Hanging in there."

"What do the doctors say?"

Jill looked around the room. Gwen and John sat on the sofa. Joya was in the kitchen helping Thomas prepare Communion. Nathan and Rob were out in the backyard looking at a sprinkler head that needed to be fixed.

"The doctors say…," Jill began. "They say they don't know."

Caye walked downstairs with Stephanie.

"She looks horrible," Stephanie whispered. "How is she really doing?"

"It doesn't look good. She was getting better, but now she's not."

Stephanie shook her head. "I can't believe it."

All the members had arrived. Caye sat in the circle and looked at each member, one by one. She looked at Jill last. She sat by Rob on the couch and held his hand. Caye was aware of her secret, of the baby she carried inside her. Nathan thought they should tell the Fellowship and get it over with. Caye wasn't so sure. She convinced him to wait at least another week. They'd decided to tell Audrey and Andrew that afternoon after Fellowship.

Thomas led them in communion. He broke the bread and served each member. "The bread we break is in remembrance of Christ's body," Thomas said. "He gave his body that we might live and have eternal life." Together, the Fellowship ate the bread.

Next he poured the juice into a pewter chalice. "This cup represents the communion of Christ's blood," he said. "Christ's blood was spilled to cleanse us. Just as our blood cleanses our bodies, his blood cleanses our lives." He served each member the juice from the chalice.

When he finished, he looked at Jill.

"Tell us, Jill, what God is teaching you."

Caye shifted her weight on the hard chair and looked around.

"I've been painting again and praising him for the people I love. He's teaching me to let go—"

"Let go!" Joya exclaimed, her voice low and incredulous. "How can you give up?"

Thomas put his hand on Joya's leg.

"I'm not giving up," Jill said. "I'm letting go. I'm not trying to control things that I can't. I'm trusting God more deeply than I ever have before—with my life, with Rob, with the boys—with all of this."

Thomas nodded.

Caye crossed her legs and leaned forward. Nathan began rubbing her back.

"We've seen your faith," Thomas said. "You're an inspiration. We'll keep praying for a miracle. In the meantime, if God should call you home, are you ready to go?" Joya looked at Thomas with fierce eyes.

"Yes."

Rob pulled his hand from Jill's and put it up to his face. Jill looked at him.

"I'll never be ready to leave Rob and the boys—and all of you," Jill said. "But I can still be ready to go."

The word *go* reverberated through Caye's head. *Go.* As if Jill were preparing for a long journey.

"I've heard of people," Thomas said, "who, once they were ready to die, were then healed. We have no idea what God is doing. We know that the cancer has metastasized to your liver. We also know that God can still heal you."

Jill nodded.

Caye expected Summer to cry or Joya to speak again or Gwen. Everyone was quiet.

"Let's pray silently," Thomas said.

❧

Jill looked around the room. She did not pray. She soaked in the scene. The people against the blue gray walls with heads bowed, some with hands clasped. Rob prayed with his hands held open, resting on his thighs. He wore khaki shorts, a plain white T-shirt, and Nike sandals.

She wondered if they were all praying for her.

She loved them, all of them. She praised God for them. She hoped they were praising God for her.

She thought of Stephanie with the kids. She prayed a blessing on her. *Poor girl didn't know what to think of me.* Jill would forget how much her appearance had changed until a neighbor stared when she walked from the car to the house or a short way along the sidewalk. Jill would wave and say hello, and the neighbor would continue to stare. "I'm sick," she'd say. Some of them, after seeing her, had brought meals and flowers to the house.

"Amen," Thomas said after what seemed like hours.

Joya turned to Jill. "God has not changed his promise to me," she said. "He's promised to heal you. I can't understand why you aren't claiming that."

"I am. I still believe he's going to heal me. But right now I'm getting worse."

"But why?"

"I can only assume it's for his glory."

"His glory?"

"Like the man born blind. Christ said that he wasn't blind
because of his sin or his parents' sin, but so that God could be
glorified."

"You think," Joya said slowly, "that by not healing you God could
bring glory to himself?"

Jill nodded.

"Jill," Joya said, "the man born blind was healed. That's the whole
point."

❧

"I am not giving up," Jill said to Caye. Caye sat on Jill's bed and fingered the afghan that she'd crocheted. The rest of the Fellowship had
left. Rob and Nathan had taken the kids to the park. "Do you think
I am?"

"Do you still believe you can be healed?"

"Yes. Didn't I say that during Fellowship? Did anyone hear me?"

"Then you haven't given up."

"God will heal me," Jill said. "Either in this life or the next."

Caye reached over and squeezed Jill's hand.

"How do you feel?" Jill asked.

"Okay. Not finding out for the first two and a half months sure
has made for a quick first trimester."

"You didn't suspect you were?"

"No. I felt tired and nauseated, but I thought they were sympa-
thetic symptoms. I just thought I was being a good friend." Caye
paused. "It's embarrassing that I didn't know, didn't figure it out."

"I'm happy you're pregnant," Jill said.

"I feel really guilty," Caye said.

"Why?"

"Because you wanted more babies."

"Don't feel guilty. It's not fair to God. He's blessed you. Feeling guilty doesn't thank him."

Caye smiled. *Quick-to-speak-the-truth Jill,* she thought. "Okay," she said, flashing her dimples. "Lesson learned."

"When are you going to tell everyone?"

"Soon. Andrew and Audrey today," Caye said as she continued to finger the afghan. "There it is. There's the dropped stitch that threw the whole thing off."

"What are you talking about?" Jill asked.

"This mess of an afghan. I hate that I dropped the stitches, that it gets skinnier toward the end. All I need to do is rip it out to here and recrochet it." Caye flipped the afghan over and started picking at the knot at the end.

"No," Jill said.

"What?"

"It's mine. I won't let you."

Caye laughed. "Why not?"

"I like it the way it is."

"Okay." Caye dropped the afghan into her lap. Life was like the afghan, she decided. She thought about Joya and the way she dealt with David's death. How she never told the Fellowship, never talked about it. That wove a pattern with a missing stitch. And Marion— what if she had told Jill about her breast cancer when it happened? And about whatever else she was keeping secret? Marion had created a flawed pattern years ago.

"Don't you wish we could go back, rip out the stitches of life, pick up the stitches again, and do it over?" Caye asked as she wadded the afghan into a big ball and tossed it to the end of the bed.

"No," Jill said. "I don't want to do any of it over. It's life, Caye. It's supposed to be this way."

❧

Jill sat in the waiting room. The nurse had already taken her blood. She was waiting to start the chemo.

Caye was at the playground with the kids.

"Jill." The nurse directed her into a consulting room. "Your blood count is down. I called Dr. Scott, and he recommended that we don't do the chemo."

"Really? What does that mean?"

"Blood counts vary—it could be nothing."

"Or?"

"Talk to Dr. Scott. When is your next appointment?"

"On Thursday."

"Call him sooner. It really might mean nothing. Plan to come in next week—sooner if your count is up and he recommends it."

Jill walked out the double doors of the clinic onto the glaring asphalt. She'd left her sunglasses in the Suburban. She could barely keep her eyes open in the bright light.

She followed the sidewalk around to the front of the hospital. She stopped at the steps and leaned against the handrail. She felt beads of sweat on her brow. She looked down at her protruding belly. A stranger might think she was on her way to the maternity ward.

She started walking again to the patch of shade in the far corner of the parking lot. She could hear the kids at the playground before she could see them. She stood against the little picket fence and waited for her eyes to adjust.

"Jill—why are you here? Is everything okay?" Caye asked as she stopped walking Simon around the playhouse. It was obvious that he would be walking soon on his own—within a day or two.

"Mommy!" Hudson shouted.

"Mommy!" Liam mimicked.

"Hi," Jill said.

"What is it?" Caye asked again.

"My count is down," Jill said. "They wouldn't give me the chemo."

❧

"Pull over," Jill said. "I'm going to be sick." She hadn't even had the chemo. Why was she sick now when she hadn't been all these weeks?

Caye slowed the car. They'd only gone a mile from the hospital. "Audrey, throw Jill a diaper from Simon's bag."

A disposable diaper came bouncing onto the front seat. Caye grabbed it and handed it to Jill.

Jill retched into the open diaper. All she'd had for breakfast was a sip of a banana smoothie. She retched again.

"I'm sorry," she said to Caye.

"Don't worry about it."

"Now what?" Jill rolled the diaper and taped the ends shut. Her hands shook.

Caye pulled into a parking lot. "Audrey, throw me a plastic bag, okay?"

A wadded plastic bag just cleared the front seat.

"You guys make quite a team," Jill said.

Caye dropped the diaper in the bag.

"We all make quite the team," she answered.

Jill thought of last spring when she'd gotten the Suburban stuck on Mount Ashland. It was Caye, with her farm-girl confidence, who finally maneuvered it out of the mud.

"Jill, did you know we're going to have a baby?" Audrey asked, leaning forward.

"Yes," Jill said. "It's such wonderful news." She turned to Caye and smiled weakly. "Do you have my cell phone? Could you call Rob? I want him to phone Dr. Scott and ask what the blood count means."

## 28

Rob talked to Dr. Scott Monday afternoon. "It doesn't mean anything definite," Rob told Jill and Caye when he got home.

Later, after Jill had fallen asleep, Rob told Caye that Dr. Scott had said the blood count was a bad sign. Caye knew that. She'd done enough research. She knew how fast and furious pancreatic cancer could move. She'd read the biographies on the Internet. Feeling good one week, dead the next. But she'd also read the biographies of people who were near death one week, better the next, and then fine two years later. Not many of those stories, granted, but a few. One woman even went on to have a baby.

That's what Caye wished for Jill. Hoped. Prayed. Wished. Pleaded.

But Caye was afraid that Jill was shutting down. She wasn't conversing. She spent her time painting or sleeping. She wasn't eating—only drinking juice and water, a few sips of broth and two bites of the custard Caye had made the day before.

Tuesday was a particularly hard day. Liam clung to Jill before nap time. In the late afternoon he stood beside her bed and jumped up and down. Caye heard Jill's frantic voice come over the intercom that they'd set up in her room. "Caye, Caye, I need you." Liam had wet his pants again for the third time that day.

Jill cried. "He'll never be potty trained. It will be my fault."

Hudson wasn't sleeping well. He wandered, scared, into Jill's room night after night and crawled up on the end of the bed. Jill cried about that, too. And the whites of her eyes were yellow again.

On Wednesday morning Caye sat in Dr. Scott's waiting room with Jill. Stephanie was watching the kids. It was Simon's first birthday—the plan was to have dinner and cake in the evening with just the two families.

It was also Andrew's last day of school. Nathan's last day of teaching had been the day before; he was finishing up grades and cleaning out his classroom.

A high school girl sat across from them in the waiting room. She wore a baseball cap. Caye was sick of cancer.

They were waiting for the results of Jill's MRI and her latest blood test. Jill had the scan and lab work done just after breakfast. They'd been waiting an hour to see the doctor. Caye felt wiped out—she could only imagine how exhausted Jill was. She wondered how the kids were doing with Stephanie.

Andrew was convinced that cancer was contagious and that Caye was going to get sick too. After breakfast, Audrey had decided she didn't want to go to Hudson and Liam's house. She wanted them to come to her house. "They can't, sweetie," Caye said. "We need to be there with Jill."

"Why?"

"To take care of her."

"Why can't she just take care of herself?"

Caye had frowned at Audrey, given her that shame-on-you look without meaning to. Audrey started to cry. "Our girl." Caye whispered Jill's pet name for Audrey as she picked up her daughter and held her tightly. Our girl was hurting. They were all hurting.

"Jill Rhone," the nurse called.

Caye stood up. Jill sat still. Caye looked at her friend—she was asleep.

"Jill," Caye said.

Jill slowly opened her eyes.

"Our turn."

"Where's Rob?" Dr. Scott asked as he entered the examination room.

"He had a conference call at work," Jill said.

The doctor sat down in the swivel chair. Jill eased her way onto the table. She wore sweatpants. She looked down at her belly. "I wish you were my OB instead of an oncologist," she said.

Dr. Scott smiled at her. "How are you feeling?"

"Not too hot. I'm sleepy most of the time. I couldn't take chemo on Monday. You know that."

Caye looked closely at the doctor. He looked uncomfortable.

"This is such a wicked cancer," he said. "First it exhibits hardly any symptoms—then it can progress so quickly."

"What have you found out?" Jill asked. *She wants to cut to the chase. Rob should have come.*

"Do you want it straightforward?"

Jill nodded.

"The blood count is worse than it was on Monday. The MRI shows that the cancer has also metastasized to your left lung."

Caye felt as if she'd been slugged in the stomach. The liver and now a lung.

"Now what?" Jill asked.

"When your count goes up, we can continue chemo."

Jill was silent. Caye wondered if she was dozing again.

"Jill?" the doctor asked.

She nodded.

"How's the pain?"

"Painful."

"Enough for a morphine pump?"

Jill shook her head.

She leaned on Caye as they left the office, their arms linked, their steps slow.

As Caye pulled out of the parking space, Jill looked at her intently. "We need more help."

"I'll call Rita," Caye responded.

"No. It's too hard on Rita. She doesn't know what to do. Besides, she has work."

They rode in silence for a few minutes.

"Rob's parents are in Houston for a missions conference that starts next week. His mom said they could come in two weeks."

"They'd come sooner if you wanted them to."

"They're the keynote speakers."

They rode along in silence for a few minutes.

"My parents would come to help," Caye finally said.

"Would they?"

*It's the right time,* Caye thought.

"There are things we should do," Jill said. "Like order a hospital bed. I should be in the living room—it'll be easier for everyone, including the boys."

"Are you going to call your mom?"

"I don't know if it matters. She said she'd call me back. She hasn't."

"It might make a difference—in the long run—to her," Caye answered.

Jill looked out the window. Caye could barely hear her words. "Rob and I need to talk to the boys."

Tears stung Caye's eyes. She reached across the seat and squeezed Jill's arm, her thin, bone-dry arm.

Jill didn't turn her head, didn't respond in any way.

Jill sat on the couch and listened to Caye in the kitchen.

Letting go was so hard. She was irritated with Caye for bringing up Marion. There was enough to take care of right now without feeling responsible for her mother, too.

She sipped the ice water that Caye had left on the end table. It tasted like metal. She felt like a machine falling apart piece by piece. Hardly human.

*Hardly human.* That was what she used to call Marion twenty years ago.

"What do I do, God?" she asked in a whisper. "I really don't think Marion has anything to offer me."

Hardly human.

Jill thought of Gideon throwing out the fleece. "How about if I just call her, okay? I'll call her and see what happens from there."

Caye had planned Simon's birthday dinner. She asked Nathan to stop on the way home and buy a salmon to grill. She asked Rob to pick up the cake at the bakery and a gift for Simon at the drugstore at the same time he got Jill's prescriptions. Caye was too tired to make a cake. And she was tired of birthdays. Years from now, when she looked back on this time, would she remember the birthdays? Audrey's, then Liam's, now Simon's, and Hudson's next week? *Why did Jill have all of her babies at the same time of year?* This month of all months. All these celebrations of life amidst the pain and suffering and threat of death. All these birthdays and a new baby, growing, dividing cell by cell while Jill's cancer did the same.

Andrew was home from school. A friend's mom had dropped him off. Caye felt guilty for not being there to pick him up the last day, but she didn't want to leave Jill alone. And Jill was right; it was harder to find people to come in to help now. She'd called Rita and Gwen. Both were busy. She didn't bother calling Joya.

Caye sat at Jill's mahogany table. Andrew, Hudson, and Audrey were playing in the backyard. Caye could hear Scout barking. Jill slept on the couch.

Caye tried to pray. "Heal her," she pleaded out loud. "Please heal her." She struggled with God, wrestled. All she could pray were those three words. "Please heal her."

*What will Rob do? What will the boys do? Why would God choose not to heal her?* Caye felt frantic. Her face was twisted in pain. She buried her head in her arms on the cold, bare tabletop.

❧

"I called Marion this afternoon," Jill said. "She's coming tomorrow."

Rob froze with his fork, loaded with salmon, in midair. Caye put her glass down with a clatter against the glass tabletop.

"Where will she stay?" Rob asked.

"I think she should stay at Caye and Nathan's."

Rob's eyes got big. "Sweetie," Rob said, "maybe Nathan wouldn't like that."

"Mom and Dad are coming too," Caye said, looking at Nathan and then at Rob. "We need more help."

"How about if they all stay at Caye's and Caye and Nathan stay here?" Jill interjected.

Rob looked at Nathan.

"It would be the best thing for the boys. They need Caye around—they don't need Marion," Jill continued.

"What do you guys think?" Rob looked from Nathan to Caye and back to Nathan.

"It might work," Nathan said.

Caye nodded.

Simon sat in his highchair and squished a piece of garlic bread in his fist.

Jill took a bite of salmon. It had no taste. She tried the watermelon. It felt good in her mouth but was hard to swallow. She took a sip of broth from the traveling mug Caye was constantly putting in front of her. *This feels like a Last Supper.*

The kids were playing house under the wisteria. Jill moved to the lounger and pulled her afghan around her. She knew she was drifting, moving away.

She listened to the children play. Audrey was the wife and Hudson the husband. Liam was the baby. Andrew, who didn't really want to be playing, was Hudson's boss.

Jill thought about all the positive thinking she'd done—she'd imagined her body healing, the cancer cells shrinking, the good cells taking over. She'd visualized next Christmas, another moms-and-kids' trip to Disneyland—this time with Simon, too. She'd created a trip to Paris with Rob in her mind. Imagined the boys in high school and graduating from college, getting married, having kids someday. She'd imagined it all, over and over, during the last seven weeks.

Jill turned her head toward Caye clapping. Nathan was helping Simon walk. The baby held on to just one finger. Simon laughed and swung his other arm as he marched along. Nathan slowly slipped his fingers from Simon's grasp and the baby kept on going.

Jill smiled. "Rob, grab the camera." Rob was already to the kitchen door.

Simon fell.

"Up you go, big guy," Nathan said. They started again.

Rob hurried down the deck stairs with the camera and began filming. Simon fell on his bottom again, clapped his hands together once, laughed, and got back up. He turned and headed to Jill. Rob turned the camera on Jill and caught her full-face smile. "Come on, baby," she laughed. "Come to Mommy."

Simon swung his arms, his diapered bottom covered by purple shorts bobbed below his orange-striped shirt. He reached the lounge, and Jill slowly pulled him beside her. She smelled his sweaty hair, sucking it in against her lips, against her mouth, like cotton candy ready to melt. Simon sat on the cushion and clapped his hands. She wanted to breathe him in, breathe him back inside her, to when she was well, when they were all safe. *God, don't take me from my baby, from my boys.* If she died, Simon would never remember her. Neither would Liam. Only Hudson.

She struggled to inhale as she looked up into the video camera that partially covered her husband's face, and then past Rob to Caye and on to Nathan. She looked back at Rob; he put the camera down. They were all crying. Tears were streaming down their cheeks.

*They know I'm going to die. This is the moment.*

"Why are you all crying?" Audrey asked.

"Because Simon just learned how to walk," Jill said, wiping her own eyes and then pulling Audrey to her. Rob, Nathan, and Caye all walked over to the lounger. Rob hugged her, pulling in Audrey and Simon. Nathan patted her shoulder. Caye sat on the other side. Liam, Hudson, and Andrew all milled around their feet. Jill wished they could stay that way in the garden, all together, all connected. She imagined how they all looked—the image of love and friendship and faith. Of hanging on and letting go.

That night a full moon rose outside the bedroom window. Jill opened the curtains so she could see it in the night sky from her bed. A pirate moon, Jill thought. A pirate moon for the boys.

She thought about the life she thought she'd always have: the bed-and-breakfast after the kids were grown, the grandchildren, the trips. All these years she'd been determined not to get the pan-cre-at-ic can-cer. But even in her worst fears, when she remembered her mother's dire warnings, she thought, if she did get it, that she'd be in her sixties or seventies, late fifties at the earliest. By then, surely they'd have a cure. If not, her children would be raised. She'd be a grandmother.

She and Rob had talked with Hudson and Liam as they put them to bed. They all sat on the bottom bunk and whispered because Simon was asleep. "Mommy's really sick," Rob said.

"I know," Hudson said.

"We're still praying God will heal her," Rob added.

"I know," Hudson said. "When is God going to do that?"

"Yeah. When?" Liam echoed.

"We don't know," Jill answered. "Sometimes God heals people on earth. Sometimes he heals them by allowing them to die."

"To die?" Hudson asked.

The conversation was harder than Jill thought it would be.

"We don't know," Rob said. "But Mommy's sick. Really sick. We want you to know that. She's been getting sicker this last week."

"When are you going to die?" Liam asked.

Jill looked at Rob. He looked horrified. Jill smiled. Liam started to laugh.

Hudson began to cry. "Who will take care of us?"

Rob pulled Hudson onto his lap. "I will."

"Who else?"

"Auntie Caye will help," Jill added.

"Are you really going to die?" Hudson was sobbing.

"Hudson, I don't know. I honestly don't know."

"When?" Liam asked again and started to giggle.

"That was horrible," Rob said after the boys finally slept.

"It was okay," Jill said. "They're little kids. Liam doesn't under-stand. Hudson's starting to. It makes me so sad."

"I'm going for a run," Rob said. "I need to get out of here."

She watched the moon climb in the sky.

She heard Rob come in the back door and head to the bathroom. She heard the water in the shower.

Relieved, she bade the moon good night and closed her eyes.

She felt Rob's hand against her arm, groping for her hand. She moved it toward him. He held it gently. Sometime in the night she was aware that he was sitting up in bed. *Maybe he's watching the moon,* she thought. But she didn't wake enough to look into his face.

*All things.* She thought of the verse she'd learned so many years ago in junior high group—the first portion of Scripture that she memorized. "I can do all things through Him who strengthens me."

*Even die?* She drifted back to sleep.

❧

Rob called Caye in the morning. "I'm staying home," he said.

"Oh," Caye answered. What would she do all day? She wondered. Quickly she answered herself—take Andrew to school, get the house put together for Marion and Bev and Hank. Wash the sheets. Buy some groceries.

"When will you be over?" he continued.

She shifted her thoughts again. She'd get the sheets in the wash. "How about if I come in an hour?"

"Okay."

"How's Jill?"

"I think she's giving up." Rob paused. "She thinks we should call hospice."

Caye walked to the kitchen window and looked out on her yard. The grass was browning. The garden looked parched. She needed to water before she left. "Then we should. She's the one who knows."

"Well, I can't do it," Rob said. "Marion's flying in at 11:30. I'll go get her."

Caye dropped Andrew off at school, rushed back, stripped the beds, started the washer, loaded the dishwasher, and threw a few changes of clothes for the whole family in a sports bag. She thought of the baby growing inside of her. Her bittersweet blessing. Her waistband was tight. She needed to buy maternity shorts.

❧

The hospital bed arrived right after Rob left for the airport. They set it up against the bay window. Jill took the clipboard from the delivery man and signed her name. The man grunted and headed out the door.

Caye made the bed and brought pillows in while Jill sat on the couch. All five of the kids piled on—even Simon, with Andrew's help—and jumped up and down. Hudson pushed a button, and the bed rose. Liam squealed. Caye started to stop them. Hudson pushed the button again.

"Don't," Jill said as she sat on the sofa. "They're christening it."

Caye sat back down on the couch.

Jill knew Caye thought she was being too lenient. Or would have. Maybe those things didn't matter now. Jill looked at the bed. She thought of her father. She wondered how much he'd suffered. It was a week before Christmas, right before vacation started. Jill woke up one morning and he was gone, gone from the daybed in the living room, gone from her life.

"They took him away during the night," Marion had said. "He passed on."

For years Jill wondered if "they" would take her away some night too. It wasn't until she was nine or ten that she understood what "passed on" meant. It wasn't until her late teen years that she fully grieved over her father's death.

## 29

Rob and Marion arrived just minutes after Hank and Bev pulled up. Jill raised the hospital bed to a sitting position. Hank shook Rob's hand vigorously and then gave Jill a quick kiss on the forehead. "I need me some coffee," he said and headed to the kitchen. Caye followed him, while Bev sat beside Jill and spoke softly.

Marion stood at the foot of the bed and stared at her daughter.

"Hi, Mother," Jill said quietly. "I'm glad you came."

"It's like night and day, how she looks," Hank said to Caye. "When were all of you over? Three weeks ago?"

"Two weeks ago, Daddy," Caye answered pulling a mug out of the cupboard. "All I have is decaf."

"You're drinking decaf?"

She poured the coffee and handed it to her dad.

"Oh, that's right, because of the baby. Your mama told me. Congratulations."

Caye had called Bev the night before and told her the news, asking her mom not to make a big deal about it when they came.

Caye poured another cup of coffee for herself and sat down beside her father. She missed the caffeine. She'd had headaches all week, but she figured she'd already ingested more than she should have for the entire pregnancy. She was limiting herself to just one cup of regular each morning.

She'd fed the kids macaroni and cheese for lunch. She had no idea what she'd feed the grownups. Summer had called yesterday evening and backed out of the meal she'd promised to bring. Rita hadn't called in two days. Caye hadn't heard from Joya since Sunday.

To Caye's surprise, Gwen had called and asked what she could do.

Caye said the grocery shopping needed to be done. Gwen said she'd be by for the list early in the afternoon.

There wasn't much food in the house—just a little bit of leftover salmon and rice from the night before.

"Did you and Mom have lunch?" Caye asked her dad.

"You know your mom," Hank said. "She packed a lunch for all of us to eat here—enough for everyone. Even made those Jell-O things for the kids. That's why we were late." He took a swallow of coffee. "This is pretty good for decaf."

Rob walked into the kitchen. "That bed looks pretty fancy," he said to Caye. "I hate it."

"Why don't you take Marion over to our house?" Caye said to her mother after lunch. "To rest."

"I want to go," Audrey whined. "I want to go with Grandma."

Bev and Hank ended up taking Andrew and Hudson, too. They all piled into the Suburban. Hank drove. He had a big smile on his face. "I could get used to this," he said. "This is quite a rig."

Rob took the little boys upstairs for their naps and then went into his office to make some business calls.

Jill patted the side of the bed. "Sit down," she said to Caye. "You're on your feet too much."

Caye sat. Jill scooted over. Caye leaned back on the bed. Jill had it tilted just slightly.

"Thanks for everything you're doing. You've been more than a sister to me."

"Thanks," Caye said as sadness flowed through her. "And ditto." *Please, don't say any more.*

Jill took a deep, ragged breath.

There was a faint knock on the door.

Caye swung her feet off the bed. She peered through the lace curtain as she walked to the door. It was Gwen.

Jill heard Caye say, "Hello, Gwen." Had Gwen come to confront her for her sin, for her lack of faith, for her cancer? For getting worse?

"Have you come to chastise me?" Jill asked Gwen, who stood at the side of the bed.

"For what?" Gwen asked.

"For not getting better."

"No," she said slowly, "I came to do your grocery shopping." Caye pulled the list out of her pocket.

"I don't believe you're going to keep getting worse," Gwen said, turning toward Jill. Gwen took a deep breath. "I still believe you're going to get better, but if you don't, I want you to know that I've been blessed by you. I really have."

"Thanks," Jill said and reached out and squeezed Gwen's hand. She suppressed a giggle as she thought of Gwen's face covered with the dots from the permanent red marker. What if she got better? Would Gwen still want her to know that she'd been a blessing?

The giggle turned into a choke. She missed Joya; she wished it were Joya saying those words to her.

Gwen bent down and kissed Jill's cheek. "I'd better go," she said. Caye walked out on the front porch with Gwen.

There had been other times when Joya chose not to come around. She kept her distance after both Liam and Simon were born. Thomas had visited right away, bringing Louise, but not Joya.

None of them had come for Jill's traditional New Year's Eve party last year, for the big millennium party. It was another time Jill felt that Joya had drifted away from them. "I think she really expects something catastrophic to happen," Rob said.

Jill understood Joya's fears. Jill was a little embarrassed to admit, and had only told Caye, that she had a drum of water in the basement and enough food to last several weeks. There was no reason not to plan for a disaster. It could be an earthquake as easily as a worldwide economic crash, she told herself. But no kind of fear would keep her away from her friends, from the people she loved.

The evening of the New Year's Eve party, Summer joked that if anything bad happened they could all move in with Jill and Rob. Jill, honestly, was warmed by the thought.

Rob was tense about the possible ramifications of Y2K on his work. He was anxious to know if all the programs he'd updated over the last year would come through intact. He breathed easier as 9 P.M., 10 P.M., and 11 P.M. passed. The East Coast, Midwest, and Mountain Time accounts were all secure. Only the West Coast clients remained.

Jill poured champagne for the toast. As midnight struck they all raised their glasses in a communal toast. "Kiss the person you love the most—," Jill said as Rob's cell phone rang. Rob snatched it up and headed to his office, taking the stairs two at a time. *I must have been off a minute or two on the toast,* Jill thought, as she stood alone without a husband to kiss, as the group greeted the New Year.

The call was from a Sacramento insurance company whose software had crashed. Rob had it fixed, via phone calls, by the next morning. "It wasn't that big a deal," he said. "They had a backup. I almost felt like their systems guy was trying to make me look bad." Even though he said it wasn't a big deal, Rob took it to heart. It added to his discontentment with his job. He started talking about moving back to Argentina, saying he wanted more adventure in his life.

Jill wanted anything but adventure. She wanted her stomach to settle down. She wanted a good night's sleep. She wanted Liam to sit still. She wanted life to be the way it had been before Rob was stressed out by his job, before she felt sick all the time.

❧

Caye slung the near-empty gallon of milk into the refrigerator. Yesterday Gwen was sure that Caye had made a mistake on the grocery list. "Surely the kids wouldn't go through three gallons of milk before it goes bad," she said as she carried in the sacks of groceries. "And all this food! Are you throwing a party every night?"

"Not just every night," Caye answered sarcastically. "All night long."

She walked into the living room to check on Jill. She was asleep. Her breathing was ragged. It came and went—sometimes her breathing was smooth and peaceful, other times it rattled. Simon sat on the floor by the bed and tore a page out of a *Family Fun* magazine. He looked at Caye with an impish smile. Scout was sprawled by the front door.

Caye felt so unprepared. So inadequate.

"We already cleaned your house," Bev called out to Caye as she swept through Jill's back door, Marion in tow. "Now we're going to clean Jill's. But first Marion needs to talk to her. You and I should go to the family room—with the kids."

Caye stood and looked at her mother in wonder and concern. How had she gotten Marion to do anything? What did Marion want to talk with Jill about?

She scooped up Simon and headed down the basement stairs. The three older children were playing with LEGOs—Liam was zoned out on the couch sucking his thumb and watching a *Winnie the Pooh* video.

"She's an odd egg," Bev whispered to Caye as she pulled the stair door closed.

Caye nodded her head. "I know."

"She has a bizarre story to tell Jill."

"Really?" Caye asked, thinking about Marion's breast cancer. *Could it be worse than that?* They sat down at Jill's workbench, out of earshot of the children.

"If it's hereditary, Jill got it from her father and her mother."

"From both sides of the family?"

"Not exactly," Bev said.

"Then what do you mean?"

"There's basically just one side to Jill's family." Bev shook her head, closing one eye as if it might help her think more clearly. "No, that's not entirely true. There's Marion's mother's side. And William's mother's side. And then their father's side."

"Mom, you're not making sense," Caye said, shaking her head.

❧

"This is the secret that I never told you," Marion said to Jill, standing above the bed. Her gray, short hair curled a little around her ears. She wore tan pants and a bright blue short-sleeve blouse that accented her eyes.

"I was eight when my father died from pancreatic cancer. He was in his second marriage. I knew that his mother, my grandmother, lived in the next town over, but I never met her.

"I lived with my mother until she died. I was twenty-six then. I'd worked in a men's store—selling hats and trousers and shoes—since I was eighteen. The fall after my mother's death, a good-looking man in his forties started coming into the shop. He was from Chicago. He bought expensive shirts and shoes, always carefully chosen. Sometimes he would come in several times to ask questions and look around before he made a purchase."

Marion paused a moment. Jill nodded her head. She knew the man was her father.

"He took a liking to me. I was flattered. It seemed, after a few weeks, that he was coming in to see me and just buying clothes as an excuse."

Jill thought of her mother, how she might have looked nearly forty-five years ago. Tall and thin. Dark hair. Blue eyes flashing with a quick, self-conscious smile.

"I didn't know the stranger's name. He always paid with cash, and I didn't ask. One day the shop owner said 'Hello, William,' when the man came in. William. I liked that. William was my father's name, although everyone called him Bill.

"A week or two later the shop owner asked me how long my 'kin' would be in town. He asked it an odd way. I didn't know what he was talking about, so I didn't answer.

"When William came in the next day, I asked him when he would be going back to Chicago. He said he wasn't sure. His grandmother had died, and he was settling her estate. He was staying at the hotel close to the store while he put her house in order. Said it was too sad for him to stay at the old place."

Jill moved the hospital bed into a sitting position. She patted the side of the bed for Marion to sit down. Marion pulled the dining room chair around from the end of the bed and sat down.

"My grandmother, whom I had never met, had just died too. At least that's what my busybody neighbor had told me. I'd seen my grandmother just one time. This neighbor attended her church. She told me exactly what my grandmother looked like. I visited the church—just once. I sat in the balcony and stared down at the back of my grandmother's head. She wore a big white hat with a purple ribbon. The message was on forgiveness. I was so disgusted that I left before the closing prayer.

"The next day when William came into the store to buy a handkerchief, I was nervous, practically shaking, as I asked him his last name.

"It was Linsey." Marion paused.

Jill waited for her to go on. What had she missed? This seemed to be the climax of Marion's story. What was Marion saying?

"My last name was Linsey too." Marion looked at Jill for a reaction.

"I thought it was Morgan," Jill said.

"That was my middle name, from my mother's maiden name."

"You were cousins?"

"No," Marion paused.

*Go on,* Jill thought.

"Siblings. He was my half-brother."

Jill tilted her head away from her mother.

"Are you serious?" she whispered.

Marion continued as if Jill hadn't spoken.

"We ran off together—it was an overnight decision. William gave his cousin, our cousin, Ada the old place, and he took the money from the estate and we headed to California. I had felt so cheated by my father's family. I finally was getting what I deserved—half the money, a new start, and the only son. It all began with such intensity, such passion, such abandon, but within a year we essentially lived like the brother and sister that we were."

"Essentially?" Jill asked. "Except for me?"

"Except for you."

Marion paused again.

Jill's head ached. She remembered the shame she felt as a child, shame from Marion that she could never comprehend. Pain shot through her abdomen. She struggled to breathe.

"Ada told us not to have children. Her mother, our father's sister, had died from pancreatic cancer too, just after Ada was born.

'You'll curse your kids,' she said. That was all she said when William told her we were running away. I thought her advice was well given, and besides, I never wanted children." Marion looked away from Jill.

"It turns out your father did. I thought I was going through the change before I figured out I was pregnant. I knew of a doctor in L.A. who could have taken care of things. Your father made me promise I wouldn't. He started bringing home maternity dresses and things for a nursery, all carefully chosen, top quality. It put a spark in our lives." Marion looked back toward Jill and made eye contact.

Jill shook her head, but her mother kept talking. All these years she wouldn't talk; now she wouldn't stop.

They led a quiet life, Marion explained. William sold real estate; Marion kept his books. When Jill was born, William, now in his late fifties, doted on her. He started buying rentals "to pay for Jill's college."

Jill thought of her father. She remembered the smell of his pipe, the smell of his polished wingtip shoes, the texture of his felt hat. She remembered his blue eyes. The same as Marion's. The same as hers.

"Then your father came down with the flu. Finally he went to the doctor. The doctor told him to stop drinking, said it was his liver. William stopped. But he was still sick. I told the doctor to test for the cancer. I was right."

Jill thought of her father on the daybed, writhing in pain. She thought of the graveside service. Just a handful of people—a few neighbors, a few Realtors from his office.

"I was petrified," Marion said. "How was I going to support you?"

Marion looked down at the floor. "I know I wasn't a good mother. William would have gone to your games, your art shows, tucked you in at night, been home when you got home from school. He never would have talked you into getting an abortion. I'm sorry," Marion said quietly.

"Pardon?"

"I'm sorry."

"You're sorry?"

Marion nodded. She took another breath and rushed on.

"I didn't call the doctor when I found my lump. A month later you called from Argentina and told me you were pregnant—with Hudson. When you told me you were due in mid June, I figured out you were four months along. I knew you'd waited that long to tell me because you thought I wouldn't be pleased.

"But I was pleased. I called the doctor that day and insisted on an appointment immediately.

"I knew you'd be a good parent. Like your dad."

"But you didn't want me to have kids?"

"Not at first. I kept thinking about Ada's mother dying, coming down with pancreatic cancer not too long after Ada was born. After you were pregnant with Hudson—of course I wanted you to have him—I just didn't want you to keep having more."

Jill closed her eyes.

"If I had told you sooner, that you had a double genetic dose of it, would you have taken me seriously about the cancer? Not had more kids?"

"Do you think I came down with it because I had Liam and Simon?" Jill's eyes flew open wide.

"I don't know."

"I would have been miserable without my kids. All those years you droned on and on about pan-cre-at-ic can-cer. I decided, after the abortion, that I wasn't going to listen to you, that I was going to live my life the way I wanted." Jill closed her eyes. Her eyelids felt thin and papery. "I have no regrets—except that I didn't have more of a relationship with you."

"But what if the boys get it?" Marion asked.

"Don't ask that," Jill commanded. "They're never going to get it."

"When Marion told me her story," Bev said, "I told her to tell Jill. That Jill deserved to know."

*What if it's too much for Jill to handle?* Caye wondered. The whole story made Caye feel unsettled, icky. Why had she been so sure that Jill needed to patch things up with her mother?

"You should go up and check on Jill," Bev said to Caye. "Marion's had enough time."

The video was over, and Liam was bouncing on the couch. He somersaulted off and fell on the floor.

"I'll get him," Bev said, before Liam let out a scream. "Go up to Jill."

Caye found Marion sitting silently, staring at her daughter. Jill's eyes were closed.

"Is she asleep?" Caye asked.

Marion nodded.

❧

*They were traveling, riding along through an orchard, in a pickup. Hank's pickup. Caye was driving. Jill turned to her and said, "I have cancer."*

*She felt foolish as she said it. The words sounded so improbable. And besides, she felt fine.*

*Caye turned toward her. But it wasn't Caye. It was William.*

*"I'm sorry," he said. "So sorry."*

*"Who will take care of Mommy?" she asked her father.*

## 30

"I'm going for a walk," Caye said to Bev in her most nonchalant, everything-is-fine voice. "Jill's asleep. So are the little boys. Can you keep an eye on things?"

She crossed the street and headed toward the park, past the neighbors' towering cedar tree, past the perfect Craftsman house that she often dreamed of buying, but knew they never could afford. She was walking downhill, pumping her arms, keeping up a furious pace.

She could feel the sweat bead on her brow, feel it begin to collect on the backs of her knees.

She cut down to High Street and then on to Winburn Way, swinging around to the front of the park. She was sure she'd restore some order to the swirl in her head if she could walk the familiar paths, pound out the churning emotions and thoughts.

Purposefully she walked under the towering "tree of heaven" planted by a homesick Chinese cook 150 years ago. Homesick. That was how she felt. She was mourning the world she'd lived in for the last four years, grieving its loss. There. She'd acknowledged it. Or almost.

Jill was dying.

She stopped briefly at the first pond. How many times had she and Jill and the kids fed the ducks and swans? Sat on the bench? Chased Liam away from the water?

She couldn't stay. She hurried along the pebbled walkway, eyes ahead to the bridge, the creek, the dirt trail just beyond the playground.

"Caye."

It was a familiar voice.

"Caye!"

Joya stood in the middle of the playground. She began to walk away from Louise, who sat on a swing, toward Caye.

"I was just thinking about you and Jill," Joya said. "I was praying for Jill as I pushed the swing."

"Hi," Caye said, standing with her arms at her side.

"I dropped Thomas off at the college. He's finishing up his grades. I need to go get him in a few minutes. I thought we might stop and see Jill on our way home."

"Her mom's there," Caye said stupidly, thinking she should say her parents were at Jill's too. But she didn't.

"Oh," Joya said. "That's good. Things always seem tense between Jill and her mom. Are they working things out?"

Caye looked at her blankly.

Joya kicked at the dirt with her blue canvas shoe, studied the ground for a moment and then looked back at Caye.

"Look, I know you're angry with me."

"Mom," Louise called. "Push me!"

Joya ignored her. "I know you think I'm wrong about Jill's healing."

Caye crossed her arms.

"I think," Joya said, "that you're part of the problem. I think that your spiritual immaturity has hindered Jill's healing."

Caye could feel the red splotches forming on her neck.

"Mom!" Louise called as she stopped the swing. "You said you'd push me."

"I have to be honest," Joya said. "I don't think you've sincerely believed Jill will be healed. I think you—and Nathan and Rob—have focused on statistics. On what you've read. On what you've found on the Internet."

Caye's mouth opened—as if she might have something to say. It didn't matter. Joya continued, "It's a great sin to lack faith."

"It's a great sin to lack love," Caye retorted and started walking past Joya. It was a cheap shot, Caye knew it.

"Caye," Joya snapped, grabbing her arm. Caye felt the fingers around the flesh of her biceps. "I wanted to talk with you, away from Jill. She's dying," Joya said, letting go of Caye's arm.

Caye pulled back.

"I used to work on a cancer ward, before I met Thomas. I talked to Rob this morning. He doesn't think so, but from what he told me, she's dying. In a day or two it will be too late."

Caye remembered that Jill loved Joya. She couldn't fathom why.

"Joya," Caye said, "I think that your theology is twisted."

"What do you know about theology?"

"Mom. Push me!" It was Louise. Caye was finding the girl as annoying as her mother. Louise was too old to be so demanding.

"What do you know about being a friend?" Another cheap shot.

"Mom!"

"Stop it, Louise!"

Caye took a step around Joya and kept on walking, nearly running. Her face was hot. Her heart raced. Her hands tingled.

"When's your baby due?" Joya called out after Caye.

Caye stopped and turned.

"I know you're pregnant. I knew on Sunday. When are you due?"

Caye turned away again and kept on walking.

"I hate her, God," she whispered. "I'm sorry. I know I'm not supposed to, but I do."

*First Joya blamed Jill, then Rob, and now me. And Nathan. Who's next? Simon?*

Caye stretched her stride longer.

She would pound the anger out, the anger that was wedged so deep.

Every step reminded her of Jill. They often walked in the late afternoons during the summers through the park and then up to the Shakespeare Festival grounds to watch the Renaissance dancers before the plays began. They'd sit on the grass in the courtyard and listen to the harpsichord music and watch the dancers in their peasant costumes.

"I was born in the wrong century," Jill would often sigh. It was an often-repeated conversation. Jill thought living in the seventeenth century sounded like a lot of fun.

"Without hot water? Without toilets? Without washing machines?" Caye would ask.

Jill would laugh. "I could live without all of those," she'd say. "I'd paint. Learn to play the harp. Tell the gardener what to do."

It took awhile before Caye realized that when Jill imagined living during the Renaissance period, she saw herself as nobility, while Caye saw herself as a scullery maid.

The creek rushed over the rocks to Caye's right. The undeveloped hillside rose to her left. She swung around to the upper pond and surveyed the water for the ducks. They were huddled in the middle on the little island. Caye hurried under the branches of the mulberry tree. "Here we go 'round the mulberry bush, the mulberry bush, the mulberry bush; here we go 'round the mulberry bush, so early in the morning," they'd all chanted so many times. She dashed across the street.

*Heal her. I know you can. I have faith. I have love—except for Joya. But I could learn to love her. I promise not to hate her.*

She wrestled with God. He had her in a horrible hold.

She dashed along the steppingstones to the top of the Japanese garden and sat on the bench.

*Heal her.*

No response. No peace.

She slapped her hands against her thighs. She thought of the mourners in the Bible who beat themselves, beat their breasts. She understood. She ran her hands through her hair, clasping them together at the back of her head, and pulled her chin toward her chest. She felt such grief.

She wanted to curl up on the bench.

Instead, she stood and headed across the lawn to the Sycamore Grove.

How many times had she and Jill played hide-and-seek with the kids in the rows of perfectly aligned trees? She loved the grove. Such order. Such predictability. She stopped for a moment and leaned against a tree in the heart of the grove.

*I will take care of Jill.* The words came to her clearly from inside. Not *I will heal Jill.* Not *I will give her back,* but *I will take care of Jill. And I will take care of Rob and the boys. And you. And Nathan. And Andrew and Audrey.*

She slid down the trunk of the sycamore tree, her back bumping along the puzzle-shaped bark, until she sat on the patchy grass around the roots.

*And the Fellowship. And Joya.*

She nodded her head.

She felt a measure of peace. She sat for a few minutes. *And the baby? Will you take care of my baby?*

*And the baby,* answered the voice.

She rose to her feet, left the grove, and headed to the marble Perozzi Fountain.

She climbed the stairs above the fountain, out of the park, up the hill toward Jill's house.

*Joya went to Jill's,* Caye thought with alarm. *She went after I left her in the park.* Caye started to run and then stopped. It was too hot. She was too out of shape. Her head hurt.

*I will take care of Jill. And Joya.*

She walked slowly the rest of the way.

Joya and Thomas sat on Jill's porch. Thomas stood as Caye approached the steps.

"Did you talk to Jill?" Caye asked. She was surprised at how calm her voice sounded.

"She's asleep," Joya said. "We've only been here a few minutes."

"We wanted to talk with you," Thomas said as he sat back down on the wicker settee.

Joya looked quickly from Thomas to Caye and then back to Thomas.

Caye heard Louise's voice from the side yard and then heard Audrey shout, "Don't hide where I can't find you!"

"Joya told me what she said to you in the park." Thomas clasped his hands over one knee. "This is difficult, but it's time that I speak up. Joya is entitled to believe what she perceives as truth. I want you to know that I don't believe that Jill has cancer because of any sin that she, Rob, or you committed. Nor do I believe that Jill hasn't been healed because of a lack of faith."

Joya walked to the end of the porch.

"I'm afraid that I haven't made this clear to the rest of the group—but I will. I talked to Rob just now. I'll call the others."

Caye nodded.

"And I'll talk with Jill when I can."

He stood.

"I feel," he said, "that my leadership has let the group down. That I should have addressed this long ago."

Joya walked down the side steps of the porch. "Come on, Louise," she called.

"Thanks," Caye said.

Thomas smiled. "Congratulations on your baby."

Caye nodded.

He lumbered slowly down the stairs and headed to the car behind Joya and Louise.

❧

Rob sat beside the bed with a cup of broth. "I'll feed you," he said.

Jill shook her head.

"You have to eat."

She shook her head again.

Hudson ran through the room, his feet pounding on the hardwood floor. The room shook.

"Hudson! Stop running." Rob shot his son an angry look.

Hudson turned and scowled.

"Mommy," he said, turning away from Rob, "my birthday is tomorrow. Have you planned my party?"

"What do you want, sweetie?" Jill's voice was soft and watery.

"A party. I want you to throw me a party. A pirate party."

Caye walked into the room carrying Simon. "What did I hear about a party?"

"Hudson wants a pirate party," Jill said.

"Ooh. Good choice, big guy," Caye said. "Do you want a pirate ship for your cake?"

Hudson nodded and skipped out of the room smiling.

"Caye, tell her she has to eat," Rob said. He had stayed home from work to take Jill to chemo.

"It's up to her."

"We have the appointment today. She should go to her appointment. She needs to eat first."

"I can't," Jill said. "I can't go."

"You're giving up?"

"Rob," Caye said.

Rob shot her a stay-out-of-it look.

"Go call Dr. Scott," Jill whispered. "Ask him what we should do. Tell him I can't eat. Tell him I can't go over to Medford. It's too hard. Tell him my stools are light-colored. Tell him my skin looks like I used fake tan lotion. Tell him my pain is really bad."

Rob stood abruptly. The broth sloshed out of the mug onto his hand. He turned and hurried into the kitchen.

"Every couple of minutes he's in here with food or water," Jill said.

"He's scared," Caye said.

"I know. And exhausted. He was out here on the couch all night. I kept him up."

"You two need some time. I'll take all the kids to the park. And the grandmas. You can have the house to yourselves."

✲

"What did Dr. Scott say?" Jill asked.

Rob had been in his office for more than half an hour. Caye, the kids, and grandmas had been gone fifteen minutes. Hank had stayed at Caye's, and Nathan had gone over for some peace and quiet.

"He said to call hospice," Rob said. Jill noticed the roughness in his voice. "We need more help."

Jill heard his words. She felt relieved.

"You've begun the process." Rob sat in the chair beside the bed.

"Process?"

"Of dying." Rob took a deep breath. "The white stools. The jaundice. Both show that your liver has shut down. Not eating or drinking. All of those are signs."

Jill was silent.

Rob continued. "I asked if I should bring you back to the hospital. Dr. Scott said only if you wanted to."

She shook her head.

"That's what I told him." Rob started to stand up. "He's prescribing a morphine pump."

Jill nodded. "Stay," she said. He sat back down.

She reached for his hand. "I haven't given up."

"I know."

"Joya thinks that I have."

"Don't worry about Joya."

"I was afraid you thought I had too."

Rob let go of her hand and rubbed the heels of his hands over his eyes. "I don't know what to think. I don't think you've given up. I just can't understand it."

"God could still heal me. I could still be one of the few who are healed."

"I know," Rob said. "I believe it."

"Pray for me? And the boys?"

Rob squeezed her hand.

"And you. Pray for us now?"

Rob prayed a simple prayer—for healing, for their children, for himself. He prayed that they wouldn't grow bitter, that they would look to God. After he said, "Amen," he turned toward Jill and stroked her protruding cheekbone. "He'll heal us all," he said, "in one way or another."

Jill's heart ached for Rob. Her arms ached for her babies.

"You should go call hospice," she said.

"I already did," he answered. "A nurse can come out today. This afternoon."

"I wish we hadn't canceled Fellowship yesterday," Jill said.

"Why?"

"Because I want to see them. And they're not coming around."

"They went ahead and met at Gwen and John's yesterday," Rob said.

"Really? Why?"

"To pray for you."

"How do you know?"

"I called Thomas after I talked with Dr. Scott."

❧

"She's right here." It was Caye's voice.

Jill turned her head.

"This is the hospice nurse," Caye said. "Helen."

Jill smiled. "Caye, could you go get Rob?"

The nurse asked about Jill's fluid intake, urinating, and bowel movements. She jotted down that Jill hadn't had anything to eat since Thursday night—only broth and juice to drink. She asked about pain. She asked about family, about the kids, about Jill's parents. She put down her pen when Jill said her father had died twenty-nine years ago of pancreatic cancer.

"Really?"

"And my mother had breast cancer five years ago. She survived."

The nurse picked her pen back up and jotted down more notes.

"Have you left messages for your boys?"

"Paintings. I did a watercolor for each of them." She thought of the paintings down in the basement. She had asked Caye to have them framed. She hadn't finished Caye's yet. She hadn't painted in all the forget-me-nots.

"Have you considered writing them messages?"

"I hadn't thought about that," Jill said.

"You could dictate them," Helen said. "Have your husband or friend write it out if that's easier."

Jill nodded.

"Some mothers choose to create a mommy basket," Helen continued. "They put in scarves, sweatshirts, favorite books, costume jewelry. Items their children can pick up and hold and play with. Items that will bring comfort."

Jill nodded again. She was thankful Caye was listening too. She looked at Rob.

"This is so hard," he said.

Helen walked around the bed to set up the morphine pump. Jill dozed again.

Caye and Rob stood with Helen on the porch.

"What happens when she gets better?" Rob asked.

"Then I'll stop coming," Helen said.

"Do you think she'll get better?" Rob asked, his voice lower.

Helen shook her head. "Her hands are cold. Her body is shutting down. Pancreatic cancer can be fast and furious."

"How much longer?" Rob's voice cracked as he asked it. Caye put her arm around him.

"Not long. A week, maybe. A couple of weeks at the very most."

Rob nodded. He sat down in the wicker chair on the porch. Caye walked with Helen to the car and thought of Joya's prediction of a couple of days. "I'll come by tomorrow," Helen said. "Call the office if you need me sooner, and they'll page me. Keep the morphine going. I know Jill doesn't like it, but it's the best thing."

Helen added that the hospice social worker would come in the morning. "She'll have some good ideas about the kids."

Caye nodded and thanked Helen. It was a relief to know that they had help.

Rob sat with his head in his hands. Caye sat down in the chair beside him. She could feel the heat rise from the gray paint on the porch. The house was warm, but Jill wanted to be covered with the afghan.

Rob lifted his head.

"You know that story Jill tells? The one about her plan. How she saw me for the first time, and she knew I was the husband she'd planned for."

Caye nodded.

"I saw her during the sermon that day too. I knew she was looking at me. David was sitting on my lap, and I was aware of what a great guy I appeared to be, holding such a cute little boy. For the first time I wanted to be married.

"You know how I was in college. I'd see people like you and Nathan settling down, and I thought you were crazy."

Caye nodded. Back then she couldn't imagine his getting married either.

"I was a long way from settling down until that Sunday when I felt Jill watching me."

He pulled the back of his hand over his eyes.

"What am I going to do?" he asked Caye, as if she might have an answer, might offer some pearl that he hadn't thought of yet. "It's all happened so fast. One day we had hope. The next day we had to fight for hope. The day after there seems to be no hope. Do I just give in to it?

"She's what makes everything worthwhile. Why did it take me so long to realize that? I knew it—but then I forgot. I didn't hold on to it."

Caye reached over and patted Rob's back. She wanted to pull him to her, to hold him, to lie and say that it would be all right, that he would be all right. None of them would ever be all right.

"I'm sorry," she said. "I'm so sorry."

"I know," he said. "The two of us, you and I, love her more than anyone else in the world."

*More than the boys love her? Who could measure a child's love?*

But Caye understood what he meant. They were the two who were the most committed to her.

"This stuff with Marion just adds insult to injury. All of Jill's life she felt like things were weird, shameful with her family. Marion's stupid secrets. Why didn't she tell Jill years ago? All she did was teach Jill to keep secrets too."

"Are you bitter?" Caye asked.

"Bitter toward Marion? No, I feel too sorry for her."

"How about toward God?"

"I don't know. I don't want to be."

"Caye." It was Jill's voice through the open door.

Caye stood. Had Jill heard them?

"Can I tell you what I want the boys to know? Would you write it down for me?"

❧

"Will you marry again?" Jill asked. She'd opened her eyes to find Rob sitting by her bed staring at her. The house was quiet.

"Don't talk that way," Rob said.

"Do. Please do. Find someone who will love the boys. And you."

Rob shook his head. "I'll never love anyone the way I love you. You've given me so much."

"Marry again," Jill said. "It will be a compliment—to me."

When she opened her eyes again, Rob was gone. Caye was on the couch, her head tilted back.

The pain was intense. She moved her legs to try to relieve the burning in her back.

"You're awake," Caye said.

Jill looked at her friend with wide eyes.

"Is the pain bad?"

Jill nodded.

"I'll check the pump."

"I keep thinking about Mom," Jill said. "All these years she kept talking around her secret. She talked obsessively about my dad's pancreatic cancer but never about why she was doubly concerned I might get it." Jill listened as she spoke, surprised that her words made sense. "Why?"

"I think she was riddled with guilt," Caye answered as she walked toward the bed.

"But why did she hook up with Dad in the first place? I understand that she'd already fallen for him, but why did she pursue it once she knew he was her half-brother?"

"Maybe because he reminded her of her father, of all that she had lost. Maybe revenge was part of her motivation too. She was never accepted into the family by her grandmother." Caye continued, "I've read about siblings who didn't grow up in the same home coming together later in life. Of course it's not the norm, but sometimes there's an intense attraction based on familiarity. If they act on their passion—on what's forbidden—they usually end up feeling intense guilt."

Jill took a ragged breath.

Caye looked into her friend's eyes. "Your mom was needy. She felt abandoned. And she probably felt that she wasn't accountable to anyone. Your dad must have felt that way too."

"What about Joya? Why do you think she talks so much about faith but never about David?" Jill's voice fell to a whisper.

Caye shook her head and then directed her attention to the pump. "There. You're ready for the new dose. Go ahead and punch the button."

Jill frowned. She had nothing more to say. She began to drift. She saw her father holding David.

When she woke again, Rob was on one end of the couch, and Hudson was on the other. Both were asleep.

"Rob," she whispered, "it hurts."

He moved his head away from her.

"Rob."

He opened his eyes and then stood.

"Caye thinks the meds need to be increased. That we should call Dr. Scott this morning," he said.

"But it makes me so groggy. I don't want to sleep all the time."

Rob climbed up on the bed beside her. "Roll onto your side. I'll rub your back."

"What time is it?"

"It's 4:30."

She could tell the day was ready to break.

"What day is it?"

"June 20."

"Hudson's birthday?"

"Yes."

"And tomorrow is the longest day of the year?"

"Yes. I talked to the boys last night," Rob said. "At bedtime. I told them that you are really, really sick. That it looks like you might die."

"What did they say?"

"Hudson wanted to know if you would die before his party."

Jill exhaled.

"He said he really didn't want you to die on his birthday."

"I won't."

Rob kept rubbing her back. She visualized a garden. An over-grown jungle of wisteria and clematis, trillium and columbine, native plants and English garden plants, redwood trees and Japanese maple trees, all growing together.

She should ask Rob to take her to the bathroom, she thought. She didn't really need to go, but it had been so long since she had tried.

When she woke again, Marion was sitting beside her. Liam was pulling on her hand. "Get up, Mommy," he said. "Get up."

"Leave your mommy alone," Marion said.

"It's okay," Jill answered.

Marion turned into Joya. "Rob said you wanted us to come," Thomas said. Jill reached out her hand to Joya.

"Sorry to disappoint you," Jill said.

Joya shook her head. "Don't give up."

"Deal with the stuff with David, okay, Joya? He was such a great little kid. He deserves to be talked about." Jill let go of Joya and reached for Thomas's large hand. Joya began to cry.

The next time Jill opened her eyes, Rita and Summer and Lonnie sat beside the bed.

*They've come to pay their last respects.*

"We're still praying for you," Summer said.

Before they left Jill called out to Rita. "Come here," she said. Rita lowered her head. "Thanks," Jill whispered.

The hospice nurse stood beside her, checking the pump, slipping a new cassette of morphine into the holder. "Dr. Scott increased the dosage…"

## 31

Caye rocked Simon as he drank his bottle. She watched Jill sleep. She felt as though they were all part of a somber wake. The Fellowship members tromping through. At least no one, except Marion, felt that they needed to shush the kids. If Jill was dozing, she was out. She woke only when the pain became intense.

Hospice Helen, as Rob referred to her, had come and gone. "She's deteriorating quickly," she'd said. "She's progressed quite a bit since yesterday."

The social worker stopped by before Helen left. She gave Rob the name of a counselor who specialized in children. "Each child reacts differently to grief," she said. "Liam is going to think that his mommy's death is temporary. Simon will wonder where she's gone. Hudson is just at the age where he can start grasping that it's permanent."

Caye had pulled Hudson's cake from the oven before she settled down with Simon. They were going to barbecue burgers and have a party—just a family party. Hudson was furious. "I want my friends from school to come!" he'd shouted.

Nathan and Andrew had gone out to buy presents. Hudson was upset that he couldn't go too. Rob put Hudson in the baby seat on the back of Jill's mountain bike and took him for a ride to calm him down. Hank read stories to Liam and Audrey in the kitchen while Bev made a potato salad. Marion poked around in Jill's garden.

Simon closed his eyes. Caye kept rocking. She felt his body relax. It was all so dreamlike—Jill on the bed, sleeping, her hair fanned over the pillow. All of them milling around, doing mundane chores, planning a party. The contrast was, to use a Jill word, galactic.

She rolled the baby onto the bed beside Jill and stood over the two of them, staring. Jill, with her jaundiced, olive skin, looked beautiful. She instinctively moved toward Simon and pulled him to her and brushed her lips over the top of his head. Caye pulled up the railings and went upstairs to get her camera. She'd had Nathan bring it so she could take photos of Hudson on his fifth birthday.

She took pictures of mother and child as they slept and then put the camera on the mantel. She'd take more after Jill awoke.

※

"That's so macabre," Marion said as Caye clicked the shutter.

Caye ignored her.

"Someday the boys might have vague memories of all of this. The photos will help," Jill said. It was an effort for her to talk.

Liam sat on the bed beside her and giggled.

"Come on, Hudson," she said, motioning to him.

He stood at the end of the bed and shook his head.

Marion walked into the kitchen. "That Hudson is such a pill," she said to Bev.

Jill couldn't hear Bev's answer.

"Let's eat outside tonight," Jill said to Caye. "For Hudson's birthday."

"Can you go that far?" Caye asked.

"If you help me."

They ate outside. Jill sat propped up in her lounger with her sunglasses on. Caye took a photo of Hudson holding his pirate ship cake standing next to Jill. Jill smiled; Hudson frowned. Next she took a tender photo of Rob and Jill. Rob stood above Jill, his arms draped over her shoulders.

Caye thought about what the hospice nurse said, about all of it coming together, about Jill's body shutting down as she readied herself to let go, to pass from this life to the next.

*I can see you taking her, God.* The realization felt holy. So sad and so holy all at once.

❧

When Jill woke during the night, Marion sat beside her bed.

"How's the pain?" her mother asked.

"Okay."

"When your father was so sick, he was always in pain. They didn't manage it as well back then."

"Don't let them take me away without the kids knowing. Okay?"

❧

"Mommy, look at my drawing," Hudson said, waving the paper in front of her face. It was morning.

Hudson had drawn a pirate ship beneath the water. Skeletons covered the ocean floor.

Jill looked through the rail of the bed at Hudson. "Hey, you," she whispered.

"You kept thrashing around last night," Marion said, nodding toward the rail. "I didn't want you to fall out of bed." She stood with a basin and a washcloth. "Do you want to get cleaned up?"

Jill reached for the switch and raised the bed.

❧

"I was just in a garden, a beautiful garden," Jill told Caye.

"When?" Caye asked, tucking her hair behind her ear.

"Just now."

"No. You were here. In your bed."

Jill paused. "There's someone waiting for me in the garden."

"Who?" Caye climbed on the bed beside Jill.

Jill closed her eyes again. "I don't know." She reached over and took Caye's hand. "You've shown me love. You've been my anchor. I'd spent my whole life bobbing along, unconnected, until I met you."

"Oh, Jilly," Caye said as tears stabbed at her eyes. She turned her head and kissed Jill's cheek. There was so much she wanted to tell

Jill—like that she didn't believe Jill ever bobbed along. Jill always had a plan. The difference was that Caye gave her someone—a girl-friend—to live her plan with, to share the daily domestic stuff, to turn it into fun. She wanted to say that she'd never imagined a friend like Jill was possible. She wanted to say that there was so much between them—a garden of love and faith and history and stories and children and husbands and God and jealousy and commitment and dreams. There was so much there that Caye couldn't believe there would be anything left of her if Jill didn't live.

"I want to sit in the garden," Jill said to Caye. "Will you help me out?"

Caye took the pillows and afghan out first. She helped Jill stand and then slipped the morphine pump into the pocket of her silk jade robe. They walked slowly down the hall, through the kitchen, and out the back door. They struggled along, taking the deck stairs one at a time, Jill leaning her thin, thin frame heavily against her friend.

Jill settled onto the lounger as Caye tucked the afghan around her. Jill closed her eyes. "Where's Rob?"

"He went for a run. He should be back any minute."

"Where's Nathan?"

"Over at our house."

Hudson, Liam, Audrey, and Andrew ran through the garden on their way into the house. "Hudson and Liam," Jill said weakly.

"Hudson and Liam," Caye called after them, "your mommy wants you."

They ran back and stood beside the lounger.

"I love you," she said.

Liam nodded and twirled around until his cape twisted around his boots. Then he twirled the other way until it unwound.

"I know," Hudson said, shifting from foot to foot. "Can I go play with Andrew?"

Jill nodded. Hudson and Liam ran up the deck steps into the house.

"Where's Simon?" Jill asked.

"Down for his nap."

"Would you have Rob wake me when he comes back?"

Jill smiled up at Rob.

"I'm here," he said. A trail of sweat ran down the side of his face. She wished he wouldn't run in the heat of the day.

She closed her eyes.

"I'm going to take a shower," he said.

"Wait." She forced her eyelids open.

He stroked her fingers that were poking out of the afghan.

"I'm sorry," she said.

"Why?" he asked, kneeling beside her.

"Sorry to leave."

The garden grew larger. It obliterated the house, covered every inch of the courtyard. Wisteria vines wound their way around the lounger, the afghan, Jill's body. Orange day lilies grew as large as sunflowers. Purple dahlia pompoms rose as tall as trees. The red and pink tulips grew as big as the children. There were no snakes in this garden.

She could feel the person waiting, waiting for her.

"Is it time?" she asked.

*Are you ready?* The voice came from behind the gate.

Was she ready? Ready to die? Yes.

Ready to leave?

*All things. I can do all things through Him who strengthens me.*

Caye sat on the window seat and watched Rob walk down the steps of the deck. His hair was wet. His feet were bare. She watched him bend down to Jill. Watched him put his cheek against her mouth and nose. Watched him sink to his knees.

Caye stood and started out the door. And then stopped. She grabbed the phone and hit the speed dial.

"Come quickly," she said to Nathan as she opened the screen door. "We need you."

## 32

Jill had said she wanted a memorial service in her garden. "Scatter my ashes in the Siskiyous," she had said. "But talk about me in my garden."

Thomas led the service. The scent of the roses hung sweetly in the air. They started by singing "Be Thou My Vision." Thomas read the Twenty-third Psalm. Neighbors, parents from Hudson's preschool, and the Fellowship members, except for Joya, filled the courtyard.

"She didn't come," Rita had whispered to Caye before the service started. "That's all Thomas would say." Tears filled Caye's eyes again. There were so many things she did not understand, could not understand.

Nathan stood on one side of Rob. Rob's parents stood on the other.

"We should have come sooner," Rob's mother had said earlier to Caye as she dabbed at her eyes. "We had no idea."

Caye had patted her shoulder and said, "None of us did." She had no desire for Rob's mother to feel guilty. It wouldn't have helped if they had come sooner. Now was when Rob needed them. Caye and Nathan had moved back to their house. Rob's mom and dad and Marion were all staying at Jill's. At Jill's. It would always be "at Jill's."

Hudson, with his arms crossed, stood quietly in front of Rob. Andrew stood beside Hank on the deck; Scout sat at their feet. Stephanie stood a few feet from Liam and Audrey as they played under the wisteria with the Matchbox cars. Caye held Simon.

Marion stood beside Bev.

Thomas kept the service short. Caye looked at Nathan's program, created by Rita last night. "In the Garden" was the last song.

"I come to the garden alone, while the dew is still on the roses…"

Simon rubbed his nose against Caye's shoulder. She looked down at the baby and then off toward the fading purple wisteria blooms against the brick wall.

"And He walks with me, and He talks with me, and He tells me I am His own; and the joy we share as we tarry there, none other has ever known," the mourners sang.

*Jill is your own,* Caye prayed, looking back toward Thomas.

*And so are you,* came the voice from inside. *You are my own.*

It was so easy for Caye to see God loving Jill.

*I love you, too,* said the voice.

*I feel so alone.*

*I know.*

Simon began to fuss. Nathan put his arm around Caye's shoulder and patted the baby's hand.

Thomas said the final prayer.

Bev walked into the kitchen and brought out coffee. Caye knew that trays of fruit and pastries would soon follow.

Rita hugged Caye and Simon. Summer stood back. Caye stepped forward and gave her a hug, sandwiching Simon between them. Gwen materialized and reached out to Caye.

"Are you doing okay?" she asked.

Caye smiled. She could not talk. *I will never stop mourning,* is what she wanted to say. *I will never be okay.*

She looked over at the tulip bed. She was embarrassed that the garden was in such poor shape. The tulips had never been cut back. The stalks had shriveled and dried into thin, grayish twigs. They looked like brittle bones. The forget-me-not blossoms had faded, and the foliage had withered into a silvery tangle.

Caye stepped toward Nathan and handed him the baby. She headed through the side door of the garage and found Jill's green-handled trowel on the potting bench.

Dropping to her knees in front of the tulip bed, Caye plunged the trowel into the soil, popping up a clump of bulbs. She shook off the dirt and slipped the five bulbs into the pocket of her maternity jumper. She would plant them in her own garden, plant the bulbs, plant the faith and love and dreams that God had given her through Jill.

Caye returned the trowel to the garage and then walked toward the house.

Simon saw her and began to cry.

She reached out her arms to the baby.

# About the Author

Leslie Gould lives in Portland, Oregon, with her husband, Peter, and four children, Kaleb, Taylor, Hana, and Lily Thao. Leslie held the position of curator at the Swedenburg House Museum in Ashland, Oregon, before becoming a mother. She enjoys backpacking and camping with her family. She currently works as a writer and editor. This is her first novel.

To learn more about WaterBrook Press and view
our catalog of products, log on to our Web site:
**www.waterbrookpress.com**

WATERBROOK
PRESS